TALES OF THE SHADOWMEN

Volume 1: The Modern Babylon

also from Black Coat Press

Shadowmen:
Heroes and Villains of French Pulp Fiction
(non-fiction)

Shadowmen 2:
Heroes and Villains of French Comics
(non-fiction)

TALES OF THE SHADOWMEN

Volume 1: The Modern Babylon

edited by
Jean-Marc & Randy Lofficier

stories by
Matthew Baugh, Bill Cunningham, Terrance Dicks, Win Scott Eckert, Viviane Etrivert, G.L. Gick, Rick Lai, Alain le Bussy, Jean-Marc & Randy Lofficier, Samuel T. Payne, John Peel, Chris Roberson, Robert Sheckley and Brian Stableford

A Black Coat Press Book

Acknowledgements: I am indebted to David McDonnell for proofreading the typescript.

Visit our website at www.blackcoatpress.com

ISBN 1-932983-36-8. First Printing. March 2005. Published by Black Coat Press, an imprint of Hollywood Comics.com, LLC, P.O. Box 17270, Encino, CA 91416.

Table of Contents

Mike Manley's cover rough

Introduction

It almost scared me to death.

I didn't dare get up in the middle of the night to cross the long, deserted corridor of our house and go to the bathroom, because I knew that *it* lurked behind me, ready to strike at any time.

It was, of course, *Belphegor, the Phantom of the Louvre.*

I was 11 at the time and French television had just broadcast in primetime a four-part black & white series featuring the gaunt, silent, eerie, murderous masked figure of Juliette Greco haunting the Louvre, seeking an alchemist's treasure.

But it wasn't just the Louvre. I had never been to the Louvre, and after watching the first episode of the series, I swore to never set foot inside, ever (another broken promise; so it goes). In episode 3, however, a character woke up in her own bedroom in the middle of the night and saw Belphegor standing there, looming threateningly, at the foot of her bed. Much screaming ensued. The way I figured it, if Belphegor could enter anyone's bedroom and loom over them while they slept, then pretty much all hope was lost. After that, I slept under the blankets because, as everyone knows, blankets are the ultimate protection against monsters.

Belphegor was *scary*.

(As I don't want the readers to think that my 11-year-old self would be scared by just another sock puppet monster or cheesy makeup effect, I offer on the next page as evidence, a photograph of Belphegor. Scary, huh?)

But Belphegor was also entrancing, fascinating, alluring, enthralling; he was the Snake in the Garden of Eden enticing you to taste the Forbidden Fruit, the Naughty Usher that draws you inside the Palace of Sin with a knowing wink and a beckoning index flip…

Belphegor was the Gate-Keeper. And the realm that he guarded was that of popular literature.

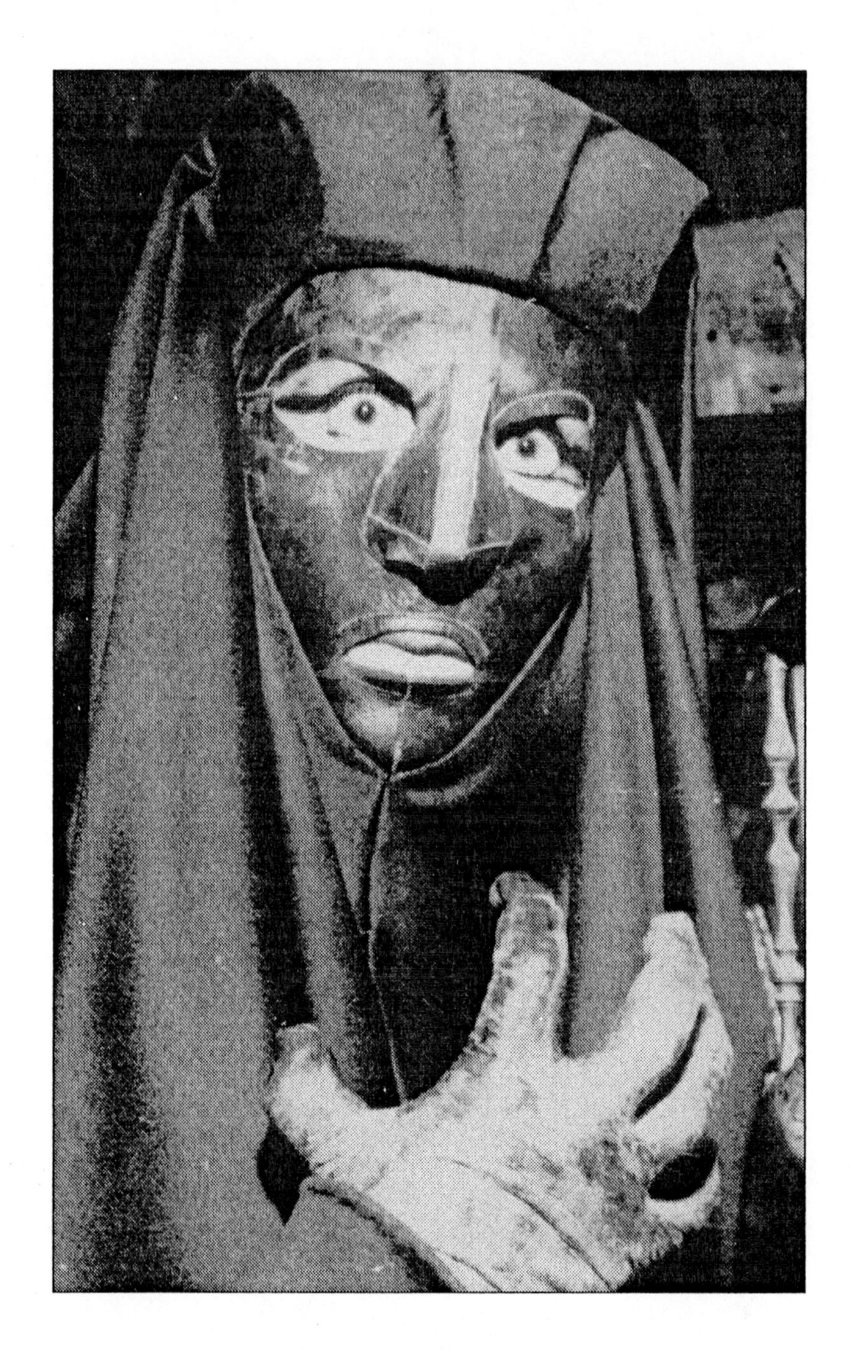

Juliette Greco as *Belphegor, The Phantom of the Louvre*

The 1960s were a bountiful decade for an adolescent eager to delve into the world of Pulp; numerous paperback imprints competed to offer a variety of classics. The point I wish to emphasize here, however, is that the French works cohabited, in the same collections, with the English and American works.

Belgian publisher Marabout published *Rocambole, The Black Coats*, the novels of Paul Féval and Alexandre Dumas next to Baroness Orczy's *Scarlet Pimpernel*. Their YA imprint featured *Bob Morane* and *Nick Jordan* next to *Doc Savage*.

In France, Le Livre de Poche's detective imprint published all the classics: *Sherlock Holmes* and *Arsène Lupin, Rouletabille* and *The Saint, Fantômas* and *Hercule Poirot, Lecoq* and *Nero Wolfe*. Plon offered both the adventures of *James Bond* and *S.A.S.* Georges Simenon's *Maigret* was only a book cover away from the P.I.s of Raymond Chandler and Dashiell Hammett at the Presses de la Cité. Editions Fleuve Noir, whose prodigious output was split between various genre imprints, published all-new *Frankenstein* novels (it was later disclosed that they had been penned by renowned screenwriter Jean-Claude Carrière under a house name) next to the adventures of the deadly *Madame Atomos* and futuristic police inspector *Robin Muscat*.

In the movie theaters, *Fantômas* and *Judex* returned to the silver screens, and Johnny Weissmuller's *Tarzan* shared the television screen with reruns of Louis Feuillade's serial *Les Vampires* and the adaptations of *Belphegor* and *Les Compagnons de Baal*.

In short, original French works and translations of English and American works cohabited happily under one single rooftop, for the enjoyment of all.

During the 1970s, when I first became aware of Philip José Farmer's prodigious fictional biographies of *Tarzan* and *Doc Savage*, I was immediately thrilled to enrich my knowledge of the formidable heritage of English-language pulp fiction. But I was also immensely saddened to discover that, with the exceptions of *Lupin* and *Lecoq*, none of my favorite heroes were otherwise included. No *Rocambole*, no *Black Coats*, no *Rouletabille*, no *Bob Morane*, etc. This was like missing an arm or an eye. The Wold Newton universe of families (to reuse Farmer's terminology) could not possibly be complete since half of its substantial essence was missing!

Of course, I understand that the language barrier, the lack of adequate translations and simply, the time it takes to become acquainted with a variety of source materials–often, let's be honest, of variable literary quality–made it impossible for even someone with Farmer's encyclopedic knowledge to expand into non-English-language areas. But then and there, I resolved to someday share both my enthusiasm and experience with my fellow devotees from across the seas. It is something that I eventually set out to do with our website *www.coolfrenchcomics.com*, which later grew into two books, *Shadowmen* and *Shadowmen 2*.

And this anthology, *Tales of the Shadowmen*, hopefully the first in a series of yearly volumes.

Tales of the Shadowmen finally accomplishes what I dreamed of since I was 11: Judex does share the limelight with the Shadow (thanks to Chris Roberson); Dracula does traverse the Atlantic on the same ship as the Ténèbre Brothers (according to Brian Stableford); Chevalier Dupin does team up with the Count of Monte-Cristo to fight the Black Coats (if John Peel is right); Maigret does cross paths with the Frankenstein Monster (reveals Matthew Baugh); and more.

Some of the folks published here are members of the New Wold Newton Meteoritic Society, newcomers to genre fiction; others are confirmed writers, American, British and French, whose credits are many and prestigious; all share one thing in common: their love for the classic pulp heroes and villains, the great mythology of the 19th, 20th and now, 21st century.

For *Tales of the Shadowmen* is not simply a collection of stories; it is the description of a meta-reality that exists in our collective minds: Sherlock Holmes and Arsène Lupin, like Robin Hood and d'Artagnan and, before them, Hercules and Jason, belong to all of us. They are the stuff myths are made of. They *are* the myths.

Further, *Tales of the Shadowmen* is not simply a collection of Anglo-Saxon myths, but it reaches across the Atlantic, across the Channel, and in an unprecedented feat of literary *Entente Cordiale*, embraces its French counterparts and creates an even bigger mythology.

On the other hand, it also is a whole bunch of wonderful stories.

Now, you must excuse me: I need to look for a blanket.

Belphegor is back.

Jean-Marc Lofficier

Matthew Baugh takes us to the golden age that just preceded World War I. The streets of Paris are abloom, the sweet smell of flowers is in the air. No one yet has an inkling of the massive slaughter looming just over the horizon. Justice is simple and Science is wonderful–or are they? Already, cracks are beginning to appear in the social edifice...

Matthew Baugh: *Mask of the Monster*

Paris, 1912, Early Summer

In all of Paris, perhaps the last place you would expect to hear a woman screaming at 3 a.m. is in the fashionable quarter of Auteuil.

The screams came from the upper floor of an isolated home on the west side. They were loud enough that some of the closest neighbors could hear them, but they stopped so quickly that no one assigned much importance to them. Not until the following morning.

After the screams stopped, the lights began to come on in the house. A second story window burst open and a large man in dark clothing stepped out. He carried a bundle wrapped in bed sheets across his shoulder. The bundle was the size of a human body.

Inside the residence, there was commotion. The master of the house was awake and shouting the name "Louise" over and over. The servants were stumbling out of their quarters, looking frightened or confused.

The large man paused a moment and a trace of a smile crossed his scarred face. He stepped over the rail and dropped to the ground. There was something ungainly about the man, an oddness about his movements that suggested deformity. Despite this, he moved quickly to the garden wall. It was ten feet high and topped with iron spikes but the giant clambered across it in seconds.

There was a soft grunt from the bundle as the man landed outside the fence. The ugly smile crossed his face again, and then he jogged off into the darkness.

Half-a-mile distant, a milk wagon was making its morning rounds. The driver was a heavyset man with a hard face and white hair. A lean youth sat on the cart with him. An observer would have guessed they were father and son, or master and apprentice, out on their morning route. The two were silent as their mule pulled the wagon along. The older man smoked a pipe, the younger a cigarette. Neither had heard the woman's screams or the distant commotion.

There was a movement from the brush at the size of the road. The large man stepped out in front of the wagon. The driver tugged on the reins forcing the mule to stop. The younger man tossed his cigarette to the pavement and hopped down. He moved to the back of the wagon. The big man followed him. The youth was tall but the giant topped him by more than a foot.

The youth opened the back of the wagon, there were cases of milk bottles, but the compartment was far from full. The giant placed his bundle into the opening, then eased his bulk in beside it. The youth shut the door and headed back to his seat by the driver.

"Let's go."

The driver grunted and flipped the reins. The mule moved forward, falling into that steady rhythm that all mules seem to have.

"I don't like this much."

The younger man grinned at his companion's words. He took out a fresh cigarette and lighted it.

"What don't you like? The boss's plan is running beautifully."

"You know who we've got. The police will be crawling the streets within the hour. If they stop us, there's nothing to keep them from finding her."

The young man sniggered.

"I pity the gendarme who does stop us. You've seen what our friend can do."

The older man grunted. The wagon continued in silence.

"What's that up ahead?" The driver asked suddenly.

The young man squinted into the pre-dawn darkness. Ahead there was a silhouette of someone standing in the middle of the road.

"You think it's a cop?"

"Quiet!" The older man snapped. "Whoever it is, he doesn't need to hear anything."

As they drew closer, they could see that the man wasn't wearing a police uniform. He was tall, with a stony visage mostly hidden by shadows and a black slouch hat. He wore dark clothes under a long cape; the kind gentlemen wore to the opera. As they drew near, the man raised his hand for them to stop.

The driver reined the mule in.

"Good morning, sir."

"Open the back of your wagon."

"Is this a robbery?" The driver asked. He tried to make his tone light but only partially succeeded. "You won't get much I'm afraid. We have only milk."

"You have something much more valuable than that," the stranger said. "I want the girl."

The driver swallowed and glanced at his companion. The youth's hand slipped to the small of his back where he kept his knives.

"I don't know what you mean, sir. It's just me and young Gaspard." The driver forced a chuckle. "If you're looking for a girl at this hour, you're in the wrong part of town."

As the driver spoke, Gaspard worked a finely balanced throwing knife out of his belt. At 19, the youth was already an accomplished knife fighter.

"If you'd really like to find some nice girls..."

The driver stopped in mid-sentence as Gaspard threw his knife. It happened so smoothly and quickly that the driver could barely catch the motion.

The man in black shifted his body and the knife shot past him.

"I am here for the girl that you took from the Leonard house."

With a cry of anger, Gaspard leapt to the ground, another knife already in his hand. The driver moved to join him more slowly. He held a heavy wooden cudgel. They advanced on the black-clad man from opposite sides.

Gaspard struck first, thrusting at the stranger's ribs. The man slipped out of the way and caught Gaspard's wrist with one hand. A quick twist and bones broke. The dark man threw the youth away from him casually as the knife went spinning off.

The driver rushed in with a slashing blow. The man dodged the blow and brought his foot up in a *savate* kick. His toe caught the older man in the elbow. The club fell to the ground as his arm went numb. The stranger followed up with a neat punch to the point of the chin that left the driver stretched out on the cobblestones.

Gaspard had managed to sit up and was cradling his broken wrist.

"Gouroull!" he screamed, "Help us Gouroull! The devil's come for us!"

The man in black moved toward the youth. Before he reached him, the back of the wagon burst open and the big man stepped out.

Big was a sorry word for it, the stranger realized. Gouroull was well over seven feet tall.

The giant surged forward with a suddenness that would have done a bantamweight boxer proud. Only the dark man's quick reflexes allowed him to duck past the huge arms. The man's fists shot out, landing a powerful combination of punches against Gouroull's kidneys.

Gouroull showed no signs that he had even felt the blows. He spun and caught the stranger's neck in his massive hands, bearing him to the ground.

The man in black was pinned. His throat crushed by the inhuman strength in those hands. He tried several jujitsu holds, and struck at the pressure points on Gouroull's wrists. There was no effect.

In desperation, he reached into the folds of his cloak and produced a small revolver. He pressed the barrel into the giant's massive chest and fired four shots.

Gouroull screamed in pain and staggered backwards. He clutched at his bleeding chest, but he didn't fall. He looked around for a weapon and spied a rock, as big as a horse's head half-buried in the ground at the side of the road. With one motion, he tore it loose and raised it above his head to crush his foe.

The man in black was gone.

"He slipped into the trees." Gaspard nodded in the direction the stranger had taken. Gouroull started to move in pursuit but the youth raised his good hand.

"No! We've got to get out of here. That was enough noise to bring the police."

Gouroull glared at the youth for a long moment, then nodded his massive head. He picked up the young man and placed him in the driver's seat, then stuffed the unconscious body of the driver into the back of the wagon and climbed in himself.

With the steady rhythm of the mule's steps, the wagon moved on into the dark.

Nearby, the man in black watched from his hiding place. His throat throbbed with pain and his breathing was ragged. He wanted to follow but it had taken all his strength to get away from the monster. Silently, he swore that the kidnappers would see him again, and soon.

Etienne Leonard was storming around his garden when the detectives arrived. He was a fierce-looking man of 50 with white hair and a pointed beard. His dark eyes blazed with emotion but his face was calm. A quarter of a century as a *juge d'instruction* had given him a grim dignity that even this crisis couldn't erase.

"Sir! We came as quickly as we could."

Leonard nodded to Inspector Gauthier as he entered. The anger in his eyes flared when he saw that the inspector had brought his protégé, Jules Maigret, along.

"They left a note." Leonard said, and handed a piece of paper to the detective. Gauthier read it while the taller Maigret read over his shoulder.

M. Leonard,

We have taken your daughter. She has not been harmed, but if you wish to see her safely again, you must raise a quarter of a million francs by tomorrow evening. We will contact you to let you know where and how the exchange will be made. If you value her life, you will cooperate!

"My God." Maigret whispered, "My poor Louise."

"Your Louise?" The anger in Leonard's eyes was frightening. "She is my daughter, young man! How dare you say such a thing? You are no part of her life. You are only here because you happen to be a policeman!"

Maigret flushed, but he managed to keep most of the emotion out of his voice.

"Forgive me, Monsieur le Juge. You are right of course. We will do everything possible to recover your daughter safely."

Maigret's face had settled back into its usual impenetrable expression. Leonard knew that look well, and hated it. He could see no refinement in that broad face, no hint of passion or gleam of intelligence.

"Sir," Gauthier said. "Time is of the essence. Please tell us everything, in as much detail as you can."

Leonard's anger seemed to drain out of him. He nodded and sank down into a wrought iron chair.

"It must have been half-an-hour ago. I was awakened from a sound sleep by screaming. It took me only a moment to recognize the voice as Louise's. The screams stopped, as if a hand had been clapped across her mouth. I was on my feet in an instant and seized my pistol."

"Excuse me, Monsieur le Juge," said Maigret. "You keep a pistol in your bedroom?"

"Of course I do!" Leonard snapped. "A man in my position has many enemies. I've led the investigations of many of the most dangerous gangs in the city."

"It's just an unusual thing to do," Maigret persisted, "unless there have been specific threats, of course."

"Gentlemen," Gauthier cut in, "we must focus on the heart of the matter. Maigret, these tangents won't help us to find Mademoiselle Leonard."

He turned back to Leonard with an apologetic smile. "Please continue, sir."

"Very well." The magistrate gave Maigret a poisonous look then resumed his story. "I ran to the room as quickly as I could. It couldn't have taken me more than half-a-minute. When I arrived, the window was open and Louise was gone."

"So quickly, sir?"

"Yes, Inspector. I didn't see how it could be managed either. I hoped the kidnappers might still be hiding in the house so I roused the servants and put on all the lights. We searched everywhere, but we found nothing. I don't understand how they could have escaped in such a short time."

"There was no one else in the house?"

"My wife and my other daughter are staying with relatives in at our house in Alsace."

"The first sound you heard was Lou–" Maigret paused, "was Mademoiselle Leonard screaming. Is that right, sir?"

"I've already said so, haven't I?"

"Of course, sir, but that surprised me. Don't you keep dogs to guard your house?"

"I keep two mastiffs if that's any of your concern."

"It's just that it seems strange. Why wouldn't the barking of the dogs have roused the house before your daughter's screams."

"The dogs were killed, young man."

"Killed? How, sir? Were they poisoned?"

"They were not. The gardener tells me that their throats were cut."

"Cutting the throats of two large dogs must have been a very difficult feat for these kidnappers," Maigret mused. "Especially without making any noise."

A look of disbelief crossed Leonard's face. "My God, man! Are you a detective or a veterinarian? My daughter is missing! I would think that you, of all people, would see some significance to that! Yet, here you are, wasting time worrying over two dead dogs!"

"Excuse me, Monsieur le Juge." Inspector Gauthier's voice was calm and quiet. "Please allow me to consult with my young colleague for a moment."

He took Maigret's arm and walked with him through the garden gate to the street outside.

They made an odd contrast. Gauthier was a slender man of medium height who moved with elegant precision. Maigret was taller, bulkier and called to mind the image of a Bernese mountain dog plodding along next to a whippet.

Once they were outside, Gauthier turned to Maigret.

"It's not going to work," he said.

"But, sir, I know I can help!"

"Any other time, I'd say yes, but you see how he is."

"I have to try, sir. I can't stand by while Louise is in danger."

Gauthier sighed. "I know how you feel, Maigret. Honestly, I do. But we're not going to make any sort of progress if I have to separate the two of you every few minutes. He is at his wits' end, and you are at yours."

Maigret's big shoulders sagged and he nodded. Louise's disappearance was affecting him. The taciturn patience he could usually call on was a shambles.

"Besides," Gauthier continued, "you know who he is. He could have you removed from this case in a minute. He could even have you demoted, and where would I be then?"

The Inspector smiled affectionately and clapped Maigret on the shoulder. "Don't look so glum. I'm not taking you off the case."

"What do you want me to do?"

"I've sent for Doctor de Grandin from the Faculté de Médecine. He'll be arriving shortly and I'm assigning you to assist him. You were a medical student once, weren't you? Who knows, maybe there's something to your idea about the dogs after all. In any case, that's what I want the two of you working on."

Maigret knew that the medical evidence was often critical in prosecuting a case. Every part of him wanted to help find Louise, but he could see why that was impossible. He nodded and received another clap on the shoulder from his superior.

"Don't worry, we'll find her." Gauthier turned and strode back to the house, leaving Maigret at the curb. The younger man sighed. He took a large pipe out of his pocket, loaded it with tobacco and began to puff as he watched the eastern sky lighten.

The milk wagon had left Auteuil at its slow pace and had used the Pont Mirabeau to cross to the left bank. It had turned onto the Quai d'Orsay and followed the course of the Seine into the heart of the city. As the wagon passed by the Ile de la Cité, it turned south into the neighborhoods of the fifth arrondissement. The shops and restaurants of the scenic Rue Mouffetard were just coming to life when the wagon turned into a small building with the sign '*Crémerie.*'

A few of the dairy workers glanced at the wagon, but their eyes didn't linger. All manner of items came in and out of the dairy in those trucks and the workers never took any notice. It benefited them not to know too much.

Once the wagon was parked out of sight, Gaspard opened the back. The towering Gouroull joined him with the sheet-wrapped bundle in his arms. Gaspard opened a hidden door for the scarred giant and the two went down a stair. They came to a set of passageways at the bottom of the landing. Most of these were blind alleys, designed to delay a police search if the secret of the dairy ever became known.

Gaspard knew the passages well. He followed a twisting route that emerged in a good-sized chamber. Bright lights came on revealing the two men while the far portion of the room was left in impenetrable shadow.

"Report."

The voice from the shadows was cultured and business-like, with just a trace of a foreign accent.

"We have the girl, sir." Gaspard indicated the bundle the giant held.

"Your partner is not with you and you are injured?"

"Gouroull too, sir. He's been shot in the body several times. Philippe is unconscious. I left him upstairs."

"The police?"

"No, sir. It was the work of one man."

"A stranger?" A second voice asked. It was similar to the first, though it lacked even the trace of an accent. It seemed less business-like than the first, yet sharper at the same time.

"He was a tall man, sir," Gaspard said. "I couldn't see him well because he wore a long cape or cloak, and a big hat to hide his face. He fought like a devil, but that didn't help him against Gouroull."

"Was he killed?" The first voice asked.

"No, sir. Gouroull hurt him, but he managed to give us the slip."

"I am aware of this man," the first voice said. "It is regrettable that Gouroull didn't kill him. He has become a thorn in the flesh of the Red Hand recently. It is good that you escaped from him. Go and see to your injuries."

Gaspard bowed to his unseen masters and left the room.

"Gouroull," said the second voice, "the girl is unharmed?"

With a small nod of his head, the giant indicated that it was so.

"Please uncover her."

Louise Leonard gasped as the sheets came away and she saw the scarred face of her captor. She started to back away, but a giant hand closed on her arm. When she felt the iron strength of those fingers, she made no effort to struggle.

"Don't be frightened. Mademoiselle," the first voice said. "Gouroull may look like a monster, but he won't hurt you. Not without cause."

"What do you want?" She tried to sound brave though her voice trembled.

"It is better for you if you don't know too much."

"My father won't rest until he's found you!"

"It's true your father is a hard man," the voice replied. "It's also true he loves you deeply. He will behave intelligently."

"Why are you telling me this?"

"We wanted you to have a good look at Gouroull. You have felt his strength. You have seen what he can do. The police cannot stop him, your dogs couldn't stop him and even bullets mean little to him. We want you to know that, even after we release you, you will always be in the palm of our hand. Let your father know this so he doesn't entertain foolish thoughts about us in the future."

Louise looked up at the towering man who held her. Her eyes held as much curiosity as fear.

"I expect you find him hideous," the second voice said. "His face is a veritable mask of scars, isn't it?"

"A mask," she repeated. "I'm not frightened of masks."

She reached up tentatively. When Gouroull didn't pull away she touched his face.

"Skin as white as snow, lips as red as blood, hair as black as ebony."

Gouroull's brow furrowed as he let the girl's slender hands brush across the mass of scars and crude stitches.

"These stitches," she murmured. "It's as if you had been..." She turned toward the darkened part of the room. "It can't be!"

"Congratulations, Mademoiselle," the second voice said, "You may have a better deductive mind than your father. You are correct about what and who Gouroull is."

She turned toward the voices. "You've shown me his face. Are you afraid to show me yours?"

"That is as much for your safety as for ours, Mademoiselle," the first voice replied.

"Gouroull," the second voice said, "please escort Mademoiselle Leonard to her room. Then return to me and I shall attend to your wounds."

The scarred giant released Louise's arm and gestured for her to follow him. The two left the chamber the way they had come.

When they were gone, a remote mechanism shut and bolted the door. The spotlights went out and a diffuse glow filled the room. The chamber was empty except for two well-dressed gentlemen sitting behind a large table.

"What do you think, Cornelius?" the first man asked. He seemed to be the older of the two. He wore a conservative suit and round spectacles. His heavy moustache and unruly mane of greying hair gave him an air of dignity. He looked like someone's stern but kind uncle.

"She seems an interesting girl," Dr. Cornelius Kramm answered. He was smaller and thinner than his brother, with the kind of massive head that suggested genius. He was mostly bald with a fringe of dark hair. He was dressed in a black suit as well. Behind his round glasses, his black eyes were lit by a fierce intelligence.

"She is quite pretty, too," Fritz Kramm replied. "I wonder what Gouroull would do with her if we weren't guiding his actions."

"I think you know the answer to that, Fritz, and it's an ugly picture. The rules of human society have no meaning for such as our friend." Cornelius paused. "It would be interesting though. I should certainly want to study any offspring that might result."

The elite of society in Munich, Paris and New York would have been shocked to hear this conversation. Fritz Kramm was one of the wealthiest and most reputable businessmen on the continent. His brother, Cornelius, had an even more spotless reputation. A famous surgeon, Doctor Cornelius Kramm was as well-known for his philanthropic gestures as for the brilliant procedures he had pioneered.

"What was that she said about his skin?" Fritz asked.

"She was quoting a story from the Brothers Grimm. Mademoiselle Leonard is a great admirer of fantasies and fairy tales. She is an avid reader of Féval, Radcliffe, Edgar Poe and, of course, Mrs. Shelley. I believe her special favorite is Madame Jeanne-Marie Leprince de Beaumont, and that is most interesting."

"Interesting? In what way?"

"Interesting, my dear brother, because one of Madame Leprince de Beaumont's most famous stories is of a young woman held captive in the home of a monster. By her goodness and beauty, she eventually breaks the Beast's curse. It seems his hideous nature is only a mask and he is really a charming prince underneath."

"Hmph!" Fritz Kramm grunted. "I wonder if Gouroull has read that one."

Cornelius smiled coldly. "I suspect the fantasies of the Italian, Collodi, would be more to his taste. He wants to be a 'real boy' after all. As for Mademoiselle Leonard, she may not be expecting the sort of tale the Brothers Kramm have written."

"I'd best go up and find out how the police investigation is proceeding," said Fritz.

"See if you can learn anything of our mysterious man in black."

"I will. It bothers me that we know so little."

"Yes." Cornelius' voice was frightening in its lack of emotion. "We'll just have to be prepared when he turns up at our doorstep."

Fritz nodded and rose. He crossed to a folding door, which opened, into a small elevator cage. He touched a button and rose from sight, leaving Cornelius alone in the large room.

Maigret had met Jules de Grandin about four years earlier, during his abortive stint at medical school in Nantes. De Grandin had come as a visiting lecturer and Maigret had been impressed with his energy and encyclopedic knowledge.

The forensic doctor hadn't changed. He was a tiny man, full of energy and strange oaths, who had set the young detective to gathering evidence at the crime scene. He had been commanded to take what seemed an absurd number of samples and to make measurements in precise detail. Now, back at his laboratory, Doctor de Grandin was dissecting the bodies of the slain dogs.

"Move closer, man." De Grandin's tone was impatient. "I need you to angle the light so I can see."

Maigret complied, though he didn't understand why the forensic man was so intent on seeing deep inside the gash on the animal's throat.

"Surely, Doctor, there's no doubt about what killed the poor brute?"

"Ah bah!" the little man snapped. "You know the general cause, but not the particulars. We mean to catch a devil, my young one, and the devil is always in the details."

"I'm afraid I don't see much point. How is any of this helping to find Mademoiselle Leonard? I feel I should be out helping in the search."

"The search? That is a charitable description of what is happening. At this moment, Inspector Gauthier and his men are kicking down the doors of known criminal establishments and rounding up wagonloads of street apaches in an effort to pick up the trail of the kidnappers. All in vain. No, my friend, what we do in this room will be of much greater help to your Louise than all the frantic activity of the Sûreté."

Maigret started to protest, then realized what de Grandin had said.

"Why did you call her that?"

"Your Louise?" the Doctor's eyes twinkled. "Do you think that I have never been in love? How could I mistake your sighs, your long face unless I was blind? You are her lover, or else you hope to be."

"We had hoped to be married."

"But her father forbade it?"

"Yes. How did you know?"

"I have met that pompous ass of a magistrate on several occasions. His daughter must be a rare beauty indeed if you would even consider him as a father-in-law. Tell me, what pretext did he use to forbid a wedding?"

"He says he won't have his daughter marry a common policeman. He tells me that I am too crude for Louise." Maigret smiled sadly and opened the back of his pocket watch. "I confess, I sometimes agree with him about that."

He showed the picture in the watch to Jules de Grandin. It showed a sensitive round face, framed by a wealth of brown curls and dominated by wise, black eyes.

"She is lovely."

"She is more than that. She is an angel." Maigret shrugged and looked embarrassed. "I know that is what a lover is expected to say, but you would understand if you met her. She is sensitive and gentle, and not only to those in her social circle. I've seen her talk to servants, shopkeepers and beggars, always with the same respect she shows her father's friends. She often goes to the orphanage as a volunteer and reads her fairy tales to the children."

"And she loves you."

"Yes, sir, she does." Maigret shuffled his feet awkwardly. "I am a lummox compared to the elegant gentlemen her father introduces her to. Yet she says she sees something in me..."

Jules de Grandin grunted and ran a critical eye across the young detective.

"I think she must be more discerning than the silly girls one often meets. It is a shame her father sees you so differently."

"Even if he liked me, there are religious differences." Maigret said. He was surprised at himself for revealing so much. There was something about de Grandin that inspired his trust.

"Ah," Maigret saw a look of pain cross the older man's features. "The old intolerances will raise their ugly heads. I once loved a girl, but she was a Catholic and my mother forbade the match. The good God cannot be pleased when young lovers are kept apart for such reasons."

"Still, I must agree with Monsieur le Juge on one point." De Grandin's tone was suddenly lighter. "Why should a lovely and refined girl want to marry a man who insists on moping when he has such an excellent chance to rescue her?"

"Rescue her?" Maigret brightened. "Do you mean you have found something?"

"Something?" the little man looked scornful. "I have found many things, and you, my friend, are clever enough that you could have found them yourself if you were not so occupied in wishing you were somewhere else. I saw much more potential in you than that in medical school."

"What have you found?"

"Let us start with the footprints," de Grandin replied. "You took the casts yourself. What do you think?"

"I think that I failed to do a good job. The man's foot must have slid, distorting the print. As a result, it looks much larger than a human foot could possibly be."

"Not so!" De Grandin crossed to the table that held the plaster cast of the single footprint that had been recovered from the garden. "Look at the sharpness of the edge of the sole, especially here, at the heel. If the foot had slid, the sharpness of the print would have been blurred."

"Are you saying that is really the size of his foot?"

"Of his shoe, yes." De Grandin replaced the cast. "We have only the one good print but there were other marks to show where he went. By using the measurements I had you take, we know the length of our man's stride. I compare it to the stride of a running man whose height is known, a little math and we learn that our man is eight feet in height."

"But surely that's not possible?"

"I tell you it must be possible. The evidence is not like an eyewitness. It cannot forget or tell a lie. What it says must be believed."

Maigret frowned, as important as evidence was his inclination was to probe the people involved first.

"Then, we must find a giant," he said. "Surely a man like that can't hide in Paris."

"Not by himself, but look at this." De Grandin pointed to the plaster footprint again. The well-formed shape, the nail marks on the heel, they all indicate that this is a shoe of the highest quality. For such a colossal foot, it must have been custom-made. It would have cost a small fortune."

"Then, the giant has a friend?"

"Very good, my young friend. We would certainly know it if there was an eight-foot-tall millionaire walking the streets of Paris."

"So, this giant has a wealthy friend," Maigret said slowly, "And he is involved in a well-planned, well-executed crime. Does that mean that his friend is a criminal?"

"I believe it does. What else do we know?"

"We know that our giant is athletic enough to climb the high garden fence." Maigret paused to think. "Before he climbed it though, he must have lured the dogs to the gate and killed them."

"That sounds reasonable, but we must be cautious of what sounds reasonable if it is not supported by the evidence. The bodies of the dogs, and the blood from their wounds, were found well inside the garden."

"So he climbed the fence before he attacked the dogs?"

"It seems strange, but the evidence does not lie."

Maigret shook his head in wonder.

"Sir, you make it so clear. It's as if you were Sherlock Holmes."

De Grandin frowned. "Fah! That one is overrated. I should prefer to be compared to the great Dupin."

"Or perhaps the brilliant Rouletabille?"

De Grandin thrust out his chin. The points of his waxed moustache seemed to stand at attention.

"That puppy? He is the one who should be flattered to be compared to Jules de Grandin!"

Maigret had to smother a laugh. His new friend wasn't lacking for ego, comparing himself so favorably to two men who were arguably the greatest living detectives. He decided that it was probably a good idea to get back to the topic of the crime.

"Is there anything else you have learned, sir?"

Jules de Grandin nodded.

"There is something strange and most disturbing about the wounds on the dogs. Look at this..." De Grandin moved to allow Maigret a clear vision of the mastiff's body.

"His throat has been slashed."

"Yes, but no knife made these wounds. See?"

Maigret bent closer.

"Teeth marks!" he exclaimed. "I don't understand. No one saw or heard any other dog."

"Perhaps that is because these are not the teeth marks of a dog," de Grandin said. "These marks were made by human teeth."

"My God! What sort of man could do such a thing?"

"I would like to know that as well," said a voice from the shadowed section of the lab behind them.

Maigret and de Grandin spun to see a dark-clad man standing in the center of the room. He wore a black cape and a slouch hat, which hid much of his face. He had entered without a sound.

"Who are you?" Maigret demanded. When there was no immediate reply, he started forward.

"No." Jules de Grandin laid a restraining hand on Maigret's arm. "This man isn't our enemy."

Maigret looked back and forth between his friend and the mysterious newcomer.

De Grandin nodded to the stranger.

"You're Judex, aren't you?"

Judex! With the mention of that name, Maigret understood. For two years, the Paris underworld had been haunted by a mysterious figure who acted as self-appointed judge over the criminals the law couldn't reach. Gauthier had mentioned the cloaked figure several times, always with anger and a touch of awe. The Inspector had little use for vigilantes. An infallible vigilante who seemed able to appear and disappear like a ghost was even worse.

Others had a more charitable view of the cloaked man. Maigret had heard some compare him to a modern Rocambole, a figure of superhuman cunning and strength who acted outside the law but who targeted only the worst of criminals.

Maigret had suspected the reports of the cloaked figure had been exaggerated, or even manufactured by the older members of the force as a story to tell to rookies. Now, facing the stranger in black, he realized that it was no fabrication. Judex, the self-appointed judge of the underworld, was real.

"I am Judex," the man said, "and you are Constable Maigret and Doctor de Grandin. The same Jules de Grandin who studied for a time under Sâr Dubnotal, if I am not mistaken."

"You are well-informed, Monsieur," de Grandin said with a little bow. "I did spend six months with the Sâr, though I am hardly the psychagogue that he is."

"I fought the man who took Mademoiselle Leonard," Judex said. "I call him a man for I don't know what else he could be. The criminals working with him called him 'Gouroull.' "

"What sort of name is that?" Maigret asked.

"An appropriate one," Judex replied. "I don't know what it means but it sounds like 'ghoul,' 'gargoyle' or 'gorilla.' I can see how any of those names could be applied to the creature I fought. He was bigger than any man I have ever seen, with a hideous face and the agility of a devil."

"Could he have actually been a gorilla?" Jules de Grandin asked, "Or an orangutan? It wouldn't be the first time an ape committed crimes in Paris."

"I don't believe the creature I fought was an ape. It stood upright and its face was human, though terribly scarred."

"Perhaps it was an ape-man," Maigret suggested, "Like that creature Balaoo who terrorized the city only months ago."

De Grandin nodded.

"I was not involved in that case, but I did help in the arrest of the madman Otto Beneckendorff. He experimented to create a hybrid of ape and man. Could this creature be the successful result of such an experiment?"

"As I said," Judex replied. "He isn't like any man I have ever seen. I had hoped you could tell me what he is."

He produced a sealed test tube from the folds of his cloak and tossed it to de Grandin.

"I wounded Gouroull when we fought. I shot him four times in the chest with my pistol, but he didn't fall. This is what bled from his wounds."

Jules de Grandin's brow was furrowed as he smelled the fluid.

"This is not blood."

"No," Judex replied. "It is not blood, and I don't believe Gouroull is any natural creature. I'm hoping you can tell me what he is. This ichor is beyond my ability to analyze."

"But not beyond the ability of Jules de Grandin, eh? Don't worry, Monsieur; I will justify your faith in me. Maigret, bring me the microscope."

Jules de Grandin placed a single drop of the dark fluid onto a glass slide and applied a cover. He slid the specimen under the microscope and peered at it intently.

"Name of the Devil! I have never seen anything like this before. It has a cellular structure like that of blood but it doesn't seem to be organic. It will take me some time to be certain, but I think this is a synthetic blood."

He looked up from the microscope. Except for Maigret the room was empty. Judex had disappeared as mysteriously as he had come.

A small red light came to life on the surface of the mahogany desk. Fritz Kramm noticed it at once, but didn't acknowledge it. He was sitting in his brother Cornelius' office at the charity clinic on the Rue Mouffetard, listening to one of the staff doctors.

Fritz raised his hand to interrupt the young physician.

"Forgive me, Doctor Lorde. I'm afraid all this medical terminology is my brother's domain and not mine. I'll be happy to ask him to speak to you but beyond that..." He raised his palms face up.

"Of course, Monsieur Kramm." The young doctor smiled. "I'll appreciate it greatly."

Fritz rose and showed Lorde to the door. Then, he crossed the room to a set of bookcases. He pressed a hidden release and one of the cases slid aside revealing the hidden elevator. As it did, the light on the desk winked out.

"Who was that?" Cornelius Kramm asked as he stepped into the room.

"That was that Lorde fellow. He's hoping to do some research and wanted to talk to you about carrying on a study in the clinic."

"He has a first-rate mind," Cornelius replied. "I'd like to see where his research goes, but I can't allow it. The studies he would like to do would result in unaccountable deaths and I can't have the reputation of my clinic sullied."

"How is your patient?"

"He was resting comfortably when I left him." Doctor Cornelius reached in his coat pocket and produced four light caliber slugs. "His ability to withstand damage is astonishing. And his recuperative powers are greater than those of any natural animal. Victor Frankenstein was a genius!"

Fritz nodded.

"If we had a few more like him, there is nothing we couldn't accomplish. If only we could count on his loyalty."

"You worry too much, Fritz. After all, we have the thing he desires most in the world. The Monster wants to look like a man, to walk among normal humans and attract as little attention as possible. Who else could give him that except the 'sculptor of human flesh?' My carnoplasty techniques can make even a monster into a matinee idol."

"And then what, Cornelius? You know what happened to his creator. The same thing has happened to every human who has tried to use him since."

"Technically, Gouroull didn't kill Frankenstein," Cornelius shot back. "It was the man's mania to destroy his creation that did that. But your point is well-taken and I have already planned for it. I am certain Gouroull would betray us as soon as he had his new face. That's why he will never wake from the anesthetic."

"Really? You aren't completing the surgery?"

"I'm afraid not. It's a shame too. Making that face into something human would have been a wonderful challenge," Cornelius shrugged. "Unfortunately for him, there's so much I can learn by doing a vivisection. His amazing vitality should keep him alive for days, possibly weeks. In that time, I'll be able to learn all of Frankenstein's secrets. Then, I can create your army, dear brother. Undying, superhumanly strong and possessing much more tractable minds than our unhappy Gouroull."

Fritz brought out a decanter of cognac and two glasses.

"We should toast the success of your studies."

He poured the liquor; never suspecting that every word they had said had been heard. Behind the bookcase, in the hidden shaft, a huge form dangled from the elevator cables. Gouroull's eyes twinkled with hatred and inhuman cunning.

It was early morning when the two investigators made their report to Inspector Gauthier. His face paled a bit when they mentioned Judex's appearance.

"That outlaw!" Gauthier snapped. "I'll be certain to have two gendarmes ready to catch him if he tries to approach you again."

He listened patiently to their estimates of the size of the kidnapper. De Grandin left out the details about the synthetic blood and his suspicion about what that meant. The two had discussed the matter ahead of time and decided to hold back some information until Gouroull was captured. Telling the Inspector that his men were looking for the Frankenstein Monster wouldn't help them at this point.

Gauthier listened patiently until the report was done.

"Thank you, gentlemen," he smiled tolerantly. "We have not found such a giant yet, but I now know we have our prime suspect as soon as we do."

He had asked Maigret to stay for a moment after de Grandin had left.

"So, Maigret, how are you getting on with the good doctor?"

"He is a remarkable man."

"He is certainly full of remarkable theories," Gauthier said with a chuckle. "We're to deliver the ransom tonight so you have only a little longer under his tutelage. It will be good to have you back doing real police work soon. Monsieur Leonard has raised the money and I think we will have Mademoiselle Louise safely home by late tonight and the kidnappers behind bars soon after that."

Maigret had gone home and slept for a few hours. He arrived at the laboratory to find the little doctor still working on the bodies of the dogs. They worked together through the early afternoon, until Maigret managed to persuade the older man to take a break. They walked to a nearby café that de Grandin knew and had a late lunch and a glass of calvados.

After lunch, de Grandin lit up a fat cigar. He offered one to Maigret, but he politely refused and loaded his pipe.

"There is something to be said for this, my friend," the forensic doctor said. "Sometimes, I become so obsessed by the evidence that I forget the needs of the body."

"This is the only way I can think clearly," Maigret replied. "I have to let things sink into my bones before I really understand them."

De Grandin nodded and the two sat in companionable silence until the little man's cigar burned down.

"I thank you, my friend, but now it is time to get back to my laboratory."

"I'll go with you."

"No, it may be better for you and your bones to stay here and ponder a little longer," de Grandin grinned. "No, I am not making fun of you. What you said is right. Each man thinks best in his own way. For me, it is in the close study of the evidence, but not so for you. Not every man can think like Jules de Grandin, but there is great value to thinking like Maigret too, I think."

They said goodbye and the little man hurried off.

A peculiar man but a good one, Maigret thought. He thought of his other new ally, the mysterious Judex and wondered what drove a man like that. Surely, it wasn't some abstract concept of justice. More likely he had suffered a very specific injustice in his own life and had brooded on it so long that he could no longer bear to see injustice anywhere. He preyed on criminals to avenge his own wrongs by proxy. What a grim life that must be.

The mention of Judex had provoked an unusual reaction in Gauthier. It was as if the Inspector actually feared the man. Was it just that the caped man was an unpredictable element in the investigation, or was there more to it than that? Also, it had seemed to Maigret that his superior had actually believed the story of an eight-foot man. Had he simply not known what to do with such an odd detail? Perhaps now that Monsieur Leonard had agreed to the ransom, he was focused on other things.

Maigret paid for his meal and began to trudge the streets. The afternoon breeze was warm and brought the aromas of the nearby park to him. There were young couples out, holding hands. He thought of Louise and felt a stab of worry. How foolish he was to risk losing her to something as foolish as her father's displeasure. When he rescued her, he should marry her as quickly as he could.

Who had taken her, and why? She wasn't the sort of person a reasonable kidnapper would go after. Her family was well-off, but there were many wealthier people in Paris, most of whom would make much safer targets than the daughter of a juge d'instruction. It didn't make sense.

Then, Maigret realized that it did make sense.

His meanderings had brought him back near the laboratory. That was good, but he had spent several hours walking and thinking and the Sun was nearly down. He and de Grandin would have to hurry.

"So this kidnapping is not what it seems?"

Jules de Grandin sat next to Maigret in the carriage as it sped along the boulevards. He had taken the young detective at his word and left his examinations behind to accompany him.

"I don't believe so," Maigret replied. "You said that the supplier of the giant's shoes must be wealthy. Why should someone like that blackmail a man like Monsieur Leonard for money?"

"But what if he were being blackmailed for something else?"

"I believe that is indeed the case," Maigret said.

"Then, perhaps the money is a way to distract the police. They will focus all of their attention on the ransom, leaving the kidnappers free to play another game."

The carriage pulled up to the Leonard house. All of the windows were dark.

"I knew he had sent the servants away during the investigation," said Maigret, "but where are the police?"

"They may have left to try to apprehend the criminals when the ransom is delivered," de Grandin offered. "Still, to leave the house empty is strange." Abruptly, he pointed as a light came on in an upper window.

"There is someone here!"

The two left the carriage and hurried to the house. The doors were unlocked and the foyer was empty. De Grandin motioned Maigret to silence as they went up the stairs. The door to the study was ajar and de Grandin caught Maigret's arm before he could enter.

Inside the room, Etienne Leonard stood, tears streaming down his face. It shocked Maigret to see the stoic man with the fierce eyes so vulnerable. In one hand, Leonard held a sheaf of papers; in the other, a small revolver. As they watched, he opened the grill and thrust the papers into the fire. He pulled another paper from his pocket and read it through before dropping it into the fire as well. He shut the grate and raised the pistol to his head.

"Name of a blue man!" Jules de Grandin hissed. "We must stop him."

They burst into the room.

"Monsieur Leonard, stop!" Maigret called. "There is another way to save your daughter!"

The magistrate froze in place, a look of pain and confusion on his face as Jules de Grandin opened the grate and pulled the burning scraps of paper onto the carpet, then tried to stamp out the flames.

"Maigret? Doctor de Grandin? What are you doing?"

"We know the truth, Monsieur," Maigret said. "The true ransom has nothing to do with the quarter million francs, does it? Your silence will not save your daughter. Only your cooperation can help her now."

Leonard slumped heavily into a chair. The pistol fell from his fingers.

Maigret turned to his friend.

"The papers?"

"A loss, I'm afraid," the small man answered. "We may be able to piece together a little from the fragments, but I don't hold out much hope."

"Monsieur le Juge can tell us." Maigret turned back to the stricken Leonard.

"The last paper you tossed into the fire. That was the note that told of the kidnappers' true demands, wasn't it? What was it you were investigating?"

Leonard raised his eyes. All of his defiant anger was gone.

"Do you know of the criminal syndicate called the Red Hand?" he asked.

"Of course," Maigret said. "They're one of the most dangerous organizations on the continent. I've heard that their influence extends even as far as America."

Leonard nodded.

"I've been investigating them for years and recently learned the names of the two individuals who lead them. I was going to prosecute them, but I had to be sure. They are powerful men with impeccable reputations. To accuse them without final confirmation would have been folly."

"And this confirmation?" de Grandin asked.

"It came yesterday evening," the magistrate said. "The night Louise was taken."

"You received two ransom notes?"

"Yes, the first was for money. It was to occupy the police so they wouldn't suspect the real demands. I was to burn all the evidence against the two men, and then I was to take my own life. They can't afford for anyone who knows what I know to live."

"You must tell us what you know, sir." Maigret's voice was agonized. "If we're to have a chance to save Louise, we have to know everything."

"The Red Hand will kill her whether you take your own life or not," de Grandin added. "You must know this."

Etienne Leonard nodded his head.

"I do. I hoped that somehow this could save my little girl, but that hope is gone."

"Tell us the names, sir."

Leonard raised his head. Whether he intended to answer Maigret's question or not wasn't clear. When he looked at the doorway, a fresh look of surprise crossed his face. Then, there was a gunshot. A small round hole appeared in Leonard's forehead and he sagged into the chair.

"I beg your pardon, gentlemen." Inspector Gauthier stepped into the study, pistol in hand. "I'm afraid the names of my employers must remain a secret."

"Gauthier!" Maigret had half-suspected his mentor. Even so, it was a shock.

"I am sorry to admit it, but I have a passion for betting. Sadly, I am not very good at choosing the best horse or the fastest dog."

"But the Red Hand told you they could make your debts disappear, didn't they?" Jules de Grandin's voice was contemptuous.

"Your deduction is correct, Doctor. I've always regretted that you chose medical investigation over the regular police force. We could have used you." He turned to Maigret with sad eyes. "And you, young Maigret, you have the makings of an outstanding detective. It's a shame such a promising career must be cut short."

He raised his pistol.

"Maigret, be ready to rush him," de Grandin hissed. "He can only shoot one of us, then the other will be on him."

Gauthier looked worried. He backed into the doorway, trying to cover both men.

"Don't try it. I'm an excellent shot. I can kill two men as easily as one."

"What about three?" said a voice from the darkness.

Gauthier started to turn to face the speaker. Before he could move, a black-clad arm chopped against the side of his neck and he fell senseless.

"Judex!" Maigret cried. "What perfect timing."

The black-cloaked man stepped into the room.

"I'm glad to have gotten here when I did," he said, "but if my timing had been perfect, Monsieur Leonard would still be alive."

He scooped up Gauthier's gun and tossed it to Maigret.

"You'll need this before the night is out."

"But it's evidence."

"If you want to save Mademoiselle Leonard from Gouroull, you'll need more than evidence."

Maigret looked to de Grandin. The little investigator nodded and picked up the pistol Leonard had held.

"Now that her father is dead, your Louise's life can probably be measured in hours. We must act immediately."

"But how? We are no closer to knowing where she is being held than before."

"On the contrary," Judex nodded to Gauthier's unconscious form. "He will tell us."

The ride to Judex's lair had seemed to take hours, even in the mysterious man's powerful motorcar. He had sworn Maigret and de Grandin to secrecy before driving them to the ruins of Château-Rouge. On the way, he had told them of his investigation of the Red Hand. He had learned of the plan to kidnap Louise too late to do anything more than try to intercept her abductors.

Château-Rouge had been a stone castle overlooking the Seine Valley. It sat at the top of a sheer cliff and had been an impressive stronghold in its time.

Now, it was a crumbling ruin, but one which still functioned as a stronghold. A hidden hatch led to a maze of passages that Judex had outfitted with the most modern equipment.

Gauthier sat in a small, windowless cell. The men could watch him using an electronically-controlled mirror. The room held some rudimentary furniture including a chair, a cot and a glass screen of a type Maigret had never seen set into one of the walls.

"He will wake soon," Judex said. "I've given him a hypnotic drug to make him more susceptible to my methods."

"I never thought I would be a party to such things," Maigret said softly.

Judex gazed at the policeman.

"I do as I must to find justice, Monsieur Maigret. If you believe that police methods will have a better chance at saving the young lady's life, I will gladly hand over the prisoner."

Maigret said nothing. He was willing to go along with Judex in these extreme circumstances but he couldn't help but sympathize with the man in the cell. Inspector Gauthier had been his superior and his friend. It was painful to see him like this.

"This is a remarkable place," Jules de Grandin commented. "And that cell, I've never seen anything quite like it."

"It is as much as a monk's cell as it is a place of confinement," Judex replied. "In that room, a man must face his sins. He is made to see all that he has done so that he can seek atonement. I designed it for another, but his time of judgment has not yet come."

"He's awake!" Maigret pointed at the mirror. The others saw that Gauthier had risen and was looking around the cell.

Judex crossed to a desk where a futuristic-looking typewriter sat. As he typed, words formed on the screen in glowing red letters.

ROBERT GAUTHIER, YOU ARE MY PRISONER. FOR THE CRIMES YOU HAVE COMMITTED, I SENTENCE YOU TO CONFINEMENT IN THIS CELL FOR THE REST OF YOUR LIFE.

"What is this?" the Inspector cried, "You have no right to hold me! I demand to be handed over to the police at once!"

THIS IS NO LONGER AN AFFAIR FOR THE POLICE. I HAVE TRIED YOU AND FOUND YOU GUILTY. I NOW PASS SENTENCE ON YOU.

"Who are you?" Gauthier's voice rose with the beginnings of panic.

I AM JUDEX.

"Judex? The madman who has been terrorizing the underworld?"

THOSE WHO HAVE KNOWN TERROR AT MY HAND HAVE BEEN DESERVING OF JUDGMENT. LIKE THEM YOU HAVE BEEN JUDGED AND FOUND WANTING.

NOW, BID FAREWELL TO EVERYTHING YOU HAVE KNOWN.

"You cannot frighten me!" the Inspector shouted. "I will never give in to these childish tricks!"

"He's telling the truth," Maigret said. "I know him, he's too strong to break."

"Perhaps not," Judex replied. "But it may be that you underestimate me."

For hours, it continued and Maigret watched his former friend's sanity slip away bit by bit. The drug made it impossible for him to ignore the flaming letters promising just punishment for his crimes. At one point, Jules de Grandin whispered in Maigret's ear.

"This Judex is relentless. It is only a question of whether Gauthier's will breaks first, or his mind."

It was past midnight when the end came. Gauthier hadn't spoken for an hour. He had simply sat and stared at the screen with its fiery messages of judgment.

Finally, the policeman let out a loud wail.

"No! Please! Is there nothing I can do?" Gauthier sounded desperate. Maigret shook his head in sorrow. The man he had trusted and admired was reduced to something barely coherent, wild eyes filled with panic.

WHY DO YOU DESERVE MERCY?

"Because I repent!" the Inspector was sobbing now. "I will do anything I can to atone for my sins! I will tell you everything I know!"

WHERE IS THE GIRL?

"She is being held at the Red Hand's headquarters. It is a secret basement beneath the dairy on the Rue Mouffetard!" He paused, breathing raggedly. "I've told you. Will you show me mercy?"

I RESERVE JUDGMENT. I WILL RETURN SOON. IF THE GIRL IS UNHARMED, YOU WILL GO TO THE AUTHORITIES. IF SHE IS NOT, I SHALL PASS SENTENCE ON YOU.

Judex left the final words glowing on the screen as he turned to the others.

"Our course is clear, gentlemen. We cannot call the police, they are not prepared to deal with Gouroull, and Mademoiselle Leonard would certainly be killed the moment they approached the building."

Jules de Grandin held up his revolver.

"I am not certain that we are any better prepared to fight that monster."

"I have thought of that." Judex reached into his desk and pulled out a strange weapon that looked like an oversized version of an automatic pistol. It had a very long barrel and was obviously hand-crafted.

"Among my allies is a gunsmith of considerable talent," the caped man said with a trace of a smile. "When I realized that we faced the Frankenstein Monster, I asked him to make this. It has the compactness of a pistol, but it fires the rounds of a high-powered hunting rifle. I thank God for his efficiency and speed."

"You knew that we were facing the Monster?" Jules de Grandin seemed slightly put out that he was not the only one to reach this conclusion.

"What else was I to think after your comments about synthetic blood?" Judex crossed to a file cabinet and produced a folder. He dropped it on the desk in front of the detectives.

"Once I knew what to look for, I had my agents comb the newspaper morgues. Here is his trail. Frankenstein created the Monster at the end of the 18th century. The events of Mary Shelley's novel seem to be accurate in most regards.

"After the Monster's supposed death in the Arctic, his body was recovered by an Ulsterman named Blessed. Blessed returned to his homeland where he made an exhibit of the body. In 1875, the Monster revived and killed a man. It was lost in the bogs and was thought dead until it turned up in Scotland several years later. The records are confused, even hysterical, but it seems that the Monster was involved in a string of horrible deaths in the village of Plosway.

"The last appearance I have found was in the Swiss Alps, near Ingolstadt. The Swiss are usually so meticulous about times and dates but my men haven't been able to sort out whether this was 10 years ago or nearly 20. In either case, Gouroull had taken up with a mad clergyman named Schleger. Their activities together are too horrible to relate. They eventually had a failing out. Gouroull murdered the pastor and fled into the mountains."

"Frankenstein... It's so hard to believe." Maigret shook his head. "But, if it is true, will even a weapon like that be enough?"

"I am told that it would kill a tiger, an American grizzly bear or even a Cape buffalo. As for Gouroull," Judex shrugged, "we will know that soon enough."

Doctor Cornelius Kramm sat at his desk in the clinic on the Rue Mouffetard, reading through a great pile of notes on anatomy, biology and the alchemical treatises that had inspired Victor Frankenstein. Suddenly, the red light on his desk came on.

Cornelius frowned. Fritz was away on other business and none of the members of the Red Hand knew of the secret elevator. Best to be safe. He pressed a hidden button on the underside of the desk. The soft swishing sound of something large sliding filled the room. He smiled and pressed the button that caused the bookcase to slide back.

Gouroull stepped out, his massive form nearly filling the elevator.

"Ah!" Cornelius said, "I thought it might be you, my friend. It was very clever of you to find my conveyance. What do you want?"

The creature gazed at the surgeon with hate-filled eyes and his thin red lips pulled into an ugly grimace.

"I see," Cornelius' voice was as calm as if he were discussing the weather. "You're here to kill me then?"

The Monster surged forward, giant hands reaching for the doctor's throat. A few feet from the desk, he stopped abruptly as he collided with something that was invisible but very solid.

"If you found the elevator shaft, I suppose you must also have been eavesdropping on my conversations with my brother Fritz. That was very careless of me, I'm usually much more discrete."

Gouroull ran his hands across the unseen wall. He began to pound at it with his mighty fists. This produced a loud, vaguely musical "bonging" but had no other results.

"Useless, I'm afraid," Doctor Cornelius said pleasantly. "Even you can't beat your way through my barrier. It's a bulletproof glass of my own design. The transparency is marvelous, don't you think?"

Cornelius' hand slipped beneath the desk again.

"Were you going to ambush Fritz after you'd killed me? Or perhaps, you were going to take the Leonard girl and disappear into the countryside?" The doctor shook his head. "You seem to be forever trapped into repeating the same patterns."

Cornelius hand slipped beneath the desk and his finger pressed another button. There was a quiet hiss as a dozen tiny jets began to fill Gouroull's side of the room with a greenish gas that smelled of mimosa.

"It's a shame it has to end this way. I would have preferred your cooperation."

The giant covered his mouth and nose with one hand while the other flailed around, smashing bookcases and hurling their contents against the unseen barrier. As Cornelius watched, he noticed that the books were forming a large pile against the center of the glass wall.

Gouroull stopped his rampage and pulled a box of wooden matches out of his pocket. He bared his teeth at Doctor Cornelius in what might have been a grin as he struck a match and dropped it on the pile of books.

"Very clever!" Cornelius murmured. "Even I have underestimated you it seems."

It was raining heavily when Judex's car pulled to the side of the Rue Mouffetard and stopped. The three men had a good view of the dairy.

"How do we get in without raising an alarm?" Maigret asked.

"We need a distraction," Judex replied. "I wish I had thought to bring my hunting hounds. If we sent that pack into the building, the Red Hand wouldn't know what to make of them. We could slip in easily."

"We may not need any such thing. Look!"

The others followed Jules de Grandin's pointing finger. Smoke was starting to pour out of the second floor of the charity clinic next to the dairy.

"My God," Maigret cried. "Those poor people."

"The two of you see that the clinic is evacuated," Judex snapped. "I'll use this opportunity to find the way down to the Red Hand's headquarters. Join me there as soon as you can."

Maigret and Jules de Grandin raced to the clinic where a slender man with fierce black eyes and a high, bald head was directing the evacuation.

"Monsieur, we are here to help."

"Excellent!" the man said. He was admirably calm. "Are you with the police?"

"I'm Constable Maigret."

"Good! I am the clinic's director. The fire broke out on the second floor so the patients are safe for the moment. All the beds are on the ground level. Just the same we need to get them out quickly."

"Why is that?"

"We store a great deal of ether on the upper floor. When the fire reaches it, there will be a terrible explosion. Can you send for help?"

"I'll do what I can."

Maigret managed to round up several gendarmes. The pouring rain hampered their efforts but it also slowed the progress of the fire. Before long, the building was evacuated and the fire brigade was setting up to fight the blaze.

Maigret and Jules de Grandin regrouped at the door of the *crémerie.*

"We had best see what Judex has found."

Maigret nodded at his friend's comment and the two turned to go in.

The explosion threw them both to the ground. The fire had finally reached the volatile materials and the effect was much greater than Maigret or de Grandin could have expected.

The next day, the newspapers reported that the blast had shattered windows for a quarter mile in every direction. Thanks to the heroic efforts of the police and Dr. Cornelius Kramm, no lives were lost. Unfortunately, the clinic was blown to bits. Nothing remained of it to show that there had ever been anything like a bulletproof glass barrier or a hidden elevator.

Inside the building, Maigret and de Grandin found the unconscious bodies of several men, including Gaspard, the young knife fighter. Judex had found the hidden door and was struggling to force it. Maigret added his shoulder to the job and the barrier slowly gave way. They hurried down the hidden stair, Maigret in the lead.

When they reached the bottom, they discovered a maze of passages.

"By all the Devils of Hell!" Jules de Grandin swore. "It is a labyrinth, with a beast more terrible than the minotaur at its center!"

They heard a woman's scream through the passages.

"Louise!" Maigret raced forward.

More through luck than anything else, the three managed to follow the girl's cries through the maze.

"I hear running water!" Judex said in a low voice.

"The Rue Mouffetard sits above a section of the old Roman sewers of Lutetia," de Grandin whispered back. "The Red Hand must have connected their passages to it as an escape route. But the sewers are small. A brute like Gouroull would scarcely fit."

"Then we have him."

Maigret redoubled his speed and nearly left the others behind. Moments later, he saw the entrance to the old sewer and stepped through.

It was much larger than he had expected. Whether through ancient design or later modification, this section of the sewer was clearly meant to be easy to traverse. The arched ceiling was 12 feet at its highest. Water ran through an eight-foot channel in the center of the tunnel and a narrow walkway flanked it on either side.

All of this, Maigret registered in the fraction of a second before a huge hand closed around his arm and another caught him by the neck. He heard Louise scream his name as the creature lifted him like a child and flung him across the sewer. He hit the stone wall on the far side and fell to the walkway.

He heard pistol shots and cries. Then, there was a louder retort followed by an inhuman howl of pain. Maigret forced his eyes open to a bizarre tableau.

De Grandin was down and Maigret couldn't tell how badly he might be hurt. Judex stood over him protectively, an electric torch in one hand and his strange pistol in the other. The heavy bullet must have hurt Gouroull. He held Louise in front of him like a shield against Judex's bullets. His clothing was burned away in many places but his flesh seemed unharmed. Louise was still wearing the pale nightgown she had worn the night before. Maigret thought, absurdly, that it made her seem an angel in a crowd of black-clad devils. Her face and the Monster's were very close, the warm olive of her skin against the dead pale of his.

Maigret shook his head and tried to think more clearly. Gouroull's eyes were locked with Judex's and his mouth was clamped on Louise's neck. He remembered the dead mastiffs, their throats slashed by those teeth. Lower the gun, those inhuman eyes said. Lower the gun, or I will kill her as I killed the dogs.

Maigret raised his hand. Somehow, he had managed to hold onto his pistol. He aimed as best he could, said a quick prayer and pulled the trigger.

The bullet struck the Monster in the head. It failed to pierce his massive skull but Gouroull cried out with pain and let go of Louise. She twisted away as she fell. He tried to bite her but his teeth merely carved a bloody gash down the side of her face and neck.

Judex fired two more shots. Gouroull clutched his chest and fell backwards into the water. The current was swollen by the heavy rain and began to carry him away. Judex fired another shot and moved after the floating body.

"Louise!" Maigret called, stumbling to his feet.

"I have her," de Grandin said. "You go with Judex. Try to catch the Monster."

Jules de Grandin bent over the young woman and daubed the blood from her face.

"It's not a serious wound, Mademoiselle, though I'm afraid it will leave a scar."

"It's all right." Louise's voice was distant with shock but still lucid. "A scar is only a kind of mask and masks don't frighten me." She tried to smile. Pain and shock were making her giddy.

"There are many kinds of masks, aren't there, Monsieur?" she added. "I thought his concealed his true nature but the mask was his real face after all. His soul was more horrible than his face could ever be."

"Perhaps so, little one," de Grandin said, "but there is no need to think such morbid thoughts. You are safe and Gouroull's moments are numbered. You should think only of getting better."

"What about...?"

"Maigret? Your young man will be all right I think. And I believe he would love you no matter what your scars. Happily, there is no need to put that to the test. You have the promise of Jules de Grandin that your face shall be as lovely as ever. Tomorrow, I will call on the greatest surgeon in Europe. He is a German living in Paris and they say he is a veritable 'sculptor of human flesh.' "

Maigret had kept pace with Judex as they had moved down the walkways, but neither man could keep pace with the current. Maigret saw the giant raise his arm to grab at the embankment but he failed to get a good grip.

"He's still alive!" he shouted.

Judex fired another shot. It was impossible to tell if it struck home.

"No!" Maigret shouted.

"Are you insane?" the caped man shouted back. "You want to save this thing's life?"

"If we can."

The look in Gouroull's eyes had chilled Maigret to the soul. There had been intelligence there, but no sign of the higher qualities of compassion or empathy. He sensed that this was a creature that would kill without remorse for its own, strange purposes. There was no room for dialogue with such a creature.

Still, it was alive, and he couldn't help but sympathize with its struggle to continue living. In his own way, Gouroull had even reached beyond the need for survival and sought some kind of meaning in his existence.

"We must turn back!" Judex yelled. "The water is rising too quickly."

"But the creature," Maigret returned, "we may still be able to catch him!"

"He'll drown soon. We'll join him unless we go back now."

Maigret nodded. He had mixed feelings about giving up but he saw the necessity of what his companion said.

Judex trained his light on Gouroull's bobbing form again. As the two men watched, he was soon borne away by the waves and lost in darkness and distance.

Bill Cunningham's approach to Tales of the Shadowmen *was to find one of the most obscure characters in French pulp fiction, the short-lived* Fascinax *(only 22 issues were ever published), and make it entirely his own. In Bill's story, the gentle world of pulp battles between Hero and Villain is replaced by a more gruesome, modern reality...*

Bill Cunningham: *Cadavres Exquis*

Fascinax is really George Leicester, M.D., a young surgeon who saved the life of the mystic Nadir Kritchna while in the Philippines. Kritchna rewarded the young doctor through a mystic ritual, which expanded the doctor's mind to nearly 100 percent, giving him superhuman capabilities. Fascinax has dedicated his mystic abilities to stopping Numa Pergyll, Fascinax's doppelganger in mental prowess. Pergyll has utilized his abilities to become the hidden puppet master behind all of the world's crime and villainy. Aiding Fascinax in his quest to stop Pergyll is the young Detective Simon Scott of Scotland Yard, and Fascinax's fiancée–the beautiful and adventuresome Françoise de la Cruz.

London, 1928

It began, as with all things, in a storm.

In the brick-faced townhouse, the butler opened the door to the evening to see the familiar dripping-wet figure standing in the entry. He quietly nodded his head, knowing of the shadow's business.

"I'll get the Doctor presently, please come inside, sir."

"Thank you. I wouldn't come, but it is of the utmost importance," said the figure.

"Of course, sir. I'm sure the master understands. If you would?" The butler motioned to the carpet for the figure to wipe his shoes. He thought that it was a much easier time when the master lived in the Philippines–hardly anyone wore shoes...

The dark figure stepped into the townhouse, revealing the nervous features of Scotland Yard's Detective Simon Scott. A broad-shouldered and handsome man in his late twenties, Scott had recently risen in the ranks of the Yard, due in no small part to the personage he had come to visit.

"And I'm telling you, George, that a woman likes to hear those things once in a while–at least in between your 'adventures.' " The feminine voice boomed throughout the house. Scott had come at a bad time.

And then, another voice, male this time, echoed throughout the foyer, "Tell the Detective I'll receive him in my study, Carstairs."

Scott turned to see the object of his visit standing at the top of the stairs. A tall dark shadow of a man with the most piercing blue eyes Scott had ever seen. Crystals that glowed with an intensity of purpose no man had ever known before. Scott was always relieved that such eyes were on the side of the law.

The butler gestured and Scott took off up the wood paneled stairs to the familiar second floor study. He had been here many times before. Too many times, thought the detective.

With each step, Scott thought of the groove he must have worn in the floor by now. Many of their adventures had begun with Scott paying a call on his host just as he was doing now. The Doctor had introduced himself to Scott's superiors at the Yard saying he had an interest in any of the Unsolved Files at the "morgue." The good Doctor, just returned from living in Southeast Asia, and without ever leaving the file room, had opened up lines of questioning that broke many of the most baffling cases. Those that were still unsolved he attributed to a scoundrel he named as Numa Pergyll. It wasn't until months later, when he intervened and saved the life of the Royal Family itself, that the Yard took the Doctor's involvement and abilities seriously.

The PM and the Home Office instructed Scotland Yard to give the Doctor their every assistance. Thus, Detective Simon Scott was assigned as liaison–a duty that never fell into boredom. *Especially now*, thought Scott.

His host sat by the fireplace as Scott quietly closed the oak door of the study behind him. A small library and meditation center, the study fit the man staring at the ebb and flow of the fire before him. Scott knew better than to come right out with it. It was their game–he would deduce everything from Scott's words, his gestures, body language, and something that Scott always found hard to believe–his aura. Over the many months of "investigations," Scott came to realize that the man he regarded as an oddity, was indeed a "superman"–one of rare body and spirit who accomplished the impossible.

George Leicester, M.D. a.k.a. Fascinax, was in tune with forces and energies (within his body and without) that science had yet to explain, but nonetheless existed. Scott had witnessed it with his own eyes in their "Case of the Terrible Templars." Fascinax had been able to remain under the icy cold current of the Thames for over seven minutes, evading the guns of a secret sect that planned to steal a hidden treasure of the Crusades.

"Fasc–," he started, but caught himself. He almost broke their second rule–"Never call me by that silly name the tabloids have saddled me with. I'm simply glad they have given me a secret identity to hide behind. Imagine the talk..."

"Excuse me, Doctor Leicester," he began again, "I was wondering if we could speak?"

"You most certainly may not," came the irritated voice behind Scott.

The lovely Françoise de la Cruz, Leicester's fiancée, stood in a separate doorway of the study. Stunning in her tightly wrapped lavender gown, she walked over to her man and stood beside him as he rose to his feet. Scott, even with his limited human abilities, could tell they had been arguing.

"Good evening, Miss de la Cruz," stammered the awestruck detective, "I wasn't aware I was interrupting. That is a lovely gown." She held out her hand and he kissed it, instantly satisfying her in some way that she had been missing.

Scott couldn't believe that she could be dissatisfied. Looking at the couple, and they were a couple–they were together in every sense of the word. They finished each other's sentences and each knew exactly the location of the other at an event. They were of one mind, one heart, but often Scott wondered, in light of her tone, "whose mind and whose heart?"

They had been the talk of the social pages, attending many an event together–charities, opera, grand balls–the things that Scott was usually assigned to guard, not attend. Scott often looked at the headlines where the exploits of the supernatural superman "Fascinax" had solved some dire mystery, only to find the calm and unassuming Doctor Leicester's name mentioned in the gossip column regarding he and his fiancée's polite social graces. If they only knew that in addition to Leicester being the superhuman Fascinax, the lovely Françoise de la Cruz was a crack shot, could ride in the steeplechase, and was a pupil of martial arts taught by her lover and mentor. She was the perfect woman for Fascinax, the perfect man.

Oops, there goes that name again, thought Scott. *I swear, he knows every time I even think the word, as if he were reading my mind.*

Fascinax smiled. "Forgive my Françoise, Scott. She has spent all week finding the right dress for the gallery opening tonight. She is going to let nothing stand in the way of her social standing." Scott was right. He did walk into the middle of a fight. He hesitated, but off Fascinax's stare he plunged forth.

"It is I who must be forgiven, Doctor. I know that invitations for tonight's London Royal Gallery Showing are very hard to come by. My subordinates at the Yard have drawn the duty of guarding the artwork for the event." Scott hoped that little bit of information would help calm the situation, but Françoise still fumed.

"Thank you for that, Mr. Scott. George is hesitant to go out unless there is some life-threatening peril. He would prefer to sit on the floor and meditate until another danger threatened mankind," said the young woman. "You would think it would kill him to 'rub elbows' every now and then."

"I know you would want to hear this information immediately," said the young detective, choosing his words carefully.

"You know Françoise is privy to all of my affairs, Scott," said the tall Doctor. His face furrowed into a statue of pure concentration. Scott hated that gaze. He always felt he was being dissected, probed by the man like an ant under a magnifying glass, which wasn't far from the truth. Leicester's sight, hearing, smell, touch, taste and that elusive sixth sense were all trained on the detective before him.

Leicester's senses continued their sweep over Scott's person. His brain analyzing every bit of sensory input he received. He reached out with every sense he had. With uncanny accuracy he knew what Scott had for dinner, where he had been that day, and what sort of tea he preferred. Then he recognized it–*No!*

Scott stumbled for the words as he looked at Françoise. Her eyes told him everything–*you're ruining our evening.*

Leicester held up his hand. He knew why Scott had come. And Scott was right–this was far more important. Françoise de la Cruz saw the grave urgency in Scott's eyes, and then looked to her fiancé for answers.

"Give me a moment. I shall meet you and your men downstairs in the car."

Scott nodded and gracefully exited the room. Leicester took a deep breath and exhaled. Françoise was puzzled. What could make her fiancé drop everything–an event they had been planning for months–to go off with Scott? What terror did the London night hold for her love?

But it wasn't George Leicester, M.D., who answered that questioning gaze, it was Fascinax. "It's not a 'what,' Françoise, it is a 'who.' I can smell him on Scott's clothes. His presence is unmistakable." He caught his breath.

"Numa Pergyll is here in London. "

Before she could utter a sound, she knew her George was lost to her. Fascinax was once again entering the fray.

Cold silence gripped the interior of the car as Fascinax and Scott sped toward their destination. As was their custom, Scott told Fascinax nothing of the "scene of the crime." The Doctor often found that the police made the wrong assumptions, and he preferred to deal with the facts that his heightened senses revealed to him fantastic as they may be. Lightning flashed by the windows of the vehicle throwing it into white. Scott flinched and hung on. The lightning and driving rain didn't distract Fascinax as he concentrated on Numa Pergyll. Such was his amazing mind that he could re-experience every encounter he had with his archenemy as if it were happening right then, even with such distractions as a storm.

Numa Pergyll was a scientist, a philosopher, a writer, a supernaturalist, a genius–and a butcher. He had much villainy to answer for. Wherever Fascinax had found chaos in the world–war, poverty, disease and slavery–the unseen hand of Numa Pergyll was often pulling the strings.

Fascinax had also uncovered several hidden "lieutenants"–politicians, generals and heads of business–awaiting a command from their master. It was not known how many were held sway by Numa's mental powers. *But where you find one rat, there are many to be had*, thought Fascinax. It was only his superhuman abilities that had, thus far, held Pergyll in check. Trapping them both in a master's class of world chess–with humanity as the pawns.

But that struggle wasn't without certain rewards as it was the diabolical machinations of Numa Pergyll that brought Fascinax and Françoise together in India. Pergyll had mesmerized her Spanish ambassador father into exporting rare artifacts from the Thuggees–the Indian cult of assassins. Fascinax was barely able to stop Pergyll from resurrecting a pantheon of demons trapped within the stone statues.

Françoise had seen him in action, and she knew at that instant she would be his, body and soul. And despite the many adventures across the globe, his mental cleansing retreats, and the occasional wagging tongue amongst society folk, she had been beside him–as a lover, a friend and, soon, a wife. Françoise was an exquisite specimen of humanity. *I've done her a disservice by making her wait this long, by taking her for granted. She deserves someone who will be with her always.* Fascinax vowed that his first order of business after this affair with Numa would be their wedding. And yet, how many times had he said that only to involve himself in some other case and postponing his life?

Damn Pergyll, thought Fascinax, *you are forever between my Françoise and I.*

This time he would finally put an end to this bloody game of theirs. This time he and Françoise would have all of the time in the world for the things she had been waiting for–their wedding, children, peace.

But deep down, Fascinax knew that there would be no peace as long as Numa Pergyll was lurking about. The villain had vowed as much in their last encounter:

Paris, 1927

"Damn your soul, Fascinax!" spat the outraged Numa Pergyll as Fascinax and Jules de Grandin stormed his secret laboratory. They freed the subjects strapped to the operating tables awaiting surgery. Cryptic plans and designs showed the future horror he had planned for their bodies–soldiers augmented with mechanisms and weaponry–living robotic zombies answerable to their mad general. Numa raised a spear and launched it across the room, allowing him time to disappear into a hidden passage.

Fascinax's unique brain "sped up" his senses so that the deadly poison-tipped spear seemed to glide slowly in the air. At the precise moment, his hand shot out and snatched the spear away before it impaled de Grandin. Fascinax dropped the spear and rushed to the dark entryway only to hear Numa's footfalls echo this way and that, disguising the direction of his escape.

Then, Numa's voice echoed in Fascinax's mind...

Remember this, Fascinax! You started this. When next we meet, I will rip away your very life, and leave you with a most exquisite corpse!

De Grandin came up to thank him when he saw the blood drain out of Fascinax's face. In his mind's eye, Fascinax could see Numa's glowing green eyes fill with hatred for him. This had become personal...

London, 1928

The car stopped in front of a rundown tenement in what would kindly be termed "the bohemian section" of London–Limehouse. Bobbies stood outside the apartment as the landlady sobbed to one of the detectives. These tenements allowed crime to walk hand in hand with refugees from war-torn Europe. Starving artists also made it their domain, painting quietly in the parks or sketching the seedy existence of their felonious neighbors. Opium dens, pubs, dancehalls and "Sporting Houses" also colored the landscape.

Criminals and artists, thought Fascinax, *what an appropriate combination for Numa Pergyll.* Fascinax exited the car and attuned his senses accordingly. He increased his focus, heart rate and flooded his system with adrenaline, steeling himself for anything. Crowds were a problem for the superman–full of thoughts, smells and colors as they were–and he being a human divining rod for sensual activity. And this was most definitely a neighborhood where anything could happen, and often did.

Fascinax brushed Scott's shoulder. "Come, Scott, let's see what Numa Pergyll has for us this time."

Scott instantly flinched. Fascinax at once knew the detective was leaving something out. Fascinax's probing stare asked the question. "I'm sorry, Doctor," Scott stumbled, "I wasn't clear... There's a body... But it is Numa Pergyll's. He is dead."

The police parted as Scott and his companion burst through the mass of people. The Bobbies, even though they didn't recognize the man with their superior, had heard enough rumors to know they were in the presence of someone of supreme authority. Scott followed as Fascinax stormed inside.

Taking the dark stairs two at a time, Fascinax flew up the five flights as Scott wheezed right behind. Long shadows haunted the hallways and the air seemed to get colder around them. Fascinax concentrated harder, filtering out the varied distractions, and continued his quest. Cigars, cheap booze, a baby crying, a man and wife arguing–all things that had nothing to do with Numa and his exquisite taste. Later, Fascinax would have to tell Scott of all the goings-on in these rooms. He could sense gunpowder, dynamite, and illegal alcohol–what the Americans called "bathtub gin."

This isn't you, Numa, he thought. Numa Pergyll was a grand meticulous planner. He crafted. He was an artiste, especially in torture and death. It was his trademark, and a small indication of the depth of his evil. The surroundings Fascinax found himself in were not Numa's territory–this, the lowest of the low. *What is your purpose here*? questioned the superman, his brain and physique aroused to the point of prickling his skin. He couldn't even allow himself the luxury of referring to Numa in the past tense.

Fascinax shoved the two puzzled Bobbies away from the door. Scott came up behind and waved them off. They were not to be disturbed. The Bobbies went away, shaking their heads and whispering to one another. A dead body in this neighborhood had never before aroused this much attention from the Yard.

Fascinax pushed open the door, which opened the rest of the way on its own. Then, the Doctor smelled it. Death.

A tall form lay prostrate on the hard wood floor. Even after having seen the body already, Scott gave a sharp gasp, but kept his gaze on the Doctor. *This is the moment of truth,* thought the Detective.

For Numa Pergyll, "Arch-Nemesis of Fascinax, The Master of Evil," the hidden puppet master behind many of the world's deepest, darkest ills, was dead, naked on floor. His body, an emaciated white canvas laced with dark blue veins. Skin drawn tight to the bone, as if dried like a beef jerky. This was a solemn, unassuming ending for one who lived his evil life like an opera. Scott expected something more dramatic. This corpse before them was simply pathetic.

Fascinax furrowed his brow, and Scott could have sworn the Doctor's blue eyes were glowing with activity. Those same senses, that gaze which disturbed Scott, were now fully focused on the corpse before them.

"Has anyone been in the room?" asked Fascinax as he walked around the body, taking in all the information his keenly tuned senses could provide. Simple plastered walls stained with water surrounded them. A few simple sticks of furniture made up the décor. In front of the body was an artist's easel and implements, as if the corpse had been lain down as a sacrifice to the art. A wet canvas covered the painting on the easel. It appeared that Numa Pergyll finished painting, lay down and died.

"Only the landlady who discovered the body and the two policemen you've seen," replied the detective, checking his notes. "I came to you as soon as I realized who this was."

"And no one has touched the body, nor been in its proximity for a period longer than a minute?" continued the Doctor. He wasn't asking a question, merely confirming what his senses already told him. He could smell the landlady's cheap liquor and perfume. He also knew she had slept with the man two floors down. Something her husband, no doubt, would find interesting. Scott nodded, frightened at where his simple confirmation would lead.

"Good. Then we can begin."

And detective Scott broke out in a sweat...

The car had come for her up promptly at 7 p.m. Big Ben's tones had confirmed it. Françoise estimated that they would arrive at the gallery at 7:30. She would have to come up with another excuse for her fiancé by then. She could imagine it: sipping wine and discussing the art with someone like Man Ray or the rest of the surrealists, when someone in the crowd would whisper and point in her direction. Usually, it was that she and her fiancé were living together in the same townhouse before marriage. That was an easy scandal to handle by now.

But tonight she had gone out on a limb and guaranteed her fiancé would accompany her to the gallery opening. Everyone in the art world would be there, and it had been Françoise's chance to silence the clucking of the hens. Now, as many times before, she would be alone.

And knowing that the main source of the world's troubles, Numa Pergyll, was in London made her burden even heavier. George would not let her come with him of course, although he understood her need in the matter. The villain had killed her father right before her eyes.

"And for that, good sir, I shall dance over your grave."

"Excuse me, ma'am?" the driver inquired. "May I be of service?"

The thick–bearded man looked in his rear-view at the stunning beauty in his transport. His accent indicated a European background, the Balkans maybe. His face indicated years of service as did the greying of his neatly trimmed beard.

"No, thank you, driver. I am just thinking out loud."

"I'm sorry that the Doctor couldn't accompany you tonight," offered the driver, seeing her slight frustration. "I know that the gallery will be disappointed as well. It's not often they send a car."

"The Doctor was called away on important business. Another matter of life and death, I'm afraid."

Upon saying the words, Françoise instantly knew that her lover's work was far more important than a few missed events. The responsibilities of Fascinax were many and the rewards few. Mainly that the public was never to know her man's true identity. To most, he was a handsome successful doctor who had inherited some sort of wealth and social standing–a playboy. She imagined that some of the society gossips pitied her, thinking Françoise was one in a long line of conquests for the man. Only her, a few members of Scotland Yard's upper echelons and, of course, Detective Scott knew the truth. Her man was the only being capable of dealing with certain terrors of the world. It was a responsibility he didn't take lightly, as she began to understand when he first told her of his life.

It was the burden she willingly undertook when she looked into Fascinax's eyes. She smiled at that thought. Calling him Fascinax, while irritating to him, was a more accurate description of her true love. He was more Fascinax than he was simple George Leicester, M.D. For once, the tabloid papers had gotten it right–he was a superman. But did her superman have no room in his life for joy? For her?

Scott's revolver shook in his hand as he trained it on Fascinax.

"Don't be a fool, Scott," uttered Fascinax, "Can't you see I'm trying to uncover what's really going on here?"

"Please, raise your hands, Doctor. I understand your feelings. I even agree that this… man… is, was, a threat, but I can't condone what you're about to do. It is against the laws of God and Man. Have some respect for the dead."

Fascinax stared at the detective. His eyes bored through the man's down to his soul. He read him like a book, and that made Scott sweat even more. He tightened his grip on the pistol.

"Well, if I, an upstanding citizen, am breaking boundaries, then imagine what a devil like Numa Pergyll is doing."

Scott hesitated as he looked in the man's piercing blue orbs. *He makes sense*, thought the detective. *I may not entirely like this man but...* He relaxed his grip slightly, and that was all Fascinax needed.

He shot his arm out, grabbing Scott by the throat with blinding speed. Nimble yet powerful fingers found the appropriate nerve clusters laced around Scott's neck and squeezed. He followed it with a quick manipulation of the blood vessels to the brain, and Scott spasmed. *What's happening to me?* he thought (for he couldn't utter a sound). Then the feeling left his arms and legs. Scott's pistol dropped to the floor.

Fascinax gently lay the detective down next to his pistol. He checked the man's pulse and pupils. He would be fine. Immobilized for a short time with no permanent damage. "I'm sorry, Scott," he apologized.

Fascinax began. He stripped his shirt, removed his shoes and stripped his pants and undergarments. He stretched his body this way and that, focusing all of his being onto the task at hand. He pressured specific nerve endings in his body and cranium sensitizing it to his surroundings. Spinal flexing opened pathways throughout his body releasing his Qi energy. In his mind, he recited endless arcane formulae designed to focus his thoughts as the Qi energy heightened his awareness even further.

As his body became a finely tuned instrument, Fascinax felt even the slightest shift in the air. Temperatures became part of the rainbow of the spectrum as his eyes shifted and became more sensitive. His core temperature rose and sweat broke out as his body worked to cool his brain and brainstem as it went into overdrive, processing all of the input it was receiving. The buds on his tongue isolated and identified the particles it tasted in the air, including the decaying body that was smeared with feces and urine. He knew what Numa's last meal was. He knew that there was blood mixed with paint underneath his fingernails.

He just knew.

You, my dear Doctor, are damned, Detective Scott thought in his paralyzed state. His mind struggled to force some limb to move–any limb. Even to twitch his nose would be a feat. Nothing. Fascinax turned and stared into Scott's paralyzed eye. Had he "heard" the detective's thoughts?

"What you believe, and what is, are two different matters, Scott," he said. "I do not require your belief in me, or my methods. What I am about to do, I do because I have to. You will be my witness on this adventure."

And what a terrible task it was.

The whole of Fascinax thought of Françoise at that moment. His right lobe was disturbed that he associated his love with his enemy. Then his left lobe realized it was because the language center had used the word "adventure." When Fascinax had proposed to Françoise, he had used her that very same word...

India, 1926

"Will you go on an adventure with me?"

He looked in her eyes, the crystal blue that matched his own, glowing with their own fire. Françoise came up to him, put his hand on her cheek and felt the warmth there. Then she placed his hand on her breast and he felt the warmth there.

He and Françoise made love that night–their bodies and minds intertwining. He lay her on top of his body, matching her heartbeat, her breathing and her very thoughts. By the time she was ready for his body to be inside her, he already was. Fascinax felt her first few orgasms. He felt for both. They were one, and, in that moment, the whole being named Fascinax knew everything about her–her memory, her energy, her soul. And from that pure moment...

Nothing would ever come between them.

London, 1928

After that night, he never again attempted such a taxing feat. Until now...

Fascinax' naked form lay down on top the body before him. Scott turned his head away. He could not even contemplate confessing to his Vicar what sort of necromancy he was witnessing. Fascinax relaxed, molding his body to his nemesis. His skin, the largest organ of the body, touched Numa's, matched, and became Numa's.

His breath was Numa's. His eyes were Numa's. With each heartbeat, Fascinax sank further into the darkness that was Numa Pergyll.

Slower...

Slower...

Until he reached that point of calm, of focus, where he was Numa. He was the dead thing underneath him-cold and unmoving. He fell into the darkness that was death, and embraced its cold love. He felt everything the body "felt"; the splinters in the floor, the cold of the air, and the intense pain in the back of his head.

Fascinax lay over Numa, seeing Scott with his dark, blue eyes. He lay immobile as Scott maintaining contact with Numa's skin. Matching the electro-conductivity of his aura to Numa's. Seeking his energy to learn its secrets.

But Numa's aura wasn't there!

This was wrong. Fascinax's lobes each independently processed that even the dead still retained some residual energy of their inhabitant's "soul." This thing Fascinax was linked to, was a husk, a shell–a darkness that was soaking up every ounce of his energy. Fascinax felt as if he were swimming in black syrup. No, not swimming, drowning!

Fascinax went numb as he sank deeper. Feeling his lungs not breathing. Feeling his heart not beating. Feeling the searing pain in his skull. Nervous spasms wracked his body as his mind reeled with images and pain... lots of pain... he had to get back to his own body!

Françoise accepted another glass of champagne from the waiter as she wandered through the huge glass-enclosed gallery. So far, she had been spared the direct confrontation of the social hens, but noticed several stares and whispers. *Oh well, they simply won't receive an invitation to the wedding*, she thought.

She did notice that her gown had the desired effect on the male population in the gallery. Too bad there wasn't a real man among them, she thought. At least not one who could hold a candle to her George. He burned too brightly for them.

Oh, I have been such a fool. He is Fascinax, a superman among men. I have pressured him to be something he is not–ordinary. And that is why I love him so ...for no ordinary love would ever satisfy me.

She vowed to stay for a respectable amount of time and then hurry home. She would get some roses and scatter them around. Find the right bottle in the cellar. Yes, it would be the right apology for her foolishness. No more pressure. No more "hints." She loved him and that was enough. Nothing would ever come between them.

"Excuse me, madam."

Françoise held onto her drink as she turned to see who had tapped her–only to see her driver. He was dressed anew in a formal uniform with a wonderful smile across his features.

"Oh, I wasn't aware you were still here," said the startled Françoise.

"Yes, madam. I was told to conduct you to the VIP area of the gallery. That is where the special exhibition tonight is being held." The driver gestured toward a set of grand curtains set off by a velvet rope. "Only honored guests such as yourself will be allowed to see the exhibit. The artiste was quite specific."

Oh how grand, thought Françoise. *At least, I will be able to slip out from there and proceed home.*

She followed the driver's arm toward the curtains and slipped behind them. The placard to the side announced the show as *Exquisite Corpse* by Guy L'Lampern, Artiste.

Fascinax choked out the words, "Again... har-der."

Scott hit him again. Nothing. Fascinax still wasn't breathing. The Doctor choked out the last of his air, "Hit me you spineless...!"

Whack! Scott increased the force of his blow. On a lesser man, it would have broken his jaw, but Fascinax wasn't responding! Scott reared back and hit Fascinax again! And again! And again, building his rage, as killing blows rained down on the Doctor. Scott didn't know how much more of this he could take, much less Fascinax. Whack!

Suddenly, Fascinax's hand shot up at supernatural speed and halted Scott's fist in mid-air. Steel-like sinews gripped the detective's and sent burning agony through his muscles. "That will be quite enough, Detective Scott. I am back."

"Thank goodness," said the detective, nursing his hand, "and thank goodness, I was able to overcome your paralysis. I do however, take offense at your commentary."

"But I am alive because of it. I do apologize, Scott, a side-effect of being linked to that thing," uttered the now-breathing Fascinax. It was a statement of fact, said with such finality that Scott was confused.

"Numa Pergyll is gone."

Fascinax could see the puzzlement on Detective Scott's face. "Numa is dead to be sure, but there's no residual energy in his body. This is a shell. Numa's mind is... elsewhere. It was taken out of his body."

Scott couldn't believe what he was hearing, even though he had no doubts that Fascinax was telling the truth. The Doctor was too far exhausted to have undergone anything other than the most hellish of experiences.

"Transferred? But where could someone transfer a mind? There must be a clue around here somewhere." Scott began canvassing the room.

Fascinax hung his head in exhaustion. Using his body to its full capacity took everything from him. But he had to recover, and quickly. If Numa had developed the ability to transfer his energy, then he could be unstoppable. He turned and saw Scott padding over to the painting, ripping the canvas off the work. There, in oil paint, was a surrealistic nightmare self-portrait of Numa, screaming in agony.

No, it wasn't agony.

It was rage.

"Scott, don't look!" but Fascinax knew it was already too late. Numa had him.

Scott's blood ran cold. He "felt" like he was drowning, and couldn't find any air. Yet, there he was, standing in that artist's loft. He had taken a look at the painting–its colors and textures and design. Odd, geometric, hardly realistic and yet, compelling. Compelling–that was an apt description. There was something compelling about it; something that drew him in. And when the words suddenly came out of his mouth, he knew he could do nothing to stop them. He could only listen and know he was doomed.

Fascinax crouched on the floor as the body that was once Detective Scott, but was now in Numa Pergyll's thrall, held the pistol up to its head.

"Greetings, mighty Fascinax! How does it feel to have a pistol drawn to your head, knowing that your greatest enemy has declared checkmate?"

Fascinax instantly surmised that the painting had been for him, and not Scott. It had been "instructed" to mesmerize him and give him a message from Numa Pergyll.

"It must be quite daunting to realize that you have somehow lost. I imagine your superior brain is wondering how I did it. The truth is if you hadn't destroyed my complex in Paris, I wouldn't have explored my psyche to the extent I needed to cure myself. You have but yourself to blame for your loss tonight."

A wicked laugh escaped Scott's lips as his eyes began to bleed.

Cure himself? Fascinax concentrated on every word, fighting back his own rage.

"Though you will never get to see it, I have had a cancerous tumor in my skull. A tumor, which doctors around the world have said was inoperable. A tumor, I later discovered, that endowed me with all of my superior intellect and mental ability. It is a conduit for all areas of my brain, allowing them to work in complete concert. I determined to defeat this irony one way or another. Radical surgery was one option, but that would have left me 'normal,' and I, and my organization, are anything but normal. Therefore, after the Paris debacle, I turned inward and unleashed my creativity."

Fascinax tried to increase his adrenaline flow and force his lungs to process more oxygen into his bloodstream. He tried to focus on the gun. If he could just get that pistol away…

Scott gyrated as he fought, with every ounce of his being, the demon inside his skull. Pulling the strings and watching him dance. Blood streamed down his cheeks and was matched by rivulets from his ears.

"I would say goodbye now, Fascinax, but I have your funeral to attend. I told you I would leave you with an exquisite corpse–your own."

Fascinax moved as Scott's hand tightened on the trigger, but the bullet tore through Scott's skull and streamed grey matter across the white plaster walls before Fascinax could reach him. The detective hit the floor, and Fascinax could already hear the Bobbies rushing upstairs. He grabbed the painting and tore it to pieces.

And then, he saw the signature at the bottom of the canvas.

"Who is the artist?" asked Françoise of her escort as they walked past the curtains.

"One moment, madam, as I must turn up the lights," replied the servant. As the soft glow of the gas lamps rose, Françoise saw the menagerie of artwork before her. A multitude of paintings placed randomly about the room. In the center was a circle, supposedly where one stood to see the panoply of work. Françoise gazed at the variety of color around her as she moved into the circle.

Then, just as she reached the nexus of the exhibit, she could see them all. Each painting was a little story of its own, but all a part of the greater tale to be told. She was immediately entranced, drawn in by the textures and the color. The surrealists were not usually her artistic ideal, but these paintings...

"Oh, this is quite lovely," she gasped as her eyes darted this way and that. "It's a tale isn't it? Like the newspaper strips?"

"Oh no, madam," murmured the driver, "this is something far greater than that. My master says it speaks to you. He is a new artiste of the surrealists. I am pleased to present the life's work of Mr. Guy L'lampern!"

And then, Françoise watched as the walls themselves began to move around her. She could see it now, each wall was held by a car rolling on a track around the room. As the paintings moved she stood in rapt attention.

"Oh, I see. This is like a kinescope! This will be fun!"

As the walls picked up speed...

Fascinax struggled against his manacles as Bobbies tore plaster away from the wall revealing more bodies. Some could barely keep their dinner down as they looked at the bloated, pustuled skins of the victims. Each one was tortured without mercy, and in specific ways. Some were bludgeoned with something dull. Others looked as if they had specific organs removed. And yet others were killed in ways too horrid to contemplate.

Fascinax was dressed in his clothes, which he had managed to drag on before the officers broke the door in. He had to get out of here!

"Please! If you will call the Home Office, they will explain!" he cried.

"Home Office! No, we're going straight to the Yard, we are," replied the slough-eyed officer. Fascinax knew they had already made up their minds about him. He couldn't afford to waste any more time. He concentrated on his hands, compressed the muscles and tendons and slipped off the manacles. He launched one of the officers away with all his remaining energy and raced for the window.

He crashed through the cheap glass and flew into the night. As he fell toward the ground, he tightened his muscles just so, reached out for the gas lamppost and swung around to the street. He raced down the cobblestones and disappeared into the night as whistles broke the silence.

Françoise eyes grew heavy as the whirling paintings indeed formed a kinescope in front of her. This image and that flowed together forming pictures in her mind: Pictures she couldn't turn away from. Pictures that spoke to her. Pictures of evil.

And as the images floated about, coming off their canvases, they became part of her. Each picture one speck in a huge collage. A collage of pain and suffering; of genius and madness; pleasure and perversion.

Françoise felt the story these paintings were telling. Experienced the images that assaulted her mind, infiltrating her very being and nesting within the electrochemical bonds of her memory. Tears flowed out of her eyes as she tried to turn away, but couldn't. In her mind, she pictured herself doing the very things that the pictures depicted–rape, torture, murder, death, destruction, manipulation.

She saw her father, no, not her father, but someone she recognized as a father beating her repeatedly. She felt the headaches in the back of her skull. She heard the words of the physicians as they told her that it was an inoperable brain tumor. She heard that it would only get worse, and indeed they were right.

She saw the lifetime of potions and addictions to subvert the pain. She saw the quacks and the treatments and the explorations of the mind and the body brought to her by the ever-faithful Franz Krypfer, her servant. And then she saw the first time she had sex (for it could never be called "making love"), when she raped the head of a crime family in front of his wife for refusing to obey her wishes. She beat the man with a baton. Then she raped the wife with it. In the last moments of their lives, she wallowed in their blood, painting her naked body with the slick fluids. She was 16.

And after that moment of revengeful horror, she saw her only relief from the slicing pain in her skull being the infliction of that pain on others. Thus began an unending darkness of pain and misery that haunted her thoughts.

No, not her thoughts, not quite yet...

Because slowly, methodically, as her mind was being raped by the images, she knew that her George, her Fascinax would somehow avenge her. Nothing would ever come between them.

And as her eyes shed their last soulful tear, she blinked; and those orbs of crystal blue turned green.

Françoise de la Cruz, daughter of Ricardo and Lita, lover of Fascinax was gone.

He rounded the corner, and Fascinax saw the blaze of orange engulfing the building. The fire brigade was already there hosing down the structure. Dozens of patrons watched as the gallery was consumed by the inferno.

Fascinax ran through the crowd, trying to find Françoise, disregarding the fact that the sensory barrage about him assaulted his mind. He shouted her name, but none could hear over the roar of the flames. He pushed aside the crowd and began a frenzied search, tearing further toward the flames. Faces blurred together. It was if he were blind. Colors/scents/sounds/tastes/emotions washed over him. Like daggers of steel, they ripped him asunder. It was too much.

And the superman the tabloids had dubbed “Fascinax” fell to his knees and cried.

Far down the street, Numa Pergyll watched through the curtains of her limousine. Her green eyes felt the pain and suffering of the young Doctor who tore through the crowd behind her, and it was the sweetest honey she had ever tasted.

“Franz?”

“Yes, Master–forgive me, Mistress?” the driver offered, unfamiliar with the tones, if not the manner, in which he was addressed.

“We shall call a meeting of all my lieutenants. We shall meet in Germany. There is much work to do there, and I want them all to know that there is a new head of the organization.”

Numa smiled for the first time in a long time as Franz Krypfer drove them out into the London darkness.

Epilogue: Germany, 1934

Adolph Hitler began a Top Secret program to selectively breed a pure Aryan superman–*Der Ubermensch.* Heading the project for the Fuhrer was a mysterious, unidentified green-eyed woman. The project was abandoned after the debacle of Aryan athletes losing to black runner Jesse Owens in the 1936 Olympic Games. The green-eyed woman has never resurfaced.

Terrance Dicks is not only the man who masterminded Doctor Who *for years, but he is also a huge fan of detective fiction, a genre which he has ably essayed with his own young adult series,* The Baker Street Irregulars. *In this story, Terrance has brought together two of his idols, Maigret, a character whom, at one time, he tried to produce for the BBC, and G-man Lemmy Caution, who seems forever incarnated by expatriate American actor Eddie Constantine, and asked himself what happened...*

Terrance Dicks: *When Lemmy Met Jules*

Paris, 1951

So I am kickin' my heels on temporary assignment in Tulsa, Oklahoma, chasing some guys who been selling oil-wells with no oil in 'em to some mugs in New York with more dollars than brains when the Agent-in-Charge sends for me.

"Lemmy, you're off the hook. We gotta tip your old friend Willie-the Goof Santana cleared half-a-million on the Zelda Van Huyten kidnap and took off for foreign parts with the loot."

"Did they get the girl back?"

"Yeah. Dead. Willie don't like witnesses."

Just to put you guys are in the picture, this Willie-the Goof is a small-time hood from Chi. His gimmick is he looks and acts like a sap, not to mention he looks like Mickey Mouse's sidekick. He looks like a clown but Willie's mean as they come. He's a quick-draw artist too. Last time we meet he puts a slug in me before I could unsling my rod... Lucky for me, Willie is a vain kinda guy and packs a .22 so as not to spoil the set of his suit. I have time to break his jaw before I keel over.

I say, "Willie's going up in the world. Holding up Mom-and-Pop grocery stores used to be his limit."

The boss shrugged. "So he branched out and got lucky. Anyway, the Director wants you should go and bring him back before he spends all the Van Huyten spondulicks."

"Do we know where he's at?"

"He's gone where all good Americans go when they die–Paris, France! Since you been there before on a couple of jobs, not to mention you and Willie are old buddies, you're a natural for the assignment."

So I shake off the dust of Tulsa–believe me, they got plenty of dust in Tulsa–and head for Gay Paree...

When I arrive, I report to the main cop joint on the Quai des Orfèvres and show my credentials to the Chief. He says in the interest of Anglo-American relations, he'll assign me one of their top guys to help. He goes off for a minute and comes back with this big, sleepy-looking pipe-smoking guy, who looks more like some hick farmer than a cop. To be honest with you mugs, I'm wondering just how much use he's gonna be. He looks half-asleep, dead on his feet.

The pipe-smoking guy tells he is currently tied up having a little chat with some poor mug who took a knife to some dame who gave him the air. This chat has been going on for 18 hours, and he reckons the guy will crack in another three, tops, after which he personally will be going home to catch a few z's. He suggests we meet for a drink later that night.

I say this is fine by me as I am a guy that will take a drink anytime and Willie is the sorta louse who won't show himself in daylight anyway...

They sat at a corner table in a Montmartre nightclub called *Picratt's*. Two big men, one considerably older and heavier than the other. There was a bottle of champagne on the table, but it was only for show. The older man sipped a glass of cool white wine from the Loire and placidly smoked a pipe. The younger, a broad-shouldered tough-looking type with a pleasantly ugly face, drank Bourbon and smoked cigarettes from a pack of *Lucky Strikes* on the table before him.

The little nightclub was crowded, the air full of the buzz of excited chatter and the drifting fumes of *Gauloise*. On the tiny stage, a plump young girl removed a spangled G-string, the last of her clothes, posed awkwardly for a moment in the spotlight, then disappeared through the door behind her, to a scattering of desultory applause.

Immediately, another girl took her place.

The younger man gazed at her with approval. "Back home, girls get arrested for an act like that."

His French was fluent and idiomatic, though with a broad American accent.

The other raised his eyebrows. "*C'est vrai?* I understood *le striptease* was originally an American invention."

"Maybe so. With us, there's always more tease than strip! Swell joint this, Jules."

"You asked to see one of our typical Parisian *boites*. A place where American tourists might come."

The other looked around. "Don't see any."

"It's early yet. The boss of this place bribes taxi-drivers and the doormen of other clubs to hand out cards to departing clients... 'Finish the night at *Picratt's*, the hottest spot in Paris.' "

"And is it?"

The French detective shrugged. "The place pretends to be very wicked but it is harmless enough really. That's Fred Alfonsi, the Proprietor." He nodded towards a short, thick-set man in evening dress standing close to the stage. "One of his girls was murdered a while ago. A messy business, one of my young inspectors was in love with her. Fred was a suspect for a while, turned out to be innocent–well, innocent of the murder. He's a rogue, but likeable in his way. Somehow we became almost friends."

The younger man nodded. "I noticed we weren't being hustled any."

In between doing their acts, girls were circulating amongst the tables and booths, blandishing the customers into buying them champagne. Always champagne– if you believed the label. They made no attempt to approach the corner table, though several nodded and smiled at the pipe-smoker and stared appreciatively at his companion.

The older man sighed and puffed smoke from his pipe. "I always seem to get on better with villains than with respectable people–like magistrates! And speaking of villains... How do you propose to set about finding this Willie Santana?"

"I already started. Apart from being a killer, a kidnapper, a robber and a hood, Willie's just your average American tourist. He's on the loose in Gay Paree with his pockets full of dollars and he ain't gonna be hitting the monuments and museums. He'll turn up somewhere where there's drinks and dames–somewhere just like this."

"Do you realize how many places just like this there are in Montmartre alone?"

"So I see a lotta strip shows and drink a lotta Bourbon–a tough job but someone's gotta do it. Unless I get lucky..." He tensed. "Jules, I think I just got lucky."

A tall man in evening dress had just lurched into the club, a bedraggled girl on each arm. He was loose-limbed and gangling with a long, comical face.

The American sprang to his feet and strode across the floor to meet him.

"Willie! Long time no see!"

The tall men flung off the two girls, freeing his arms. "Lemmy! I shoulda smelled the stink of Fed when I came through the door."

"Let's not be unfriendly, Willie. I came all the way to Paris to escort you back to the States. I hope you haven't spent all that ransom money." His hand moved inside his coat as he spoke, but suddenly there was a gun in the gangling man's hand. A big gun.

"I see you changed your tailor, Willie."

"I changed my gun as well. I don't make the same mistake twice. This is a .45, Lemmy. It'll blow you apart. This is it, G-man."

Something spun across the room and struck the tall man on the shoulder. It was a heavy champagne bottle. He staggered a little as he fired and the shot went wide, shattering a wall-mirror. Women screamed. Before Santana could raise the gun, the other sprang forward and struck. There was an audible crack and the gangling man crumpled to the floor.

His attacker looked down at him. "Waddya know, I busted his jaw again!" He looked back at the table. "Thanks, Jules."

"*De rien.*" The pipe-smoker snapped his fingers and two men in raincoats came through the door. "Lucas, Torrence, escort Monsieur Santana to Headquarters, by way of the Infirmary. Take his gun with you. Oh, and find out where he was staying and get a warrant to search the premises." He turned to the thick-set man. "Sorry about all this, Fred, it's all over." He turned to the younger man who was rubbing his knuckles. "I am sorry to cut short your stay in Paris, Lemmy, but we don't tolerate people like that here. Let's celebrate your success. Fred, some champagne. Real champagne, mind..."

We found the loot in the mattress at Willie's hotel and he's currently residing in the Tombs, waiting for a trip to the hot seat. So that was my trip to Gay Paree, short and sweet. And I'm telling you mugs, I learned one thing. That big French cop just ain't nearly as sleepy as he looks...

Guy d'Armen's Doc Ardan, *a 1928 proto-*Doc Savage *whom no one would have remembered had it not been for a 1973 anthology devoted to the Golden Age of French science fiction, has gained a new lease on life thanks to our 2004 translation of* City of Gold and Lepers. *Win Scott Eckert, the very soul of the New Wold Newton Meteoritic Society, latched onto the character to depict what might have happened 20 years later...*

Win Scott Eckert: *The Vanishing Devil*

Prologue: New York, 1949

In an empty penthouse suite on the 86th floor of the grandest skyscraper in New York, the telephone rang five times before the line clicked over. Inside a cherry-paneled box in the telephone alcove, a mechanical arm lifted the receiver. A pre-recorded vinyl disk was inserted against one needle, while a fresh wax cylinder was inserted and aligned with another.

A voice began reciting, "This is the Doctor. Please speak–"

"Doctor Ardan! This is Louise–"

"–into the receiver loudly and clearly enunciate your words. State the nature of your business and how we may contact you. Your message will be recorded and immediately conveyed to the Doctor or one of his associates. Thank you. Begin speaking now."

"Doctor Ardan–Francis! This is Louise Ducharme. My daughter, Justine, has disappeared!"

Sussex, 1949

Doctor Francis Ardan reflected that the Great Detective was quite spry for a man of 95 years. The tall, lean, grey-eyed man moved freely about the cottage, filling leather-bound footlockers with books, clothing and other personal items.

Ardan had been in London for a scientific conference and had taken the opportunity to visit his old mentor. Or rather, one of his former mentors who had participated in the strange training program devised for him by his father. The program had been instituted from Doc's birth and was designed to create a superman capable of tracking down and defeating evil all over the world.

There had been many others involved in his preparation for the fight against the criminal element. Professor Kennedy, who had instructed him in scientific detection. The sallow Frenchman, M. Senak, who had taught him the trick of temporarily paralyzing an attacker by pinching the nerves where neck met shoulder. Wentworth, who, along with Indian fakirs, had coached him in adding or subtracting six inches from his height. The list went on. Of all, though, Ardan reserved his highest admiration for the hawk-nosed man bounding about the Sussex cottage.

Now, observing the elderly Detective, and considering his mastery of disguise, Ardan wondered if the excessive wrinkles and liver spots weren't a sham. However, by unspoken agreement, Ardan had never pried into the Detective's beekeeping activities, even when he was a boy brimming with curiosity. In turn, his former instructor in the fine art of detection and deduction had never inquired into Ardan's synthesis of the African Kavuru elixir received from their mutual cousin.

As the Detective packed the trunks, Ardan finished relating details how he and a masked vigilante called the Yellow Jacket had disrupted the annual assassin's auction being held in the French Quarter of New Orleans.

"And you?" the bronze man asked, finishing his story. "Where are you off to this time, sir?"

"Tibet, Ardan." The Detective tossed a copy of *The British Bee Journal* in a bag and sat down on the divan, curling his legs under him like a cat. "An extended stay. I'm afraid you arrived just on the eve of our departure. Russell is up in the City, finalizing our legal and financial arrangements with M."

"I'm sorry for dropping in unannounced, sir. The neuroscience conference in London ended earlier than expected."

"Not at all, not at all. You know you are always welcome here, my dear Francis." The older man's grey eyes twinkled.

"It's been a long time since I went by 'Francis Ardan.' " In fact, it was the name he had used a boy, when he had spent summers being coached by various experts on the Continent while living with his great aunt Michelle Ardan; here in England learning the fine art of detection from the Master, as well as Thorndyke and Blake; and later still when adventuring in Asia in the 1920s. "The only ones who still call me that are you and Lupin."

The Great Detective's eyebrow arched at the mention of the notorious thief, with whom he had finally made his peace some years before, but the ringing telephone cut off his retort.

"Hallo? Yes? Yes, Violet, tonight will be fine. Yes, we depart at first light tomorrow. Very well. Yes, goodbye." He wrapped his mouse-colored dressing gown around him, curled up again, and started to fill his clay pipe with a foul smelling shag. "My niece, Violet, you know. Recently widowed, she was married to one of M's men. She's letting the cottage in our absence with her son, Clive. Dickson will keep an eye on them for M while we're gone."

The Great Detective lit the pipe, inhaled deeply and continued to speak when the telephone rang again.

"Confound it," he said, borrowing a phrase, "what does she want now?"

On the other end of the line, a mechanical voice intoned, "*Important message for the Doctor. Important message for the Doctor. Important message–*"

Bemused, he handed the receiver to Ardan. "Apparently this is for you."

Ardan took the telephone. "This is the Doctor."

As Ardan spoke, an audible click indicated that his voice had been recognized, and over a trans-Atlantic hiss, a tinny message recorded on a wax cylinder in New York began to play back.

"Doctor Ardan–Francis! This is Louise Ducharme. My daughter, Justine, has disappeared from her laboratory above Le Chateau Mireille club! All the doors and windows were locked from the inside, and there's no trace of her! If you get this message, please come to Paris immediately. I've been instructed not to contact the authorities, but I am desperate. I've tried your friend, Captain Morane, but he's away on a case. You're my last hope. Please help me. I'm staying at–wait. That smell. Like ozone… What is that blue light–?" There was a sound of a high-pitched whine, followed by the dull thud of the phone hitting the carpeted floor, after which the message ended abruptly and the line clicked off.

"That's quite ingenious," the Detective said as Ardan hung up the telephone. "How did the machine know to ring you here?"

But Doc didn't answer the question. Instead, he asked, "Would you contact M, or his successor if necessary? I need a favor."

Doc Ardan was not sure he would ever become accustomed to jet travel. His first supersonic flight over a year ago was marked by the eerie silence associated with faster-than-sound flight. This craft was not supersonic, but was close enough.

The RAF pilot, Major Roger Gunn, had shown him around the two-seater plane, a de Havilland DH 113 *Vampire* NF Mark 10, before takeoff. The British military were testing this prototype, which had a maximum speed of 545 mph at 30,000 feet, and a range of 1,200 miles. Although the dual tail craft was a night fighter, Doc's reputation and years of fighting wrongs across the globe had led the British government– and it had been said occasionally that M was the British government–to place the *Vampire* and her pilot at Ardan's disposal for the hop to Paris.

Periodically through the short flight, Major Gunn had attempted to break the monotony by drawing Doc into conversation, regaling him with anecdotes of his recent holiday at the estate of the 14th Earl of Marnock.

"The Lord of the Manor is a real gentleman, that he is. And of course the estate, Greensleeves, is kept up impeccably. But that boy of his, Brett, is a bit of a wild one. Oxford lad. Turn in the Service would do him good. Do you know the family, sir?"

"No," Doc replied.

Gunn was quiet for a bit, and then tried again, telling Doc about his plans to eventually retire and move his family to Kenya.

"Even at three months old, I can already tell that my boy James is going to be a real strapper. Do you have any children, Doctor?"

This time, Doc didn't even reply, but Gunn wasn't offended. Doc's mind was clearly elsewhere and the two lapsed into a companionable silence.

As they entered French airspace, Major Gunn reduced thrust to the DH Goblin 3 turbojet engine, and the *Vampire* began to descend. Nearing Villacoublay airfield, Ardan and Gunn simultaneously noticed several dark blobs materialize in the sky above them. The plane descended, and the blobs tumbled down along with them, finally coalescing into what appeared to be large chunks of dirt, rock and pavement flying through the sky.

"Taking evasive action!" the RAF man said as he swung the fighter around in a tight arc. The hunks of rock missed the jet by an uncomfortable margin and continued speeding downward to rain on the ground.

"Damn. What the hell was that? They came out of nowhere!"

"Yes," Ardan agreed. "They certainly did."

As the plane approached the military airfield, both occupants noticed what appeared to be giant gaping holes in the runway. The plane pulled up and began to circle for a new landing approach.

"I'm being directed to a different runway," Gunn explained to Doc. "Seems there's construction or some such on our original landing strip."

As the plane began its second approach, several large dark spots appeared in the new runway. From this distance, they looked like small potholes on an upcoming stretch of highway, but both men knew that the dark spots would prove significantly more dangerous to their small craft if they tried to land.

"Aborting," Gunn said as the thrust increased once more and the *Vampire* pulled up–right into the path of more tumbling chunks of concrete and debris. Swinging violently aside, Gunn and Ardan's plane barely avoided being pummeled as the pavement flew past them.

However, one large mass of rock remained directly in their flight path. Gunn reacted instantly, firing the *Vampire*'s four 20mm nose cannon and blasting the chunk into tiny fragments though which the plane blazed.

"I suggest landing as soon as possible," Ardan said. "We're not going to be able to avoid this flying debris forever, and if the intakes get clogged..."

"I'm way ahead of you, sir." Gunn brought the plane around fast and headed for the nearest undamaged runway, this time landing at Villacoublay without incident.

As the fighter slowed and taxied toward a cluster of outbuildings, an official French police vehicle came alongside. The plane stopped and Gunn popped the canopy. Ardan exited the plane at the same time that a middle-aged man in an overcoat and fedora exited the car.

"Doctor Francis Ardan?" the policeman inquired.

"Yes."

"I am Inspector Maigret of the Sûreté." Maigret displayed his identification to the bronze man. "I must speak with you immediately. In private. Will you come with me, please?"

Doc dryly thanked Major Gunn for the interesting flight and entered the Inspector's vehicle. Maigret promptly sped away, dodging the gaping fissures in the pavement which looked as if they had been smoothly dug out of the ground, as if with an ice cream scoop.

"Doctor, do you have any idea how these giant craters in the runway came to be?" the Inspector asked.

"It appears that the rubble we were dodging as we tried to land came from the holes," Doc replied.

"But how is this possible?" asked Maigret with disbelief.

Instead, Doc responded with questions of his own. "What is this about, Inspector? Why did you meet me at the airfield?"

In reply, Maigret handed Ardan a slip of paper. "I received this very strange note this morning. It did not come by normal post. I had momentarily turned away, studying a case file, and when I turned back, the note was spiraling down through the air to land upon my desk. When I noticed this, I went to my office door and checked the hall, but there was no one. My office is situated such that I surely would have seen a messenger, and yet as I say there was nobody. This would have been extraordinary enough, but the contents of the note were even more peculiar, especially given what we both have just witnessed." He gestured that Ardan should read the note, and drove on.

My dear Inspector Maigret [the note began]–

Please excuse the unusual nature of this missive's delivery, but I implore you to treat it with the utmost seriousness. You will note the impending arrival this a.m. at Villacoublay airfield of Doctor Francis Ardan of New York City. He will arrive via RAF jet, and though he shall encounter some small difficulties upon landing, I trust he shall arrive intact. It is not my intent to discourage the good Doctor's advent in Paris. Far from it. Rather, this morning's unique exhibition should demonstrate to you both my utter power over this situation, and the futility of any opposition.

You shall meet the Doctor's plane immediately upon his arrival. You shall not notify your colleagues or anyone else of the contents of this message, with the exception of Doctor Ardan. You shall immediately escort Doctor Ardan to the clinic on the Rue Mouffetard–you know the clinic to which I refer–and leave him there.

Do not deviate from these instructions in the slightest. The fate of two brilliant women depends on it. I would very much regret depriving the world of their future scientific contributions. Ardan understands.

Doctor Natas

The stone-walled chamber was smoke-filled, scented with a hint of jasmine incense. The lavish Oriental decor reminded Louise Ducharme of her time in Shanghai, China, when she was a researcher at the School of Medicine.

"Welcome to my humble clinic, Doctors." A man with the face of a devil, resplendent in his silk robes, emerged and ensconced himself in what was essentially a small throne. He fixed his diabolical gaze on mother and daughter, Louise and Justine Ducharme.

Louise visibly blanched.

"Yes, Doctor Ducharme, it is I," came the sibilant reply. "It has been a long time. But not so long, I see, that you forget your former opponent. I am honored." He turned to the younger woman.

"Doctor Ducharme–I shall call you Justine, in order to distinguish from your honored mother–Justine, I will come straight to the point. You are a recognized expert in theoretical physics, specifically the disassembly, transmission and reassembly of solid objects. Your experiments with Professor Rushton are legendary among my scientists, and I expect great things from him. But you are in Paris, and he is not. Thus, your presence here."

"Professor Rushton!" Justine exclaimed. "But that research is classified!"

"My dear, nothing is hidden, nor remains hidden, if I wish it to be revealed. You, Mademoiselle, have knowledge which I require, expertise in the area of accurately directing and controlling the integrity of the matter transmission over large distances. You shall be escorted to my laboratory, where you will consult with several other professionals in my service. They will brief you on the precise information which we require from you. Your mother is here to ensure your cooperation. That is all."

"Who are you?" Justine demanded. "How dare you?"

"Your mother knows me as Doctor Natas, and I dare much, my child." There was no flicker of recognition in Justine's gold-flecked eyes. "I see you are not familiar with the name."

Natas directed an inquiring glance at Louise. "So you never told her the tale? The story of our adventure together in Tibet? Never told her of Doctor Ard– "

"That's enough," Louise interjected. "We are here. You have us. Get on with it."

Natas' cat-like green eyes blazed briefly, but his visage quickly calmed. "You are right, of course. Time is of the essence." He clapped once, and two lascars emerged from behind the throne. Natas pointed to Justine. "Escort the doctor to the laboratory."

The two burly men took Justine by each arm and directed her to a wall of bookcases, one of which slide aside to reveal a hidden elevator. As the three entered the elevator cage, Justine turned and looked imploringly at her mother, but Louise merely nodded reassuringly. Then the elevator's folding door closed and they were gone.

Louise looked at the satanic visage of Doctor Natas. Twenty-two years ago, he had held her and Doctor Francis Ardan captive in his "City of Gold and Lepers," hidden deep in the wasteland of the Koko Nor desert of Tibet. Then,

Natas had mastered the alchemy of converting base matter to gold. He had captured dozens of eminent scientists–including Doctors Francis Ardan and Louise Ducharme–as well as thousands more menial workers. All the prisoners had been held as slaves, hostage to an especially virulent form of leprosy. Only the City's Z-Rays, another of Doctor Natas' discoveries, held the sickness in check. And thus had held Natas' slaves captive to toil in the City, for to flee was to die.

Natas had aspired to world domination, and would have achieved it, if not for Francis Ardan and Louise Ducharme.

Now, Louise's face took on an expression of profound disgust. "What do you really want from her?"

"Information, Doctor Ducharme, merely information."

"You won't get it."

"By hook or by crook, I will."

"She is but a girl!"

"She is of age. And she is genius... Just like her father. She will share her secrets. They will be safe with me."

Two more lascars appeared. "Take Doctor Ducharme to her room." The three entered the hidden elevator and disappeared from sight.

Another Asian man came forward from the shadows behind the throne. "You play a dangerous game, Master."

"Perhaps, Pao Tcheou, perhaps. I have been patient, have waited 22 years. I am close. The danger is necessary."

"But to lead Ardan here. It is hazardous," Pao Tcheou said.

"I decide what is necessary or not. Remember that, honorable cousin. When you lead the Council, you may decide."

"Master, you have my allegiance. But the other Council members do not have your foresight. They do not understand your plans. Fen-Chu, in particular, grows restless."

"Pao Tcheou, all is unraveling as I planned. I brought Doctor Ardan and Doctor Ducharme together all those years ago. I set them in the perilous circumstances that drew them to each other. Though they destroyed my City of Gold, it was I who won in the end. All is as it should be. You will reassure the Council," Natas said.

"Very well, Master."

"Excellent. And now, go to check in the laboratory. Ensure that Doctor Caresco is obtaining what he needs."

Pao Tcheou bowed deeply and withdrew.

"It is time," the villain Natas said to himself. Turning to a large apparatus in the corner of the throne room, he activated several switches. A screen came to life, and focused on the outside of the clinic, just around the corner from the nearby dairy. A police vehicle pulled up to the corner.

Arriving at the clinic on the Rue Mouffetard, Doc Ardan instructed Maigret to wait outside, but to bring police backup if he did not appear after four hours. Maigret agreed and turned to enter his vehicle. At the faint sound of a high-pitched whine, he looked up and saw a slight shimmer in the air, almost as if he were looking through waves of heat on the desert, although the waves were tinged with blue light.

And nothing else.

Ardan was gone, leaving nothing but the faint hint of ozone in the air, although he couldn't possibly have rounded the corner so quickly in the time Maigret had been turned away.

Doc Ardan materialized in Natas' throne room, appearing in mid-air and dropping to the floor. Cat-like, Ardan landed on his feet. He stared for long seconds at the Asian man standing by the apparatus in the corner, an assemblage of electrodes, antennae and globes topping a control panel of knobs, switches and sliding levers.

"Congratulations, Doctor Ardan," Natas said, assuming his seat in the room's center. "You are as agile as ever. The perfect physical and mental specimen."

"That's an interesting trick," Doc said.

"Oh, that. Merely a refinement of a technology developed by another of your many foes, which was in turn based upon Nemor's Disintegrator."

"Yes, I know, the teleporter. That's how you abducted the women. Delivered the note to Maigret. And cast debris into the air at my plane."

Doctor Natas was only momentarily nonplussed. "Very clever, Doctor. I will not underestimate you again. Since you are familiar with the technology, you also know that the teleporter as originally designed only worked in a straight line, limiting its range. We have strengthened the integrity of the transmission stream considerably, but the device's range is still not to my satisfaction. Perhaps you would care to 'take a crack' at it?"

"I don't think so," Doc replied.

"Come now, Doctor. You and I are giants, supermen. Immortals, even! Does not the science of this device intrigue you? I fail to understand how you could let this technology languish these 14 years."

"I'm not surprised," Doc said wryly.

"Nevertheless, you will assist in the completion of the teleporter," Doctor Natas said. Six more brawny dacoits appeared from the shadows and took positions circling Doc.

"On no less than three separate occasions you have interfered with my plans," Natas continued, raising three long, clawed fingers.

"Tibet, 1927. The destruction of the City of Gold and Lepers. The dispersal of my labor force. That was a considerable inconvenience, Doctor." One finger curled inward.

"Limehouse, December 1931. You and Allard interfered with my plans and those of my colleague, Yu'An Hee See." The second finger closed, leaving one long forefinger pointing at Ardan.

"Haiti, April 1940. The complete destruction of my arsenal, including various advanced aircraft and submersibles." Natas closed his last finger into a fist.

Throughout this recitation, Doc had remained standing as motionless as a Greek statue, evincing no sign of emotion.

"You are a worthy adversary, Doctor Ardan, deserving of my respect." Natas paused. "But the scales must be balanced. Debts must be repaid. You will assist me with the teleporter."

"Enough of this charade, Natas," Doc said. "You've already kidnapped Justine Ducharme, and she's the expert in this area. Louise Ducharme is a medical doctor, so if you're only seeking to perfect your teleporter, then you have no reason to capture her, except to force Justine's cooperation. You don't need me at all."

"Au contraire, Doctor. You were present when the teleporter was first used. Doubtless you analyzed its secrets. You are a scientific genius in numerous fields of study, a genius perhaps only second to my own. Do this thing for me, and in consideration of our distant... familial relationship, I will release you unharmed."

Ardan's silence was his answer.

Natas gestured for the dacoits to close in on Ardan. "Take the Doctor to the laboratory," instructed Natas, but before the men could act upon that order, Ardan was a blur of bronze motion.

Two solid punches sent the first two men immediately to the floor.

As two more adversaries approached, Doc tore hanging shreds away from his already ripped shirt, took a classic Baritsu stance and waited for the men to press their attack. They coordinated their assault, and faster than thought, the men were flying through the air in different directions, hitting opposite walls and collapsing insensate on the ground.

The final two lascars appraised Ardan with more caution.

Ardan leaped, and before they could react, he was behind them, with each cabled bronze hand gripping them at the base of their necks and working at the junctures of neck and shoulder. Both attackers slumped to the floor, unconscious.

By this time, however, Doctor Natas had made it to the apparatus in the corner, manipulating several switches and dials. The granite ceiling above Doc's head was already enveloped in the shimmering blue light. Before even Ardan could react, chunks of stone were raining down upon his head, knocking him unconscious. Only the skullcap resembling his natural bronze-colored hair protected Ardan from suffering a concussion.

Natas pressed another button, and shortly thereafter Pao Tcheou appeared from the elevator hidden behind the bookcases.

"Put him with the others. We are almost done here," Natas said.

Pao Tcheou bowed deeply.

Ardan, Louise and Justine sat in a dank cell deep below Natas' throne room.

"Louise..." Doc had just awakened from the blow to his head.

"Francis," Louise asked with concern, "are you all right?"

"Yes, there does not appear to be any permanent damage."

"I gave you a quick once-over while you were still out, and I agree. Although I have to say this is obviously not the first time you've taken such a blow to the head. Or elsewhere, given all those scars."

Doc looked uncomfortable, and shrugged slightly, but didn't say anything.

"Thank you for coming."

Doc finally looked up and took in Louise's milky complexion and raven hair. Memories and emotions buried for 20 years came swirling back unbidden, but he quickly suppressed them. "Thus far, my presence here has been unproductive," Doc said ruefully.

"But you came. So thank you."

"You're welcome." Ardan looked over at Justine. Her eyes, swirling with gold-flecks, stared blankly into nothingness. "Is that...?"

"Yes. That is Justine. She appears to be hypnotized. They brought her back half an hour ago in this state, and she hasn't come out if it. I've examined her, and she appears to be unharmed, but nothing I do or say elicits a response."

There was an awkward silence, broken only by the incessant sound of water dripping outside the cell door.

Finally, Doc said, "I respected your wishes. I stayed away from you after Tibet. I didn't realize it was because we had a daughter." There was a hint of anger in his voice, although his face remained a bronze mask.

"I had hoped to spare Justine from incidents just like this one by raising Justine alone. You were prepared, trained in that strange program your father arranged, to fight evil all over the world. That is no life for a wife and daughter, and who was I to try to dissuade you from what you had spent your whole life preparing for?"

"Perhaps if I had known, I would have made a different decision."

"That is easy to say," Louise flared, "but it is rather less easy to overcome a lifelong program of indoctrination. Your path was set. It didn't include me. I missed you, and occasionally wondered... But I have not pined away for how it could have been. Justine and I have a good life, happy, safe and healthy. And from all the news accounts, and all the stories I've heard over the years of the people you've helped, I think things turned out the way they were supposed to."

Doc was quiet for a bit. Then, he ventured, "Many of those accounts are drastically exaggerated."

"Nevertheless." Louise was firm.

"Yes. Nevertheless." Ardan inhaled, exhaled deeply. "I had another child once, a son. Before we met."

"You never told me."

"No... It didn't turn out well."

"I'm sorry."

"You needn't be." Ardan looked over at Justine, noting her coppery blonde hair and bronzed skin. "She is a beautiful young woman. And intelligent. Her scientific reputation precedes her."

He paused, and then looking back to Louise, told her, "You've done a wonderful job raising her. You made the right decision."

Louise took Ardan's hand in hers and squeezed it, smiling. Then she took him in her arms. "Thank you, Francis," she whispered.

At a slight moan, they both looked over at Justine, who started to come out of her trance.

"Justine, Justine. Are you all right?" As the girl nodded, Louise went over to her. "This is my... colleague, Doctor Ardan."

"How do you do, Doctor Ducharme," Doc said formally. "How do you feel?"

"I feel very well, thank you. As if I have slept for hours...." She stretched.

"What happened in the laboratory?" Louise asked.

"I don't remember... We went to the lab. There were several men there, all in white coats. One gave me a brief physical exam, and took a tissue sample, which I thought was odd. Then he gave me an injection. The next thing I remember, I woke up here with you."

"Clearly," Ardan interjected, "Natas' men have managed to extract the information they wanted while you were under. Why else return you here so quickly? He must be stopped. Now that Justine is awake, we can leave."

"How do you suggest we do that?" Louise asked. "Shall we just ring for the porter and tell him we're ready to check out?

Without answering her directly, Doc unloosed his belt, aimed the buckle at the heavy cell door, and depressed a tiny switch. After about 30 seconds of this, while the two women stared at Ardan and began to doubt his sanity, the door latch started to glow with heat. Doc aimed a massive kick at the latch and the door flew open. He glanced at Louise expectantly, with one eyebrow raised ever-so-slightly–a habit he had also picked up from his old master M. Senak–and gestured for the two women to follow.

"I withdraw the question," Louise said.

Unhindered, the three traversed several maze-like corridors of the abandoned dairy underneath the clinic before they finally found the elevator's lower entrance. When they emerged on the top level from behind the hidden bookcase, Natas' throne room was deserted, save for the telltale hint of ozone.

Doc went over to the teleporter apparatus in the corner and examined it. Looking closely at the rematerialization settings, he noted that they were set for latitude and longitude coordinates which were across the globe. In China.

Doc, Louise and Justine emerged from clinic onto the Rue Mouffetard, and introductions were exchanged with Inspector Maigret. Ardan was quiet, reflecting that their escape was too simple. However, before Ardan could bring Maigret up to speed with the details of their ordeal, the call box outside the erstwhile clinic rang.

Ardan exchanged glances with the other three, and then walked over and picked up the receiver.

"*Oui?*"

A familiar mechanical voice recited, "*Important message for the Doctor. Important message for the Doctor. Important message–*"

"This is the Doctor."

Once again, a click indicated recognition of Doc's voice, and another wax cylinder in his New York headquarters carried its message over the Atlantic.

"Greetings, Doctor Ardan! I wished to set your mind at rest that, despite your interference in my affairs, I have extracted the information I needed from Mademoiselle Ducharme. The teleporter can now be aimed much more accurately and at much longer distances, as you no doubt saw when you examined my equipment. No, do not bother attempting to follow me, the apparatus has already self-destructed in the time it has taken you to evacuate the clinic and receive this message. And to further ensure that you do not attempt to follow me, I have arranged a further distraction for you, which, I assure you, you will ignore at your peril.

"I also pledge to you that Mademoiselle Ducharme will remain unmolested by me in the future. Please convey to Justine, and to her mother, my deepest regrets at inconveniencing them, and my warmest regards. They are both the finest examples of their gender, and come from excellent stock, as you well know. I have nothing but the highest admiration for them both. And for you, my dear Doctor. Goodbye."

The line clicked off and Doc hung up the telephone. He conveyed the gist of Natas' message to the two women and the Inspector. Natas' statement about Ardan interfering in his affairs struck him as strange, in this instance. Ardan had really done nothing substantial in terms interfering with Natas' plans and rescuing the two women, and yet Natas clearly wanted him to think he had. Why?

Nonetheless, Ardan kept his lingering doubts to himself. Instead, he told the two women that he had been considering a semi-retirement from his life of adventuring, in order to focus more of his energies on scientific research. He concluded by cautiously suggesting that he visit Louise and Justine when they had more time to become better acquainted. Louise looked skeptical, but Justine was enthusiastic.

"Yes, Doctor, I would like that. In fact, I would very much appreciate your input on a new area of research I've been contemplating with my British colleague, Dr. Rushton. It may be that in addition to teleporting objects from place to place, we can actually dematerialize them at one end of the process, and rematerialize them at a different size."

"The laws of physics–"

"Yes, yes, and just a few years ago conventional wisdom dictated that we would never exceed the speed of sound. The laws of physics state that objects cannot travel faster than light, and yet I firmly believe that as we learn more about the universe, the laws of physics will be rewritten to account for practical interstellar travel. Given your own inventions and scientific discoveries, and what we have seen today with that fiend Natas' teleporter, how can you disagree?" Justine challenged.

"In truth, I cannot," Ardan admitted.

"Very good. Now, if we can attain a practical means of rematerializing objects wholly intact, but at a much smaller size, why the possibilities for surgery, engineering–"

"Doctors, Doctors, please!" interjected Maigret. "There will be plenty of time later for these discussions. Right now I must insist that you all accompany me to headquarters, where I must take your statements and file a report on the kidnappings."

Ruefully, the three scientists agreed, and started to move toward Maigret's vehicle.

The call box on the Rue Mouffetard jangled again.

Doc raced back and picked up the phone.

"Doc, Doc, is that you?" a high-pitched male voice squeaked.

"Yes, you've tracked me down."

"Well," the squeaky voice continued, "it wasn't tough with that phone-tracker thing you invented. Lissen, anyway, Doc, you've got to get back here, quick! Somethin's up in Port City, just up the coast from Innsmouth. Some kinda creature washed ashore, complete with gills and scales and webbed feet and bulging eyes. Johnny's up there now, and even he can't identify it for sure. Best he can say is it's some kinda amphibian frog-thing."

"All right, Mo–"

"Hang on, Doc, there's more! There's some nutjob up there, calling himself Doctor Ariosto! He's stirring up the local Chinese immigrants with stories about this frog-boy, and it ain't helpin' that some of them are starting to disappear without a trace. Me and the boys are heading up there now! Lissen, Doc, where are you, anyway?"

"Go up to Port City to check it out. I'll meet you there as soon as I can," Doc said, and he hung up.

The distraction, Doc thought. He turned to Maigret. "I need to get back to Villacoublay airfield right away. Can you drive me, Inspector?"

Epilogue: Honan, 1951

Doctor Natas' eyes were heavy-lidded and opaque in the darkness of his reception chamber, which was only dimly lit by a few inadequate flickering sconces. The room was redolent with the fragrance of jasmine from a single cone of incense burning in a jade brazier.

Pao Tcheou's light footsteps padded quietly across the stone-tiled floor and stopped in front of Natas. He waited patiently for Natas to acknowledge his presence.

Natas' green-flecked eyes glistened as their nictitating membranes slid back. "Well?"

"Success, Master. As you know, after instigating the growth of a clone from the cultures and samples we took from Mademoiselle Ducharme in Paris, that madman Caresco was able to stimulate the clone's rapid growth to child-bearing age."

"Yes," Doctor Natas reflected, "Doctor Caresco may be mad, and his resistance is growing, but he remains under my control, for the time being. We shall dispense with him shortly. And the clone... That magnificent example of the female of the species has been scientifically selected from all the women of the world. And not only selected, but bred, by me. These Westerners are so charmingly predictable. It was frightfully easy to place her parents together in a situation which caused them to gravitate toward each other, so many years ago. Going back generations, Justine Ducharme had better breeding than one could have hoped for, even through a purposeful eugenics program. Justine Ducharme is among the most perfect women, both intellectually and physically, in the entire world. And so is her clone."

"It was a stroke of genius to cause Ardan to believe that once he had rescued the two women the matter was concluded," Pao Tcheou said.

"Yes," Natas agreed, "despite the vast resources at my disposal, I had no wish to suffer the ongoing distraction of making a permanent enemy of Ardan by kidnapping his daughter. His daughter's clone is more than sufficient, and Ardan need never know the truth."

Doctor Caresco entered the far end of the chamber and approached Doctor Natas and Pao Tcheou.

"Speak!" Natas commanded.

Doctor Caresco's face gleamed with dementia and the strain of continually trying to fend off Natas' controlling drugs. "As you know, Pao Tcheou successfully impregnated the clone of Mademoiselle Ducharme. The pregnancy has come to term successfully. The baby girl is strong and healthy."

"I am pleased," said Natas. "The girl will be called Ducharme, in honor of her 'mother' and 'grandmother.' She shall be prepared for a life in my service."

"Yes," replied Caresco, his voice thick with resistance, "the experiment has been a complete success. Justine's clone will be ready for you after she has recovered."

"How long?"

"Most likely, in a few weeks."

"Excellent. For 24 years, ever since I brought together Ardan and Louise Ducharme, two of the finest physical and mental examples of humanity who have ever lived, I have worked toward this moment. The result of their breeding, combined with my own mental perfection, shall culminate in the greatest living weapon ever created! The finest genetic background, combined with my eugenics expertise... My son will be a great avenger, whose spirit shall rise and advance over the West, striking without warning, and executing my will and vengeance wherever and whenever I see fit.

"And then..." Doctor Natas smiled diabolically, "the world shall hear from me again!"

A book like Tales of the Shadowmen *would not be complete without an* Arsène Lupin *adventure, and Viviane Etrivert, a talented French novelist, supplies it with the necessary verve and panache, combined with her first-hand knowledge of the city of Montpellier where she resides...*

Viviane Etrivert: *The Three Jewish Horsemen*

Montpellier, 1912

"Baskerville! You fool! You weren't supposed to kill him. I wanted him to talk first."

The woman whipped her riding crop through the air. She was stunningly beautiful. Strands of copper hair encircled her Madonna-like face. Her eyes were a flamboyant, emerald green.

"He was about to, Countess, but his heart just gave out." The man was gaunt, in his 20s and spoke with a British accent. "I had no way to know..." He turned his head, looked at the dislocated body which lay grotesquely twisted on the floor of the small Parisian apartment. "In any event, we still have the parchment."

"Don't make me regret having taken pity on you at the Conclave of the Black Coats in Sartene, last year," snapped the woman. "You were nothing but the bastard child of a discredited family traipsing aimlessly across Europe..."

"As opposed to a criminal hunted by the police forces of five countries, you mean?"

"Enough, you two. I'm not altogether sure that the Italian held the key to the mystery," said a third man, in a deep and perfectly modulated voice. He stood in the shadows, a haughty silhouette hiding his features beneath a black mask.

"My information was accurate," said the woman, still smoldering in anger. "That fool Perugia wouldn't have lied to me. I never fail! I always succeed in everything I undertake."

"Yet, if I recall, there was one man who..." interjected Baskerville.

"Don't mention him! Ever!" said the woman in an icy-cold tone that was even more frightening than her previous display of emotion.

"You must learn to let go of your hatred, my sweet Josephine," said the masked man., "as I once let go of the angel I worshipped, my beautiful Christine... Come, proud daughter of Cagliostro," he continued, gallantly kissing her hand, "let us concentrate on deciphering this ancient document together... You too, Sir Baskerville..."

The long, bony finger traced the contours of a coat of arms engraved on an ancient parchment covered with Latin writing.

They read:

"*Today, as Death at last nears, I live in fear that soon the Heavenly Judge will weigh my sinful soul. No one in this town knows who I truly am, Bernardin de Ganges, Knight of Malta, murderer of the beautiful Diane, my own brother's wife who spurned my advances. I am a miserable sinner and must unburden my soul before I depart this Earthly realm. I have hidden in the town of Mont Pelier, a treasure given by the Jews of Sauve to the Bishop of Maguelonne in 1246, entrusted to Diane and which I stole after committing my heinous crime. I have never dared spend that cursed gold. It stands as a witness to my crime. May the Black Madonna forgive me!*

Sub antiquae majestatis pedibus
Ac in scutuli gurgite
Tres equites jacent."

The woman stretched, looking more than ever like some beautiful, feline creature, unveiling sharp, white teeth under her full, purple lips.

"My carriage awaits. Let's ride to Montpellier then."

A few weeks later:

"Where did you get this document, Béchoux?"

Jim Barnett traced the contours of a coat of arms engraved on an ancient parchment covered with Latin writing. It was a copy, of course, but executed with a style and assurance that indicated a genuine artist.

"From an Italian artist who shared a studio with Vincenzo Perugia, a man we questioned in connection with the theft of the Mona Lisa last August. We cleared Perugia of any suspicion. We found his friend murdered in his lodgings a few days ago, and I discovered this drawing when I rifled though his papers. I wondered if it could have any connection with his murder?"

The grisly vision of the murder scene came back to Béchoux in all its horror. The policeman shivered, wiping his face with a handkerchief.

"What about Perugia?" asked Barnett.

"Disappeared. A few months ago. But he's got nothing to do with the Mona Lisa. I'd stake my reputation on it. The concierge reported seeing a beautiful red-head with an Italian accent, a tall Englishman and a third man who sulked in the shadows. Does that tell you anything?"

Barnett smiled a secret smile, as if enjoying a joke he shared with no one. He read the Latin inscription, translating it as he went:

"*Sous les pieds de la Majesté Antique
Dans l'abîme de l'écusson
Les trois cavaliers gisent.*"

[Under the Feet of the Ancient Majesty
In the Abyss of the Shield
Lie the Three Horsemen .]

"I'm sorry, Béchoux, but this means nothing to me at all... This time, you're on your own."

The Vicomte Raoul de Cherisy walked up the new boulevard that led from the royal square of the Peyrou, in the ancient center of the Southern city of Montpellier, to the neighborhood known as the Aiguillerie. His face was thoughtful; his steps slow. A recent visitor to Montpellier, he was, with his old mother, staying in a posh hotel located in the heart of the old town. The doctors had recommended she stay in a warm climate, he had told the concierge.

The hackney carriages, their white Camargue horses stamping their feet, red bobbles hanging around their necks, drove by at leisurely speed; there were very few motorcars outside of Paris. Passers-by stopped to chat, exchanging news in a sing-song blend of Occitan and Provençal French. The pure blue sky, hardly smeared by a few bright, white clouds, lifted Raoul's spirits.

Raoul stopped briefly in front of the Prefecture, admiring the classical balance of its architecture–during the 16th century, it had been the noted Hotel de Ganges–and the superb Napoleon III-styled covered market nearby. A boy selling newspapers yelled: "Mysterious Gang Strikes Again! Another Murder Reported! Police On Alert!" Raoul bought a newspaper and started to read it, tapping on the sidewalk with the metal tip of his cane.

"Watch out," he thought. "Don't let this peaceful, serene setting of the perfect provincial life distract you. That she-devil is out there, sharpening her claws..."

Back in his suite, Raoul grabbed the hands of a middle-aged woman who sat on a sofa and dragged her into an impromptu waltz. Then, after he let her go and she sat back down, out of breath, he exclaimed:

"Victoire! My dear old Victoire! I'm near my goal! I can feel it! The *Abyss of the Shield* is the *district de l'écusson*, the center of Montpellier, the heart of the old town. From above, the old town does resemble a shield, or a coat-of-arms. The new boulevards follow the path of the old city walls. The inner part of a coat-of-arms is called the 'abyss.' The abyss of this shield is, therefore, the Prefecture and the covered market. The treasure is right under our noses, or rather, I should say, our feet. It's been buried there for centuries, waiting for me, Victoire! For me. But now I need to figure out who the *Three Horsemen* are... And who is the *Ancient Majesty*?"

Still out of breath, Victoire sighed: "I don't know, Raoul, but don't forget that you've invited the priest of Notre Dame des Tables for dinner tonight."

Raoul burst out laughing.

"The man who might have the answers I seek! Victoire, remind me to order a bottle of that excellent Bourgueil wine which has gathered dust for far too long in the magnificent *cave* of this hotel..."

The aged priest cheerfully surrendered his empty glass to the young waiter. The hotel dining-room was decorated with red velvet curtains and a grandfather clock, ponderously beating time. Its chandeliers glittered, their light sparkling on the gold cutlery used by the guests.

"You are a marvelous host, my dear Vicomte." The priest took a sip of the wine and lightly clicked his tongue against his palate, savoring the subtlety of its prestigious bouquet. "The identity of the murderers who are plaguing our benighted city has proved most elusive. The Prefect of Police himself hasn't got a clue. It's all Greek to him."

"Speaking of dead languages," said Raoul, "I read a Latin inscription recently that referred to a *Magesta Antiqua.* Would you know what it meant?"

"The Ancient Majesty. You could hardly have found a better man to ask that question of, dear Vicomte. It's a strange and mysterious local legend, that few know. It refers to a Madonna, a beautiful statue, made of finely carved ebony, brought back from the Crusades in the 12th century by Guilhem VI, Lord of Montpellier. A Black Virgin, as it was called, which attracted the pilgrims on their way to Compostelle. She was said to perform miracles, heal the sick, that sort of thing. The doctors from the old University treated those who weren't worthy enough for her to cure."

"Where is she now?"

"No one knows. She disappeared. She was in the oldest church in the town, Notre Dame des Tables, not the one where I serve today, but the first one which was destroyed, first by the Huguenots, then by the Revolution. It was a wonderful Gothic edifice erected on top of the original Roman church. All destroyed. How sad. They've built the covered market where it used to stand. That ugly Napoleon III building you can see from your windows."

"Was there anything left of the old church?"

"Not as far as I know... Perhaps the cemetery... A boneyard... Who knows? It was such a long time ago. I'd give anything in the world to see that Black Virgin."

"Maybe she rules the abyss," said Raoul. "The *Abyss of the Shield.*"

But the priest did not hear him as he had started to nod off, snoring in time to the beat of the grandfather clock.

Raoul lifted the lamp high, lighting the stone wall that his workers had reached. They had labored for several days, digging through the yellow clay, in the cellar he had rented near the covered market. He had already mapped out the location of the catacombs by tapping on the sidewalks near the Prefecture with his cane and noticing where they sounded hollow.

Raoul grabbed a crow bar, pulled out a few stones, causing the others to crumble and fall. Before him was a room, small and circular, filled with a musty smell. He stepped inside and saw a hundred faces staring at him from dark, empty eye sockets. This was the ancient boneyard of Notre Dame des Tables. He was looking at hundreds of skulls, piled on top of the other.

He took a few steps forward. He had a strange feeling that something was moving in the shadows, watching his every move, but told himself it was only the product of his imagination. No one had been inside this room for centuries. He continued his exploration, probing the walls with the crowbar. Suddenly, he heard a noise and was felled by a violent blow to the head. He saw two hideous yellow eyes and the grinning face of death staring at him before blacking out.

Raoul awoke in the dark. He felt for his lamp. It was of no use to him, it was broken.

A light shone in front of him, lighting up a room draped in black and red material. He stepped forward and hit a thick, glass wall. He was in a prison. Three figures, wearing black Venetian Carnival masks, stared at him. Their dark cloaks blended into the darkness that was filled with ancient ivory bones. Raoul guessed that he was in a chamber hastily arranged, in the catacombs deep under the city.

One of the figures made an exclamation from her sensual mouth:

"Raoul!"

"I was hoping we'd never meet again, Josephine."

The mask fell revealing the delicate oval face of Josephine Balsamo, Countess Cagliostro. "How can you say that, Raoul? You were 20. I was your first love – the one you never forget..."

"No, Josephine. Clarisse was my first love. And you killed her."

"She took you away from me. She was nothing. She stopped you from being what you've become–Arsène Lupin! What you are today, you owe to me, Raoul. Together, we would have been unbeatable."

"We're wasting time," said the man with the English accent, taking off his mask, as well. "It's obvious he knows where the treasure is located. I'll make him talk."

"Like you tortured and murdered the others, all in vain, Sir Baskerville? And they call me a monster..." The third mask fell, revealing a hideous, skull-like face.

"So that was you watching me in the ossuary earlier?" said Raoul. "I've heard of you, You were the one who haunted the Opera? Still alive ? Or still undead?" When he was fighting for his very life, when danger was at its most pressing, he always felt the urge to mock, to scoff, as if to shout "I still live!" to the face of the world. This time was no different. "What a mismatched trio of rogues: a harpy, a rat and a scarecrow. Congratulations, you've kept the Prefect of Police awake for weeks now! I'm sure he'll thank me when I deliver you bound and gagged, with a card in my name..."

Raoul saw greed struggle with hatred in Josephine's eyes. The hatred of the woman scorned won once again.

"We'll find the treasure without him," she spat.

Without a word, the three figures disappeared into the darkness. Raoul knew the trap was about to turn deadly. He waited for a sign, all his senses on alert. Suddenly, he heard the sound of trickling water. Water from above, from the sewers perhaps. They intended to drown him.

Quickly, Raoul took off his shirt. On his back was taped the disassembled segments of a metal-tipped walking stick. He put them together and struck the glass, repeatedly, with all his strength. Water now reached his knees, then his waist, but he continued to strike the glass methodically, without panic. Finally, a fissure appeared and shards flew. Water began to flow out through the hole. Seconds later, the entire shattered pane fell to the floor.

Raoul was free.

He searched the catacombs until he reached an ancient chapel. It was small, no more than a crypt, guarded by the statues of the dead. Over its entrance, he noticed the same coat of arms engraved in the stone. There were the arms of Guilhem VI. Raoul pressed the metal point of his cane to the center of the shield. The clover moved slightly, starting a mechanism, causing a roman column to rotate and reveal... the *Ancient Majesty*!

The delicate Black Madonna sat on a throne, a child in her arm. Raoul lifted the statue carefully and underneath, he saw a niche containing the Three Horsemen... Three horsemen of the finest gold riding horses once made by the Jewish goldsmiths of Sauve as a present to the Bishop of Maguelonne... Waiting eight centuries to be found by–Arsène Lupin.

Suddenly, a man jumped up from behind a tomb, trying to stab Raoul. He would have succeeded had not the Black Madonna at that very moment tipped from her pedestal, causing him to move forward to catch her, thus escaping the fatal bow.

"I knew you would escape and lead me to the treasure," said Sir Baskerville. "The others are gone. I'll kill you. I won't have to share with them."

"How English of you. Always ready to betray your associates, eh? Worthy of the Perfidious Albion, indeed!" joked Raoul.

Better men than Baskerville had tried to kill Lupin; none had succeeded. Soon, the villain lie disarmed on the ground, tied with ribbons made out of Raoul's shirt.

Then, Raoul thought he heard a strange music, a majestic and sad melody, coming from deep within the catacombs. A pure, crystalline voice accompanied a funereal Requiem like a silver filigree on a black curtain. Lupin rushed down a corridor, pushed aside a heavy tapestry and saw Erik, hunched over an organ, playing madly, sobbing, as if wracked by some tremendous grief. Next to him was a beautiful, blonde girl, singing.

Raoul pounced on the Phantom, but his hands only grappled empty air. The music continued for a short time, then stopped and did not start again. The image of Erik and the girl vanished, melting away into nothingness like morning dew.

Raoul looked around and, in a corner, found what he knew had to be there: an ingenious device combining crystal prisms and phonographic records. He recognized it at once. "Orfanik's machine... A recording of both sights and sounds... Wherever he goes, he carries her image and voice with him... Poor Erik..."

That next morning, two men in Montpellier found their heart's desire at the foot of their beds when they got up: for the Prefect of Police, it was the bound and gagged body of Sir Lionel Baskerville, the assassin who had terrorized the city, and for the priest of Notre Dame des Tables, it was the Ancient Majesty, the Black Madonna of Guilhem VI.

Those in the know claim that a skeletal phantom still haunts the catacombs under the old city; others believe that Arsène Lupin himself has made it his new refuge; the more romantic souls say that he shares his underground throne with a lady with scarlet hair, forever young... Let the reader beware and believe what he will!

[*translated by Joan Bingham & J.-M. Lofficier.*]

When Greg Gick first pitched the concept of The Werewolf of Rutherford Grange, *it was so ambitious, and yet so fascinating, that we decided to make an exception and publish it as a serialized novella, of which this is the first installment. This can also be construed as an homage to the old serials; one can easily imagine Louis Feuillade at the helm of the camera filming the adventures of a young Harry Dickson (the German-Dutch-Belgian-French Holmesian pastiche) as he prepares to face...*

G.L. Gick: *The Werewolf of Rutherford Grange*

Surrey, 1911

Looking back, I am glad I never entrusted this tale to paper before now.

Frankly, I've spent most of my adult life trying to forget the incident. But, after our recent experience against the Germans, with that mysterious French Duke and his allies, Tom Wills had issue to take me aside and ask me again whether, after all we've encountered over the years, I've ever really believed in such a thing as the *supernatural.*

I looked at this young man I had once taken under my wing, now with a family and agency of his own, and had to reply I still just didn't know.

And it is that not knowing that makes me so damn uncomfortable.

My name is Harry Dickson. By trade, I am a private detective, although now I consider myself retired. Indeed, if I keep my hand in at all, it is for my own amusement or by the request of the Government, as in my recent case mentioned above. Still, I am glad to say I have had some little success in my chosen career, to the extent that the press once dubbed me "the American Sherlock Holmes." Although proud of the moniker at first, as the years go by, I find the title more and more noisome. While I was indeed born in America, the son of a stage magician, I was educated in Britain, live in Britain and, in all ways, view myself as a full citizen of that sceptered isle. I enjoy regular tea-times, speak with an Oxford accent (put on, I admit, at first, but now such a part of me I cannot speak "normally" without it), and am far more concerned about who's going to be my local MP than who the President is. I haven't set foot in the country of my birth in years. No, British I am and British I will be 'til the end of my days. To call me American does me a disservice.

But further, the title is an offense against my mentor. To even *begin* to consider myself an equal to the Master Detective, who so kindly took an interest in me and guided my early career despite my arrogance and youth, is an affront I would never dare to take. Even S.P., an even more dedicated student of the Master than I (and with whom I have never gotten along), would balk at being described as such. I owe the Master nothing less than my career, talent and whatever little fame I have achieved. I will not tolerate the lowering of his genius so someone as unworthy as I can be placed above him.

Not that many of my adventures over the years wouldn't have caused him to raise his eyebrows in disbelief. Professor Flax. Cric-Croc. Gurrhu and the Temple of Iron. Strange cases, with even stranger criminals. But in just about every instance, even when I was fighting self-styled Babylonian "gods," in the end, I discovered a motive and an explanation that, while perhaps sometimes stretching the boundaries of the laws of science, nevertheless did not break them.

But then, there was *the* case, so early in my career.

Just as my mentor had *the* woman, so I have *the* case. The case that showed me that, perhaps, just perhaps, there were things that could not be explained by Rationality alone.

For years, I have shoved the incident to the back of my mind, trying not to think about it, but now, all these years later, I am forced to put it to paper, to try, one last time, to make sense of it all. I doubt I shall. That is why, when this is over, I shall place this manuscript into a safe-deposit box I have rented and promptly try to forget it ever existed. For all my adventures, this is the one that disturbed me the most. The adventures where I learned that there might, just might, be more to the world than mere Reason could define. The adventure where I met the man who, while never my mentor and perhaps not even my friend, gave me my first glimpse into a world that, despite my best efforts, I still cannot explain.

I still wish he hadn't.

It was the summer of 1911. King George V had just ascended the throne. The House of Lords would soon give up its power of veto, making the House of Commons dominant in Parliament. The White Star shipping lines were putting the finishing touches on a new ship called the *Titanic*, offering a sparkling new future in comfort and speed on the oceans. And in a tiny room in London, a crass youth of 21 named Harry Dickson had just completed his third year at university, and was preparing to go to work.

Oh, he was an impatient, arrogant youth, this young Dickson. Full of himself and his dreams of the future. True, such could be said of any young person in any era. But this young man particularly thought the world was his for the taking. And why shouldn't he–I–have? For unlike so many of those other youths, my path was already set. I was going to become a private detective, and a great one. Oh, yes. There was no doubt of it. Like my fellow countryman Sherman, my march was inexorable. Had I not already a dozen successes to my credit? Small cases, yes; amateur cases, but each one brought to a successful conclusion, and by none other than myself. And there was more. Had I not met and worked with the Master Detective, who pronounced me "promising" and become my own guide into the world of detection? Had I not, through his offices, met several others famed in the same line of work–Triggs, Hewitt, the late Mrs. Dene, that unassuming country priest–and each one declared me the same? There could be no veering from the path. As the Commandments, my future was set in stone. I was going to be a detective.

But first, I was told, I would have to pay my dues.

It seemed my mentor was concerned with me. I was "promising," yes, but in his view a far too tempestuous and impatient youth to strike out on my own just yet. The art of criminal detection was an exacting one, demanding great sacrifices in time and attention, he said. But I was obviously still under the impression most cases a detective handled were like those his chronicler had so romantically exaggerated in *The Strand* when nothing, he said, could be further from the truth. Detectives had bills to pay, just like everyone else, he informed me, and competition was fierce. For every case involving red-haired men and orange pips, there were ten cases accepted solely to put bread on the table and fire in the hearth. Everyone had them. Even in the early days, before he had made his name, my mentor explained sternly, he had been forced to take whatever he could get to keep the money coming in. Minor matters of blackmail. Dull divorce investigations Even simply looking into the prospects of a would-be suitor. What I needed, the Master said, was a lesson in the actual day-to-day drudgery and boredom most cases actually consisted of. And so he had arranged for me to spend my summer serving an apprenticeship with a Mr. Blake.

I had felt quite elated, at first. Not about the majority of the lecture, which I heard but did not listen to, but rather to the fact I was to work with Blake. He was second only to the Master in fame and talent, and would prove to be one of the kindest and most encouraging of men. Looking back, I find that I did indeed learn much from him. But he had listened to the Master more closely than I, and, as a consequence, what he had me doing for him was, as my countrymen might say, as "dull as watching paint dry."

The stipulation of my working with Mr. Blake was simple: at no time was I to be permitted to work directly on a case of any import. I was solely to be used to assist in gathering whatever background research he might need, or to do legwork in whatever small, negligible cases Mr. Blake might have accepted to kill time in between the next big one. And so I did: for the past two months I had spent most of my time muddling through dusty old books in the British Museum or engaged in chemical experiments while Blake was off on his own adventures. While he fought a notorious Devil Doctor in Limehouse, I examined mushy fingerprints gathered after a clumsy burglary. While he sloshed through the sewers of Paris searching for the secret hideout of a black-coated conspiracy, I followed a husband through the seedier parts of Soho to see which brothels he frequented. While Blake hung upside-down trying to free himself from a runaway balloon, I spent long hours searching through Burke's *Peerage* to discover the supposed birthright of an obscure chimney sweep. I also fed and walked the dog. It was incredibly frustrating. Here I was, declared one of the most promising (that word again) would-be investigators of the 20th century, and I was wasting my talents on discovering the spousal possibilities of the local butcher instead of being on the scene of master crimes looking for clues. And, although I never said as much, my feelings were obvious to all who worked with me.

This particular day, however, I was in rather high spirits. Mr. Blake had just praised me for some research I had done on the secret meanings of *orghum* which had cracked a puzzling case for him, with the implicit promise I should be rewarded somehow. It was a pleasant summer morning, the Sun was out, the sky a deep sapphire blue and I decided to forego the expense of a cab and walk to work. The streets were busy, even at this hour, but almost all had a smile on their face and many nodded pleasantly to my greeting. I saw only one thing that disturbed my bonhomie: in a new storefront, someone had placed the sign: "Dr. Tin Zen: Spiritualist–Make Contact with Your Loved Ones Beyond the Veil! Prices negotiable." Beneath was a picture of a fat, balding, middle-aged "Chinese" man–obviously in makeup–wearing a turban, hovering with what he evidently thought was a "mysterious" air over a crystal ball. In point of fact, it looked as if he was about to fall over on it.

I sighed and shook my head. Tin Zen was a ridiculous name. No self-respecting real Chinaman would have it. But more than that, I loathed the very premise of Spiritualism. I have never been a religious man. I have my own beliefs, of course, but if asked at what altar I primarily worship, I would have to answer at only two: those of the Twin Idols of Logic and Reasoning. My mentor taught me that. Everything could be explained if only one used his mind, he told me; there was no such thing as magic to a true detective. So you may imagine that the very idea that someone gazing cross-eyed into a crystal ball could somehow call up the spirit of your deceased Uncle Charlie, who would then tell you the secrets of Heaven in such a vague, nondescript way that you were even more puzzled when you went out than when you came, was anathema to me. But what appalled me most was how many otherwise normal, intelligent people believed in it. I had seen them; these were men (and women) who would smile indulgently at the thought of life on Mars and laugh aloud at anyone who claimed to see a sea serpent, but would spend hours in line to sit holding hands in a darkened room calling for their deceased mother. Perhaps I should not have been so biting toward people who simply wanted to see their loved ones again, but I was. As a magician's son, I had seen all the tricks mediums used to fake "spirits" performed a hundred times. I knew them to be nothing more than illusions, and in my mind I expected everyone else to as well.

But enough of that. If the foolish and gullible had nothing else better to do with their money, then so be it. I had my future to think about. I turned my mind to fantasies of the reward Mr. Blake was to give me–a raise? A real case? Dare I say–a *partnership?*–and almost skipped up the steps of his Baker Street quarters. Nothing could destroy my mood this day!

So you may understand my surprise when I walked in to a chorus of angry voices issuing out of Blake's private office.

"Damn it all, Blake, I don't want one of your wretched men! I want you!"

"Sir Henry, I already told you–"

"I don't care what you told me!"

I looked inquiringly over at T., Blake's full-time assistant, sitting at his desk. He waved me to silence, a look of concern on his face. From behind the door, I could hear the patient voice of the detective himself:

"Sir Henry, I'm afraid it's impossible for me to personally come to your home at this time. I'm already deeply involved in another case, and it looks as though the trail is leading to Geneva. I may have to leave for the continent at any moment. I simply cannot break away. My men are perfectly capable–"

The first voice, loud and tinged with arrogance: "If I wanted a second-rate constable in charge of this, Blake, I would have hired one. London is full of them! This conference is too important to my fu–to the future of England to trust to inferiors, and I promised the attendees a top man to ensure its safety!"

A third voice, much younger and quieter, but stiff: "Mr. Blake, perhaps you don't comprehend the situation here. Security is of great importance to this conference, and–"

Mr. Blake's voice, sounding very patient: "I comprehend the situation perfectly, Mr. Westenra. But as I understand it, your father has already hired agents from eight firms to help provide security. I know these men and they are all quite competent. Surely you do not need–"

"None of them are as good as you, Blake!" snarled the first voice.

"I appreciate the compliment, sir, but–"

"I never make compliments," thundered the speaker. "I only speak facts. And in your case, that's little enough, Blake. I don't believe half the stuff that's published about you. But you owe me, and–"

As the argument, whatever it was about, continued to rage, Blake's assistant and I exchanged looks, then shrugged. I took out my pipe and began to light it. As I did, the door to Mr. Blake's office opened and his dark, handsome face peered out.

"Ah, Master Dickson!" There was a smile on his face, but the cheerful tone behind it seemed distinctly false. "Good to see you! Would you be so kind as to step into my office a moment?"

I felt a sinking sensation in my stomach. I glanced back at T., who shrugged again. There was nothing else for it. I put out my pipe, obediently chimed, "Yes, sir," and went inside.

I had always liked Mr. Blake's office. I wanted one just like it when I got out on my own. It was sumptuous, yet comfortable, with fine leather-backed chairs and an expensive mahogany desk. The walls were lined with bookcases, save for behind the desk, which was a full plate-glass window, offering him a fine view of the comings and goings of Baker Street. It was also unnaturally crowded. In addition to Mr. Blake and myself, two others stood in the room.

The eldest stood fuming before Blake's desk, literally, as clenched in his mouth was a large, ill-smelling cigar. He was probably somewhere in his early sixties, and his hair and thick mustache were already grey. He was actually relatively tall, but his hefty paunch, distorting his otherwise expertly-tailored clothing, made him appear much shorter. His skin was florid and beaded with perspiration even in the relatively cool room. Black eyes snapped arrogantly at my employer through a pair of expensive, but slightly cockeyed, spectacles and I had a feeling that if he could have raised his nose any higher without bumping the ceiling, he would've. Looking at him, I was reminded of nothing so much as a caricature of G.K. Chesterton out of *Punch*–but without the *bon homine*.

The second man was much younger, perhaps 26 or so. He hung back in one of the corners, arms folded, looking bored. He was handsome, it must be admitted; with dark eyes, a firm, strong chin, and a thin, straight nose, but it was a chilly, unemotional handsomeness. Compared to his elder–who was at least active, for all his girth–this man was a contemptuous mannequin. He had a queer little smile on his face, like someone who knew a great joke he was playing on all the world, and they simply couldn't recognize it.

But now Mr. Blake was speaking: "Dickson, may I present Sir Henry Westenra and his son, Alexander. Gentlemen, my employee, Harry Dickson."

"Gentlemen." I bowed slightly and proffered my hand. They stared at me. I looked back and forth, from one to another. Neither moved. I lowered my hand.

"No," Sir Henry barked. "No, no, no, no, no, no, no. He won't do at all. Boy's barely out of short pants. What are you trying to hand me, Blake?" He glared at my employer, as if daring him to speak

Mr. Blake closed his eyes and sighed, very low and long. "Mr. Dickson is perfectly capable of handling the requirements of your situation, Sir Henry. He has worked for me and several other detectives, and we find him most promising."

"That would be fine," bristled Westenra, "if I wanted someone *promising.* I want someone *competent*, Blake, with experience." Suddenly he wheeled toward me. "You, boy. Where'd you go to school?"

"I've just completed my third year at South Kensington, sir."

"Kensington?" Alexander Westenra, the mannequin, spoke for the first time. I was amazed his lips could move. "Isn't that the school Geoffrey Rutherford attended?"

Immediately, Sir Henry snorted derisively and raised his eyes to heaven. "The Rutherfords," he spat contemptuously. "Don't even speak to me about the Rutherfords."

"Well, it's not Christina's fault Peter made such a hash of things," Alexander replied calmly. "She's not responsible for him being what he is." Suddenly, he smiled wickedly. "Besides, look at it this way–at least now we can be sure your grandchildren won't howl."

"Enough, I say! Damn it all, Blake!" Sir Henry twisted back toward my employer. "I don't want children! I want *you!* Now are you coming or aren't you?"

"No, Sir Henry," Blake said through gritted teeth. "I am not." He strode to his desk and sat. "For the last time. I am deeply involved in another case the Prime Minister himself asked me to look into I cannot–*cannot*–break away right now. Either you take Mr. Dickson, or you take nothing. Or would you rather take it up with Mr. Asquith himself?" He lifted the phone receiver. "I can ring him up, at any moment. Now, what's it going to be?"

For a long moment, Westenra stared at Blake, eyes boggling as if they was about to burst His head twisted toward me sharply, glared me up and down, and finally snarled: "All right, Blake. I'll take him. But he won't be in charge. I'll take that on myself. And mind you–the slightest mistake and he's out. And believe me, I'll make certain everyone knows he's your employee!"

He whipped around quickly for such a fat man and stalked toward the door. Over his shoulder, he called: "I'll expect you by two o'clock tomorrow afternoon, young man! I'll have someone waiting at the station to pick you up! See that you're not late! Come along, Alexander! Let's get out of here!"

With a flourish, he threw open the door and left. Alexander Westenra, after a cold nod to each of us, followed. A moment later, we heard the door to the street fling open and slam shut.

Mr. Blake sank his head to his desk with a groan. "That," he said, "was Sir Henry Westenra."

"So I gathered," I replied wryly.

Blake sighed. "Don't be impertinent, Dickson; it doesn't suit you. Do you know anything about him?"

"No, sir."

"Well, you're about to learn. Sit."

I did so. He spun his own chair around to face the window, steepling his fingers together thoughtfully "Sir Henry Westenra has come to that title only five years ago, when he was granted it due to his work in India. At least, that is the story; in point of fact, he received it due to nepotism and his one great talent, as you will see While up until now his family have never been granted titles or peerages, they're extremely rich and influential–they're apparently distantly related to the Westenras of Whitby, whom you may have heard of–and are based in a remarkably ugly domicile in Surrey called, with all due modesty, Westenra House." Mr. Blake turned to face me, a little smile playing across his lips. "Are you with me so far?" I nodded.

"Good. Now. The Westenras have always had interests in India. They helped found the East India Company, and apparently quite a bit of their money is invested there. As a result, the sons of the Westenras have, as a rule, entered either the Army or the Foreign Office, specializing in the subcontinent. Henry Westenra was the latest scion to do so. He became a small functionary in the Office, and was based, I believe, in Bombay. There he married–very late, and to a very rich woman–and had two sons, Alexander, whom you met, and Peter, the youngest. Still, nothing much was expected of him. It is well known Sir Henry was not the brightest light in the Office." Mr. Blake turned back toward the window, thoughtfully. "However, this is where it all matters. For all his incompetence–and he is *very* incompetent from what I've heard–Sir Henry Westenra has one great ability. He is very, very good at being in the right place at the right time.

"What happened was this. There was what appeared to be a small uprising in Bombay A group of native Muslims had walked into a small white community, and Sir Henry just *happened* to be on the scene when it occurred. He managed to escape, get the Army and lead them back, where the 'uprising' was put down in a most bloody manner." He sighed. "As it turned out, the natives were there to protest the mistreatment of their women by certain British officials. Among them, it seems, Westenra's son Alexander. They had no intention of doing violence, they simply wanted to lodge their protests with the local officials. We–that is, the whites–overreacted. There were no survivors"

For a moment, Mr. Blake did nothing but sit silently. Then: "The whole affair was hushed up, of course. No questions were asked. Natives vanish in India all the time, I'm told. If not addressed, no one cares. But some of Westenra's relatives higher up in the Office heard about their nephew's 'heroics,' and insisted he receive some kind of reward. They made such a fuss that to finally shut them up, Sir Henry was granted his knighthood and has used it to advance his career ever since. Two years ago, he was recalled to England, and now works directly for the Office. Which brings me to why he was here today."

Mr. Blake turned and leaned towards me intently. "You need to understand, Dickson. Sir Henry is a racist, an ass and as self-centered a boor as I've ever had the misfortune to meet. But he knows where to be and when, and he knows how to curry favors and when to call them in. As a result, he has made himself look far more important to the Foreign Office and the outside world than he actually is. And there are a great deal of important people who are in his debt. One of those people is myself."

He pulled out his pipe and lit it, indicating that I could do the same. I was grateful for the chance. I had the terrible sensation this was not going to be something I would enjoy.

"Two years ago, while working on a case, I was obliged to go to Sir Henry for some information the Office had on a certain suspect," Blake said quietly. "The information was very sensitive, and something I should not have had, but without it a dangerous murderer would've escaped the gallows. Sir Henry gave it to me, but with the stipulation that I, as a private investigator, would owe him one favor when he needed it. Yesterday, he called that favor in."

Once again he spun around toward the window. "This weekend, there will be a conference between Great Britain and France. Through his sources, Sir Henry has somehow managed to get permission to host the entire affair at his estate. Why, I do not know, but it undoubtedly involves puffing himself up to his superiors. *Supposedly,* this conference is merely on matters of various economic aspects of our respective colonies, particularly Ceylon and India. You know, discussions of tariffs and such. But I suspect it involves rather more than that. Firstly, a man like Sir Henry does not take an interest in something so mundane as importation fees. Secondly, the main attendee from France will be the Duc d'Origny himself."

I stifled a gasp and nodded. The Duc d'Origny! Although fairly unknown to the general public, even in his own country, the Duc was a near-legend in government circles. In his younger days, he had been a government agent for France, traveling the Far East and South Asia and infiltrating dozens of rebel groups. It was he who had been instrumental in revealing to the West just how fully the fingers of Russian imperialism were spreading in the East and, it was said, had personally stemmed an invasion of Tibet by the Tsar's forces several years earlier. No one knew more about the influence of Moscow in our colonies than he. The Duc was very old now, and had for the most part retired, but he was often called in on an advisory capacity by his own government, and, on occasion, ours, when problems arose in the East. If he was attending, then this conference was definitely concerned with anything but tariffs!

"Naturally enough," Mr. Blake was continuing, "such a important conference would need adequate security. And that is why Sir Henry contacted me He wanted me to take charge of it personally. You saw that I refused–but nevertheless a favor is a favor. Therefore, someone from this office must go in my place. That someone is you, Dickson."

I'm afraid I groaned rather more loudly than I intended. From all that I had heard, I should have expected something like this, but really! Security detail? Mere security detail! And here I had been expecting a reward for good work! How much further could my career sink before I drowned in it?

Mr. Blake was staring at me, then chuckled. He reached over and patted me consolingly on the shoulder. "Now, now, Dickson, it isn't as bad as all that. It's something every detective has to do now and then. We have to deal with all sorts of people in our trade, and you'll find that very few of them are actually pleasant to work with. Particularly the aristocracy." He smiled briefly. "Do you think this is a punishment, Dickson?"

I coughed, cleared my throat, and started, "Well, sir, I–"

"Well, it isn't," Blake interrupted sternly. "Nothing of the sort. I must admit, I've been very pleased with your work thus far. Like your mentor, for your age I find you very promising. In fact, I was going to recommend to him that I go ahead and place you in full charge of some of my smaller cases to see how you did, but this takes precedence. It'd be good practical experience for you, and you need that. Without such, you can spend your career ratiocinating about murders all you like, and it will make not one whit of difference to you as a detective." He picked up a pen and fiddled with it. "It's only for half-a-week, Dickson. Besides, you'll be in a position of more responsibility than you think. With Westenra 'taking charge' of things himself since I'm not there, he's bound to make a mess of it, and I'll need you to help keep things on an even keel. The other agents he'll have there are good-hearted chaps but rather vacuous, so try to keep an eye on him and guide him as best you can. Besides, before the conference, you might even get some time to go sightseeing. The country's very beautiful down there. Very steeped in folklore and occult history, too, I hear. Are you at all interested in the occult, Dickson?"

"No, sir," I replied honestly. "I have no belief in the supernatural at all. The Master once told me that when it comes to the rational mind, no ghosts need apply. I have never seen any reason to disregard that advice."

"Hmmm," Blake murmured thoughtfully. "He would say that. Never likes to admit anything. One day, I should tell you what he and I encountered once in the catacombs under Bayonne. But that's neither here nor there. You'll find some notes on the Westenras and their guests on your desk, Dickson. After you walk Pedro, I suggest you spend the rest of the day studying it. You leave first thing tomorrow morning."

He glanced up at the clock in the corner. "And I have to get busy. I'm lunching with the Becks today, and have to get this paperwork finished. Dismissed."

There was nothing else left to say. Feeling a great weight on my shoulders, I stood to go. Then I thought of something. "Sir?"

"Yes?"

"Excuse me, but you told Sir Henry that the Prime Minister might have you leave for Geneva at any moment. I was unaware he had retained you for any case."

"Oh, that," Blake smiled. "I'm sorry, Dickson. I lied. If I had gone to Westenra House, I should have throttled the man before the weekend was out. Never could stand him. You know how it is. Rank Has Its Privileges and all that." He smiled broadly. "Cheer up, Dickson! As I said, it's only for a couple of days! Besides, it's *Surrey,* for God's sake! What could possibly happen there?"

Despite my disappointment, never let it be said a Dickson ever shirked his duty. I arrived at the station bright and early, taking one of the private compartments Mr. Blake had kindly booked for me (Sir Henry having apparently not bothered). I had brought with me the file I had been given, and while the train was beginning to pull out, I opened it to reacquaint myself with its contents.

There was little about Sir Henry I did not already know, save that his wife had passed on a few years earlier. Currently he lived in his ancestral home,

Westenra House, some few miles outside the town of Wolfsbridge. I had never heard of it.

Of rather more interest were his two sons, Alexander and Peter. Both were also members of the Foreign Office, albeit at lower levels than their father, and both would be attending the conference. Both had been born in India, although Peter, the youngest by two years, had proven a very frail, sickly child. Photographs of the two showed the waxly handsome Alexander looming over a sallower, thinner young man, with fair hair and pale eyes. There was a quiet sadness about the image of Peter Westenra that caught my attention. It seemed as though he really didn't want to be there, in that family. Knowing what little I did of his family, it was difficult to blame him. Still, there was very little in the files about him; he quietly did his work, avoided trouble, and had remained a bachelor.

Alexander was the more intriguing. After Blake's assertion that the younger Westenra had been considered something of a rake while in India, I found the file added that there were reports of other incidents he had been involved in, which Sir Henry had often been forced to extricate him from. The details were vague, but it was said he was often seen in the company of characters of unsavory repute, and had often been involved with fights with the native population. Since returning to England, however, he had married, maintained a home in London and apparently had calmed down.

So intent was I on my reading I almost didn't hear the voice ask: "Pardon me, are these seats taken? It's too noisy in the other cars."

I looked up to see a tall, lean, but well-built man gazing with regal amiableness down at me. He had obviously seen much travel in foreign climes over the years, for his face and hands were bronzed and toughened by storm and sun. He seemed vaguely familiar to me somehow, but I could not place him. Besides, it was his two companions that garnered most of my attention.

Unlike my mentor, I have never been totally... impervious to the presence of the fairer sex. And the two that accompanied this man were fair, indeed. The youngest was a beautiful girl of about 18 years, brandishing a glorious crown of sun-gold hair that seemed to shimmer with every movement. High cheekbones, a pert nose and intense blue eyes completed the ensemble. A lovely picture, indeed, but compared with her companion, still shallow. She was standing behind the others, but was almost as tall as her male associate. Porcelain skin and a flowing mane of cascading black hair seemed to cause her perfect features to glow, even in the sunniness of the train car, demonstrating her obvious Mediterranean ancestry.

I instantly stood and bowed, more to her than to her companions, although she was clearly my elder by some five or six years. "No–no, not at all," I managed to stammer like a schoolboy. "Please, do come in."

They did, the man sitting next to me, the women across. From the look in their eyes, I could see they noticed my attraction and were amused. I flushed, but managed to introduce myself.

The man accepted my hand, shaking it vigorously. "Lord John Roxton," he said, and instantly I realized why he seemed so familiar. There was hardly one in the British Isles who had not heard of the famous aristocrat, hunter and explorer! He was on the level of Burton and Quatermain. He had first made his name with his trip to a fabled South American plateau and his renown had only grown since. He was one of the few white men to have ever penetrated Mecca (in disguise) and had fought pirates in the Malay jungles. He had even (it was said) spent over a year in the desolate Sahara, searching for a legendary lost city supposed to be the last outpost of Atlantis. Seeing he had been recognized, he smiled and indicated his companions: "And may I present Miss Christina Rutherford of Wolfsbridge and Miss Gianetti Annunciata, late of Milan."

Christina Rutherford, I thought, *What an odd coincidence.* But most of my attention was on the lovely Miss Annunciata. So you may imagine my heart trilled more than a bit when she asked in her charming, perfect English: "And whither are you bound, Mr. Dickson?"

When I answered, Miss Rutherford laughed–and I must admit, her voice, too, was enchanting "Why, how wonderful! Wolfsbridge is where we're heading, too! It's my home. We can all get off together."

My eyes wanted to keep drinking in Miss Annunciata, but it would be impolite to ignore the rest of my company. "I'm sure that would be delightful, Miss Rutherford," I said.

"Oh, please, call me Christina," Miss Rutherford interjected. "I hate ceremony, and so does Gianetti here. Uncle John does, too, but he's old-fashioned when it comes to women."

I saw Lord John look sharply at her, but Miss Rutherford merely stuck out her tongue at him. "Very well, then–Miss Christina," I said.

"And you may call me Gianetti, too," added Miss Annunciata, "or Miss Gianetti, if you must."

"If you'll pardon me, Mr. Dickson," Lord John interrupted, obviously wishing to change the subject, "but do I hear a slight American accent in your voice?"

"Very likely, sir," I replied. "I am American. But my father wished me to have a British education, so I was schooled here."

"An excellent decision," Roxton nodded. "Finest schools in the world here. Went to Brookfield, then Eaton. You?"

"Pertwee, sir."

"Dickson, Dickson," Miss Gianetti was murmuring. "Would you by chance be related to a detective I've heard of called Allan Dickson? But he's Australian, I believe–perhaps you aren't."

I smiled broadly. "But as a matter of fact, I am related to him. Quite closely. He's me. That is, Allan's my middle name. I went by it for a time a few years ago."

"I see," replied Miss Gianetti, "but you're American."

"Oh, that's very easy to explain. My father was a magician. While touring in Sydney, he met my mother. In my youngest years, I spoke much like her. Still can, if I want to. If I remember correctly, I picked the accent up again to annoy my Latin professor. He never could stand to hear me conjugate with a Brisbane twang. *Veni, vidi, vici.*" I added in my thickest Antipodean

Miss Gianetti and Miss Christina laughed, and even Lord John gave a little smile. "So you are a detective, then, Mr. Harry?" Christina asked.

"Well," I squirmed a moment, "not quite as yet. That is, I don't have my own practice. But I've been involved in a few cases on an amateur basis. Solved every one of them, too." I was bragging and I knew it. But then, I was trying to get the attention of two beautiful women Still, my conscience eventually got the better of me, for I was forced to add, a bit abashedly, "Actually, I'm surprised you've even heard of me, Miss Gianetti. 'Allan' Dickson didn't last long."

"Oh," she replied airily, " I probably wouldn't have, but my guru had a habit of collecting files on unusual crimes. It's one of his hobbies." She smiled pertly, and I felt a bit crushed. Clearly my fame hadn't preceded me as much as I'd hoped.

"Yes, your mysterious teacher," giggled Christina. "When are we going to meet him, Gianetti? Mother invited him, you know."

Gianetti nodded. "I know, but he'd already made plans. Besides, he doesn't attend many anymore. He's much too busy with his own research."

"What type of research?" I asked automatically, and wished I hadn't. After all, their private matters were none of my affair. Beside me, Lord John was looking uncomfortable.

"Why, séances, of course," Miss Gianetti replied as if it were the most natural thing in the world.

I couldn't believe what I was hearing. Surely, these two lovely, obviously intelligent women, and a famous aristocrat who had seen so much of the world, weren't serious! Spiritualists! Sadly, I was reminded again of just how pervasive such irrationality had become in the world. If such a man as Lord John Roxton could believe in such nonsense, what chance had we to stop it?

My thoughts must have been plain on my face, for Miss Gianetti said, "Ah. You don't believe in Spiritualism."

For the sake of truth, I was forced to shake my head. "I'm afraid to say I do not, Miss Gianetti. I am a Rationalist. I believe in Science and Reason, not superstition."

"But so do I, Mr. Dickson!" Miss Gianetti leaned forward intently "Very much so! And so does my guru, who taught me so much. It was he who first discovered my potential as a medium, and it was he who taught me how to approach it the way I do–as a Science! He knows very well all the fakery that's out there and despises it. But he also knows that there are some things that cannot be explained by the use of the mind alone, Mr. Dickson. We can only discover so much, because we can only comprehend so much. The rest we have to leave up to faith."

I'm afraid I smirked a bit. "Faith, Miss Gianetti?"

"Yes, faith," Christina put in. "Faith that there's something out there greater than ourselves, and faith that somehow, we continue on after death. You see, my father just recently passed on,"–she fingered her hat wistfully–"and Mother was absolutely devastated. They were so much in love. She has to know that he's all right; that he's in Heaven and happy. So I've gotten a number of mediums, including Gianetti, to come and hold a séance to prove that he's still there; that we don't just turn to dust when we die. We're going to make contact with my father again, Mr. Dickson. And then you'll see the true power of faith."

I coughed uncomfortably. "Be that as it may, Miss Christina, but–"

"Come, young man," Lord John interrupted suddenly, "let's go out and get a smoke."

"I've got cigarettes, Uncle John," Christina protested, reaching for her handbag.

"Women shouldn't poison their lungs with such things," Roxton snapped as he stood.

"Oh, pooh." She lit a cigarette just to prove the point.

Roxton sighed; this was a battle he had apparently fought many times. "This way, Dickson," he said, ushering me out into the train's corridor. Then, once out of earshot of the compartment, he turned and said soberly: "Young man, I know what you're about to say, and under ordinary circumstance I'd agree with you. I don't believe in any of this Spiritualism guff myself–not a word. But the Rutherfords have been friends of mine for years; they're related to a zoologist I know and Christina's become like a daughter to me. No, I'm not really her uncle; she just calls me that. I would not see them hurt. Althea–Mrs. Rutherford–was heartbroken when Geoffrey died. So much so she nearly lost her mind. She's convinced the only way to assure herself of his continued existence is through this séance foolishness. I'm concerned about her–*of course* they're going to pull off some sort of hoax; I totally expect that. But if by it Althea's mind is set at ease, I'm going to let it happen. Anything to help her get back on the road to recovery. I'm going to make sure they don't gouge her financially, and that' s all. So I ask you–please don't get involved with this. Let me handle it."

After a moment, I nodded. "As you say, Lord John," I said. "But if I may, what about Miss Annunciata? Miss Christina seems very fond of her."

"That she is," Roxton nodded, "Christina is good at making friends instantly. And I have to admit Miss Annunciata is a beautiful and charming young woman. She's a fraud, of course–she can't be anything else–and yet strangely enough, something's telling me she's honest That is, I get the feeling she genuinely believes she's a medium of some kind, rather than engaging in open chicanery. She's clearly not mad, but delusions run deep. I hope this mysterious 'teacher' of hers isn't some sort of second Svengali, tricking her for his own ends–I guess we'll see."

There was nothing to say to that. After we smoked, we returned to our compartment to find the ladies waiting. Christina had finished her cigarette. Gianetti looked calmly at me. She clearly had guessed what we had been talking about, but wisely said nothing. Instead, she merely asked: "And why are you going to Wolfsbridge, Mr. Dickson?"

"Just to do some research for my employer," I lied carefully. Seeing as the conference was supposed to be so sensitive, early on I had decided not to tell anyone my business.

"Oh," replied Christina, "you mean you're going to Sir Henry's silly meeting."

Now I know my thoughts showed, for the girl burst out laughing. "Oh, dear, *everybody* in town knows about this big secret conference!" she chortled. "The man's practically bragged about it to everyone in a five-mile radius! Sir Henry's such a pompous ass! He just loves to show how much more important he is than the rest of us poor peasants! And Alexander's exactly the same way. I feel so sorry for poor Peter–he's so sweet, and they treat him so badly. Especially after Sir Henry tried to get us–"

"Christina, don't tell stories," Roxton said sternly.

"Oh, all right," Christina sighed, "But it's a shame about Peter. He's such a dear man."

"Yes," replied Lord John, "but that's enough."

I decided it was time to change the subject. I didn't want to talk about the Westenras, or the conference, or about Spiritualism, any more. So I turned the discussion to some of Lord John's previous adventures, of which he was more than willing to speak about. Despite my doubts of her, Miss Gianetti proved both fascinated and fascinating, and so the rest of our journey passed in a most pleasurable fashion

I was pleasantly surprised to find the town of Wolfsbridge much livelier and bustling than I had anticipated. I was expecting a tiny, rather insular village; what I received was a fair-sized market town, with busy streets and shops, paved roads, a telephone and telegraph line, and even cars roaring through town. Who knew–there might even be a place with indoor plumbing! I was holding Miss Gianetti's bag; Lord John had Christina's, and we had just stepped off the train together. Miss Christina's expression was one of happiness in familiar surroundings and we set off to look for her mother, whom Christina stated would meet them.

As we did, a particular feature caught my eye and held it. A small, pale-white stone bridge, arching over the small rivulet that passed through town. Unlike the rest of the architecture, which was typically Tudor, there was something distinctly Mediterranean about the bridge, with its ionic columns rising from the water and the faded images of nymphs and fauns carved in its sides. Someone had taken much time and care to build it many, many years ago. Miss Christina had followed my eyes and nodded. "Yes, it's the oldest thing in the village. Dates back to Roman times, I've heard. Isn't it beautiful?"

"It is," I said. "And that's obviously the 'bridge' in 'Wolfsbridge.' But where does the 'Wolf' come from? Do you know?"

"Oh. Well, that's rather difficult to explain. But there's Mother; come and meet her!" And before I could protest, the young lady had grabbed me by the elbow and was propelling me eagerly forward; Lord John and Gianetti following.

At the edge of the station, a long white motorcar stood waiting by the kerb, engine running The driver stood smartly beside the door, while resting in the back seat waited a woman. "Mama!" Christina called out, steering us toward her

"Christina, my dear." She raised herself up eagerly enough to meet her daughter's kiss, but it was clear it was an effort for her. Mrs. Althea Rutherford was still a comparatively young woman, somewhere in her late forties, and had obviously been a great beauty in her youth. I would see a portrait of her later, showing the figure of a uniquely handsome, somber, but self-confident woman. She still possessed her daughter's hair and coloring, and, as maturity had set in, her features had grown more and more dignified. She looked, to me, like one might expect a princess to become in a fairy tale after Prince Charming whisked her away balancing compassion, regality and just a little mischief in her eyes.

But that had been before her husband's death. Now, her appearance was drawn and sallow and she lay in the back-seat of the motor covered with blankets as if she might get a chill even from the summer air. Christina had informed me that her parents had been deeply in love and, upon Geoffrey Rutherford's death (by a heart attack), his wife had suffered a complete physical and mental breakdown. For several months, she had been a recluse, nearly a complete invalid, and only recently had recovered her strength enough to start taking up her life again. But it would be some time before she could regain her full health.

"I do hope you didn't pick up any of those awful cigarettes in London, my dear," Mrs. Rutherford was saying. "You know how your father disapproved of women who smoked."

"Of course not, Mama," Christina said cheerfully. "Everyone knows a real lady wouldn't poison her lungs with such things." She shot a mischievous glance over at Roxton, but the latter wisely ignored it. Instead, he bent to kiss Mrs. Rutherford's hand and say, "Althea It's truly wonderful to see you up and around again. We were all so concerned."

"Thank you, John. But nothing will be right until I can speak with dear Geoffrey again."

"That's what I wanted to speak to you about, Althea. Please–do you really want to go through with this? With all due respect to Miss Annunciata, I–"

"John, please." She took his hand weakly but determinedly. "I *must* know. I must know that Geoffrey's safe and with the Lord. He was never a religious man. How could I possibly go through the rest of my life knowing I might never see him again in the one to come?"

"That's what we're trying to do, Mama," Christina interrupted, reaching out to take Gianetti's hand. "This is Miss Annunciata, the assistant of the Sâr Dubnotal. She's going to help us, just like you asked."

"It's a pleasure to meet you, Mrs. Rutherford," Gianetti spoke softly, taking the elder woman's other hand. "And I hope I can help. I know well the pain left behind when a loved one crosses the veil."

"Oh my dear, I do hope so. I miss him so much."

"We'll try. It's much harder to contact, truly contact, the deceased than one might think. But keep faith–for faith is power, and love is the strongest faith of all. We'll find him. Now–you said in your letter than you had contacted other mediums as well as the Doctor? Are they here yet?"

"No; they'll be arriving tomorrow. Rosemary Underwood, who is a local medium everyone tells me is excellent, and a very, very famous psychic from Russia, Count Gregori Yeltsin. Do you know him?"

"Yeltsin?" Gianetti frowned thoughtfully. "No, I'm afraid not. I've never heard of him. Which is odd–*El Tebib* makes it a point to keep up with any mediums operating out of Russia. He's never told me of any named Yeltsin."

"Really? He's reputed to be an associate of Blavatsky, and to have studied under the Hidden Masters in Tibet."

This was too much for me to pass up. "If I may, Miss Gianetti," I put in, "just *why* does your employer go out of his way to keep track of Russian mediums?"

Everyone's attention was now turned to me. "Mama, this is Mr. Dickson," Christina introduced me. "He was on the train with us. And guess what, he attends Papa's old school! He's a detective, and is going to be working security at that conference Sir Henry is holding this weekend."

"Really?" She smiled weakly but with genuine warmth. "My dear young man, words cannot express how sorry I am for you. I'm afraid you're in for quite a time."

I chuckled a bit and bowed. "Thank you, Ma'am. But, if you please, Miss Gianetti, if I may, just who *is* this employer of yours? What does he do for a living? What did you call him again–Sir Dubnose?"

Miss Gianetti burst out laughing. "Oh, how he'd scream if he heard you call him that! He'd yell at you for hours! No, no, that's the Sâr Dubnotal, although he prefers to be called *El Tebib* or the Doctor. He's... he's... well, it's hard to explain just *what* he is. I guess the best way to describe him is as an explorer."

"Like Lord John?"

"Not quite. Lord John, bless you, sir, only explores *physical* realms. *El Tebib* studies more than that. His explorations are those of the higher planes; of the *psychognosis.* The realm of the powers of the mind and spirit; of the mysteries of life and what lies beyond."

I was confused. "He's an alienist, then?"

"No, not exactly, although you could call him one. The Doctor explores the hidden recesses of the mind, yes, but also that of the soul, of the powers and secrets we all have within us. But to find those secrets, we sometimes have to reach beyond life, to those who have already passed on. I merely use my small abilities to assist in his research. But we both use our knowledge for the betterment of others As for his interest in Russia–well, let us just say there are those who seek the same secrets, but for their own purposes. The Doctor doesn't approve of that."

"I see," I said, and felt disappointed. So this "Sâr Dubnotal" was simply some sort of would-be occultist. Another Spiritualist who thought they could find all the answers to life's problems from the dead. Lord John sidled up to me and whispered in my ear. "I've heard of him. Some Frenchman who visited India and went a bit native, or so they say. Probably just as much a fraud as the rest, but that's my concern."

"Would you care to attend the séance with us, Mr. Dickson?" Mrs. Rutherford asked. "It's not until this Friday."

I coughed. "I doubt I'd be able to break away, Ma'am. The conference begins that night as well."

"Well, come to tea if you can," Christina said. "We'd love to have you. Rutherford Grange is our home, just down the road from Westenra House. Do come, if you can."

"I'll try, Miss Christina," I said, but had my doubts. From what little I had seen of Sir Henry, it was unlikely he'd permit a mere peon like myself to leave during the conference for any reason, and besides, the more I thought of it, the more uncomfortable I felt. The Rutherfords were lovely and charming people, but far too gullible for my taste. As for Miss Gianetti–well, it pained me to see such an intelligent, beautiful woman waste her time indulging in confidence tricks. She could have been so much more.

"And we need to get going," Roxton put in. "You're exhausted, Althea; we should get you back home." He turned to me. "Goodbye, Mr. Dickson, it was a pleasure meeting you." We shook, and he shot me a glance that read *I'll take care of everything. Let me handle this.*

"Goodbye, Lord John, Mrs. Rutherford. Goodbye, Miss Christina, Miss Gianetti." I watched as they all piled in the car and slowly drove away. I waved as the young women waved to me, and stood as the motor pulled out of the village and vanished into the countryside. I remained there musing for a moment, then looked around. Fortunately, the post office was right next to the station. I went inside and said, "I would like to send a telegram to Paris, please."

I knew a reporter there, a young man about my own age. I sent this message:

Joseph:
I need a favor. See if you can find anything on a metaphysician calling himself Sâr Dubnotal. It's important.
Harry

I told the man to have it delivered to Westenra House as soon as an answer came back, and left. No, it was none of my business, but I had to admit that Mr. Blake had been proved right after all–a little background research never hurt anyone.

With my "extracurricular" activities finished, I went looking for the ride Sir Henry had promised me. I finally found it: a small trap carted by a pony, driven by a taciturn Scot whose main capacity for dialogue seemed to be the word "Urmmm." "Lovely day, isn't it?" "Urmmm." "Are you well today, sir?" "Urmmm." "Is it very far to Westenra House?" "Urmmm." "Did you know I'm secretly prince of the Ubangi warriors come to steal your women?" "Urmmm" A most scintillating conversationalist. Suddenly motoring with the Rutherfords was beginning to look better and better all the time.

Westenra House was some three miles east of Wolfsbridge, so it would be a bit of a ride. Fortunately, the Sun was out, the air was fresh, and the scenery was most pleasant I have always loved the English countryside. It is, in part, one of the reasons I never returned to live in my home country. Yes, America has its places of beauty, sometimes great beauty, but there is something soothing about the ancient green fields surrounded by hedges, the small, unpretentious farms, and the wildflower-ringed walking paths of England, a refreshing of the spirit very few other places can offer. Certainly the grimy, crowded, impersonal streets of New York cannot compete. Here and there were fresh, grassy pastures dotted with sheep or cows, there, a farmer out in his fields plowing behind an old horse. Yes, I sound quite the fool romantic, but I cannot help it. That is the way I truly felt. I felt myself relaxing for the first time in two days and mused that perhaps serving as a mere security agent wouldn't be such a bad thing after all. Not if the weather kept up like this.

Still, one did have the need to talk once in a while. So I attempted one last parley with my driver, casually mentioning that I had met neighbor Christina Rutherford on the train.

The old Scot turned his head, looked at me, and asked:

"Aye? Did she howl?"

"Howl?"

This was the second time I had heard that word used in conjunction with the Rutherfords. "No! Whyever did you say that?"

"Nothin', lad," the Scot replied, turning eyes back to the road. "Nothin' at all. Be comin' up on the House in a minute."

And indeed very shortly the cart reached the border of a long, high brick wall, stretching out alongside the road. We traveled beside this for several hundred yards until we reached an open, wrought-iron gate, and the driver guided the pony through it We entered into a thick clump of trees, which quickly thinned out into a spacious, well-kept garden, and I received my first look at Westenra House.

It was, without doubt, the most pompously dull edifice I have ever seen.

I have been in many manor houses over the years, from the richly opulent to the genteelly decrepit. But Westenra House... Westenra House... ah. Even after all these years I find it difficult to find the words to describe just how the appearance of the house put me off. It wasn't that there was anything wrong with the physical structure of the place: a large, three-story mansion with two extensive wings jutting off from the main hall. If anyone else had been living there it would have been quite attractive. But with the Westenras owning it... well. Perhaps this will help me explain. In all the houses I have ever been in, from palatial to worn, magnificent to shambles, there was always an air of individuality, of familiar comfort, of actually being lived in. Even with the most conceited, socially-climbing matron you can name, in a house filled with the most expensive furniture and priceless bric-a-brac you can think of, there was always a sense of a place where memories were made and kept precious, where hearts were found and broken and mended again. A sense of home.

Westenra House had none of that. As said before, it was physically attractive enough, but there was something missing. The sense of comfort, of individuality, was totally missing. It was too cold, too austere. If the young Westenras had been raised there, there would have been no laughter in the halls, no toys on the floor. It was a building meant only to show how rich and important the owners were, how far above they were over all others, a museum to the Westenra's greatness and nothing more. They just happened to have a bedroom inside. A mausoleum trying to be the Coliseum.

I could tell my silent driver felt it, too, for a veiled look of disgust passed over his face as he gazed at the place. But he said nothing and guided the trap around to the back, then pointed me roughly to a small door. Obviously one of the servants' entrances and not a very important one. I certainly stood highly in Sir Henry's esteem.

"Knock loud," the driver advised me in a mutter. "Someone'll hear ye eventually. Prob'bly Colleen." A brief half-smile twisted his face as he said this. But then he was nicking the reins, and I barely had time to grab my bag and leap out before the trap started moving back toward the stables.

"Thank you!" I called, but the driver only replied back with an extra-loud "Urmm." I took that as an "You're welcome" Then I turned towards the door. No sense turning back now. I walked up and rapped the knocker loudly. There was no answer. I knocked again.

While I did so, I pondered the driver's odd words. Hmmm, I thought, a maid named Colleen. Suggestive of an Irish lass, young, red-haired and pretty. And possibly lonely. I had already had the great fortune to meet two extraordinarily beautiful women today and it had put my youthful imagination in a mood for feminine company. Already I was slicking my hair back, envisioning goldenred hair and eyes as emerald as the fabled Isle. I knocked once more and unconsciously leaned forward to impress the undoubtedly gorgeous creature that would answer.

The door flew open, a cat dashed out and got entangled between my legs. So surprised was I that I involuntarily stepped back, right on the creature's tail; it yowled and swiped my calf with an extended claw. Now I yowled, made an odd sort of jiggy dance with my feet, slipped on the cat again and fell right down. With an indignant "Mrrrowrr!" the cat dashed off and left me sitting upon my dignity.

A howl of laughter met me. I looked up, reproachfully, to see a darkskinned, square-jawed and unquestionably masculine figure leaning against the doorpost, laughing uproariously.

My greeter was no Irish beauty. Instead it was a young East Indian youth about my own age, with quick, intelligent eyes shining with mirth at my predicament. I had to admit he was quite handsome. The unfortunate stereotype of the Indian is that of a wasted, stick-thin figure with ribs showing, dressed in a dirty loincloth and turban. But this man was tall and strapping, broad in shoulder and thick in arm. His rough hands and hard build showed many years of hard labor, but his dark, smooth skin was unblemished by weather, acne or disease. His head was bare, but a neat pointed beard bristled on the tip of his chin. Even his teeth were excellent, better than many Europeans I knew. An air of pride and confidence hung about him, and, if it were not for the older, patched clothing that marked him as some sort of servant, one might almost have taken him for the master of the house.

He laughed immoderately at me for quite a while. I could only sit and look at him. It, the laughter that is, seemed to be something he hadn't done in a long time "A–are you all right?" he finally managed to get out at last, between guffaws. "Did you hurt anything?"

"Only my pride," I grumbled, feeling my backside. Grinning, the young Indian reached down and helped me up.

"I'd advise you to stay out of Colleen's way from now on if I were you," he told me. "She has a long memory and doesn't take kindly to things like that."

"Colleen's the cat?"

"Of course. This is her favorite door. Open it once and, swoosh, she's gone. What were you expecting?" He read the look on my face and laughed again. "Oh, I get it. Old Jack's been playing one of his jokes on you. No, Colleen's just the kitchen cat–not an Irish beauty."

"Wonderful," I muttered, dusting myself off"

"Seriously, can I help you?"

"Harry Dickson. Here to help with security for the conference."

"Oh. So you're one of the detectives, eh?" The young Indian rolled his eyes. "Gods, that conference. For the past two months, Sir Henry's been on nothing but 'conference, conference, conference' and he blows up at the slightest delay. Everyone in the House will get on their knees and give thanks when that thing's over. I thought it was supposed to be some sort of secret, anyway. By now everyone in the whole bloody county knows about it. Anyway, come in. Mr. Appleby's in the kitchen–he'll probably be the one to talk to."

I entered a long, narrow servant's corridor, whitewashed and bare. It ran the entire width of the house, terminating at one end and turning a corner towards the rear That, I surmised, lead toward the kitchen. "This way," the youth said, and guided me in that direction.

As we walked, I commented, "I'd rather like to know whose hospitality I'm currently enjoying."

"Kritchna. Darshan Kritchna."

"Harry Dickson," I said again, and we shook hands. "If I may ask, what do you do here?"

Kritchna paused for a moment, thinking, and then said simply, "Whatever it is the whites don't want to."

"Ah. Well." There seemed to be nothing to add to that, so I changed the subject. "So, how long have you been with Sir Henry? Did you come with him from India?"

"*No*!" Kritchna burst out so suddenly and sharply it was nearly a shout For a split-second his dark eyes flashed fire. But just as quickly it was gone. "I mean, no," he said, in a much quieter, calmer voice. "I... came over on a ship about a year and a half ago. Working my way over. I've only been at the House about six months now."

"I see." To say I was puzzled would be putting it mildly. Why should Kritchna have such a strong reaction to such a simple question? It wasn't anything unusual. Many brought back particularly favored native servants with them when they came back home.

I mused, but put the questions to the back of my mind. No use looking for mysteries when there were none. "You speak English very well," I said.

Kritchna nodded absently. "Self-taught, mostly. A little missionary schooling," he muttered, but distantly, as if thinking about something else. But by now we had entered the kitchen, and put any more conversation aside.

The kitchen was, to all appearances, the antithesis of the cold, too-showy exterior of the House. It was smaller than most from similar-sized houses, but was comfortable and warm, like a well-loved family dining area. Utensils and other kitchen paraphernalia hung in a cozily haphazard fashion everywhere–those with a beloved, absent-minded aunt or uncle will know what I mean–and the air was thick with the friendly, clean scents of soap, onions, linen and fresh-baked bread. A flour-haired old woman was bending over a huge pot of spicy-smelling soup. "Where's Mr. Appleby, Mrs. Mulligan?" Kritchna asked her.

The old woman looked up from her stirring and smiled kindly. "Out," she said with a thick Irish accent. "Th' Master called for him He should be back any moment. Who's this?"

"Fellow named Dickson. Here to help with the conference."

"Oh." She nodded pleasantly at me. "Nice t'meet you, Mr. Dickson. Darshan, Colleen didn't get out when you opened the door, did she?"

Kritchna shrugged, smiling. "Have you ever known her not to?"

"Oh, Darshan!" She tossed the spoon aside with a clatter. "Now I'll have t'go find her. You know how the Master hates to see her wanderin' around the yard. Here, you get over here and stir this soup. I'll be right back." Removing her apron, she toddled out of the kitchen. Unruffledly, Kritchna picked up the spoon and took her place "Want some soup?" he asked casually.

I was about to decline but a growl from my stomach overruled me. "Yes, please. Thank you."

Kritchna poured a thick, steaming goulash of vegetables and meat into a bowl and shoved it over toward me. "Tea's in the kettle over there," he offered, and I was quick to help myself. The soup was excellent, and my stomach thanked me over and over again. But I also wanted to know more about my curious companion. So I attempted to steer him into conversation again: "Are you the only Indian on the staff?" He nodded briefly, his attention on the soup. "Do you like working for Sir Henry?"

Instantly, his head shot up. "Would you?" he demanded.

I had to admit he had me there. "From what I've seen of him, no," I finally confessed. "To be perfectly frank, I'm only here because my employer wants it. But if he's that bad, why do you stay?"

"I have my reasons," Kritchna said gruffly. "And, 'to be perfectly frank,' they're not any of your business."

I was properly abashed. "You're right. I apologize. It was rude of me to inquire."

Kritchna sighed deeply and gave me a sheepish smile. "Don't be. I shouldn't have been so gruff. Sir Henry doesn't have the monopoly of boorish behavior. I'm the one who should apologize. Seriously, working around here is fine–as long as you stick to the rest of the servants. They're all right. Mind you, Mr. Appleby can come on a bit strong at times–but you'll see that for yourself. Beyond that, though, he's fine–a bit too dignified, but fair." He sighed again.

"But, as for the Westenras... they're... they're..." He paused, taking a deep breath as if searching for the words. Or trying to erase a bad memory. "I get along well enough with Peter," he said at last. "He, at least, isn't a bad sort. Weak as anything, and, well, you know, being that he's–"

"What?"

"Nothing."

"No, what? If I'm to work here I'd better know something about who I'm working for."

"Well..." Kritchna mused a moment. "All right," he said, "But if you ever tell anyone I told you this, I'll deny it. Understand?" I nodded. "All right. Peter Westenra is... well, he is..." Kritchna raised his hand. Then he waved it limply. Very limply. "See what I mean?"

"Oh," I replied, realizing. This was interesting. There had been no indication in the files that Peter Westenra was believed to be homosexual, and little wonder. It would mean, at the very least, scandal and social ruin to his family– and they could not have that. Not a man like Sir Henry. That explained the business with Christina Rutherford–many homosexuals hid, or were forced to hide, their behaviors under a guide of legitimate marriage. Sir Henry must have tried to arrange one, and it had fallen flat. I wondered why. From all reports, Peter was an intelligent man, certainly smarter than his sire. Surely he would have seen the benefits a marriage, even a fake one, would have given him career-wise and socially.

"It's a bit of an open secret around here," Kritchna was adding "Everyone in town knows. But the fact is everybody likes him. Far better than his brother or father. He's... well, he's good. Not at all like the rest of the Westenras. They..." The young Indian's voice trailed off. Then his jaw clamped smartly shut, as if he had definitely decided not to say something. "Let's just say Sir Henry doesn't get on too well with his younger son. He's too embarrassing. But he also can't just deny him because of the effects it'll have on his position. So they simply keep things quiet. Peter'll be at the conference, but he'll be expected to do little but sit and nod and agree with whatever his father or brother says. I have to say I feel a bit sorry for him."

Silently I agreed. I could imagine it–a pale, sickly child, probably quite sensitive, born into a domineering family like the Westenras. And then discovering he was gay. It must have made for many painful experiences.

Kritchna was looking away, seemingly lost in thought. Then he said: "Look, let's just forget the whole thing. I'm sorry, you're sorry; let's start over again. Would you like more soup?"

"Please," I replied, and about that time Mrs. Mulligan returned, carting a small black-and-white tabby: "There's my Colleen. There's my pretty lass." I swore the feline gave me the most miffed look. I made a mental note to keep away from her in future. Just in case.

Kritchna had been eating a late lunch himself when I knocked and joined me at table. We had just finished eating when the door opened and a pudgy, middle-aged man in butler's dress strode in. He was small and balding, with grey hair on the sides, but comported himself with the regality and dignity of all butlers (which was sometimes more than their masters could do). He was holding a thick, black book beneath his arm. "Ah, Darshan, there you are," he said. "I need to speak with you. Yesterday afternoon, I–oh, hello, young man. Who might you be?"

I stood. "Harry Dickson, here for the conference."

"Ah, yes, one of the security men. A moment, young man, and I'll escort you to the library. Sir Henry will give you your instructions from there. Now, then, Darshan–early last night I called you and couldn't find you for about an hour. Where were you?"

"Oh," Kritchna squirmed in his chair, "I was doing something for Sir Henry, Mr. Appleby."

Appleby drew himself up. "I doubt that, for I asked the Master if he had called for you, and he said no. Now, really–where were you? And don't tell me you were out helping at the stables. I checked there, as well."

"All right, all right." Kritchna threw up his hands. "I confess I snuck into town for an hour and went to the cinema."

"Darshan!"

"It was a *Little Neddy* picture!"

Appleby groaned and put his hand to his forehead. "Darshan, Darshan, what am I going to do with you? You know how I feel about cinemas! And sneaking off from your duties, too!"

"Well, if it's any consolation, the picture wasn't very good."

"It isn't, but I'll deal with you later. Come along, young man, and I'll take you to the library. But don't you go anywhere, Darshan–we have some things to discuss."

With a sympathetic glance at Kritchna, I rose from the table. Appleby escorted me out from the servants' quarters into the House proper.

It was just as bad as the outside of the House. Now I knew why the kitchen had seemed so homey and comfortable–clearly the Westenras never bothered to set foot there The servants' area could be decorated any way they wished. But out here, where they lived–things were different. Everything had to reflect the glory of the Westenras. Here was a great portrait of Sir Henry; there one of Alexander. Between them were dotted pictures of older Westenras, dating back to at least the 16th century. All of them held the same snotty, superior look. At no time did I see any portraits or photographs of Peter. The furnishing were all excellent, of museum quality, but that's the way they were meant to be They were meant to show off, not be used. I had to wonder if Sir Henry actually had to lay in his bed, or if he had found a way to just hover over it. It was cold. I couldn't imagine the conference being a success here. Everyone would be too afraid they'd track mud on the carpets.

As we walked, I taking in everything I could to learn my way around, Appleby suddenly spoke up. "If I'm not overstepping my bounds, sir, may I ask–are you a believer?"

"Hm?" I looked at him in puzzlement. Thinking back to my train ride, I inwardly groaned. God, not another Spiritualist, please! "A believer in what?"

The butler held up his book–which I now saw was the Bible. "A believer in the Word, sir; in the Holy Bible and the death and resurrection of Our Lord, the Holy Son of God."

I breathed a sigh of relief. "Oh, that! Thank goodness–I thought you were going to say Spiritualism."

"Spiritualism? Oh, heavens, no, no, no. Total rubbish, and Satanic rubbish at that! I'll have none of that!"

I smiled. "Well, then, we have something we can agree on–at least in regards to Spiritualism being rubbish. I don't believe in the Devil, though. I'm not a Christian."

"I see, sir."

"Does that offend you?"

"No, sir; that's your concern. But I must admit it disappoints me to find so few Christians these days. The Spiritualist obsession in this country..." he shook his head. "The Bible explains the existence of life after death perfectly well! Where is people's faith?"

I shrugged "Faith is fine, until you actually reach a point where all you've heard about faces you. Then you want facts. You want to know your loved one is all right; you don't want pats on the head and comforting murmurings of 'have faith.' Ergo, the popularity of Spiritualism Why do you need faith when you can simply 'talk' to your loved one and find out the truth?"

"I suppose," the butler said. "But I still think it's evil. The Enemy will use all at his disposal to lure men from the Truth. Spiritualism is just another tool in his arsenal."

"Perhaps," I said, not wanting to get into it. I thought of Sir John. "Then again, perhaps if it makes some people happy, then there's a reason for it."

"You're speaking of the Rutherford séance?"

"Yes. How did you know?"

"It's common knowledge, I'm afraid. I must admit, it truly upsets me to see Mrs. Rutherford so wounded. She and her daughter are fine Christian people. Even if Miss Rutherford, if you'll excuse me for saying so, can be a bit too exuberant at times. But their faith should have been strong enough to see them through this. I'm sorry to see that it is not." He paused before a door. "But enough of that. Gossiping is a sin, and one I must overcome. Please pardon me. This is the library. If you'll wait in here, I'll fetch Sir Henry."

"Thank you," I said and went inside. The library was much as I had expected. Filled wall-to-wall with rare and expensive books, not one which had ever been cracked open. It was a shame to see a library treated so poorly. The best ones were those with the pleasant scent of wood pulp all about, with the pages of each volume yellowing and well-thumbed, underlined at the best scenes, used and loved. I was disliking Westenra House more and more.

I glanced around, looking at the titles. As I suspected, no real attempt at ordering had been done; they were simply shoved inside according to size and color of cover. Here was a first edition of *Pickwick Papers*, there a history of South America, there a old, rare of volume of Arronax's sea life encyclopedias, there *Hamlet*. I found myself reaching up and plucking one of the books off the shelf at random. If the Westenras would not use their own library, I thought, I would. Pulling down a large, black, folio-sized volume, I checked the spine. There was no title. Carefully I opened the cover to the title page and read:

JOURNAL OF CHRISTOPHER WESTENRA
(1663-1664)

A journal! I never would have thought a Westenra would have kept one. Well, I never thought a Westenra would have the intelligence to read or write, but that was cruel. Licking my finger, I flicked a page open at random, near the middle of the book. It read:

"*I have buried the body under the bridge where no one will think to look for it. As soon as we have a good flood, the grave will be smoothed out. I dare not let anyone know what I have discovered. If it should be learned, I would be the one hanging off the edge of the bridge, not the Rutherf–*"

Voices behind me caused me to slam the book shut and quickly replace it back on the shelf. The door opened and Appleby came in, followed by a very red-faced, very indignant Sir Henry.

"Sir Henry, this is Mr. Dick–" the butler began but Westenra cut him off.

"So, you finally decided to come, eh?" he snorted, glaring at me. "I'm surprised you even had sense to get on the right train. Very well, now that you're here, you may as well be useful. The rest of the security staff won't be arriving until tomorrow, so there's nothing for you to do–so go out to the stables and see if you can lend a hand out there. They always need someone to clean up after the horses. Not what you signed up for, I'm sure, but I never waste men or time. I won't have any layabouts here. Later, you can get the feel of the place. But whatever you don't, don't mess up! This conference is too damned important. I spent months trying to get the wretched French over here, and I won't have anything spoil it now! Damn them anyway, miserable Frogs and their concerns about what we're doing to the natives in India. They're our wogs, not theirs.

We'll do what we like to them. Frogs and Wogs, what a combination, eh?" He glowered at me, as if expecting me to answer. I could swear his mustache actually flapped.

I wouldn't give him the satisfaction of answering. Appleby just looked embarrassed. Instead, I said: "Whatever you like, Sir Henry. And may I ask about my sleeping quarters?"

"Oh," Westenra shrugged dismissively. "Yes. Well, space is at a premium here with the conference, so most of the arrivals' aides will be rooming with the servants. I planned to have the security staff sleep out in the stables with the men out there. Since you're here, I guess we can put you up with our house Indian, what's his name, Appleby?"

"Darshan, sir, Darshan Kri–"

"Yes, Deershan. Whatever. You can sleep with him tonight. Ordinarily, I wouldn't think of putting any white man with a wog, but you have to make do when you have to. What do you think of that, Mr. Dickson?" He looked at me smugly.

"I think that would be fine," I replied coolly. "I've already had the opportunity to meet Darshan, and would be glad to have him as a roommate."

Sir Henry looked at me bemusedly. Clearly he had been expecting another answer. Then he shrugged: "Suit yourself. Appleby, show Mr. Dickson to the stables for now. I'm sure they can find something useful for him to do." He turned to leave.

"Oh, Sir Henry," I called, "one more thing."

"What?"

"I look forward to meeting your son Peter. Is he here?"

"Peter?" Sir Henry wheeled about. "Why would anyone want to meet him? Yes, yes, he'll be here, if he's not too drunk to walk. But I wouldn't get too friendly with him." He gave a wicked smirk. "He might take it the wrong way." He turned on his heel and stalked out.

I glanced over at Appleby. Once he had been certain his master was no longer in sight, he had leaned against the wall and gave a groan. "Sir, I apologize... it's just Sir Henry's way..."

"Never mind, Mr. Appleby," I said. "Just take me to the stables After the air in here, horse dung would smell far sweeter."

After a rather filthy rest of the afternoon, I ate dinner with the rest of the staff in the kitchen. I sat next to Kritchna, and Appleby led the table with great dignity and good manners. To his credit, he forced neither of us to join him and the rest in prayer before and after the meal. Afterwards, most of the staff left for bed or their other duties, while Appleby sat reading his Bible, waiting for any call. Tomorrow, I would learn my exact duties and master the grounds of the House, and so wanted to retire early. Kritchna had no other duties, so we both said goodnight and trooped upstairs.

Kritchna's room was at the very top of the House, just off the attic. At the door, he paused. "Welcome to the Wolfsbridge Savoy," he said, "Please, make yourself comfortable." And he opened to the smallest, most wretched garret I had ever seen.

It was barely bigger than a closet. There were no furnishings for there was no room for them, just a small, rickety bed with a pillow shoved inside. There was barely enough room for one man to walk beside it. One lone window, a porthole really, let in what light there was. And there was precious little of that even in the daytime, for the roof above slanted down, neatly blocking the majority of the view There weren't even actual walls, for the builders had simply left the bare wooden skeleton of the timbers showing. Kritchna slipped in, bent under the bed and pulled out a candle. With a match from his pocket, he lit it and then grandly gestured me inside. "The Royal Suite."

"Good Lord, this is ridiculous," I exclaimed. "The other servants get regular rooms, even the tweenies. Why do you get this?"

In reply Kritchna simply ran his hand down his skin. I bit off an obscenity.

"I'm used to it by now," Kritchna said, starting to pull off his clothes. "Just something else my people have to put up with."

"Oh, for–but, look, Kritchna... Darshan. I don't know you very well, but you're obviously an intelligent, gifted man. Why are you in Service? Surely there's something else you can do than this. Working for the Foreign Office as a translator, perhaps, or..."

"As I said, I have my reasons for being here," Darshan said sharply "Now, move over, I've got to put this blanket out in the hall."

"Whyever for?"

"Where do you think I'm going to sleep? You get the bed."

"You mean Sir Henry expects you to give up your own bed for me?"

"For a white man, yes."

"Nonsense." I was appalled. "I'm not about to kick you out of your bed just so I can have one. I'll sleep in the hall."

"No, you won't. If Sir Henry catches you, he'll have both our heads. He may not like you, but you're still white. He expects you to behave that way."

"I'd be ashamed to call myself a white man if I kicked another man out of bed just so I could have it. Look. There's just enough room for the two of us. Why don't we share?"

Darshan looked skeptical. "Share the bed?"

"Why not? At least that way we both get a bit of mattress."

"If you can call this piece of petrified timber a mattress. I've slept on iron bunks that were softer. But–all right. But you get the side by the wall. If someone comes up here, I have to hit the floor fast."

"Fine," I replied, and quickly changed to my own nightshirt. I crawled in next to Darshan (the mattress groaning as I did) and he blew out the candle.

"Just like Ishmael and Queequeeg, eh?" Darshan chuckled.

"You've read that?"

"I've read lots of things. Just as long as you keep your great white whale to yourself, sahib."

"No problem there." We turned our backs to each other and closed our eyes.

I couldn't sleep. Which was unusual: for all my life I've been able to sleep anywhere, unfamiliar surroundings or not. Irritably I drew the lone blanket up closer. I felt cold. But no matter how tight I pulled, not matter how I curled up my body to converse heat, I could not get warm. And this on a summer night that would ordinarily make me perspire. Further, I was starting at every sound: the gentle whisper of bat wings over the roof, the creaking of settling floorboards, the hoot of an owl. Finally, I jerked up as the sound of tiny, regular pattering sounded on the tiles above us. Pat-pat-pat-pat-pat-pat. It traveled quickly down the slope of the roof, then up, then back down again. A rat? I wondered. Then I heard a piping little mew.

"It's Colleen," Darshan murmured sleepily next to me. "She climbs the roof at nights. You get used to it."

"Mmm," I mumbled, slipping back down. Mentally I admonished myself. It must have been all the talk of Spiritualism earlier, I thought. Playing games with my subconscious, making me jump at every little sound as if afraid a Spirit might jump out and seize me. Foolish. You know better than that, Dickson.

Above, Colleen continued with her contented mewling. "Mew. Mew. Mew." Enjoy yourself, my girl, I thought and started drifting to sleep again.

That was when I heard the other noise.

I say without exaggeration that it was the strangest sound I have ever heard. Heavy, and regular, spaced precisely like footsteps. Thump. Thump. Thump. But there was something odd, something wrong about each thump. Something incomplete I should say, as if whatever was causing it was something very big and very heavy and yet–not all there, if you know what I mean. It sounded almost as if someone had a great rubber bag half-filled with water and was steadily dropping it upon the roof, so it sounded more like Schtwhump. Schtwhump, schtwhump, schtwhump.

"What the hell is that?" Darshan grunted, rising up in the bed. "I've never heard that before."

"Dunno," I replied. "Could someone have gotten on the roof?"

Whatever it was, it was moving steadily, if wetly, down toward the edge. Directly above us, Colleen the cat was still meowing, but suddenly fell silent just as the schtwhumping stopped. We could hear her hiss violently. Then there was a great, frightened "MRRROOWWWWWW!!!" and suddenly the little porthole that served as our window shattered into pieces! Darshan and I both clambered up clumsily, knocking into each other and trying to avoid falling glass, as we stumbled to the edge of the bed and over.

"Damn!" roared Darshan. "What the bloody hell is going on? Where's that damn candle?" There was the scratch of a match and the tiny pinprick of flame shone dimly. Darshan raised the candle up. "What happened?"

"Something came through the window," I snapped obviously, climbing back upon the bed. My hands pressed against several pieces of glass, cutting myself, but I ignored it. "But God knows–oh my!" I drew back. Darshan leaned forward, holding the candle out. He swallowed.

There on the bed, lying in a bloody heap, was the tiny, twisted body of Colleen.

Her head had been completely severed from her neck.

END OF PART ONE

(*To Be Continued in Volume 2*)

Rick Lai easily wins the prize for the story with the most pop culture references; he also wins the prize for the most interesting juxtaposition of myths: French pulp fiction and Italian Spaghetti Westerns, with a dash of Hong Kong cinema. A delightful smorgasbord (or bouillabaisse*?) of plot twists, which will cause many to turn to the back of the book to trace the origins of all the characters...*

Rick Lai: *The Last Vendetta*

New Orleans, Mardi-Gras 1900

In the course of his 83 years, Arthur Gordon had been a fighter for Texas independence, a captain of a slave ship, a gambler, a duelist and a bigamist. He had been married to both Hermine de Chalusse of Paris and Francine Xavier of Austin at the same time. He was living a quiet existence in El Paso when a letter arrived that would revive an old vendetta.

The author of the letter was Ignacz Djanko, alias the Undertaker. Descended from Croatian immigrants who settled in the American West, Djanko had been one of the most bloodthirsty gunslingers of the West. He had slain easily over 50 men in the course of his brutal career. Gordon first met Djanko along the Pecos River in 1878. At the time, Gordon was selling Lee Bailey's machine guns. Bailey had been a Confederate gunsmith who had been forced to flee to Mexico when he got into trouble with the Federal troops stationed in the South during Reconstruction. Bailey was a genius who had made a vast improvement on the Gatling gun over a decade before Maxim invented his version of the machine gun. Wishing to reside in obscurity in Mexico, Bailey had gone into partnership with Gordon to market his machine guns. Gordon had sold one of these weapons to Djanko with the understanding that the Undertaker would convince a group of Mexican revolutionaries hiding out in Texas to purchase more. These revolutionaries were stragglers from General Santilla's aborted attempt to overthrow Porfirio Diaz in 1877. Unfortunately, Djanko's impatience and greed had caused the potential Mexican clients to prematurely return to their country and be massacred by Diaz's forces.

Many people mistakenly believed that the Undertaker's machine gun was an 1884 Maxim. This misunderstanding always irked Gordon. This fallacy was largely spread by Stanley Corbett's recent dime novel, *The Undertaker's Big Gun*. Djanko was feuding with the Red Scarf Gang, a group of ex-Confederates who took over a Texas town after the Reconstruction. In the dime novel, Djanko had his final showdown with the Red Scarf Gang in a cemetery. Djanko had sought shelter behind a grave that bore the inscription *1889*. This was not an error by Corbett. The local gravedigger had gotten intoxicated one day, and transcribed 1889 instead of 1869 on the marker. If Corbett's narrative was read carefully, it would be noticed that Djanko was depicted as a young man in his late thirties who fought for the North during the Civil War. Also Corbett's narrative accurately described Djanko's revolver as an 1873 Peacemaker, a weapon that would have been outdated by 1889.

Sometime in the 1880s, Djanko had shocked his criminal associates by suddenly becoming gripped by religious fervor. Seeking atonement for all the blood on his hands, Djanko had joined a monastic order in Mexico. Two years ago, Djanko had suddenly broken his vows and returned to a life of mayhem. He had written to Gordon seeking replacement parts for his old Bailey machine gun. Unfortunately, Gordon couldn't help him because Gordon had retired from the armament business when he reached his 70th birthday. He had no idea whether Bailey was even still alive. Gordon had informed Djanko to try other arms dealers. Despite his failure to satisfy Djanko's request, he and the old gunslinger continued to correspond. Gordon perused Djanko's letter.

Dear Arthur,

While receiving some replacement parts for my machine gun from a Swedish arms dealer, I received an unusual invitation from some of his associates. It is for the New Orleans Assassins' Auction, a gathering being held for a rather unique clientele during Mardi-Gras. The items being offered for sale include various weapons that have been used to murder our fellow human beings over the centuries. They even have a Bailey machine gun. I am unable to attend because of other business matters. My Swedish friend suggested I pass on the invitation to one of my friends. I have chosen you because there is an item of fairly recent vintage that will interest you.

Sincerely,

Ignacz

Besides the invitation, enclosed with the letter was a detailed catalogue of items being offered for sale at the auction. One of them immediately caught Arthur's attention:

#37 - C96 Mauser Pistol. Formerly the property of the Mute Shootist of Utah, a man who conducted a violent campaign against bounty hunters by either shooting off their thumbs or killing them outright. In good working order. Capable of firing 10 bullets.

Josephine Balsamo, also known as Countess Cagliostro, was holding the Assassins' Auction in a large mansion on the outskirts of New Orleans. She was an attractive blonde woman of 32 years. Her personal office had been made virtually soundproof with steel paneling just in case it was necessary to liquidate any customers who refused to pay. Her partner in this unique endeavor was the American known as Aguirre.

His real name was not Aguirre. After a career as a bounty hunter in Utah, this American decided to leave the state because the Governor had ordered an investigation into his activities. Josephine had christened her partner Aguirre because she believed that only the notorious 16th century conquistador of the same name had matched him in bloodthirstiness. During his travels in the West, Aguirre had been able to locate numerous firearms and knives that belonged to many of the most notorious gunfighters. This huge arsenal would be dispersed at the auction.

For her own part, Josephine was making contributions to the auction from various different sources. Since the 18th century, her family had engaged in extensive dealings with the secret societies of Italy. Josephine had come into possession of the diabolical inventions of the Camorra, the Red Circle and the Brotherhood of the Seven Kings.

In additions to her assortment of Italian instruments, Josephine had also profited from her brief love affair with the French swindler Ballmeyer. During their torrid romance, the pair had amused themselves by plundering the evidence rooms of leading police departments of the United States. In Baltimore, they had purloined the complete paraphernalia of the mass murderer known as the Butcher. His instruments included a hook, a meat cleaver, a rapier and a single-shot revolver. From the San Francisco authorities, Ballmeyer and Josephine had stolen the seven idols that had been left beside the victims of Professor Malaki. After Ballmeyer deserted Josephine to return to France in 1897, he had left such plunder with her as a token of his affection while absconding with the undivided loot from their joint murder of a New Orleans merchant. Ballmeyer had assumed that he had saddled Josephine with items of questionable value in exchange for a more tangible asset. The trusting Ballmeyer had been totally unaware that Malaki's statues were made of ivory. Josephine would soon convert Ballmeyer's legacy into substantial money.

The final supplier of Josephine's stockpile of death devices had been the mysterious Dr. Antonio Nikola, a man who had ties to various secret societies in Italy. Nikola had also journeyed substantially in the Far East. In 1898, Nikola had announced his intention to leave Europe and meet his final destiny in an Asian monastery. In exchange for assistance that she had rendered him in the past, Nikola had bequeathed Josephine an assortment of Asian weapons that he had collected during his travels.

On this morning in 1900, all the participants for the auction had arrived. Before the bidding began, the potential bidders were allowed to view the items in a massive ballroom. Numerous armed guards were present to make sure nothing was pilfered. The guests had been allowed to gather together with one notable exception, Arthur Gordon. He was being held in a separate room by two of Aguirre's guards because his invitation was not in order. Arthur was clearly not Ignacz Djanko. While he was examining the prisoner, Aguirre sent a guard to inform Josephine.

Josephine was interrupted in her office as she was perusing an Italian novel that concluded with a violent bloodbath.

"As you know, Countess, Peterson delivered an invitation to Djanko with our permission" explained the guard. "Then this fellow Gordon showed up with Djanko's invitation. He claimed that Djanko sent him the invitation because the Undertaker purchased his Bailey machine gun from him years ago."

"Could you describe this man Gordon?"

"A tall, elderly fellow. Must have been an athlete in his youth, but now he looks like he has one foot in the grave."

When Josephine was escorted into the prisoner's presence, Arthur stared at her in shock.

"Josine, is that you? My God, you are the splitting image of your mother!"

"And the splitting image of my great-grandmother. This is quite a surprise, Arthur."

"You know this man?" queried Aguirre.

"Yes, Arthur was an old friend of my mother's in the late 1860s. In fact, he helped my mother to become a hostess in Paris shortly before the Franco-Prussian War. Upon my mother's tragic death, Arthur arranged that I be properly educated. When I was 12, he paid the cost of my enrollment at the Marie Gilbert School in Paris. When I reached the age of 15, Arthur arranged my transfer to the Fourneau College for Young Women near Avignon."

"Josine, I never expected to find you in New Orleans," Gordon said. "I heard you were in France six years ago."

"A dispute with a business partner prompted me to come to America. I recall that you knew the father of my treacherous ex-associate. He's the son of Theophraste Lupin."

"If the son is anything like the father, then he's the last person in the world that I would ever trust."

Josephine had ample reason for hating Theophraste Lupin. He had been indirectly responsible for her mother's death. Josephine devoted her existence to ruining the lives of his descendants. Her first act of vengeance against the Lupin family had actually transpired at the Fourneau College. The mistress of that school had chosen Josephine to be the senior prefect of all the girls and entrusted her with helping run the school. It had initially been very difficult at the Fourneau College for Josephine. She had been exiled there after being put on probation at the Marie Gilbert School for the relatively harmless prank of putting a frog in the bed of a classmate. Discipline was incredibly sterner at the Fourneau College where corporal punishment was not unknown. With grim determination, Josephine had risen to a position of power.

A younger girl known as Mademoiselle Tupin was later enrolled at the school. Having access to all the school's records, Josephine uncovered that Tupin was actually the illegitimate daughter of Theophraste Lupin. Tupin was seemingly a variation of Lupin. By the time that Josephine graduated, she had thoroughly corrupted Tupin and recommended her to the headmistress to be the new chief custodian of all the other students. Josephine had been far less fruitful in her efforts to dominate the son of Theophraste.

"Is your uncle here as well?" wondered Gordon.

"Yes, Uncle Leonard is working in the showroom." Turning to Aguirre, Josephine asserted, "Please release this old family friend. His presence at the Assassins' Auction is most welcome."

When Gordon entered the showroom, he was immediately struck by a large metal Chinese abacus on display at one of the tables. According to the catalogue, it had once been the property of the Bookkeeper, a member of the Ten Killers of the Underworld.

Next to the abacus was a large circular metal object that that looked like some sort of hatbox. Blades extended from the side of the object almost making it resemble a buzz saw. Gordon looked up the item in the catalogue:

#235 - Flying Guillotine. This weapon was created on the orders of Emperor Yung-Cheng (1722-35). Execution squads armed with multiple versions of this device roamed the Chinese countryside inaugurating a Reign of Terror similar to that which transpired in the French Revolution. This instrument is not only designed to behead the victim, but to capture his head as a grisly trophy for the executioner. According to Kegan Van Roon's Secrets of the Shaolin Temple's Thirty-Sixth Chamber *(New York: Golden Goblin Press, 1897), Yung-Cheng was slain by rebels who had captured one of these Flying Guillotines. The Manchu Dynasty allegedly obfuscated the assassination by pretending that the Emperor had died a natural death. This particular model offered for sale was used by a blind assassin who reported directly to Yung-Cheng.*

"I see that you are admiring the glorious handiwork commissioned by the enlightened Yung-Cheng," remarked a small Chinese gentleman dressed in Western attire. Accompanying the diminutive Asian, who appeared to be his fifties, was a fellow Chinese attendee, a tall thin man in his very late thirties. The older man identified himself as Hong Chen and his younger companion as Huan Tsung Chao. Both identified themselves as the envoys of an enigmatic Dr. Natas. They neglected to mention that Natas was an alias adopted by the powerful Governor of the Chinese province of Honan.

"I must confess that I am appalled by the misleading representation of this artifact in the catalogue," complained Hong Chen. "Did you notice the glaring historical error, Mr. Gordon?"

"I am afraid that I haven't."

"Does not the description imply that the Emperor ordered the creation of this instrument in order to emulate the guillotine introduced into Europe with the French Revolution?"

"Yes, it does."

"When was this Chinese artifact invented?"

"In the early 18th century."

"When was the guillotine invented?"

"Well... It must have been manufactured during the early years of the French Revolution. Let's see ... The Bastille fell in 1789... I see your point. The guillotine didn't originate in France until decades after the reign of Yung-Cheng."

"In our country, this device is known by another name that would more properly translate into English as the 'Flying Executioner'," noted the younger of the two Chinese aristocrats. "The term 'Flying Guillotine' was completely a concoction of Kegan Van Roon, a mountebank who pretends to be a serious scholar."

"It is regrettable that such an error occurred in the catalogue considering the ancestry of our hostess," interjected Huan's older colleague.

"I don't understand your comment, Mr. Hong," replied Gordon.

"Her great-great-grandfather, Count Cagliostro traveled extensively in Asia. There he encountered Yung-Cheng's great contribution to the science of capital punishment. Cagliostro became obsessed with our Flying Executioner. Upon his return to Europe, he tried to persuade others to create a similar wondrous means of death. Initially, he prevailed upon the Brotherhood of the Seven Kings to investigate the practicality of an equivalent device. Unfortunately, that Italian secret society could only achieve decapitation with a rather crude Iron Circlet. The Brotherhood's creation is another item on display in this showroom. Cagliostro didn't achieve his dream until he met Dr. Joseph Guillotin, and ordered him to propose that France manufacture a decapitation machine in the Constituent Assembly."

"But I also thought that Cagliostro was a mere confidence trickster. You talk about him as he was a personage of incredible influence."

"I can not fault you for your lack of knowledge, Mr. Gordon. You and most of the world have fallen victim to the Masonic campaign to hide the true facts of history."

"What in Heaven's name do the Freemasons have to do with all this?"

"Cagliostro was the secret Grandmaster of the Masonic Lodges. In this role, he orchestrated the French Revolution from behind the scenes. The Cagliostro family is famous for hatching convoluted schemes in which others are manipulated. The Count later instructed his Masonic minions to alter all the historical records concerning him when France nearly conquered all of Europe. All the so-called facts about Count Cagliostro are false. These distortions involve his physical appearance as well as his death. Only the great French novelist Alexandre Dumas was aware of the truth. He portrayed the real Cagliostro in a series of novels."

"Why didn't the Masons murder Dumas if he was revealing their secrets?"

"Not being a Mason, I do not know. Possibly they concluded that most readers would simply surmise that Dumas was spinning wild yarns from his own imagination."

"I would never have envisioned that a Chinese Emperor was indirectly responsible for the adoption of the French guillotine as a means of execution. I guess that Van Roon's account of Yung-Cheng's death is false."

"You are correct," inserted Huan Tsung Chao. "The story is simply the legend that Shogun Ietmitsu of Japan was beheaded by one of his own Yagyu assassins transposed to a Chinese setting. Our lord, Dr. Natas, was particularly inflamed by Van Roon's lies concerning the Emperor's death. Our noble master swore that if Van Roon ever set foot in China, he would meet with a violent death. Please excuse us; we want to express my grievance considering the depiction of the Flying Executioner to one of the managers."

The pair left Gordon and approached a grey-haired Frenchman at the other side of the vast showroom. Gordon recognized the man as Josephine's uncle. The Chinese duo was expressing their outrage in a loud manner that caught the attention of many spectators. Gordon suddenly heard an old familiar voice. "Well, Arthur, it looks like our old friend Leonard has been captured by the Chinese."

"Good Lord! Count Bielowsky. I though you would be dead by now."

"That's a strange comment coming from a man who is 12 years older than me."

The speaker was dressed in the uniform of an officer of the Second Empire. His face sprouted whiskers in the style of Emperor Franz Joseph of Austria-Hungary. His hair was parted in the middle. Both his hair and his whiskers had been dyed dark brown.

"When Napoleon III abdicated, you suddenly disappeared from Paris. Where did you go, Count?"

"I have been serving as an aide-decamp at the court of Antinea, the Sultana of Ahaggar."

"Ahaggar? I never heard of such a kingdom. Where is it located?"

"You are better off not knowing. The Sultana believes in keeping the knowledge of her kingdom's existence confined to her loyal subjects. The Sultana is a woman of unusual pursuits. She has dispatched me here to bid on one particular item, a group of small statues, apparently of Sumerian origin, that materialized in San Francisco a decade ago. Queen Antinea suspects that they were actually plundered from the tomb of the wizard Surama in her own kingdom. I am somewhat concerned that I may not been able to acquire the idols. One of our fellow attendees is Oliver Haddo, a man rumored to be the purchasing agent of a wealthy consortium of occultists. Haddo has also expressed an interest in bidding on the idols. But that's enough about my commission. Do you still live in Germany during the summer and in France during the winter?"

"Those days are long gone. Like you, my fortunes were severely depleted by the consequences of the Battle of Sedan. I tried to borrow money from my son Wilkie, the heir to the Chalusse millions. That spoiled brat refused to have anything to do with me. I was forced to return to Texas where my son John helped me establish a munitions business. I haven't been in Europe since except for a few trips in the 1880s to sort out some family matters."

"I wasn't aware that Hermine bore you another son."

"She didn't. Hermine wasn't the only woman that I married."

"Wilkie's behavior towards you was really quite extraordinary. I generally find daughters to be more considerate of their parents than sons. It's too bad that you never had a daughter."

Gordon was tempted to reply that he had a daughter, but he hadn't been married to the mother. Furthermore, her late mother had made him promise never to reveal his parentage to her. Instead, Gordon decided to change the topic of conversation.

"Well, my dear Count, it looks like Leonard has escaped Chinese captivity only to be assaulted by a female blizzard from Hell."

Leonard had been able to placate the Chinese delegates by promising to publicly announce that the catalogue contained errors about the Yung-Cheng's execution device. As soon as the Chinese duo had left satisfied, a Japanese woman in a white kimono accosted Leonard. She was complained that a large wooden baby cart with concealed muskets was a forgery. She screamed that the genuine baby cart had been destroyed in the 18th century.

"Josephine's uncle has no luck," continued Gordon.

"I am confident that Leonard will sidestep this lady's thrusts. He is a very slippery eel. You won't believe the story that he told me in a Bourbon Street bar last night. He was an extremely caring brother."

"What are you implying?"

"Leonard just pretended to be the brother of the earlier Countess Cagliostro. This deception permitted the Countess to have another lover who thought that she was his exclusive mistress. Leonard told me all this in confidence recently, but he didn't mention the name of the other man. When Josephine was born, the Countess then told her deluded lover that he was the father. In truth, Leonard is Josephine's father. It is very funny, is it not?"

"Yes, it is," Gordon acknowledged with a bitter laugh.

"In fact, Arthur, I heard it stated that Leonard convinced the other man to fund Josephine's education after she was left destitute following her mother's death. The poor fool sent her to the Fourneau College, the place where all our old comrades sent their illegitimate daughters. I heard from a Frenchman who visited Ahaggar that this unique learning institution was closed down by the authorities due to a scandal. The principal's son apparently became overly affectionate with several of her students."

"He tried to emulate Casanova, I presume."

"I suspect Bluebeard was more the boy's model. Believe me; you don't want to know the details."

Gordon proceeded to show the Count numerous items from the American West that were being exhibited. These included the knives of Manuel Sanchez, Doc Holliday's revolver that had been recently found in the Arizona town of Clifton, and a banjo that contained a Winchester rifle inside it.

Gordon motioned the Count over to a table in which several unusual rifles as well as a large derringer were situated.

"These weapons, my dear Count, were all the handiwork of my partner, Lee Bailey. I sold them to Gunsight Eyes, a bounty hunter who was one of my best clients. Bailey and I even developed special ammunition for Gunsight Eyes. These were capsules that seem to be bullets, but really were harmless and contained a red liquid that looked like blood."

"Why would Gunsight Eyes need those?"

"He needed to join a circus in order to track down a counterfeiter. The capsules with fake blood were used an act in which he functioned as both a marksman and an illusionist. He and other people pretended to kill each other in the act.

"Here is another of Bailey's great creations. This is one of his famous machine guns that were developed years before Hiram Maxim's. Looking at the serial number that Bailey inscribed on the weapon, I can verify that's it the one utilized by the Rojos Brothers to ambush Mexican soldiers at Rio Bravo in 1873."

"Pardon me, sir, but perhaps you can settle a friendly disagreement between me and another gentleman."

The speaker was a tall muscular man with curly black hair. He was dressed in a black suit with a white carnation in his lapel.

"My name is Washburn. I am the sales representative of Washburn-Peterson Armaments."

"I believe that I am familiar with your company," declared Gordon. "You sell arms throughout the Caribbean. Has business been good?"

"Yes. We are even branching out into new territories. My brother John, who runs the company with a Swedish partner, is currently filling a rather large African order for a client aptly known as Killer. Countess Cagliostro was invaluable in negotiating the contract. Please allow me to introduce my friend, Monsieur Satanas of Paris."

Satanas was a thickset man in his thirties. He wore a monocle over his left eye.

"My friend, Mr. Washburn, and I were debating about a weapon of similar nature. I am a devotee of the novels of Corbucci. One of his best works was a fictionalized treatment of the real-life outlaw known as the Undertaker. He described such a weapon being employed by the Undertaker in the 1880s. Mr. Washburn insists that the Undertaker's exploit really happened in the 1870s."

Gordon was thoroughly confused.

"Who the dickens is Corbucci?"

"Count Corbucci, the late Camorra leader of Naples and a very close friend of our charming hostess. He was a rather ingenious fellow who once rigged a grandfather clock to fire a pistol. His clock is being offered for auction here. He became infatuated with the stories of the American West during an extended visit there in the 1870s. The various gunfights of your country reminded him of the blood feuds in his native Italy. Corbucci loved American dime novels so much that he decided to write them himself. His ambition was to be the Ned Buntline of Italy. Having researched several actual events, he wrote a series of books about the West. Being multi-lingual, he first wrote them in Italian and then translated them into English himself. His stories are incredibly popular in Italy. Foolishly, his American publisher, Pickman and Sons, refused to distribute the English version of Corbucci's greatest work, *Il Grande Massacro*, because it had a brutally depressing ending."

"I never heard of this Corbucci. I did read a dime novel about the Undertaker by a man named Stanley Corbett."

"Stanley Corbett is Corbucci's pseudonym in America. In Italy, his novels appear under his real name."

Gordon then proceeded to elucidate how a gravedigger's error must have misled Corbucci.

"That explains everything," concluded Satanas. "Corbucci did mention to me that he had visited the graveyard in the ghost town where the Undertaker disposed of the remaining members of the Red Scarf Gang."

"Being such an aficionado of Corbucci, do you intend to bid on the machine gun?" questioned Count Bielowsky.

"If the Undertaker had owned this weapon, then I would have been tempted. I am more interested in finding something that could be put to usage in my own business endeavors. I have my eye on a small cannon here that was made by Professor Schultz in his factory at Stahlstadt, Oregon."

The group clustered around the machine gun was then joined by a thin young man clad in a white suit with a flamboyant blue scarf. He gave his name as Adam Saxon, and was curious as to where one might purchase a machine that was more portable and lighter than the weapon being auctioned. Washburn began to enunciate various models sold by his brother's company.

Gordon was intently listening to this litany of machine guns when he was accosted by another newcomer. The fellow was a tall mustached man in his fifties.

"Are you the Arthur Gordon who fought for Texas independence in 1836?"

"Indeed, I am."

"I also fought for Texas. I was an 18-year-old lieutenant in the final year of the War Between the States. People now called me Nine Fingers. May I have the pleasure of shaking your hand?"

As he shook the hand of the Civil War veteran, Gordon noticed that his new acquaintance was missing the top joint of one of his fingers."

"I see that you are missing the tip of your trigger finger. You must have difficulty in handling a gun."

"There is still enough of my finger left to pull a trigger."

"You're lucky that you weren't wounded in the thumb. A man can't hold a gun if he is missing a thumb."

Gordon remembered how he had once told the same thing to a young boy that he trained how to shoot.

"Have you ever been to Utah?" inquired Gordon.

"Utah? No, why do you ask?"

"It's just that I knew a lot of Utah bounty hunters with injured hands. You weren't ever a bounty hunter?"

"No, but I was a close personal friend of one of the best bounty hunters that ever lived. I even served with him in the Confederate Army. He was called Gunsight Eyes."

"I was also his friend." Gordon paused for a few seconds. "Wait a second. You aren't the fellow who lost 5,000 dollars to Gunsight Eyes in a poker game and then skipped town without squaring the debt."

"You are confusing me with another man, sir. The Major and I have always been on the best of terms."

"Major? Gunsight Eyes was a Colonel."

"He was a Colonel when he served in the United States Army before Fort Sumter. During his time in the Confederate army, he only rose to the rank of Major."

"I remember now. That's correct, but he preferred to be called Colonel."

"To me, he will always be the Major. Did you know the Major long, Mr. Gordon?"

"Yes, in fact I sold him his derringer and rifles."

"Are you planning to bid on the derringer?"

"Why would I? I sold it. Why buy it back now?"

"I am glad to hear that. I intend to bid on that item. It has a sentimental value for me. Since you are such a close friend of the Major, perhaps you could settle a matter of some mystery to me. In 1879, I suddenly stumbled upon the Major in a circus using a very weird alias."

"Yes, I know all about that. Let me see. What was the name? Some Spanish name. Wasn't it Zapata?

"That's close enough. Why did the Major change his name?"

"Gunsight Eyes had a younger sister. While he was off fighting the Yankees, she and her husband were killed by a Mexican bandit known as the Indian.

When the War ended, Gunsight Eyes tried to find the Indian. In 1867, he got a lead that took him to Mexico when the Juaristas were about to finally finish off the forces of Maximilian. There was a mercenary fighting with the Juaristas against Maximilian's forces. This soldier of fortune was named Zapata, but he was also called the Black Indian."

"Black Indian? Was he an African?"

"No, he just had a horrible taste in fashion. He wore the most outlandish black outfit that you could ever imagine. Mistakenly concluding that Zapata was really the man that they were after, old Gunsight Eyes killed him. He was deeply upset when he realized the truth. Years later, Gunsight Eyes would be reminded of his tragic error in judgment.

"In 1876, there was a corrupt Justice of the Peace in Utah. In partnership with an equally dishonest sheriff, he wanted to get rid of a gun runner who settled there. The man was selling guns to Mormon settlers whose land the two corrupt officials were hoping to steal. The devious pair of officials came up with a plan to frame the gun trafficker for a crime that he didn't commit. In order to keep their own hands from getting dirty, the duo then opted to trick a famous bounty hunter into killing their enemy. The man that they decided to dupe was Gunsight Eyes. At first, old Gunsight Eyes didn't suspect a thing. His target had a rather common surname in this country. The name didn't mean anything to Gunsight Eyes until he viewed his quarry. The wanted man greatly resembled an older man with whom Gunsight Eyes was friendly. It turned out the intended victim was actually the son of the old friend. Gunsight Eyes did some investigating and discovered the truth.

"That's why he took the name Zapata. Gunsight Eyes had almost killed an innocent man again. By taking the name Zapata, he was constantly reminding himself never to make that mistake again."

"I remember reading a recent scandal about bounty hunters in Utah massacring Mormon settlers," recalled Nine Fingers.

"That whole mess was caused by the same Justice of the Peace," maintained Gordon. "He was able to finally master the art of orchestrating bounty hunters to further his ambitions. The Mormons responded by hiring a gunslinger to kill the bounty hunters. The conflict in Utah's Snow Hill County in 1898 was nearly as bloody as the Lincoln County war that erupted in New Mexico during 1878."

"Well, thank you, for clearing that matter about Gunsight Eyes, Mr. Gordon. Please allow me to take my leave. I have to make some arrangements concerning a poker game that will be held in Dr. Mabuse's hotel suite tomorrow."

When Nine Fingers left, Gordon turned around and suddenly saw Count Bielowsky. The Count had been standing behind Gordon the whole time during the discussion about Gunsight Eyes. The shrewd aristocrat had heard everything.

"You didn't trust that mountebank enough to confide in him the whole story, Arthur. Reading between the lines, I can deduce that there's more to the tale. Gunsight Eyes must have left Utah to warn his old friend that his son was marked for death. Am I right?"

"Yes, nothing seems to get by you. Of course, the father rushed to his son's assistance."

"Did the father arrive there in time?"

"No. The sheriff and his partner decided that they had wasted enough time toying with bounty hunters. They personally shot the son and his wife. Both were dead when the father arrived."

"But there was another family member."

"Yes, there was a grandson. The killers didn't waste any bullets on him. They just cut his throat. He would have bled to death if his grandfather hadn't rushed him to a doctor. He lived, but he never spoke again."

"That's... very tragic."

"It's not as tragic as it might have been. As the grandfather told the boy, you don't need vocal cords to learn how to handle a gun."

At the auction, Count Bielowsky purchased the Punjabi wires, but Oliver Haddo beat his bid on Malaki's six Sumerian statutes.

Washburn was quite surprised that Gordon spent a substantial amount of money on a Mauser pistol. Such a weapon could be bought for a much cheaper price from Washburn-Peterson Armaments.

Very late into the evening, Josephine Balsamo invited Gordon as an old family friend to have a drink of rare Amontillado with her and her partners. Both Leonard and Aguirre joined Arthur and Josephine in her office.

"I must say, Josine, you presided over the auctioning of those items with the grace of an Empress."

"In a sense, you are responsible for that talent of mine. I learned how to affect a regal bearing by closely observing the headmistress of the Fourneau College. I owned much of my success in my profession to the training given by that skilled lady."

Josephine was totally sincere in her praise. She had learned the fine art of manipulation from the headmistress of the finishing school. Nevertheless, Josephine always resented the indignities that were inflicted on her person in the early phases of the tutelage of the matriarch of the Fourneau College. Josephine succeeded in a diabolical revenge on the headmistress. Josephine's patron had kept her teen-age son segregated from the female students. Unknown to his mother, Josephine secretly contacted the boy during her last days at the school. She suggested an idea to him regarding the remaining students. Following Josephine's departure, the boy acted on her advice and brought ruination to his mother.

"I am curious, Arthur. Why did you buy this Mauser pistol that's lying on my desk?"

"You probably know that I sold a lot of Bailey's weapons to bounty hunters. A lot of those men were my close personal friends. That damn Mute Shootist murdered some of my best clients. I intend to break that pistol with a mallet in order to honor their memory."

"Well, sir," intoned Aguirre in a nice Southern drawl. "There is a piece of information that you might find interesting."

"What's that?"

"I'm the man who gunned down the Mute Shootist. I set an ambush for him with a few of my friends. I shot him in the head, and then I removed that Mauser from his stinking corpse."

"Well, Mr. Aguirre, I think that you and I should shake hands."

Aguirre extended his right hand. Gordon seized the Mauser from Josephine's desk. His first bullet blasted into Aguirre's right thumb. As Aguirre fell to the ground screaming, the second bullet from the Mauser stuck the thumb on his left hand.

"You murdered my grandson!" yelled Arthur as he sent his third bullet into Aguirre's forehead.

"As for you, Leonard, there is the matter of the unnecessary tuition that I paid to the Fourneau College."

Arthur fired the Mauser at Leonard. The Frenchman fell to the ground. His forehead was covered with blood.

"Josine, you're just a treacherous tart like your mother."

Arthur fired three times at Josephine. Her blouse was covered with red stains. She slumped lifelessly to the floor.

Another gunshot was suddenly fired. Arthur felt a sharp pain in his right hand and dropped the Mauser. He saw Leonard standing with a revolver. Josephine Balsamo lifted herself up from the floor and picked up the Mauser. Aguirre also rose up and laughed.

"You all should be dead!" shouted Gordon

"Have you forgotten the special ammunition that you and Bailey made for Gunsight Eyes?"

"The fake blood capsules..."

"Yes, Arthur. We knew all about you relationship to the Mute Shootist."

"How?"

"You may thank the late great Corbucci for that. Satanas told me about your conversation concerning my late friend's literary effort. His *Il Grande Massacro* is actually a sensationalized account of your son's death. It even mentions the mutilation of your grandson."

"But why did you let me attend the convention if you knew I wanted to avenge my grandson's death?"

"Your arrival here was planned from the beginning. I lured you to this auction."

"But I received a letter from Djanko."

"A letter that Djanko was prompted to write by the Swede who is co-owner of Washburn-Peterson Armaments, a firm that is indebted to me for their lucrative African deal. If it is any consolation, Djanko was totally unaware that he was being used as a pawn. He really thought that he was helping you take revenge for your grandson's death."

"How could Djanko trust that Swede so implicitly?"

"The Swede is one of Djanko's bastards. In fact, he's the spitting image of his father except his hair is blonde. Illegitimate children can't always be trusted by their parents. This is a painful fact that you are about to learn, Father."

"Stop it with those lies! Bielowsky told me the truth!"

"Bielowsky made that supposed revelation as part of a deal that we made. His old friendship for you is outweighed by his need to please Queen Antinea. He needed to procure at least one of Malaki's statues to keep her content. I sold him one of the seven idols before the auction, and then he competed unsuccessfully for the other six. Part of the price of that one idol was the telling of a lie to you."

"Is Leonard then really your uncle?"

"No, that part of Bielowsky's story was true. However, don't harbor any doubt about my parentage. My mother told me that you were my father on her deathbed."

"What was the point in having Bielowsky pretend that you aren't my daughter?"

"To cause you to suffer, Father. I want you to suffer."

"Why do you hate me so?"

"You incarcerated me at the Fourneau College! A purgatory for the unwanted daughters of the wealthy! You can't imagine the depravities that I had to endure there in order to survive!"

Josephine removed the phony ammo from the Mauser. She then inserted a real bullet into the gun and gave the weapon to Aguirre.

"Do what you do best," she advised.

Aguirre pressed the barrel of the Mauser against Arthur Gordon's forehead.

"Give my regards to your grandson when you see him in Hell."

Dear Mr. Djanko,

Mr. Peterson has graciously agreed to deliver you this letter. As you have probably heard by now, my beloved father has tragically perished.

My father was overjoyed to see me when he arrived at the auction. Together we both plotted to avenge the death of my nephew. Unknown to us, Aguirre had discovered my father's relationship to the Mute Shootist. He was betrayed by an old friend, Count Bielowsky, who was acting on the instructions of Queen Antinea of Ahaggar. The price of the Count's treachery was an ivory idol.

When the auction concluded, my father and I were alone with Aguirre in my office. My nephew's Mauser was lying on my desk. Aguirre put out a revolver. I grabbed the Mauser, but I was too late. Aguirre shot my fath

Peterson explained why the letter ended abruptly to Djanko.

"She was so overcome with grief that she just couldn't finish writing it, Dad. She loved her father with her whole soul."

"Did Aguirre die a painful death at least?"

"She shot off both his thumbs, and then drilled him through the head."

"What a woman! It's too bad, son, that you don't have a sister like her. Where is this Ahaggar?"

"It is located in the Hoggar Mountains of North Africa."

"You remember my saying that if any harm came to Arthur, I would slaughter those responsible. I am packing my machine gun and taking a trip to North Africa."

Belgium is so important to the field of French-language popular fiction–from Harry Dickson *to* Tintin *to publisher Marabout–that it simply had to be represented here. And it could have no better spokesman than Alain le Bussy, a renowned author who is also an authority on Sherlock Holmes and Arsène Lupin–it is about the latter that le Bussy has chosen to write here...*

Alain le Bussy: *The Sainte-Geneviève Caper*

Paris, 1920

Count Sainte-Geneviève was justifiably proud of his ancestors. One of those had fought alongside Godefroid of Bouillon, the first Christian King of Jerusalem, at the Crusades. Another had had the honor of being beheaded the same day as Louis XVI. Although he did not dare mention it in his wife's presence, he was far less proud of her ancestors. In fact, he only knew one: her father. It was unclear where he had been born, at what he had studied and what kind of job he held between the ages of ten and 30. Sometimes, the Count thought that it was better not to inquire. In any event, if he was not proud of his father-in-law, he was at least grateful to him. For without his money, his castle would have long become a ruin and he would have had to work for a living, a ghastly fate which no true gentleman could contemplate without a feeling of horror.

The Count's happy marriage–financially speaking–enabled him to maintain a proper lifestyle as befitted his rank. Every year, on the eve of the day of Sainte-Geneviève, all the French nobility, as well as some foreigners, were invited for a commemorative *fête* held in the family castle at Sainte-Geneviève-des-Bois, near Paris.

The following events happened on that fateful day, or rather, that night.

"I must say, my dear friend, I don't think I've ever seen so much beauty gathered under a single roof before," said one of the guests to another.

"I agree. Have you ever seen so many diamonds, sapphires, rubies, pearls and emeralds...? And all that gold, too! You're quite right, my friend. It's truly a dazzling *fête*!"

The two elderly gentlemen who spoke, each with a glass of champagne in hand, were looking down at the castle's celebrated Knights' Hall from the gallery on the first floor above. They had thus an unobstructed view of the crowd. Everyone was dressed in lavish 18th century costumes, as if the French Revolution had never happened.

"I was not referring to that kind of beauty," said the man who had been introduced as Edward John Moreton Drax Plunkett, 18th Baron Dunsany. He was slightly taken aback by the other man's comment. "I thought of all these lovely ladies who, alas, already have husbands and their maiden daughters of marriage age but fiercely protected by those same husbands who turned into fathers years ago. Ah! Were I only 10 years younger, I would risk..."

"I know someone who, irrespective of age, would risk everything, but for the more tangible beauties I spoke of earlier."

"Surely, you don't mean...? No, even he wouldn't dare!"

"It's precisely because you, and many others, think that he wouldn't dare that I, for one, believe that he will. He steals from the rich, which if you think about it makes sense, since the poor have nothing worth stealing. But I think it's also a nearly-sexual experience for him. And his pleasure increases with the danger."

"Is there any danger to be found here? Do you think that our host, anticipating that this *fête* may be the sort of challenge to which he likes to respond, decided to lay a trap for him?"

"Well, the Count Sainte-Geneviève may sometimes appear somewhat guileless, but his father-in-law, Herman Mayer, is anything but. I believe Monsieur Mayer has hired some private security. I even heard that Sherlock Holmes himself is here, disguised somewhere in that crowd... He's also enlisted help from the best of French Police..."

"So that would explain your presence here tonight, Monsieur Ganimard."

"How... How did you recognize me?" asked the astonished Chief Inspector.

"You are a famous man, Monsieur. I've often seen your photograph in the newspapers–even the British ones."

"These damned reporters! They're no help to us. Everyone knows my face but I'm never sure of his! He could be anywhere in this crowd and no one would recognize him."

"From what I understand, no one seems to know what he really looks like, not even himself. But don't worry, Monsieur Ganimard, I'm sure you'll catch your man sooner or later... Now, if you excuse me, I've just spotted a Duchess friend of mine whom I must congratulate on her daughter's recent marriage. Be seeing you."

"Be seeing you," replied Ganimard, who was now busy again scrutinizing the guests in the grand hall; he spotted one of his men here, another one there.

He was not only trying to find–if only by some kind of miracle–Arsène Lupin (for it was he whom he had been discussing with Lord Dunsany) but also Sherlock Holmes. Although their methods were a world away, he could not help but admire the results obtained by the great British detective. It would be a shame for him if Holmes succeeded in arresting Lupin before he did.

Most of the dances played that night were from the *Ancien Régime*, before the Revolution, but these were the "crazy years" that followed the Great War.

Sometimes a concession to the spirit of modernity had to be made and the orchestra occasionally performed some of that new-fangled music from the other side of the pond they called "jazz." And the younger folks contorted to its tunes with primitive movements they claimed constituted "dancing."

Count Sainte-Geneviève was proud of the great crystal chandeliers which made the Knights' Hall as bright as a garden at midsummer noon. His wife, on the other hand, was more attuned to modern sensibilities. Upon her instructions, a footman fiddled with a switch to slowly decrease the light intensity. Therefore, no one was surprised when, just as midnight had tolled, all the chandeliers suddenly stopped flooding the great hall with their glare.

Some kisses were exchanged, or stolen, in the darkness. Then, uncertainty began to creep in. The orchestra threw a few false notes. The dancers stopped dancing. There was complete silence for a few seconds.

"My necklace!" screamed a Duchess.

"My wife's broach!" roared a Marquis.

There were many other similar screams and panic set in, made worse by some noxious fumes out of nowhere that made the guests cough and gasp. Everyone rushed out in the garden. Someone had the good idea of lighting some candles, which had been put there purely for decoration. Finally, the panic subsided and the lights came back.

Ganimard made an immoderate use of his official police whistle, inside, then outside. That, at least, alerted the men he held in reserve outside. The uniformed policemen, who had been waiting in the park since the *fête* began, surrounded the castle, making an impressive human fence. It must be noted that Ganimard had been more than cautious: he had brought with him nearly half of the Paris police force, and even men from some of the neighboring precincts.

Ganimard smiled. This time, he was certain that Lupin had fallen into his trap.

The next day, the eastern skies were greying. So was Ganimard's hair. He was staring at a business card that had been found on the electrical switchbox when a footman had gone to turn it back on. It said:

With the sincere salutations of
Arsène Lupin,
Gentleman Burglar

It was not the first card of that type he had held. Sadly, he had nearly a drawer-full of them in his office. However, it confirmed his suspicions. The master-thief had paid a visit to Castle Sainte-Geneviève the previous night.

Nearly all of the Count's guests had to return to their respective homes and hotels. Their identities were double- and triple-checked: Chevalier de **, Marquis de **, Earl **, Viscount **, Duke **. All were not members of the nobility.

Some were bankers, high-ranking civil servants, captains of industry–even politicians. They all had to prove that they were not Arsène Lupin.

They were also searched–a rather delicate job. However, they all agreed to submit without making too much of a fuss after the Count and his wife volunteered to be the first "victims" of such an indignity. No stolen jewels were found.

Everyone appeared innocent of the nefarious deeds that had happened the previous night.

But what nefarious deeds exactly, one may ask?

For the policeman in charge of taking down the complaints and the descriptions of the stolen jewels made the following report to Ganimard, who grew very upset:

"Sorry, Chief, but no one has filed a complaint yet."

"What do you mean?"

"Just as I said. No one has filed a complaint because nothing was stolen."

"How could that be? What about the screams? The panic?"

"Nobody I spoke to admitted to being the ones who screamed."

Ganimard suddenly seemed to age, putting on years in the space of a few heartbeats. His composure crumbled like a sand castle assaulted by the rising tide. Then, after a few seconds, he regained control of himself.

"We're returning to Paris! Quick, bring the car! And you tell everyone they're free to go."

His driver drove at the breakneck speed of 30 miles an hour and, consequently, they reached the Préfecture de Police only an hour later. Ganimard went to his office and began to wait for the bad news he knew was sure to come.

He was not disappointed.

The first man to show up was Herman Mayer, the Count's father-in-law. He was the kind of man used to giving orders–and having them quickly obeyed. This morning, however, he was just another ordinary poor man.

"He stole my Rembrandt, my Rubens, my David and a few lesser known paintings," said Mayer. "I also had a reserve of gold in my safe, Napoleons, double-eagles, pesos, taels, ever bars. He took it all. He just left this."

And he put down a familiar business card on Ganimard's desk.

He was not the only visitor the Police saw that morning. Taking full advantage of the relative absence of policemen in Paris, Lupin's gang had been very busy the night before...

Somewhere else in Paris, an elderly gentleman who had impersonated a Marquis for a few hours and a middle-aged woman who had played the role of a Duchess, but who in reality were unemployed actors were counting banknotes.

"More money that I ever made in two years just to say one line. Marvelous. And I don't even mind that my name was not on the bill," said the pseudo-Marquis.

"Well... in that kind of play, the bill just mentions the star, you know," replied the pseudo-Duchess.

[*translated by Alain le Bussy & J.-M. Lofficier.*]

It is not becoming to introduce oneself, so suffice it to say that, since 2002, we have written a trilogy of French graphic novels (beautifully drawn by Gil Formosa) starring a more dynamic version of Verne's notorious science-pirate, Robur the Conqueror. It is that Robur whom we have reused in the story that follows, the concept of which was initially created for a video game...

Jean-Marc and Randy Lofficier: *Journey to the Center of Chaos*

Tibet, 1928

Even though the Monsoon hadn't yet come to the Nepalese border, the streets of Gezing were already hot and muggy. In this corner of the western district of Sikkim in the late 1920s, westerners were still a relatively rare occurrence, and the presence of Professor Alexander Whateley of the Miskatonic University of Arkham, Mass., and his companion, John Green, could only attract attention.

Green alone would have been noticed in any crowd, anywhere. He was a tank of a man, one eighth of a metric ton of bone and muscle; he could go through anything on Earth and come out wondering mildly why other people were so excited. Whateley, on the other hand, was thin, almost skeletal, and bookish. Unlike his companion, he was visibly more at ease locating a rare dusty tome in an ancient library than he was horse-trading with the merchants of Northern India, as he was presently attempting to do.

Only the most inept observer would have failed to notice that the two foreigners were watched intently by a small posse of natives, one peeking out from behind a doorway, another slithering behind a bead curtain, others peering from a neighboring windowsill. Whateley was blissfully unaware of the spies–but not so Green, whose hard-edged, clean-shaven face began to show some concern.

"Dahoor... Dahoor," repeated Whateley, addressing a merchant trying to sell him a vase that was such an obvious forgery it would not have fooled even a first year archeology student at the Louvre. "Surely you must know who he is? I've come all the way from America to see him..."

But the merchant remained obdurately dense. He kept trying to shove the vase in Whateley's hands. "Beautiful vase. From the Gupta period. Very rare."

Green, increasingly concerned about the attention they were getting, tugged at his companion's arm.

"Come on, Professor. We're wasting our time here."

The archeologist, resigned to not getting the information he sought, dejectedly walked away from the merchant's stall.

"He was lying to me, Mr. Green. Dahoor is one of the biggest antique dealers in Northern India. He's been selling to us for years. If anyone can help me put together an expedition to K'n-yan, he can."

"If you don't mind my saying so, Professor, I think you're chasing after one of those demented heathens' opium dreams. There is no lost city of the Mi-go. It just doesn't exist. This is a wild goose chase."

Whateley pulled a small carved cylinder from his belt.

"My map says you're wrong, Mr. Green."

"It's got to be a forgery. I've seen dozens of fake maps sold by unscrupulous babus in the back streets of Benares. Why should this one different from the others?"

"You insisted on joining me, remember?"

"Not quite. Meldrum Strange, who financed this expedition, asked me to do it. And he was right, too. It's not safe for someone like you to travel alone in this part of the world. He's only protecting his investment."

"Please, Mr. Green! This is just as safe as Harvard Square!"

While the two westerners were crossing the souk market, the mysterious figures that had been shadowing them had gathered into a dangerous-looking mob.

Suddenly, the thuggees–for that is what they were–pounced on the two explorers. Three of them tried to wrest the map away from Whateley.

But Green had already detected the threat. His massive fist crashed into the face of one of the men, and with a kick, he sent two of the other would-be thieves flying into the stall of a nearby merchant.

Green knew what he was doing. The merchant, who looked like a Punjabi, was understandably irate, and better yet, he had five surly brothers ready to rush to his aid.

Rush they did, and in seconds, a fierce melee had erupted between the Punjabi and the thuggees.

Judging that there was still not enough chaos for them to make a discreet exit, Green took a handful of copper coins from his pocket and threw them into the air, shouting, "Gold!"

At that point, real pandemonium broke loose.

"I think you've just started a riot," said Whateley.

"Good! That'll make it harder for them to catch us."

Grabbing Whateley by the arm, Green began running away through the narrow aisles of the street market, looking for the convenient refuge of the houses beyond.

"I bet that never happened to you in Harvard Square," he said.

"I accept that you were correct, but we'd better save our breath for running. Some of them seem to still be after us."

This time, Whateley was right. Two of the thieves had not lost sight of their prey despite the commotion. They had managed to slip by unscathed and were now running after the two westerners. In their hands were long kris knives, and the expressions on their faces plainly showed that if, before, their intent had been to get the map from Whateley dead or alive, that had now been updated to simply dead.

Green grabbed a rather vulgar statue of the god Ganesha from a stall.

"*Isakii kyaa kimat hai*? (How much does this cost?)" he asked the seller, who quoted him a wildly inflated figure. The strong man did not haggle and told Whateley, "Pay him!"

Then, using the statue as a club, he waited for the two thuggees. He quickly disposed of one of them with a massive swing of the statue, but the other managed to avoid the blow.

While Whateley was paying the merchant ("*Dhanyavaad*!" said the grateful man who had never dreamed he would ever get his asking price), the other thug approached him with murderous intentions.

Whateley escaped the deadly swish of the native blade by stepping aside with a dancer's grace, and kicked the man hard in the crotch. The thug fell to the ground, writhing in agony. Green temporarily put him out of his misery by hitting him on the head with the statue, which he then gave back to the merchant, who blessed the gods for having put these two generous strangers on his path that day.

"That's a side of you I've never seen before, Professor, and I have to say it surprises me."

"It comes from growing up in a rough neighborhood, Mr. Green."

"Let's go before the others come," said Green.

"But I need a receipt!"

Taking a number of detours through the small, grimy streets to mislead any followers, Whateley and Green finally reached their hotel, or rather what passed for a hotel in Gezing. In reality, it was more of an inn, a rest stop for caravans en route northward to Mongolia and beyond. The place was managed by an old couple and their two boys; it had seen better days in the 6th century.

"Those thuggees coming after my map proves that it's authentic," said Whateley.

"What makes you think that's what they want? Maybe they're common thieves."

"You don't believe that yourself, Mr. Green. In any event, we're not any closer to finding Dahoor, and it will probably make our job more difficult."

"If you'd let me organize a proper expedition back in Bombay instead of rushing to get here, I could have found as many reliable guides as we wanted."

"Yes. Sometime next year."

"What's the big hurry? If K'n-yan exists, it isn't going anywhere. Let's have a drink and figure out our next move."

The inn came with its own bar attached, where locals and travelers mixed and dealt in various commodities in its suitably smoky and darkened atmosphere. As the archeologist and his companion sat at a table, one of the innkeeper's sons came to take their order.

"Any messages for me? Professor Whateley?" Whateley expected a letter from the University and had left the inn as a forwarding address in Bombay.

The boy did not answer. A look of total, uncomprehending blankness washed over him.

"Professor..." said Green, tugging at the archeologist, who had his back to him.

"A minute, Mr. Green. I'm trying to ask this boy if I've got a message."

"It can wait," said Green, forcing his colleague to turn around.

Whateley then saw what had caused such stupor in the waiter. The six thuggees who had chased the two men in the souk were framed within the doorway. Some of them exhibited nasty bruises and their clothes were partially torn. Consequently, they were all in a particularly foul mood. They looked like a pack of hungry wolves. Their daggers were out, and only God knew what else they had hidden within the folds of their kaftans.

The boy vanished as if by magic. The few other patrons meticulously absorbed themselves in the contemplation of the bottoms of their glasses.

The thug leader stepped forward, grinning evilly, his hand extended.

"Map, now!"

Green sighed. There was going to be a massacre. It could no longer be avoided as he had hoped. The question remained, whose? The odds were far from good and he now wished he had enlisted several of his friends to come with him on this trip. Still, it was too late for regrets.

One of his hands lie deceptively quietly on the chair in front of him. He calculated that he could swing it to hit the first man, then use the pieces to keep the others at bay, until he could reach for his gun...

Before he could move, there was a sudden and amazing change of expression on the thug's face. The sneer of rapacious savagery was replaced by pure, unadulterated fear as quickly as the tide erases a drawing in the sand.

Green immediately saw the cause of such an astonishing metamorphosis.

A Herculean figure, dressed in an incongruous white tuxedo, had just stepped out of the backroom of the tavern, undoubtedly summoned by the servant boy.

"Well well if it isn't my old friend, Ali. Come here, you son of a dyspeptic camel!" said the newcomer.

Ali–no fool he–stayed rooted in place, but the stranger stepped forward and proceeded to grab him in what is appropriately called a bear hug. Green looked up in admiration. Whateley, on the other hand, could not prevent himself from wincing when he heard an ominous crunching sound.

Ali, to his credit, remained silent, but after being released, collapsed on the floor like a rag doll. The other thuggees looked properly impressed–and properly scared.

"I think my business with Ali is done for today," said the newcomer amicably. Then he barked an order: "Take him away and don't come back!"

The thuggees nodded as one as fast as they could. They scurried away, carrying the body of their unfortunate comrade.

The huge man, beaming a cheerful smile, grabbed a chair and sat at the table.

"I understand you were looking for me. I am Dahoor. I believe you've received my map and seek the lost city of K'n-yan, hmm?"

High in the skies above Tibet flew the *Albatross*. The prodigious craft was a true clipper of the clouds, with its 37 masts, each equipped with two propellers driven at prodigious speed by powerful engines, the secret of which was known only to its captain–and inventor.

That man was presently going by the name of Robur. He was of middle height and weight, with a surprisingly large round head. At the least opposition, his grey eyes would glow like coals of fire. He was dressed in a leather aviator's uniform, including gloves and boots. He sat in the luxuriously furnished control room, comfortably ensconced in a leather armchair, sipping a cup of Darjeeling tea while engaged in conversation with another man.

His guest had soulful, ageless eyes, green with specks of gold. He was dressed in an odd mixture of European and Oriental clothing. His high forehead was partially covered by a white silk turban. His name was Sâr Dubnotal.

"No one else but you could have successfully guided me to this spot," said Robur.

"I'm happy to be of service to such a distinguished friend of our mutual acquaintance, Mr. Strange. I trust he is well?"

"Meldrum's under a great deal of pressure these days. Apparently the Kun Yin are staging a comeback. I thought the British had wiped them all out, but you know what they say, the bad penny always turns up. One of his agents stumbled across a survivor of the Iron Temple in London. Even though he was half out of his mind, what he said was enough for Strange to ask me to come here and, er, take care of the rest, if you see my meaning."

"I assume you're referring to the Crown of Genghis?"

"Yes. But Strange didn't have time to fully brief me. He said you'd fill me in."

"Cast your mind back seven centuries. The Great Khan has come out of the desert and used the Crown's powers to conquer China. Afterwards, he chose to cast it aside and entrusted it to Marco Polo to be delivered into the protective hands of the Yian Ho, the Wise Men of K'n-yan. There was no better place to keep it safe, away from the evil ones who would use it for their own ends. And in K'n-yan it has remained ever since."

"Strange believes that the Kun Yin are after it."

"I wouldn't be surprised. The Hour of the Scythe approaches. If they get their hands on the Crown before then, they will travel to the Heart of Chaos and release the Guardian of the Gate."

Robur stood up and pressed a button. Seconds later, his first mate, a burly American named Tom Turner arrived on the bridge.

"I'm going to leave the Sâr in charge, Mr. Turner. You will obey his every order, in every respect, no matter how... draconian, you understand?"

"Completely, sir."

Robur walked to a cabinet, pulled out a harness attached to a backpack and began strapping it on.

"I know I can trust you to do what's necessary if I fail to stop them, Sâr Dubnotal."

"The Abyss is dangerous only for those who look into it, Robur."

"If you say so." Then, he addressed Tom, who now stood at the controls.

"Release the hatch, Mr. Turner."

With a whooshing sound, a circular shaft slid open in the metal walls of the *Albatross*, letting in a gust of frigid air and a streak of bright blue-white light.

"The rest is up to me," said Robur.

He jumped into the shaft.

A couple of hundred feet down, his pack opened, releasing a delicate, origami-like structure that grew into an ingenious, ultralight glider.

The scientist-adventurer began his safe descent towards the ground.

If Robur had been able to scan the far side of the peak over which he currently flew, he might have seen a small, ant-trail line of people slogging laboriously through the eternal snows of the Himalayas. The expedition was comprised of Dahoor, closely followed by Professor Whateley and Mr. Green, while four sherpas hired in Gezing closed up the rear.

"Without you, Dahoor, we wouldn't have been able to mount this expedition on such a short notice," said Whateley.

"Your gratitude is greatly appreciated but sadly misplaced, Professor Whateley. Indeed, it is I who an indebted to you. In exchange for my miserable find, your munificent American Museum has provided me with ample funds to pay for all of this. And believe me when I say that I expect to earn a handsome profit from your discoveries."

"But, surely, anything that we uncover belongs to science," said Whateley with a certain intensity.

"Certainly, certainly, but how it gets to the scientists is where I make my money. After all, you will not be able to take everything away with you, eh?

There will be enough wealth from this expedition to last me a lifetime. So you see, Professor, the gods indeed smiled upon me when I sent you that map."

The expedition began a slow and perilous descent into a sharp, craggy ice canyon. Green thought that the ice itself appeared to be sculpted in sinister forms, but he attributed that to the same human reflex which makes us see animal shapes in the clouds. He did notice, however, that the four sherpas looked increasingly anxious.

"It all seems so–mercenary." The Professor and Dahoor, seemingly unaware of the eerie decor, continued their discussion on the professional ethics of archeology.

"Well, wealth is good," said Dahoor laughing. "What else is there?"

"Knowledge. The origins of man. Life. Everything."

"Words don't fill hungry bellies, Professor."

"So you would loot Ubar or Ys?"

"Just so. If I knew where they were."

"But the knowledge of K'n-yan could lift your country to new heights... It could be your Holy Grail..."

Suddenly, the sherpas became extremely agitated and gestured for Dahoor's attention.

"*Shahajjo*! *Rakkhosh*! *Mi-Go Khokkosh*!" they shouted.

The lead guide walked back to confer with his anxious men.

"What is it? *Ki*? *Ki*?" he asked.

The sherpas all began talking at the same time while gesticulating wildly. Dahoor's face became a worrisome shade of purple as he began screaming at the men. More shouting followed, until finally, the big man pulled rolls of coins from his bag.

"What's going on?" asked Whateley.

"One of them claims to have seen a Mi-go," replied Green. "A Yeti. They're scared. They want to turn back."

"What? They can't do that!"

"Actually, they can. But Dahoor is taking care of it. He's offering them more money. It's going to cost you an arm and a leg."

"Hmf. He should have talked to me first."

"Stop it, Professor! He's only doing what's necessary."

After the labor unrest had been successfully dealt with by the transfer of cash from Dahoor's pockets into those of the reluctant sherpas, the expedition continued its arduous trek, deeper into the grim, windswept, icy canyons. It finally came to a stop when it reached the bottom and came face-to-face with what looked like a barren wall of ice.

"We seem to have come to a dead end," said Green. "With all due respect, have you been reading that map correctly, Professor?"

Whateley walked to the wall of ice on his right and began attacking it with his knife. He kept chopping away until he uncovered an ancient sculpted post that had been buried under the ice and was barely visible from the surface.

"Yes. We're where we should be. Look."

Green helped Whateley finish excavating the post.

"What are those symbols?" he inquired.

"They're Yian-Ho gate markers," replied Whateley.

"Good luck signs?"

"No. More the 'abandon all hope, ye who enter here' type."

After excavating an identical post on the left, the men were directed to use their picks to dig between the two. Soon, a crack appeared in the ice wall, between the two posts. With a thundering sound, the remaining ice collapsed, revealing gaping darkness behind it.

"The entrance to K'n-yan," whispered Whateley.

"Congratulations, Professor," said Green. "You've led us where no modern man has been before."

For hours, the expedition had traversed a maze of underground caverns, deep inside the Tibetan peaks. Without the map, which enabled Whateley to locate and decipher the sculpted posts that acted as markers, they would have been hopelessly lost in the Stygian complex of caves. As it was, finding their way was not their only challenge, they had to remain vigilant for chasms that suddenly appeared unexpectedly beneath their unwary feet or sudden rockfalls from above.

Green felt his hackles rise several times. A mysterious sixth sense told him they were not alone in the dark. He peered through the darkness every time he heard–or thought he heard–a distant shuffling. It was a sound that reminded him of the silken, deadly tread of a jungle cat before he pounces, a noise that few explorers lived long enough to recognize more than once.

Suddenly, a gut-wrenching scream tore the darkness like the slash of a razor. More terrifying was that the scream had been cut short, as if by a guillotine putting an abrupt end to its victim's suffering.

The scream was followed by a gun shot and a series of curses. Green recognized Dahoor's voice.

"What happened?" he asked.

Dahoor, his gun raised, squinted into the darkness. "A Mi-Go I think. He got Cibi. But I hit him..."

Unexpectedly, a pair of red eyes shone in the dark.

"Or maybe not..."

Without warning, several pairs of red eyes flashed in the night, accompanied by low, feral noises, intermingled with bits of what could best be described as an inhuman tongue.

"Or maybe he has friends," said Green.

Whateley was starting to panic. "We can't retreat now," he said stubbornly. "We're so close."

"Then let's make a run for it," exclaimed Green.

The six men began running through the caverns. They could hear the distant sounds of their pursuers. Except for the blood-red eyes and the occasional, spectral sight of a clawed hand that briefly emerged from the obscurity, as it tried to grab them, their attackers remained cloaked in darkness. Dahoor covered the rear, stopping several times to fire at the ravening creatures, but with no apparent effect.

"I'm sure I'm hitting them, but it doesn't seem to stop them," he said, frustrated.

Out of breath, one of the sherpas stumbled and fell. Before any of the others could even think of coming to his aid, something indescribably hideous had already fallen upon the man, whose screams of terror were mercifully brief. Green tried hard to not hear the awful sounds of chewing that followed.

"The exit should be just around the next bend," said Whateley, panting.

Indeed, they had reached the proverbial light at the end of the tunnel, although it was only a pallid, wan light that cast bleak shadows on the carved rocks surrounding them.

They emerged into a small, circular valley surrounded by the snowy peaks of the Himalayas. On its opposite side, carved into the very side of the mountain, was a strange, intricate, portal. The valley itself was a giant graveyard, littered with bones, human, animal and possibly other creatures' as well. It was almost sunset and the light was fading.

"K'n-yan! I've found it!" Whateley exclaimed, pointing to the sculpted entrance at the far end of the circle.

"Somehow, from reading the Veda, I pictured a more pleasant setting," said Green, looking at the bones.

The howl of the Mi-Go behind them reminded them that, although they had reached their goal, their survival was still very much in doubt and their bones might be the next ones to join those that littered the valley floor.

"We can't stand here and gape," said Dahoor. "Those–things–are still after us!"

The men began running again. The ancient bones crumbled into dust beneath their feet. Green cleared the way before them, hacking away at the remains with a machete.

Suddenly, they heard howls coming from the right. Then, from the left.

Then, the Mi-Go stood front of them as well, blocking their path.

Their bodies were stocky, apelike in shape, but with a distinctly human quality. They were six feet tall and covered with shaggy, coarse, snow-white hair, some with dark patches on their chests. Their faces were sturdy, with wide mouths featuring large teeth and prominent fangs. Their heads were conical, with a pointed crown. Their arms were long, reaching almost to the knees, and their hands sported fierce-looking claws.

The five men formed a small circle, guns ready, prepared to defend their lives.

"I regret that our short but eventful association had to come such a miserable end, Professor Whateley, Mr. Green," said Dahoor, sounding almost apologetic.

Whateley was almost hysterical. "I can't die here! Not when I'm so close!"

"You're not the only one with a problem, Professor!" rebuffed Green.

The Mi-Go slowly started moving towards them.

Suddenly, flares of all colors erupted in the sunset skies. Thundering noises echoed throughout the valley, its circular structure magnifying the rumble into a near-apocalyptic din.

The Mi-Go ran, terrified by this unprecedented display of man-made thunder and lightning.

Robur, flare gun in hand, stood on top of a huge mastodon skull and gestured at them.

"Quick! Follow me!"

As the hidden valley of K'n-yan was wrapped ever more tightly in a mantle of darkness, a small campfire burned bright inside the temple, its magnificent sculpted entrance standing as the last remains of a once mighty culture. Statues of long-vanished gods came to life in the flickering light. Robur and the surviving members of the expedition finished a meal that had been hastily cooked by the two remaining sherpas.

"Dahoor," said Robur. "I should have known you'd find your way here sooner or later. You're drawn to treasure like a fly to rotting meat."

"One is always pleased to see one's skills recognized, My Prince."

"I'm not your Prince anymore. Just Robur."

"Yes, of course, My Prince."

"You know this man?" Green asked Dahoor.

"We've met once or twice, yes," the guide replied.

"You haven't yet told us what you are doing here, Mr. Robur," Whateley interjected. Green noted that the Professor seemed rather ungracious towards the man whose sudden arrival from above had, after all, saved their lives.

"There's only one thing I want. You're welcome to everything else, including fame. In fact, I'd rather that my presence wasn't even mentioned..."

"And that one thing is?"

"It's known as the Crown of Genghis."

Whateley sniffed contemptuously. "So, you're a trafficker in antiques too, no different than your friend Dahoor here?"

Robur smiled. "Oh no! I've come to destroy it."

Whateley reacted in shock, almost as if the newcomer had punched him. "What!? You can't do that. It's a priceless artifact. You can't be serious!"

"Deadly so, I'm afraid."

"But why?"

"I could tell you that it's none of your business, but I've heard of Miskatonic University, Professor Whateley, and I believe you deserve an honest answer. The cosmos is not unlike a tapestry. Scientists like you study its patterns, trying to fathom its meaning. But there are those who have peered behind the tapestry and know what lurks there. A long time ago, K'n-yan was home to a race of wise, civilized men..."

"Yes, the Yian Ho."

"Well, they became those shaggy things that almost killed you. The Mi-go are what's left of the Yian Ho. That's what the Crown did to them, and why it must be destroyed."

The next day, they began their exploration of the Temple. From the outer hall where they had spent the night, a beautifully-decorated corridor, meant to represent a descent into the underworld, took them deeper within the mountain. Its walls were painted with images of the Djad and the forgotten gods of the Yian Ho.

Lower down, they reached another hall, this one leading into a sacred chamber where mysterious ceremonies were conducted. It was a relatively large, rectangular room with four square pillars supporting the ceiling. Two side rooms and a small inner room were accessible from it. The entry walls were adorned with representations of the gods, while the pillars were mostly decorated with scenes from the Book of the Dead. The King of the Yian Ho was represented passing through nine gates guarded by statues representing the dreadful Rakashas, demons from the underworld.

Whateley studied the inscriptions in the light of his torch. "Amazing. It's all here. The entire history of the Yian Ho, and before them, the Dzyan..."

"Interesting indeed, Professor," said Dahoor, "but where is the gold?"

Robur smiled. "You're slipping, old friend. Those carvings are made of orichalcum."

The Hindu's eyes burned bright and he developed a sudden interest in the wall decorations. Green could see him already totaling up figures in his mind.

Whateley looked at the map. "It says the Crown was kept in the next chamber, the one guarded by the Rakashas..."

They entered a smaller chamber, walking past a short corridor lined on both sides with giant statues representing demon-like creatures with claws, sharp beaks and bat-like wings.

"There are your Rakashas," said Green.

"When I was a boy, the holy man told me demons would get me if I wasn't good. Now I wish I had believed him," remarked Dahoor.

Inside the chamber was an altar and on it lay a simple gold band, just large enough to fit a human head.

"The Crown of Genghis!" exclaimed Whateley. He ran towards the altar, grabbed the Crown and placed it on his head.

"Mine, at last!"

His face began changing, twisting, as if some powerful force was intent on remodeling his features. His eyes rolled back into their orbits, then returned to normal but the irises had gone white and the expression contained in them was distant. It was as if he was not gazing upon the room where they stood, but rather the unfathomable vision of another dimension.

"Whateley, what's happening to you?" asked Green.

"You fool! Whateley is dead!" said the spectral voice which issued from the archeologist's mouth.

"The Hour of the Scythe is almost upon us and I, the Servant of the Crawling Chaos, will at last unleash His Hideous Strength upon the Earth!"

Whatever force had taken possession of Whateley, Robur was ready. The Master of the *Albatross* reacted instantly by starting an incantation.

"Nosmo Cobis... Holo Erasma Rabis..."

Whateley raised his hand, eyes blazing with unholy energies.

"That pathetic spell has been out of fashion since the Monks of Montsegur in 1244, and even they were better at it than you are."

Robur was thrown to the ground.

"We the Kun Yin have served the Old Ones since Man, and those who came before, emerged from the primordial muck. We know you, Robur and your friend the Sâr Dubnotal, and all your other allies. Come the Hour of the Scythe, you will all die."

Whateley began to advance towards Robur, his hands extended forward. Dark tendrils of force seeped from his palms.

"But you–the Dark can't wait that long!"

Green was skeptical by nature about what he usually called the "fakir tricks" of India, but was open-minded enough to not question what he saw. He had beheld the previous scene with the dawning realization that far more than the possession of an invaluable ancient treasure was at stake. He grabbed his gun and shot Whateley, twice, aiming for the legs.

The archeologist staggered from the shots, halted, but did not fall. He turned towards Green, his face filled with so much pure hatred that the adventurer could not help but take a step back.

"For that, your pain will be increased a thousand-fold, mortal!"

Whateley gestured at the demon statues in the corridor.

"You who have slumbered for millennia, now by the Crown I wear–awake!"

Dahoor let out a bellowing scream of terror as the statues of the Rakashas–statues no longer–began to shake like a man waking up after a long slumber. Their stone eyes blazed open.

Almost faster than the eyes could see, the Rakashas leapt on the two hapless sherpas who had thought it safer to stay behind, closer to the chamber entrance. The two men fell screaming beneath the monsters' razor-sharp claws. Their eviscerated bodies collapsed to the floor like deflated balloons.

Green blasted one of the Rakashas into rubble with his rifle. Dahoor also shot at the advancing creatures. But the rubble, including the claws and beaks, continued to live and crawled towards its human prey.

"Sotheby's would have paid a king's ransom for that statue. Ah, Dahoor! Why does fortune always slip through your fingers?" bemoaned the guide.

Whateley, seeing the two men's powerlessness, gloated. "The Heart of Chaos awaits! The time has come for me to release the Guardian of the Gate. The Rakashas will soon feast upon your brains. I understand those are a delicacy. Ha! Ha!"

Believing his three remaining adversaries to be almost as good as dead, the late archeologist left the chamber with a Rakasha in tow.

Upon hearing the familiar clicking sound, Dahoor realized his gun was out of ammunition. If the Rakashas had been alive, they would have whetted their beaks in anticipation of the slaughter. As they were, they just continued their lumbering progression, stepping ever closer, claws extended, beaks hungry for the blood of their victims.

"I'm sorry I won't be able to get you that Chandela chess set we discussed last night, Mr. Green," said the Hindu.

"Where we're going, I doubt I'll have much opportunity to practice my game," replied the adventurer, realizing that it was only a matter of seconds before he, too, ran out of bullets.

Suddenly, Robur stood up and confronted the Rakashas, addressing them directly, barking orders as one would to a pack of wild dogs. Before Green and Dahoor's unbelieving eyes, the creatures stopped and appeared to heed what the mysterious man was saying.

Robur rubbed a sore muscle in his right shoulder, which had borne the brunt of his fall. Dahoor looked at him with effusive gratitude.

"My Prince! You are a man of many wonders!"

"That was authentic Yian Ho, wasn't it?" asked Green.

"Yes. Professor Whateley isn't the only one to speak it." He then pointed at the motionless Rakashas. "I told them that we were dead already. Lucky for us, their ability to tell the difference between life and death isn't very good. I doubt we have much time before they realize I lied."

They ran out of the chamber and into the great corridor–and almost straight into a pack of hostile Mi-Go! The ape-men, having recovered from their terrors of the previous evening, had followed the scent of the explorers all the way to inside the temple.

"Can these truly be what's left of the Yian Ho?" whispered Green.

"Yes," said Robur. "That's what Chaos will do to you, give or take a few centuries. But despite it, they're still fulfilling their duty. They're trying to protect the Crown. It's in their blood."

However, instead of pouncing on the strangers, the ape-men remained still. Then, a younger and particularly fierce-looking Mi-Go stepped forward and began uttering a few words which Green recognized as the same Yian Ho tongue Robur had used with the Rakashas.

"My Prince, I believe he's speaking to you," said Dahoor with a wan smile.

Robur began a dialogue with the Mi-Go. Whatever was said must have been convincing for the Hindu noticed that the ape-men had begun to look if not more friendly, at least as if they weren't planning to slaughter them all in the next few seconds.

Meanwhile, Green had kept an eye in the direction from which they had come. His face grew concerned.

"I hope you've convinced them that we're the good guys," he told Robur, "because it looks to me like the Rakashas have finally figured out that we're not really dead yet are intent on remedying the situation."

As soon as the Mi-Go saw the Rakashas, it was as if a dam had erupted. Nothing could contain the unbridled fury of the ape-men. The guardians of the Crown had recognized their ancient enemies and plunged into battle. Though the Rakashas were made of stone, even that could be pulverized, ground into fine particles, with unrelenting fangs and claws. The Mi-Go seemed to feel no pain from the many injuries the revived demons inflicted upon them. Their bodies appeared to regenerate at amazing speed and nothing short of decapitation seemed able to stop them.

During the combat, Robur grabbed Green and Dahoor. "We've got to stop Whateley from reaching the Heart of Chaos. He can't...."

"We, My Prince?" interrupted Dahoor. "With all due respect, I am very sorry but this humble tradesman has more than fulfilled his obligations..." The guide picked up bits of green orichalcum rocks that had broken loose during the battle and put them in his bag. "These scraps of orichalcum will be compensation enough. You two are great heroes but you must continue without me. These matters are beyond the powers of simple souls such as I..."

"I expected better from you, Dahoor," said Robur. "You stood by my side at Sinkuderam."

"That was long ago, My Prince. Besides it involved fighting the British. No, it's time for Dahoor to move on."

Robur made a gesture, as if to grab Dahoor, but Green stopped him.

"Let him go. He's right. This is no business for someone like him. Now I understand why Meldrum Strange wanted me to accompany Whateley on this expedition. The man tricked us all, but I'll see him and his damned Crown destroyed before I leave this god-forsaken place!"

Having said his farewells, Dahoor left, vanishing into the darkness of the corridor leading to the upper hall and the hidden valley.

As he stepped outside, he looked at the sky and the sculpted entrance behind him. For a minute, he stood still, undecided. Then he shrugged, muttered a short prayer and walked away, beginning the long and arduous trek that would lead him back to civilization.

Inside the holy chamber, the Mi-Go had defeated the Rakashas. Chunks of broken statue littered the floor, where it was stomped into dust by the ape-men. The young Mi-Go who had spoken with Robur, looking bloodied but pleased with himself, stepped forward and again addressed the Master of the Albatross.

"If we're going to beat Whateley to the Heart of Chaos, we're going to need a guide," said Robur. "This one seems to have a good idea of why we're here..."

"Then, let's follow him," said Green.

Robur answered the Mi-Go in Yian Ho, and all three continued their descent. The temple had been built over miles of natural tunnels and shafts, some as old as 40 million years. There were huge underground spaces, vast enough to house a cathedral, waterfalls, crystalline formations in hues of amber, white, blue and grey. Green thought they were now more than 500 feet below ground.

Following their Mi-Go friend, they continued ever downward, climbing acrobatically through a series of perilous shafts, jumping from cliff to cliff, holding their bodies at impossible angles and positioning their weight before figuring out their way down the naked rock.

At one point, the two men stopped to take a breather on a ledge. "He says it's a shortcut," Robur said, pointing towards the Mi-Go, who was impatient to continue the descent.

"For him, maybe," said Green with a smile. Then, the explorer added: "Since you know so much, how about filling me in. Where are we going?"

"K'n-yan was built around a natural phenomenon the Old Ones called the Heart of Chaos. The magnetic power of the Earth is concentrated into one tight beam to the Heavens. My friend Seaton thinks it's like a beacon to other worlds. Me, I don't have an opinion. When the stars align to form a configuration known as the Scythe, the beam appears to cut through the very fabric of space. With the power of the Crown, Whateley can manipulate the phenomenon to open a gateway that will release, whatever you call it, the Hideous Strength, the Creeping Chaos, the Guardian of the Gate, Yog-Sothoth... It's not pretty and it's usually hungry."

After an hour of arduous descent, they finally reached the bottom of the shaft. An opening allowed an odd greenish light to enter it.

As they emerged, they stepped onto a jutting stone platform overlooking a vast subterranean realm, a savage land filled with a primeval forest of giant trees, inhabited by giant insects and strange flying reptiles, lit only by that eerie greenish light. At its center was a green beam reaching up towards the Heavens–the Heart of Chaos.

Still led by their Mi-Go ally, Robur and Green ran briskly through the jungle towards the beam's point of origin.

Despite the urgency of their mission, neither man could stop themselves from occasionally taking a closer look at some extraordinary natural–or rather unnatural–wonder revealed by this amazing environment, like an oyster revealing the pearl inside.

Robur was fascinated by a giant white mushroom with oddly shaped red spots on its top, which appeared to inflate like a balloon, then explode softly, spreading its spores in the wind. Green saw giant flowers which attracted giant butterflies, which in turn met their ends in the webs of giant spiders.

But the Mi-Go waved them ever on, shouting at them in his strange language.

"I don't need you to tell me that he wants us to hurry," said Green, who had been entranced by the sight of a black lotus.

Finally, they spied Whateley, escorted by a Rakasha, barely ahead of them despite his considerable advance. The "shortcut" had paid off. He was making his way towards the beam that was the Heart of Time.

"It looks like we're still in time," said Robur.

Whateley was only a few hundred feet away from the beam when he saw Robur and Green. The face of the archeologist, or rather the thing that had been the archeologist, became contorted with rage.

"You?! This time, you won't stop us, Robur! Not when we're so close."

Whateley sent the Rakasha to attack the two men, thinking it would dispose of them easily. But the Mi-go who, at Robur's instructions, had remained hidden to encourage Whateley to waste his strongest weapon, sprang out of the jungle and met the challenge head on. Roaring his defiance, the ape-man savagely fought the demon statue.

Realizing that he had been tricked, Whateley shook his fist angrily. When he opened it, he released a blast of energy that hit Green, who was the closest to him.

Robur seized the opportunity to jump on the former archeologist and, wrestling with him, tried to wrest the crown from his head.

Whateley grabbed Robur by the neck and stared into his face as energy poured from his fiery eyes.

The Master of the *Albatross* collapsed screaming to the ground, smoke drifting from his face.

Then, Whateley blasted the Mi-Go who had just defeated the Rakasha.

"And now there is no one left to stand in the way of destiny," he said as he stepped into the beam.

The crown... Whateley's entire figure... began radiating a shimmer of strange energies, and coruscating waves of unearthly power that mingled with the beam. The column of light began pulsating to the rhythm of an alien song that the archeologist started to sing–a song written before the birth of galaxies, that no human larynx could possibly utter, and yet which fed the phenomenon.

Above, a black tear opened up in the very structure of space itself.

Darkness began to fill the cavern. Inside the fracture, one could see the phantoms of alien stars, bizarre shapes, other worlds and other galaxies... Horrible abysses of radiance... *Yog-Sothoth.*

Outside, the phenomenon spilled out over the mountain peak. The tear in space was weirdly omnipresent throughout the celestial axis that the beam followed.

In the hidden valley, the remaining Mi-Go howled in terror.

Plowing through the snows of the icy canyon, just outside the secret passages under the mountain, Dahoor, too, saw the fracture and addressed another, more fervent, prayer to the gods..

Aboard the *Albatross*, Tom Turner by his side, Sâr Dubnotal had been using his own mysterious powers to monitor the events and his face grew somber.

"Chaos is rising, Mr. Turner. Stand by to release the Void That Consumes, but not yet. The plan that Meldrum Strange and I designed still has one last chance to succeed. But if not..."

His hand moved ominously near a red switch.

In the cavern, near the Heart of Time, Green stood up, battered and bruised, and prepared to step forward into the beam where Whateley was still chanting.

Lying on the ground, Robur, his face badly burned and charred, shouted after him: "Don't do it! He'll fry you alive!"

"Like he tried to do to you?"

"I have protection against that kind of thing–you don't!"

"I've got something better..."

Green boldly stepped into the beam.

As he embraced Whateley and held him close with his left arm, he pulled a blood-red jewel from his pocket.

Immediately, the Crown changed colors, turning from its white-gold radiance to a sickly reddish-brown shade. Whateley screamed as the metal liquefied on his head, leaving charred marks on his forehead and dripping into his eye sockets, burning his eyes to cinders.

Above, Chaos flickered.

The loss of his eyes and the pain that would have incapacitated any human did not seem to stop the archeologist. "Where did you get that jewel? Who are you?" he snarled, looking with sightless orbits at the man who had defeated him.

"My name is James Schuyler Grim. In this part of the world, they call me JimGrim. Meldrum Strange hired me to keep an eye on you and he was right. And he gave me this trinket–the Heart of Ahriman–or of Azathoth–for just such an occasion."

Whateley's entire body had begun to liquefy and melt away, forming a putrescent puddle at Grim's feet.

Grim cast his eyes above. Chaos, while still flickering, was not gone–and showed signs of breaking through.

The adventurer extended his hand to Robur, inviting him to join him inside the Beam.

"The rift needs to be repaired but I can't do it alone," he said. "I don't have your expertise."

"I've done this before," said Robur with a wry smile. "Let me show you."

They held hands, both grasping the blood-red jewel. Sweat, tears, pain, even thin rivulets of blood seeped from their faces as they strained to repair the damage, close the breach…

"It's too strong," said Robur.

"No, we can win. We must win!" said JimGrim.

Aboard the *Albatross*, Dubnotal's hand rested on the red switch. The time had almost come. Only a few seconds remained before he would do what had to be done.

Suddenly, a third, bronzed hand joined Robur and Grim's.

"Maybe even great heroes can occasionally use simple souls such as me," said Dahoor.

And on that day, Chaos rested.

Robur, Dubnotal, JimGrim and Dahoor stood on the bridge of the *Albatross*, watching the snowy peaks of the Himalayas below them.

"You and Meldrum Strange cut it rather close this time, didn't you?" said Grim to Dubnotal. "The Heart of Ahriman... My role in all this..."

"We didn't know exactly what the Kun Yin plan was... If Robur had managed to get to the Crown before their pawn–Whateley–got his hands on it... You were there mostly as a back-up precaution, Mr. Grim. One that turned out to have been a bit of enlightened forethought, I'm happy to say."

"I haven't thanked you enough for coming back," said Robur to Dahoor.

"The orichalcum from the K'n-yan are thanks enough, My Prince. I'll be the richest man in Gezing."

"But you will keep the location of the Hidden Valley a secret?"

"My lips are forever sealed. After all, I am but a simple soul..."

Samuel T. Payne hails from England and is a great fan of Doctor Who*; hence, unsurprisingly, he decided to feature in his story a remarkably similar cosmic traveler, whose origins remain steadfastly mysterious... but I should not spoil Samuel's story, which also features Edgar Allan Poe's first fictional detective, Chevalier Auguste Dupin...*

Samuel T. Payne: *Lacunal Visions*

Paris, 1845

C. Auguste Dupin clasped his watch together and carefully pocketed it in his waistcoat. "If I'm correct, it cannot be much longer," he whispered gently into my ear. I turned myself as quietly and discreetly as possible to meet his gaze.

"The sooner the better. This is quite possibly the most uncomfortable position I've ever been persuaded to adopt. My ankles–"

"Your ankles, my dear Monsieur Picard, can take another ten minutes, I am sure."

My poor feet, swollen from a prolonged crouch in the confines of a small wooden chest, were expanding in circumference by the minute. A man of my particular age, and girth– thanks to a healthy appetite–should not have to suffer such things.

"Outrageous," I hissed, glaring at his faint outline, highlighted by the firelight which penetrated our box. "This is hardly the investigative methodology I expected from the great Dupin!"

"May I remind you, Picard, of the absolute essentiality for silence? Furthermore, it was you who requested my services; as such, I would expect you to at least honor my instinct and tact."

I agreed and shifted my balance, providing somewhat more comfort for my nether regions. Peering through the slit in the chest which shrouded our presence, I saw that the empty workshop remained completely still. Nothing could be heard, save the crumbling embers of the fire, collapsing lazily upon themselves.

Fatigue clawed at my every joint and muscle, and as I gazed into the orange fragments cooling in the fire-grate, I thought of my vacant, inviting armchair at home. I could feel the lids riding lazily over my eyes as I recalled the events of the past two days.

It was on a bitter, chilly, Thursday morning, as I was departing from a small Parisian watchmaker's *boutique*, that I held the door open for an arriving customer.

"Excuse me, Monsieur," I said. "I'm afraid you'll find no service in this shop today."

The gentleman halted, removed his hat and began to unwind his scarf. An expression of disappointment and mild irritation formed on his face.

"Really? This is most inconvenient. I had hoped to have my wall clock repaired before the week's end."

He indicated the small package under his arm. There was little I could say in response. "Well, I'm sorry to be the bearer of bad news."

Sighing, the gentleman unbuttoned his long jacket, exposing his waistcoat. From it, he extracted a beautifully crafted pocket watch. He glanced up from it, raising an eyebrow.

"Can you suggest another local watchmaker or similar, Monsieur...?"

"Sergeant," I interjected, tilting my head. "Sergeant Picard. No, I'm afraid I cannot. I have come in contact with several recently, thanks to my investigations these past two weeks, but not any single store who'll be able to offer that kind of service."

"You are with the Parisian Police... investigating crime scenes," he said curiously, more a statement than a question.

"Indeed," I replied with an air of resignation. "This outlet is one of the latest to succumb to a long line of queer robberies. We're getting nowhere fast in terms of catching the culprit."

"Perhaps you can tell me more about it at lunch?" he said simply, pressing a card into my hand. I glanced at it. Printed on it in neat green letters were:

C. AUGUSTE DUPIN

The name was instantly familiar to me. It was a title synonymous with the solution of cryptic conundrums of the criminal kind; the moniker of an amateur sleuth renowned through Paris for his curious talent in unraveling the tightest knots of mystery. I cannot express the delight I felt in my heart at meeting this living legend, for it was immense. A brush with such a celebrity–for that was what he had become–filled me with great excitement, and here he was requesting my presence at table. My mind was racing and I quickly considered the prospect of inviting this gentleman to aid in my investigations, for he would be a great asset to depend upon. I decided to act quickly, to buy him into my affections.

"You may be just the man we need, Monsieur Dupin. Please, let me pay," I said, guiding him towards the cheapest restaurant at hand, where I began to explain fully the series of strange events that had been occurring.

A bottle of house red was required to prepare myself for the lengthy discourse I was about to embark upon. Dupin, declining to drink, inadvertently forced me to drain the bottle single-handedly. He sat before me; his elbows reposed upon the table and his hands supporting his chin.

"So, every single watchmaker in Paris has been broken into, in the space of a fortnight?" he said in reflection, his brow furrowed.

"Yes," I replied in a deep, thick tone. It was good claret. "Each time, parts were stolen. Small parts, bits of watches, components, tools..."

"Do you have an inventory of the missing items?"

I pushed the chair back from the table–I may have knocked into somebody seated behind me but it wasn't of any importance–and pulled from my jacket pocket the list he requested. I slapped it on the table with vigor.

"There! To the trade value of over hundreds of francs."

Dupin raised an eyebrow and ruminated over the tally of stolen pieces.

"These items... they're a strange selection of goods to covet. Very select components. One could only sell these to an engineer, as they'd be little use to the lay tradesman."

I leant back in my chair. "Perhaps it's a rival watchmaker?" I said in deep consideration.

"You said all Parisian stores were affected," Dupin stated quickly, dismissing my conjecture. "If so, it would have to be an out-of-town establishment, in which case, it hardly seems worth their while."

I could see his point. Why bother to attack a rival who isn't a threat to your local market? I looked to Dupin for his own theory, a razor-sharp deduction, but he simply handed the inventory back to me and cut a slice of cheese.

"Well?" I asked dryly. He slowly chewed his food before answering.

"It's clearly a person, an intellectual, I'd say, who is accumulating these items for some reason we're not as yet aware of. Someone who is well versed in mechanics and engineering, I suppose. But that's just a guess. At the moment, we are merely looking at the crimes themselves, not the reasons why the person may want the clockwork components in the first place."

"What... do you suggest?" I said clumsily, attempting to mask a gastric eruption with my hand. Unfortunately, the reflex of my arm was too indolent to arrive at the vital moment, and Dupin was exposed to the release. He closed his eyes.

"I suggest," he sighed, "that we visit the scene which has been exposed to the most activity."

One store came to mind instantly, "*Maître Zacharius - Horloger*?"

With that, I modestly tipped the waiter and made my way outside, where Dupin was heralding a carriage for our departure to Verdain Street, the home of Maître Zacharius.

I don't know if you've ever been there, but Verdain Street is a dull little strip, dotted with quirky houses each of utterly different heights and designs. It gives the street an inconsistent and frankly backward appearance, which is at odds with the rest of Parisian architecture. It is often a home to the homeless, who frequent the vestibules and crevices between the buildings as permanent lodgings from the cold. At the end of the street is *Maître Zacharius - Horloger*, and it was here where the driver deposited Dupin and my good self.

"An intriguing building," Dupin mused, looking over the shop's little windows, which were cluttered with a variety of clocks and watches.

"Quite so," I said, brushing past him towards the entrance. A vicious headache of a severity I can scarcely describe had formed during the journey, and the biting winter breeze outside the confines of the carriage certainly wasn't soothing the agony. I pushed the door open and stepped into the warmth. Dupin followed my lead.

Master watchmaker Zacharius was behind the counter as usual. I'd met him several times previously during my inquiries and we were now on quite familiar terms with one another. He was a quiet, distinguished little man with neat grey hair and a very trim beard and was always clad in his leather apron. Zacharius' store was easily one of the largest watchmakers in Paris and people would travel from miles around to employ the man's talents.

"Please come through to the parlor, gentlemen," he said softly, indicating the little room behind the counter. "I'll see to some coffee."

Dupin made himself comfortable at the table and I sat opposite, surveying the room. It had hardly changed from when I'd visited last week; the modest fire was well stoked and his tools were arranged on the workbench. Little else decorated the parlor apart from a large tool chest and some shelves which supported various reference books.

Zacharius brought over three small cups brimming with the steaming black liquid. The vapors alone aroused me from my headache. One had to wonder how the man could possibly repair the delicate mechanisms of a pocket watch when he was dosed up with caffeine. He was shaking like a leaf in a hurricane.

Dupin smiled, for the first time, I noticed. "A potent brew, Monsieur," he said. "You must scarcely sleep at night with measures as strong as these."

Zacharius sat down with us and gave a resigned nod. His eyes were circled with dark arcs and the whites appeared bloodshot. Dupin was right; he looked exhausted.

"I've waited, you know. I've waited up all night to catch *it* in the act, yet *it* still seems to conceal *itself*. I'm lost."

Dupin put down his cup and leant forward. "Tell me, Monsieur Zacharius... What exactly do you mean by '*it*'?"

"That godforsaken *thing* that pilfers my shop. It only happens at night, see. It isn't natural, I tell you. I've had bits and pieces stolen from the shop before but never like this. The things that go missing, they're... they're not of any use to anybody but a watchmaker. Why leave all of these valuable watches and clocks, yet run off with just mechanisms and parts?"

"Indeed," I said, draining the last of my coffee. "It doesn't make any sense."

"It will make perfect sense, Sergeant, once we discover the criminal's motive," Dupin said, tapping the surface of the table with his finger. Zacharius seemed agitated and brought his cup down heavily on its saucer.

"*It* doesn't have a motive! *It* isn't natural, I tell you."

"What makes you say that?" asked Dupin.

"The weird noises... The way things move about the place. At first, I thought I was just forgetting where I'd put things but now I've seen it for myself. Bits and pieces move from one side of the table to the other, some disappear entirely. Doors once bolted are suddenly open, others that were open are closed."

This was news to me, as he hadn't informed me of it in my earlier interviews. "When did this last happen?"

"Last night and the night before. No doubt it'll happen again tonight. That's when *it* walks, see?"

"You say '*it*', Monsieur, but you haven't seen anybody have you? Just items displaced throughout the night," Dupin stated.

"Always between midnight and 3 a.m. *It*'s something unearthly, trust me. First time I didn't notice, but now there's a pattern."

"A poltergeist?" I foolishly considered, aloud. Dupin scalded me almost instantaneously as the words left my lips.

"Rubbish. A ghost that walks the streets of Paris, selectively thieving from watchmakers? That's a ludicrous notion."

"I wasn't suggesting it was a ghost, just attempting to fill in the words for Monsieur Zacharius, here," I said indignantly. Usually, I wouldn't allow anyone to speak to me in such an arrogant manner but Dupin's response seemed reasonable and logical. The master watchmaker disagreed.

"You haven't heard the things I've heard! Weird noises in the night, footprints appearing on the floor. Devilish sounds that I've never encountered in my whole life. There's something evil at work."

"I seriously doubt that," frowned Dupin, pointing his forefinger in the air. "Here, sensation takes the place of common sense. Assume that we're dealing with a person, a person who knows how to shroud him entirely during his criminal activity. It is shroud, gentlemen, which we must discover and ultimately unveil."

Dupin stood up and encouraged me to do the same. As I buttoned my coat, I glanced down at the center of the table and pointed at a strange mark burnt into the surface of the wood.

"What's this?"

Zacharius raised his weary head. "It appeared overnight, just as all these confounded events began."

"It looks like something hot has been placed upon it," I suggested.

"Odd, isn't it?" Dupin mused. "I noticed it as I entered the room, too. Have these markings been seen at the other crime scenes, Sergeant?"

I quickly produced my notebook and found the relevant pages, revealing that such markings had indeed been noted at several other burglaries. Dupin gave a wry smile.

"Intriguing," he said, before turning to Zacharius. "I urge you to get some rest, Monsieur. We shall return tonight to continue our investigations. In the meantime, retire and get some sleep."

I seriously doubt if he took the advice. As I closed the shop door when we departed, I observed him assuming his vigil behind the counter again, his eyes wide, staring vacantly in the desperation of catching sight of his spectral adversary.

"I asked the driver to pick us up at 4 p.m. He's late," Dupin muttered.

"He's down there," I said, noticing the carriage rattling up the road. We made towards it partway down Verdain Street. "Might as well meet him halfway."

As I approached the carriage, something on the street grabbed my ankle. It was the grip of a filthy tramp, and a drunken one at that. I latched onto Dupin's arm to support myself and we both came to an abrupt stop. I shook loose the vagrant's grip, thankfully, and was about to make off when he made a comment that cut deeply into my soul.

"I've seen it. That ghost–the old man with white hair. The one that walks from the shop..."

"What?" I snapped, "What have you seen?"

The fool burst into laugher and turned away from me, groaning under his breath. Dupin pulled me towards to carriage.

"Forget him," he said. "Get inside. We'll find out for ourselves tonight."

Dupin had arranged for me to meet with him again on Verdain Street at 8 p.m. Thankfully, this gave me time enough to change my clothes and have a meal at home before rendezvousing with him outside *Maître Zacharius - Horloger*. Dupin had requested that I bring some form of restraint, such as handcuffs. That was all.

When I arrived, Dupin was waiting for me inside the shop. He stepped outside to meet me.

"You feel sure the thief will return tonight?" I asked Dupin as I stepped from the carriage, my boots crunching the fresh snow on the pavement.

"I do and we shall be there to catch him in the act."

His optimism surprised me. We entered into the welcoming warmth of the shop and I passed my coat to Zacharius.

"You'll be pleased to hear that Monsieur Zacharius has prepared our lodgings for the evening," Dupin said firmly, walking towards the parlor. The thought of sleeping in the little parlor was far from comforting and I considered my own empty bed waiting for me in my apartment.

"The box has been cleared of its contents and I've put a cushion inside for you," Dupin continued, indicating the big mahogany chest in the parlor.

"What, you want me to sleep inside the box?" I blustered, shocked at the thought.

"Of course not. We can't sleep, otherwise we'll miss him. We'll be watching the room from the holes in the front, Sergeant," he smiled. "Master watchmaker, I suggest you lock up for tonight and make your way home. We'll see you tomorrow morning, all being well."

Zacharius agreed and said his good-byes, blowing out the candles in the shop-front and leaving the two of us alone. Dupin crossed to the tiny stove in the parlor.

"Just enough time for some coffee, and then we'll get into position."

The night passed slowly and uncomfortably. From the neat holes in the front of the chest, both Dupin and I could survey the whole room quite clearly, especially with the fire raging violently, basking the room in flickering orange patterns.

On the table, in the center of the parlor, Dupin had placed a cloth directly over the burn mark. Arranged on the workbench were boxes of watch parts and mechanisms; our bait, you might say. The trap was set, and all we had to do was wait.

Time passed. It must have been about 2 a.m., and just as I felt myself dozing, Dupin jabbed me violently. There was a strange rhythmic, pulsating sound, almost like a disorganized string section of an orchestra. It rang around the room for a moment.

"That's it!" Dupin hissed, leaping from the chest like some sort of jack-in-the box. "Whoever it was, he's been and gone!"

I clambered out of the chest, noticing that the boxes were absent from the workbench and that the parlor door was open. The room was deathly quiet, with only the crackling pops of the fire occasionally breaking the silence.

"That's impossible, we've been watching this room all the time. We'd have seen him, or at least heard him."

Dupin indicated several footprints on the floor. "Not impossible. This 'ghost' not only wears size ten boots but also came from the outside. He's trailed in some snow from the street."

I rubbed the back of my neck, stiff after the claustrophobic confines of the chest.

"So, you're telling me that the thief walked in here, took the goods, then walked back out again without either of us noticing?"

"Yes and no," Dupin answered, his brow pleated in concentration. "The man–for that is what I believe him to be with footprints like these–made his mark… again."

Dupin waved me over to the table, where upon he identified a burn mark on the tablecloth. It was the tablecloth he'd placed there not five hours before.

"Whatever it was that made this mark, Sergeant, it is a tool that is essential to our malefactor's routine. As well as entering the shop, walking past the chest, taking the items and departing again, he also put something here. Something important. Something he has to do every time. We can only assume it is this object that somehow conceals him from our gaze."

I was having great difficulty in grasping what Dupin was surmising. Did he really believe that somebody could walk in front of us, invisible to our senses?

"If what you say is correct, how come neither of us saw the door open, nor heard his footsteps, or see the items move? They were there one minute, then gone the next."

"In the blink of an eye… here today and gone tomorrow."

"Exactly!" I snapped, feeling we weren't getting anywhere at all by exchanging clichés. "So we're dealing with a magician, then? Is that what you're saying?"

Dupin's eyes narrowed. He seemed to be looking somewhere distant, turning the sequence of events over and over in his mind. "A magician, no. A man of superior intellect, yes. We have encountered no observable process of change, merely experienced the disappearance of objects. As a magician may use a mirror to deceive and confuse his audience, I believe this man to be somehow abusing time to elude capture. Time, for us at least, has stood still while the man undertook his criminal tasks, undisturbed."

Dupin stood there, starring at me. It was too much to take in; to believe that a man had somehow stopped time and walked into the room, stolen the parts and left. No wonder we hadn't noticed. Usually, one would disregard such an idea as fanciful conjecture, but I failed to ascertain any other means of how the thief could have purloined the stock.

"That's… incredible!" I said. "How?"

"By means of some device which is far beyond our comprehension. No doubt the intermittent sounds we heard were induced by the source of the machine's function. It is the machine, or device, that is our criminal's accomplice and shroud. Perhaps it emits heat, enough to scorch a surface like the table. It is a device that somehow pauses time," he said, clicking his finger. "Just like that."

"If that's true, we'll never be able to catch him. He's untouchable."

Dupin smiled, "Oh, I wouldn't say that."

That was last night. This time the room was arranged similarly as before, save for a few vital differences. The table now had a long tablecloth shrouding it from top to bottom, hiding the underside from view. The surface of the tabletop had been carefully voided in the center with a jigsaw. Hypothetically, if anything were to be placed on the tablecloth, it would drop through to the floor beneath. This was the masterstroke of Dupin's plan. Beneath the table, directly under the void, was a bucket of water. Accompanying it was Zacharius, hunched around the bucket like a Buddha, ready to catch the mechanism in the bucket as it would fall.

I glanced at my watch again, angling it through the hole in the cramped confines of the chest. Enough firelight revealed that it was coming close to 3 a.m.

"He isn't going to come," I said, desperate to free myself of the infernal chest and stretch my legs.

"Just you stay right where you are!" spat Dupin irritably. "Maybe he saw us last night in the chest, maybe he didn't. My guess is that he didn't, in which case, he'll return to the scene of the crime to siphon off as many parts as he can while the stock is plentiful–especially if he's assembling a large contraption of some kind."

I was just about to argue the case for my blood circulation when that odd, pulsating sound began to reverberate through the room as it did yesterday. I turned to look at Dupin, who glanced back at me and nodded. This was it, the sting we'd been waiting for. Whoever it was, we were about to catch him in the act.

There was a flash as something blazed beneath the table, illuminating the whole room. It took an instant for my eyes to adjust as Dupin pulled me up and out of our hiding place.

Standing in the room, looking almost as surprised to see us as I was to see him, was an old man with long white hair that stuck up in a curious wave at the top. He was wearing a black velvet frockcoat and was holding one of the boxes of parts we'd left as bait on the workbench.

The man seemed to be in shock and he glanced towards the table. Whatever had been placed on it wasn't there now, as it had fallen through the hole into the bucket beneath. A dark blue smoke was rising in its place.

"The Temporal Rotor!" he screamed at nobody in particular. He seemed horrified, his expression the picture of alarm.

I took the opportunity to jump him, but moving like an insect he threw his box at me, sending me backwards into the open chest. He made for the door, but Dupin blocked his way.

"Get out of my way!" he screamed, raising a tight little fist to strike the sleuth. Fortunately, he didn't have the chance as Zacharius, who had jumped from beneath the table, emerged from behind him and grabbed the old man by the arm, twisting it behind his back. He shrieked in discomfort, scrabbling around like an animal to get free. By this time, I was on my feet again, pulling the handcuffs from my pocket. I latched them around his wrists and pushed him across the room.

"Everybody well, I trust?" Dupin breathed in relief. I answered him with a nod as I forced the old man into a chair at the table. He was furious, muttering vulgarities under his breath.

"And what do we have here then?" I asked, regaining my breath after the exertion.

Dupin smiled. "Your serial burglar, Sergeant."

Zacharius crossed the room and looked into the old man's gaunt face.

"Doctor Omega? No, surely not!" burst out Zacharius in recognition. I turned on him, surprised at what I'd heard.

"You know this man?"

"Yes, why I sold him a magnetic compass not so long ago! ...Wanted to use it for a ship or something. People say he's a crackpot inventor."

"No doubt he desired more parts for his private ventures, but wasn't willing to pay the price, is that it, Doctor? Did you want more timepieces to complete some sort of fanciful science project?" probed Dupin, quite literally with his walking cane.

"I'll say nothing!" snapped the old man. "Where is it, what have you done with it? Tell me!"

I glanced across at Zacharius. "For somebody who doesn't say anything, he certainly asks a lot of questions..."

"The Temporal Rotor!" he sneered, squirming in the chair. "It was there!"

Dupin crossed the table and reached down into the cut-out hole, pulling out a heavy silver object dripping in water. It looked like a part of an engine or something very similar. Sections of it were blackened with soot from where it had clearly fused after coming into contact with the water. Zacharius was lucky not to have been blinded in the blast.

"You fools!" the Doctor screamed. "Look at what you've done! You've destroyed it!"

I leaned forward to take a closer look at the object, momentarily diverted by its glistening, alien appearance. It was at that moment when the old man took his chance, springing from the chair and kicking the table into Dupin and Zacharius. The last glimpse I had was a flash of his coattails flapping past the doorframe of the shop-front, his hands still cuffed behind his back. I made out into the store and onto the street, but he was gone.

"We've lost him," I declared flatly, entering the parlor.

"No matter, Sergeant," smiled Dupin, casually lifting the odd contraption before Zacharius. "Without this, he has nothing."

"Monsieur Zacharius, do you know where he lives?" I asked desperately.

"Yes, about two miles from here, I believe."

"Then, we must head there immediately," I said, about the leave the room. Dupin stopped me.

"He'll be long gone now, Sergeant, probably making for the coast. From there, no doubt he'll complete the venture he started here. Quite what that is, we can scarcely guess at. One thing we can be sure of, though, is that he'll have to do without one of these for a while."

With that Dupin held aloft the Temporal Rotor, still smoldering a blue smoke. The device which, at one stage, stopped time for all but the man who operated it. Now, its spell was broken and the Doctor's veil had been compromised. The object was quite easily the strangest contraption I'd ever seen. However, in context of the events of the past few days, it seemed rather acceptable in its ridiculousness. Under the circumstances I'd come to accept, the once implausible had turned into the possible, but how was I going to explain my findings to my superiors? I couldn't.

When I returned to the station, I marked the case as:

CLOSED – UNSOLVED

After all, Dupin was right. The robberies ceased that night and the mysterious Doctor Omega was nowhere to be found. And in honesty, who on Earth, save Dupin and Maître Zacharius, would have believed the true events that took place on those nights in Verdain Street?

Dupin makes a return appearance in John Peel's contribution. John is a renowned YA writer, known to many for his wonderful Doctor Who *books, often featuring the Daleks. This story, however, showcases a lesser known side of John's fiction: the detective and the swashbuckler, as Edgar Allan Poe's sleuth teams up with another legendary hero to fight crime and rescue a damsel in distress...*

John Peel: *The Kind-Hearted Torturer*

Paris, 1842

I have had occasion in the past to note down one or two of the singular affairs that my good friend C. Auguste Dupin has resolved, thanks to his strict interpretation and application of logical thinking. I have never considered myself a dull-witted man–nor have I been so thought by my acquaintances–but if I were to compare myself with Dupin, I should certainly appear almost Neanderthal in my thinking. He was frequently of great use to the official police, but there was one occasion when he was unable to help them solve a case.

We had been out smoking pipes and imbibing a moderate quantity of a rather fine Madeira and were on our way back to our rooms at an early hour of the morning. As is generally the case with Paris, we were far from alone on the city streets. In fact, due to the press of the crowds on the main routes, we slipped from them and into a maze of the back streets that Dupin somehow knew so well. I knew only that we were in the region of the *église Ste-Mathilde*–I could see her spire about the roofs ahead of us–but Dupin led the way without hesitation or doubt.

As we drew closer to the church, a figure turned from around the corner ahead of us. He was ambling rather than walking, but still almost collided with us. His hand flashed to the brim of his hat, and he nodded slightly. "I do beg your pardon," he said, in English. Then, he added: "*Pardonnez-moi.*" I was quite impressed with the Englishman's attempt at French–very few of them ever manage to get their tongues around the Gallic consonants correctly, and he had almost succeeded. I nodded back politely, noting that he was well dressed in expensive evening clothes, though without gloves, and carried a walking stick in his right hand of some dark wood, topped with a silver fleur-de-lys. He touched his hat again, and then walked on.

Dupin made no comment–he had spoken not a single word in this short encounter–but he had an abstracted look to his face that usually accompanied his attention being focused on some mystery or other. Since he had undertaken no such investigations, to the best of my knowledge, and since he had been most genial over our glasses and pipes, I came to the conclusion that I must have mistaken his glance. We moved on, only to encounter a crowd just two streets away, in front of Ste-Mathilde.

"It would appear that there is no one in their beds this night," I commented. "Perhaps we should find another way?"

"I think not," Dupin replied, his eyes feasting eagerly on the motions and sounds of the gathered crowd. "Observe–these people go nowhere–they instead crowd around something on the pavement. And, unless I am very much mistaken, that is Monsieur Couperin, of the Préfecture de Police attempting to move them along. It seems I was correct to suspect foul play."

I confess that I was puzzled by this remark, as I had seen nothing that had alerted me to the possibility of trouble. But Dupin was like a hound who has scented the fox, and hurried along to Couperin's side. The policeman appeared surprised to see my friend, but there are few in the Sûreté who do not know Dupin by both reputation and appearance.

"It would appear," Couperin said, jovially, "that you have a nose for blood. But there is little here to interest you, Dupin. It is merely an affair of honor that has ended tragically." He scowled. "Unless you know something of this case that I do not."

"I know very little about this case," Dupin replied. "I was not even aware that there *was* a case until moments ago. My friend and I were merely heading home after a pleasant evening. But, as I am here, and a dead man is here…" He shrugged.

Couperin considered for a moment, and then nodded. He turned to the three gendarmes who were with him, and who were attempting–without noticeable success–to disperse the onlookers. Parisiennes, it has been claimed, have seen everything–but, nevertheless, there would appear to be no lack of interest in seeing a dead body on the pavement. "Let us through," Couperin said, and the policemen motioned back the onlookers.

"This has only just occurred?" I asked him.

"Within the past ten minutes," Couperin confirmed. "There was a policemen in this street who heard cries, and then saw a man fall from the roof of the church. I happened to be close by also, on an entirely different case, and arrived just moments later.

"Then how is it that you allowed the murderer to escape?" Dupin asked. He was standing close to the body, and studying it, as was his habit, with minute attention.

"I am yet to be convinced that it *was* murder," Couperin said, somewhat stiffly. "It appears to me to have been a matter of honor."

"Indeed?" Dupin beckoned me forward. "And what is your opinion?" he asked me.

I bent to examine the corpse. It was of a thick-set man in his late 20s, I should judge. He wore no coat, and his clothing was otherwise tidy. His face looked heavy, not refined, and there was a deep wound in his right shoulder. It was clear that he had been the victim of a sword-thrust. Oddly, there was not as much blood about the wound as I would have expected, nor was there a great deal on the ground.

"There is not much that occurs to me," I confessed. "He was stabbed with a sword, obviously, but the blow did not kill him. It is not in a vital spot." I glanced upward–the roof of the church was some 40 meters high. "I imagine it was the fall that terminated his life."

Dupin turned to the policeman. "And on what do you base your ridiculous theory of an affair of honor?" he asked.

Couperin scowled. "On the *facts*," he replied. "Your friend is undoubtedly correct in saying that the fall killed the poor fellow. So, we must ask ourselves: what was he doing on the roof on the church in the first place? Note the sword wound–how could he have been given one? Through a duel, obviously. Why the roof? So that he and his opponent could fight without being disturbed. His coat has been removed, clearly so that he can have greater freedom in the fight. I imagine that he was startled by being run through the shoulder, and then lost his footing and fell to his death." He smiled, pleased with himself. "As I say, an affair of honor between two gentlemen–I admit I cannot deduce if it was over a point of honor or a woman–that resulted in the tragic death of this man. I do not believe that it was murder."

Dupin snorted. "You, like all policemen, see everything with the eyes–and nothing with the mind. Do not look so annoyed with me, Inspector–you did at least see all the relevant details. The problem is that you are a romantic. You come upon a man with a sword wound, and instantly imagine that he is a romantic, as you are. You decide that the whole business is an affair of honor, when it is clearly nothing of the sort. Have you been up to look at the roof of the church yet?" he asked.

The policeman was momentarily taken aback by the apparent change of subject. "I was just about to do so when you arrived," he said. He was still annoyed at Dupin's comments, clearly, but striving for politeness. "Would you care to accompany me?"

"No," Dupin said, carelessly. "I know precisely what you will discover up there. You will find this man's jacket, which is black. You will find a pair of discarded gloves, which are white, but covered with blood. You will find a pool of blood–more than a liter, I would imagine. What you will *not* find is the mythical sword that this man used in your imaginary duel." He waved one hand. "I will await you here. Ah, before you go, which is the policeman who was first on the scene and discovered the body?"

Couperin gestured to one of the trio, who stepped forward and saluted rather smartly. "I am going to examine the scene of the battle," he told the man.

He gestured to Dupin. "Answer this man's questions as you would mine." He then stalked off, into the open door of the church, taking another policeman with him. Dupin turned to the policeman.

"You saw the man fall?" he asked.

"Yes, sir." The policeman had clearly been rehearsing his story in his mind, for he needed no further questioning to continue. "I was walking in this direction, and stood over there." He gestured to a spot some 20 meters further up the road. "I heard a cry from the roof of the church, and looked up. In the darkness, I saw some object fall and strike the ground. Hurrying forward, I saw it was the victim. People had already started to gather, and I sent one of them for Monsieur Couperin, whom I knew to be close by."

"I see." Dupin smiled slightly. "And you saw no one with a sword?"

"No one at all, sir. I should certainly have detained anyone with a weapon."

"I'm certain you would," Dupin agreed. "You seem to be a most conscientious fellow." There was a sparkle of amusement in his eyes. "Then where do you imagine that the Inspector's other duelist has vanished to?"

"I have no idea, sir," the policeman admitted. Then he looked startled. "You don't think he's still on the roof, do you? Monsieur Couperin–"

"Is in no danger at all," Dupin replied. "The murderer is quite some distance from here by this point."

The policeman looked confused, and then his puzzlement cleared. "You think he dropped his sword, then? I should have held everyone about here."

"You could hardly hold *everyone*," Dupin reassured the crestfallen policeman. He glanced at the crowd. "Though it would seem that almost nobody wishes to leave. Murder, it would appear, is something of a spectacle."

Couperin returned from the church, looking somewhat flushed. Part of this was no doubt due to the exertion of climbing and then descending the tower. The other part, I soon discovered, was from anger. "How the Devil did you know what we would find on the roof?" were his first words to Dupin.

"Because I understand what has happened here," my friend replied calmly. "You could find nothing other than I expected. Your problem, my friend, is that you are a kind person–you assume that others are like you, and give them too much credit for kindness. While this trait is admirable in the population at large, it is perhaps not the best characteristic for a policeman to possess. I, on the other hand, know the depredations that a person can sink into, and thus I expect nothing less. Sadly, perhaps, I all too frequently discover myself to be correct. I often wish that the human race did not lower itself to meet my expectations."

"All of which still does not inform me how you knew what I would find on the roof of the church," Couperin persisted, his annoyance still very evident.

"Very well," Dupin said. "Let us examine the evidence. You see a man with a sword-wound, and without a jacket. You assume from this that he had been fighting a duel of honor, and fell from the roof. Let us examine the possibility that you are right. First, look at this man. Note the heavy features, the coarse hands. Is this a man to whom honor might mean more than life itself? No, this is a man who would settle an argument not with a sword, but with a cudgel or a pistol. Is there a sword he might have used? No, you found no trace. And nor did your conscientious policeman find anyone who saw anyone carrying a sword in this vicinity."

"The other party might have hidden them," Couperin protested. But I did detect a lack of force in his words, as if he were already coming to believe my friend's objections.

Dupin waved his hand airily. "By all means, waste time searching," he said. "There was no duel. Allow me to explain what actually occurred, and I am certain that you will be able to follow my reasoning." His face took on the detached expression he always had when expounding his theories–if the word "theory" is not too light to be used concerning his mental processes. "This man's killer happened upon the man here. It was unlikely to be by chance, for the murderer clearly knew that Ste-Mathilde had a flat roof, and that it was accessible at this odd hour. Therefore, the killer knew this man, and had planned carefully for his arrival. When the victim reached the church, he was forced inside by his attacker–undoubtedly when the man brandished the weapon that produced the wound we have seen.

"He took the victim to the roof so that he might have a very private conversation with him. The wound was not inflicted in a moment of passion as two men fought–it was given calmly and deliberately. Its purpose was to induce the man to talk."

"How can you possibly say that?" the policeman asked.

"If you look at the wound," Dupin said, "you will observe that there are black threads driven into it by the point of the weapon. Since the man's shirt is white, clearly the threads had to have come from a black coat. Since the man was not wearing one, this was why I knew you would find one on the roof."

"That does not prove that the wound was given to make him talk," Couperin persisted.

Dupin sighed. "Again, look to the wound. There is remarkably little blood on the shirt, yet the wound is deep. It does not touch any vital spot, however, so it was not a killing thrust. And the man's jacket is missing. How to explain this? Obviously, the person who attacked the victim then thrust him down onto the roof on his hands and knees. The blood fell straight from the wound and onto the roof–and you discovered the pool of blood there, as I knew it must be."

"But why remove the jacket?" Couperin asked. His voice showed that he was considerably less sure of himself now.

"To restrain the man. Once he was on his hands and knees, gripping the collar of the jacket and pulling it down the arms is a very effective way of immobilizing a person. So, given that this is what must have happened, the only problem remaining is–why would the attacker act in such a fashion? The answer is apparent–the victim had some information that the killer wished to know. The attacker gave him the wound to torture him, to induce him to speak. The victim then told all. His attacker thereupon threw him from the roof. Why? For one of two reasons–to either silence the man, so that no one would know the information had been obtained. Or else... as a warning of our killer's earnest. He is a man not to be trifled with, and he takes this man's life as you or I would squash a bug."

"But how can you be sure that the attacker gained the information he needed?" asked the policeman. "Is it not possible that this man threw himself deliberately from the roof to avoid talking?"

Dupin smiled slightly. "If you wish to conduct an experiment, my friend, then perhaps you would get down on your hands and knees. I will then pull your jacket down over your arms to immobilize you. You may then see if you are able to struggle out of your jacket and throw yourself anywhere before I am able to prevent you. You would not succeed. No, the victim was thrown to his death by his torturer, who pulled off the jacket first and discarded it."

Couperin looked defeated, overwhelmed by Dupin's relentless array of logic. "And the gloves?" he asked, feebly. "How did you know I should find them?"

"Ah, there I have a confession to make," my friend admitted. "I was not absolutely certain that they would be there. It was a good guess, but by no means certain. They were stained with blood from the victim, so that the killer could not afford to be seen wearing them in public."

It was then that I realized the point that Dupin was making. "Great Heavens!" I exclaimed. "We passed by the killer!"

"Indeed we did," Dupin agreed. "And you and I both noted the oddity that such a well-dressed man was not wearing the gloves that would have completed his ensemble. That was what made me suspect they would have been left on the roof."

"You met the killer?" Couperin cried. "Why did you not say so at once? Perhaps there is still time to find him..." He looked ready to send off his policemen to search the city streets.

Dupin shook his head. "You will not find him," he assured the policeman. "He was disguised as an Englishman, and has undoubtedly discarded this disguise by now."

"Disguised?" I could scarcely agree. "Dupin, I would swear that man *was* English. His accent, his admirable attempt to speak good French..."

"My friend," Dupin said, smiling, "you heard what he wished you to witness. We are dealing with a most intelligent and dangerous man. But his accent, whilst superb, was not quite good enough to fool the ears of Dupin. He was a Frenchman, pretending a difficulty with our tongue, and that his native speech was English. I do not blame you for being deceived–very few people would not have been. Also, did you not notice the walking stick that the man carried? It had as a head the fleur-de-lys–a very French symbol, one that a true Englishman was unlikely to own. In fact, it was because of his attempt at disguise that I paid close attention to him. Why, I wondered, would this man pretend to be what he was not with two strangers who might never see him again? He was clearly behaving oddly. And so I was prepared for some strange occurrence. That is why I moved toward, instead of away from, the gathered crowd here. And, in retrospect, is it not curious that while all other people were hurrying *toward* the scene of the crime, our false Englishman was walking slowly *away* from it?"

"This is all very logical," I was forced to admit. "But the man was not carrying a sword, and you do not expect to find one here. So, where is the weapon?"

"He *was* carrying it," Dupin argued. "Undoubtedly that walking stick of his concealed a sword cane. A most useful weapon that is simple to disguise."

Couperin looked quite exhausted. "But what was this man killed for?" he asked. "What information? And how can you be certain that your fake Englishman obtained what he sought?"

"If he had not, he would not have been so pleased with himself when he ran into us," Dupin explained. "As to what that information was–I cannot yet say. Whatever it was, though it was of sufficient importance to cost a man his life, it was not of great urgency, otherwise the killer would have been hurrying away instead of walking quite casually. No, whatever it was that he learned, it is not something he will be able to make use of for several hours yet, at least." Abruptly, he yawned. "So I believe we all have sufficient time to go home and get some rest. If you will excuse us?" Then he paused. "Perhaps you would be kind enough to let us know any further facts you might unearth, my friend?" he asked the policeman. "You have our address, I trust? Just in case, please write it down–I would not wish you to mistake the house." He dictated the address where we stayed to Couperin, and then had the audacity to force the policeman to read it back so Dupin could ascertain that it had been taken correctly. I was not surprised that Couperin looked distinctly annoyed at this lack of trust. In fact, once we had taken our leave of the poor fellow, I berated Dupin for humiliating him so.

"Did I really?" he asked, showing little concern. "I am sure that I will be forgiven. But I had to be certain that the man listening to all that was said heard it quite distinctly."

"Man?" I asked, astonished. "What man?"

"You did not notice him?" Dupin asked. "He was attempting to pretend to be one of the crowd, but was paying inordinate attention to our conversation with the Inspector."

"A journalist, perhaps?" I ventured.

"I think not." Dupin shook his head. "The killer of this unfortunate is a most cunning and intelligent man. It seems to me that he may well have left an agent behind to ascertain what the police might discover from the corpse of his victim. I trust that when he receives the report, my deductions will unnerve him."

"Good Heavens!" I said. "And what will he do then?"

"Come and call upon us, I hope," Dupin replied. "Why else should I have made certain that he will get our address? I do not believe that we are in danger from this man, my friend, but it might be as well if you slept with a loaded pistol close at hand."

Thankfully, despite Dupin's warning, the rest of the night was uneventful. We had just finished a late breakfast–it might even have passed for a late lunch–when our visitor was announced. Dupin glanced to me to ascertain that I had my pistol within reach, though concealed from view, before allowing the man in.

Thanks to Dupin's assurance that this was our fake Englishman who passed us in the night, I paid careful attention to the stranger. Though he was certainly as tall and muscular as the "Englishman," had I not been forewarned that it was the same man, I would never have guessed. It wasn't so much that his features had changed, but that his complete attitude had altered, making him appear so very different. This morning he was without a single doubt a Frenchman born and bred. And, from the style and cut of his immaculate clothing, one of rare breeding and wealth. I have heard it said that great actors are able to change their appearance through nothing more than their attitude and mannerisms, but never before had I ever seen it done.

"Chevalier Dupin," the man said, bowing politely. "I trust I have not arrived too early for our appointment?"

"Not at all," my friend replied, equally politely and calmly. "Though I confess a small hesitation in knowing how to address you. Should I be addressing Lord Wilmore, Edmond Dantès or the self-appointed Count of Monte-Cristo?"

A slight shock passed fleetingly over the features of our guest. "I see that you have discovered who I am," he murmured. "May I sit down?"

"Excuse my bad manners," Dupin replied. "Of course, please take a seat." He gestured to one facing the both of us. A slight smile crossed the man's face, and I understood that he knew he would be covered by a brace of pistols.

"I assure you," he said gently, "that you have no need to fear violence from me. Had I wished it, you would both be dead by now. But I have nothing against either of you–save that you might cause me a small inconvenience in my plans."

"I assure you, Monsieur le Comte," Dupin answered, somewhat offended, "that any inconvenience I might cause you would be by no means small."

Our visitor laughed. "No, you are correct–you could cause me a major inconvenience by simply telling the police my name. Which raises the interesting question of why you haven't–and how you happened upon it."

"I did not happen upon it," Dupin replied. "I attended the details of your case with interest as it happened. I know that you were born Edmond Dantès, and were unjustly committed to the Château d'If for life. That you somehow escaped, took upon yourself the identity of the fictitious Count of Monte-Cristo and subsequently brought justice to the men who had wronged you and others. I confess, I was much impressed by your methods. I noted that in the course of your actions you adopted a number of disguises, including that of an aristocratic Englishman, Lord Wilmore. When you ran across us last night in this disguise, the details of your case sprang back to the forefront of my mind, and I was certain that I was dealing with none other than the much-wronged Edmond Dantès. It was solely because of the regard I held you in that I did not immediately pass along your name to the police. However, that is an oversight that can be corrected at any time."

"And your invitation for me to visit you was for the purpose of deciding whether to do just that, I take it?"

"You are correct," Dupin agreed. "I am willing to hear you out as to the reason you committed torture and cold-blooded murder this last night. If I am not convinced by your explanation, then I am afraid that I shall have to call in my friend Inspector Couperin and hand you over to him."

Dantès–Monte-Cristo–whatever the man was called, he was cool. "And you feel that the odds of two against one will enable you to take me captive?"

"Two armed with pistols against one who is not," Dupin corrected him.

"Ah, yes, I had almost forgotten the pistols," Monte-Cristo said. He snapped his fingers, and the door to our breakfast room burst open. Two large men entered, both with pistols of their own. Our visitor held up a hand. "No violence, please," he requested. "Simply relieve these two men of their weapons, and then leave us alone." The two men did so, leaving me, at least, feeling humiliated and rather naked. "I merely removed the pistols to prevent accidents," Monte-Cristo assured us. "Now I believe I do owe you at least my story as to the events of last night. After that... well, we shall see." He settled back, apparently quite at ease, and commenced his tale.

"After I had achieved my aim of justice against those men who had wronged me, I left France with every intention of never returning. I had a bride whom I was learning to love, and had left matters completely settled–or so I believed. My house on the Champs-Elysées I had left to the son of my old master and friend, Maximillian Morrel. He had wed Valentine de Villefort, and their life promised to be one of happiness.

"However, this was not to be. Two weeks ago, I received an urgent missive from Morrel, telling me that his wife had been kidnapped, and was being held for ransom. He feared greatly for her safety, and begged assistance. Even if I were not moved by compassion and friendship to agree, my wife, Haydée, would have forced me into it, for she and Valentine were great friends. Accordingly, we returned as swiftly as possible. Yesterday, I met with Morrel, who is a broken man after the abduction of his beloved wife, and learned the details of the story. She had been taken on the street in broad daylight, and her maid assaulted. It was clear that this was the work of the Black Coats." He paused. "I take it you know of the association?"

Dupin nodded and smiled. "I have caused that organization more than a small amount of inconvenience. I should relish causing them more."

"So would I," Monte-Cristo answered fervently. "As I say, it was swiftly apparent that they were behind the kidnapping and ransom of poor Valentine."

"They have demanded money for her return, then?" I asked.

"They have." He named a considerable sum, more than Dupin or I would make in ten years.

"There is a problem with paying this amount, then?" I asked him.

"The amount? No." He waved a hand. "Morrel or I could–and would–pay ten times that figure for Valentine's safe return. The problem is not financial, but a matter of trust."

Dupin saw that I did not understand, so he elucidated. "The Black Coats will require the ransom to be delivered before the lady is returned. However, once they have the money *and* the lady, what is the likelihood that they will set the lady free? In many cases, the victim may be considered to have seen too much."

I understood. "You think it likely, then," I questioned the Count, "that they will take the money and kill the lady instead of fulfilling their bargain and setting her free?"

"It is more than likely," he replied. "But, even if they do allow her to go free–once they know Morrel will pay, what is to stop them from abducting her again and forcing the family through this torture a second or third time?"

Dupin nodded. "Given the habits of the Black Coats, I believe your assessment of their likely strategy to be a sound one. I take it, then, that you have a different plan?"

"Indeed." Monte-Cristo resumed his tale. "It was the work of a few short hours to learn that the man whose body you examined last night was a lieutenant in the Black Coats. It was a simple matter to divert him, and his fate you know, of course."

I believed I now understood. "Ah! So you tortured him to make him tell you the whereabouts of the unfortunate Madame Morrel!"

"Had he known them, it would have been a great help," the Count replied. "But the Black Coat organization is large, and he did not know who was responsible for the kidnapping. I thought it unlikely that he would."

"You had a different aim in mind, then?" Dupin asked. I could tell that the case intrigued him. He hated boredom more than anything, and this case was proving to be of the greatest interest.

"Yes–an exchange of prisoners. If I could take as hostage someone that the Black Coats valued, then this person might be exchanged for Valentine. It would ensure the safety of my friend's wife, and also stand the Black Coats on notice that any further attempt on her person would be met by serious reprisals."

"Which is why you felt no compunction about killing the man last night?" Dupin hazarded a guess.

"They had to be shown that they were dealing with someone who would have no single hesitation in doing whatever he said," Monte-Cristo amplified. "Also, as he is dead, they can have no idea who my target within their organization is, and cannot defend that person."

"So you propose to kidnap one of their higher functionaries and then effect an exchange?" Dupin summarized.

"This afternoon." He withdrew a watch from his pocket and glanced at it. "In two hours, to be precise. Always assuming, of course, that you decide not to... inconvenience me." He looked at Dupin expectantly.

Dupin didn't need to look to me for confirmation. "Not only will we not inconvenience you," he vowed, "but I'll wager that you might be able to find the use for two stout fellows–with pistols, if you'll return them."

"Capital!" the Count exclaimed, leaping to his feet. "Your assistance in this matter will be gratefully accepted." He opened the door, and called in his companions, instructing them to return to us our pistols. Thus armed once again, we accompanied him outside to a waiting carriage. This took us to a section of the Rue de Bois–affluent, without being too ostentatious.

"The person we await will be arriving at No. 17 shortly," he informed us. "There will be a small guard, naturally, whom we shall have to overcome. This is why I am so glad of your assistance. Jacopo, Michel and I might have managed the task alone, but with the two of you as well..." He smiled his thanks.

During the wait, I could not but wonder what adventure we were in for. As Dupin had remarked, he had encountered the Black Coats once or twice, always to their detriment. They were a secretive band of law-breakers, who were willing to undertake any enterprise that might fill their coffers, no matter how vile or anti-social. Dupin had cut off a couple of their minor heads through his detection, but more seemed to constantly spring up. France, it would seem, might sometimes find itself in want of good artists or composers, but never of criminals. The same is undoubtedly true of any center of enterprise in our modern world.

"Softly," Monte-Cristo murmured a short while later, dashing me from my reverie. "The carriage approaches." From where we sat on the road opposite the target house, we could peer through the curtains of our own conveyance and see the small enclosed carriage that drew up. Along with the driver, there were two other riders on the outside.

"I am sure there must be at least one other guard within the coach," the Count said softly.

"We shall take the more obvious ones," Dupin said. "You and your men take the others."

We waited a moment, until the two guards began to disembark. At a signal from the Count, we then sprang from our own carriage. I raised my pistol instantly. At the sight and sound of our approach, the two men whirled, drawing pistols of their own. The same instant, the driver attempted to whip his horses into motion again.

I fired first, and had the satisfaction of hearing my target howl and fall, clutching his shoulder. Blood was pulsing from a wound there as I sprang across the road and seized his unfired pistol, thus rearming myself. Dupin, I noted, had also taken down his man, and was procuring his weapon also. The servant named Jacopo had leapt atop the carriage, and prevented the driver from moving it, while Monte-Cristo and his remaining retainer threw open the door of the vehicle.

There was a gunshot at that instant, and Monte-Cristo fell. I thought for a horrified second that he had been injured or killed, but he pounced onto the man who was now drawing a sword and dragged him from the carriage. In his own hand, I saw the cane flicker, and then became a sword also–the weapon that had been used to wound the man the previous evening. The Count and his opponent set to fighting with a will, as Michel, Dupin and I surrounded the coach. I confess to being startled.

I had been expecting some evil-looking man, a human spider used to spinning webs of treachery and deceit, to be within. Instead, I saw, calm and refined, one of the most beautiful women I have met. She was tall, elegant and dignified. Had we, after all, made some terrible mistake?

Thankfully not. Dupin smiled slightly. "The Countess of Clare," he murmured. "I had long suspected that there was a link between you and the Black Coats."

"Chevalier Dupin," she replied, inclining her shapely head slightly. "I have long been expecting you. This trap of yours is admirably well set."

"Not mine, Madame," Dupin answered, gesturing toward the Count. "I merely assist."

Monte-Cristo had his man by now. The guard was skilled, but the Count much better. With a final flick of his wrist, he disarmed his opponent, and then plunged the blade into the man's shoulder. The man cried, clasped his wound and fell back.

"Tell your colleagues," the Count cried, "that the Countess is captive and hostage. She will be kept alive as long as Madame Morrel is in good health. If you wish the lady returned to you, I will exchange her for my friend. The exchange is to take place at six precisely at the Bois de Boulogne." He mentioned a place. "If Madame Morrel is not there at that time, or if she is at all harmed, you will receive the Countess back in small pieces. And then we shall take another of your elite and attempt the exchange again." He did not bother to ask if his terms were understood. Instead he strode to the lady's carriage. "If you will accompany me?" he asked, politely but firmly, extending a hand.

"How can I refuse?" the Countess replied. She accompanied us back to our own carriage. Jacopo then whipped the horses, and we sprang off through the streets of Paris. The Countess surveyed us without apparent fear. No doubt she felt protected by virtue of her feminine sex and her beauty, though in her situation few women would have been so poised. "I fear, gentlemen, that you are being naive. There is a rule in the Black Coats–*coupez la branche*–cut off the limb–that the fallen are to be left behind. I am afraid that they are more likely to abandon me than to exchange me."

"I think not, in this case," Monte-Cristo countered. "They will recognize that your abductor is the same man who tortured one of their number last night and killed him. They will fear that I shall torture you to obtain your secrets. They may not want you back, but they will desire to safeguard what you know."

"I fear you overestimate their fears."

"For your sake, my lady, let us hope not."

Nothing more was said for the remainder of the ride. Eventually, we drew up outside a house in a section of the city not far from the woods. The Count led the way inside, where we were met by a young woman whose beauty surpassed even that of the Countess. There was the suggestion of the Near East about her countenance, and a definite suggestion of ferocity within her dark eyes.

"My wife," the Count introduced her.

This fresh Countess faced our captive one. Her eyes were blazing with suppressed anger. "My lady, you are no doubt feeling yourself safe from harm from these gentlemen. You are no doubt considering that you are a beautiful woman, and they clearly men who respect the sanctity of the female. You are thinking to yourself that they would not be able to bring themselves to harm you in any way." She shrugged her shapely shoulders. "And it is possible that you are correct. However, I am also a woman, and it is my friend that your scoundrels are holding to ransom. Believe me when I say that, to save her life, there is no degradation or torture I would not offer you–and with joy in my heart the whole time."

For the first time, the Countess of Clare looked concerned. She did not answer, but turned her head slightly away. I could not help looking in some small horror at the Count's wife. I, for one, had no doubt at all that the woman would cheerfully keep her promise. All the determination a man may possess is as nothing when compared to the ferocity a female may offer.

"An interesting lady, my friend," Dupin remarked. "And one I should by no means like to offend."

"That is unlikely," Monte-Cristo replied with a short laugh. "Haydée is by inclination the gentlest of women. But like a she-bear, she is ferocious in her defense of those she loves. Come, let us take refreshment as we wait the approach of our appointment."

He played the most urbane of hosts, and, it is to be confessed, his fare was more than adequate. As befitted a man of his wealth, he was able to offer us delicate pastries and a more than pleasant port. My own appetite was a little reduced due to our circumstances, but Dupin plunged in with a will.

In the eventuality, we departed for the rendezvous a shade after five. The Count showed the first hint of concern I had noticed upon his countenance. "I cannot but suspect that there will be treachery attempted," he confessed. "These Black Coats deal in dishonesty as a matter of course, and I cannot believe that they will abandon it now."

"Nor I," Dupin agreed. "You have a plan?"

"Such as it is." He gestured for his wife to take the coach, along with our captive. Jacopo and Michel accompanied her. A second coach arrived for the three of us. "I dislike placing Haydée in jeopardy," he admitted, "but she would not remain out of this. Valentine is her friend, and she will not rest until that friend is restored safely to her husband. But Jacopo and Michel will protect her with their lives, should the need arise."

"It is our task, then," Dupin remarked, "to ensure that the need does *not* arise." We took the coach to the edge of the woods. The Bois de Boulogne is a public park, and there were pedestrians strolling the grounds. Monte-Cristo's rendezvous point, however, was a little off the main thoroughfare.

"I thought that the Black Coats might be more circumspect in a semi-public place," he explained. "But perhaps we had better conceal ourselves and await their coming. Haydée and the others will arrive shortly, and I should like to be well hidden by then." So saying, he handed Dupin and myself two spare pistols, already loaded and primed. We already had our own at the ready, along with knives, should any fighting be at close quarters. We would be able to face a small party–but what would happen if the Black Coats came out in force?

We slipped from the carriage, which the driver then removed from sight, as the three of us found solid hiding places overlooking the point where the exchange would take place. It was then merely a matter of waiting, and trying to quell the doubts that my feverish mind kept raising. Had we planned well enough? Would there be sufficient of us? What might the villains arrange? Since there was no way of deducing the answers to any of these questions until the moment of truth arrived, speculation was pointless–but still my troubled mind insisted on making it.

And then the two carriages slowly approached from opposite directions. I knew ours because of the figure of Jacopo, acting the part of the driver. Michel, then, was inside the coach with his mistress. The carriage of the Black Coats had two men on the outside–and who knew how many more within. Both conveyances drew to a rest some 40 meters apart. There was a brief moment of inactivity as both sides regarded the other–and we three in hiding regarded both sides. I was concealed in bushes some 50 meters from the Black Coats' coach, and had an excellent view of what was to transpire.

The door to our coach opened, and the Countess stepped down. Haydée was as close as her shadow, and a flash of light at the Countess's throat showed that Haydée had her knife at the ready. I watched the other vehicle intently, praying that this was not some treachery. The door opened, and an unfamiliar, yet beautiful young woman stepped down, followed closely by a man with a pistol at the ready. This, I assumed, was Valentine Morrel. She looked shaken and haggard, but otherwise unhurt.

"We will both release our prisoners," the man called out. "They will then walk toward each other."

"Agreed," I heard Haydée reply, her voice firm and resolute. She took the knife from the neck of the Countess, and prodded her forward with the point. Valentine, also, began to walk steadily away from her captor.

I kept flickering my eyes all about, though I wished to follow the drama occurring before me. If there was to be treachery, this was the moment. As the two women's paths crossed, the Countess suddenly sprang forward, her arm wrapping about Valentine, attempting to make her a captive once again.

There was a rush of movement as Monte-Cristo leaped from his hiding place, and he rushed to where the two women had begun to struggle. Madame Morrel might be a sweet flower, but she was determined not to fall into the hands of the gang again. As the Count dashed forward, the man by the Black Coat coach whirled, his pistol at the ready. There was a flicker of movement from the carriage also, and two more armed men dropped to the ground.

I ran from concealment, the first of my pistols in my hand and ready to fire. Out of the corner of my eye, I saw that Dupin had done the same. The Black Coat men caught sight of us, and held their fire for a second, unsure where the greatest threat lay. I fired my pistol, not expecting at this range to hit anyone, but to draw their attention to me and away from the struggling women.

My ruse worked, fortunately for them, but not so for me. The man at the coach spun about and discharged his pistol at me. The bullet went as wide as mine had, but then he ran toward me, drawing a second weapon. I discarded my spent pistol and drew the second. Now that battle was joined, I would have to be more careful. I heard two further shots, but dared not break my concentration to see what was happening elsewhere. My attacker fired his second shot, and this time I heard the bullet whistle past my ear, and felt the breeze of its passage. Dropping to one knee, I steadied my pistol across my left arm, and fired carefully.

The man leaped into the air as if startled, and then fell to the ground, bleeding copiously from a wound high in his chest. I did not dare see what I had done, but came to my feet again, throwing aside the pistol and taking my last fresh weapon in hand. I looked for further targets, but there were none. Both men beside the coach were down, either dead or severely wounded. One had been shot by Dupin, the other had a knife in his stomach, clearly thrown by Jacopo, who was reclaiming it and wiping the blood from it.

Monte-Cristo had reached the struggling women, and immediately struck down the Countess with the butt of his unfired pistol. The villainous beauty collapsed with a cry, and Valentine finally broke free. She ran with a gasp of relief to clutch at her friend Haydée, and the two women hugged and greeted one another.

Panting somewhat, I reached the Count at about the same instant as Dupin. We looked down at the Countess, who was dazed, but conscious. "Shall we take her again?" I asked Monte-Cristo.

He shook his head. "I promised to exchange her for Valentine," he said, "and I always keep my word. I know she attempted to break the deal, but I hold myself to higher standards."

"So I note," Dupin said, a wry smile on his lips. He glanced about the battlefield. "It might be as well to depart now, before the police arrive. The Countess may have some difficulty explaining the situation, and I have no desire to see the inside of the Sûreté from the point of view of a suspect."

Monte-Cristo nodded. "Gentlemen, you have my thanks for your assistance in this matter. I will return this lady to her husband. My other carriage is at your convenience. Know that you have made yourself a friend today who will go to great lengths should you ever have need of his services." He held out his hand to both of us, and we shook it.

"It seems to me," Dupin remarked, "that we may have the better part of the bargain. You have shown what your friendship means quite graphically."

The coach we had taken to reach the woods had now returned, and Dupin and I hastened into it, and away from the scene. I looked back, and saw that the other coach, driven by Jacopo, also departed.

"It might have been a mistake to allow the Countess to go free," I remarked to Dupin.

"What else could we do with her?" he inquired. "We could not hold her captive, and we have no evidence to offer the police of her guilt in anything. She was, after all, out of town when the kidnapping occurred. No, a woman like that will get herself into further trouble, and we may be able to deal with her at such a time." He was lost in thought for a few moments, and then sighed. "Well, my friend, there is only one small task left for us to do." He rapped on the roof of the carriage, and called up to our driver: "To the Sûreté, if you please!"

Once there, we were ushered into the office of our acquaintance, Inspector Couperin. He glanced up from paperwork he was completing, and then motioned us to take seats and await him. As he finished his work, he laid down his pen and regarded us. "You have further information on the murder at Ste-Mathilde?" he asked.

"Not exactly," Dupin replied. "In fact, I have come to tell you that I now feel I can agree with you, and that I may have been mistaken."

Couperin preened himself. "Indeed?"

"Yes. I believe that you were quite correct–the whole business was over the honor of a lady. And I do not think that you will uncover the identity of the other party."

The Inspector was almost bursting with pleasure. "Well, Dupin," he said generously. "It takes a big man to admit that he may have been wrong. So it would seem that, at least on occasion, the romantic view of life might be right."

"It would seem so," Dupin agreed. He rose and shook the policeman's hand. "Good day, Inspector."

As we left, I frowned at my friend. "That was most duplicitous of you, Dupin."

"Was it?" he asked, casually. "I told him no lies. And I do not believe that Couperin will uncover the name of the man who threw that villain from the tower."

"You allowed him to believe that he was right and you were wrong," I protested.

"Let matters lie as they will," he said, unconcerned. "I have not so feeble an ego that I must be proven right every time. Besides, those who are important know the truth. And there is something else that I know."

"What is that?"

"That there are pipes and glasses of a fine amontillado awaiting us at the house of Monsieur Grunet. Let us not keep him waiting, my friend!"

Now, it is Judex (last seen in Matthew Baugh's tale) who returns, appropriately within the context of another Feuillade classic: Les Vampires. *The gifted Chris Roberson happily crosses the lines from pulp to film to comics to show that World War I France was indeed the crucible in which myths were forged...*

Chris Roberson: *Penumbra*

Paris, 1916

The morning papers all carried the story on their front pages, most with huge banner headlines above the fold. Perhaps the various editors thought their readers needed a diversion from another day's litany about the numbers of young French servicemen dead in a recent military action, or about ground lost to or won back from the Boche. Or perhaps they knew that glamorous crime, particularly so close to home, would always sell newspapers. Either way, over breakfast all of Paris was buzzing.

Ironically, of all of the reporters covering the event, Philippe Guerande of *Le Mondial* was the one most skeptical of the proposed connection to the infamous gang, the Vampires. Guerande had been writing about the suspected activities of the Vampires since the spring, even if his reports were buried in the back pages of the metropolitan section before the decapitation of Inspector Dural made front-page headlines. The editors at *Le Mondial*, though, knowing full well how many copies a Vampires-related lead story could sell, had commissioned one of their staff artists to do a somewhat hasty sketch of the figure clad in skin-tight black slinking away across the rooftop, alongside an inset photo of the victim's body lying on the pavement, the crushed remains tastefully covered in a white sheet the instant before the photographer had taken the shot.

Through the black-and-white grain of the photo, faint shadows could be seen appearing on the impromptu shroud, where the blood pooled on the body had begun to seep through the fabric. The editors then placed above the photo and pen-and-ink sketch a headline reading, "*VAMPIRES THROW VICTIM FROM HIGH WINDOW–FLEE SCENE.*"

Guerande's article, however, left open the question of whether the infamous gang was or was not truly involved, stating merely that a man had fallen to his death from a high story window of a residential building, and that a figure clad in skin-tight black from head to toe had been seen fleeing the scene of the crime, running across the rooftops.

At the home offices of the banker Favraux, the topic was mentioned in passing, dispassionately, as one might discuss the weather or the quality of one's dinner of the previous night. Not 200 miles away, war raged, and young men bled out their last strung up on wires in No Man's Land, or huddled for shelter in trenches and hastily-dug foxholes, dreading the whiff of gas that might come drifting across the lines–chlorine, phosgene, or worse yet, mustard gas–but within the cool confines of Favraux's wood-paneled study, all was peaceful and serene. Favraux and his guest had business to discuss, and the concerns of the wider world dwindled in comparison.

Favraux's personal secretary, Vallières, an older man with snow-white beard and hair neatly trimmed, was on hand as he always was on these occasions; but he kept to the shadows at the corner of the room, silent, unobtrusive, never noticed unless and until he was needed. Vallières was the most trusted of all Favraux's servants and employees, and the only one to whom the banker entrusted his most guarded secrets. Favraux never kept notes during his meetings, or a personal diary. Instead, he looked to Vallières to monitor what was discussed, and to recall specific details on demand. So it was with great care that Vallières followed the conversation between Favraux and his young guest.

Dr. Wayne, a young American in Paris on an extended honeymoon, had opened discussions with Favraux a few weeks previous about potential European investments for his family fortune. The sole heir of a considerable estate, Wayne was eager to see his fortunes grow, and Favraux had convinced the young American that he was best qualified to assist. On that morning, Wayne and Favraux were in the midst of yet another in a seemingly endless series of meetings about investment opportunities.

Wayne was prepared to invest some considerable capital into a number of funds selected and managed by Favraux, but he had need of a short-term loan while a cashier's check was drawn up and sent from the States. In return, he would provide an extremely valuable piece of jewelry as collateral. After feigning reluctance for an appropriate span, the banker Favraux quickly agreed to the arrangement. Vallières well understood why. The gem, which Wayne's wife was bringing from their rooms at the Park Hotel, was a fire-opal of immense value, mined in the Xinca region of the Republic of Guatemala some years before. Famously known as the Gotham Girasol, it was easily worth one hundred times the loan that it secured. If Wayne paid back the loan–along with the exorbitant interest rate Favraux was charging, compounded weekly–it was all to the good, but if he should default, and the gem remain in Favraux's possession, so much the better.

Favraux's distress was obvious and genuine, then, when Mrs. Wayne arrived in tears and without the gem in her possession.

"Oh, darling," she said, throwing herself into her husband's arms. "You simply must forgive me. I... I no longer have the Gotham Girasol."

Dr. Wayne stiffened, and cast an uncomfortable glance to his host before turning his wife's face upwards and looking her in the eyes.

"Martha," he said, trying to sound calm but his voice audibly strained, "whatever do you mean?" His French was as good as hers, which is to say passable, but pronounced with a thick-tongued American accent that fell hard on Gallic ears.

"It was stolen from me nearly a week ago," Mrs. Wayne answered, her voice quavering. "I was wearing it when we attended that ball on Avenue Maillot, and when I was woken by the police the next morning, I found it gone." She bit her lip, her eyes flashing. "I wanted to tell you, but I was simply so overwrought by its loss that I couldn't bring myself to mention it before now."

Dr. Wayne held onto his wife for a moment, as his gaze drifted and settled on the middle distance, thoughts racing behind his eyes. Then he released her, and slumped into a chair. Mrs. Wayne, sobbing vocally behind a handkerchief, kept stealing glances at her husband, almost as though gauging his reactions.

The Waynes did not need to explain to Favraux or to Vallières about the ball on Avenue Maillot the week before. All Paris knew about that night. It had made the front pages of all the papers, just as the murder had done that morning, and in both cases the Vampires were suspected.

Several days earlier, the Baron de Mortesalgues had held a grand ball at his home on Avenue Maillot, in celebration of his niece's birthday. Over 100 of the brightest lights of Parisian aristocracy, from financiers to artistes, rushed to the reception. At the stroke of midnight, the doors were locked from the outside and, by all accounts, a strange gas entered the salon. All of those trapped within found themselves succumbing, passing into unconsciousness and not waking until the authorities arrived in the morning. No one was hurt, but the Baron, his niece and all of the jewelry and valuables in the room were missing. Neither the Baron nor his niece had been seen since that night. Authorities feared the worst, that they had fallen prey to the infamous Vampires, or to the criminal organization led by the villainous Moreno, only recently escaped from jail. Parisians had not been so fascinated with criminal exploits since the days of Fantômas, as the circulation figures of the daily newspapers certainly proved.

After a long moment, Dr. Wayne composed himself, and rose from the chair, straightening his waistcoat.

"Mr. Favraux, you must accept my apologies," he said, turning to his host. "It appears that I will not be able to provide you collateral, after all, and as a result my wife and I might be forced to cut short our stay in Paris."

Favraux bristled visibly. Vallières knew his employer's moods and tempers well, and could see that the banker was pained at the thought of not laying hands on the precious gem, to say nothing of the interest he had planned to collect on the loan. However, if Dr. Wayne were to return to the States without first investing in the banker's funds, Favraux stood to lose a great deal more. Just a few days' grace, and the cashier's check would arrive in Paris, but without the short-term loan to cover expenses, Wayne and his wife would have to leave almost immediately.

"Well, my dear Dr. Wayne," Favraux answered, visibly pained by what he was about to say, "we cannot allow the criminal element and the capricious whims of fate to interfere with the business of men, now can we? Absent the security of the gem as collateral"–he paused, his face flushing red with suppressed anger and anxiety–"I am still willing to loan you a small sum, sufficient to allow you to stay on in Paris until our business is concluded."

Dr. Wayne took Favraux's hand, visibly relieved.

"I cannot thank you enough for your generosity, Favraux," he said. "It would have been most... unfortunate, if our long negotiations would have been for naught."

The hard glance Dr. Wayne gave his wife made it clear to Vallières for whom such an outcome would have been the most unfortunate. Wayne was not the most doting husband, and for all of his wealth and refinement, he had a certain rough edge that Vallières found unsettling. No wonder his wife spent so much of their honeymoon by herself at cabarets and restaurants, while he whiled away his hours in business meetings with Favraux.

Once the arrangements for the loan were completed, and polite words were exchanged all around, Dr. Wayne and his wife took their leave.

When they had gone, Favraux dismissed Vallières for the rest of the day. The banker's daughter Jacqueline, had convinced him that his grandson needed more masculine attention, since her own husband had died nearly three years before. As a result, Favraux had reluctantly agreed to take his daughter and grandson to the circus for the afternoon, though it was obvious that he regretted the decision.

Vallières, unaccustomed to being at his liberty so early in a working day, saw nothing for it but to go home. Pausing only to pick up a copy each of the day's papers from the newsagent on the corner, he returned to the apartments he kept in another quarter of the city.

Once safely in his study, Vallières dropped the newspapers on his cluttered desk, piled high with papers, notes and photographs. He laid his coat carefully across the back of a chair, and crossed the floor to an armoire with a full-length mirror set in its door.

With practiced motions, Vallières removed his snow-white beard and mustaches, and pulled off his wig of snow-white hair. Dropping them into a bowl on a side table, he stood straighter, an intense scowl on his young, lean face. He smoothed back his short black hair, and regarded himself momentarily in the mirror. Having put aside the mask of the ever-loyal, always patient Vallières, he stood revealed for who he truly was: Judex!

Of course, Judex himself was something of a mask. Not the name with which he was born, he chose it by necessity, to help him fulfill the oath he made to his mother, so many years before. An oath to avenge the death of his father, the Count de Tremeuse, who took his own life after losing the family fortune to bad investments. Investments made on the advice of an eager young banker, Favraux.

That his father died just as news arrived that a gold claim he had in Africa had come through, making him the owner of a fabulously rich gold mine, was an irony almost too cruel to bear.

Instead, fate had decreed that Judex would own a gold mine, along with his brother, who was currently in Africa overseeing its operations. His brother would return before the year was out, to help put into motion the next and final stage of their revenge against the banker. For the moment, though, Judex would continue to play the faithful servant, learning everything he could about Favraux and his dealings before making his terminal move.

And at the moment, Favraux's dealings included the young American couple, the Waynes.

Judex sat at his desk, and looked over the piles of newspaper clippings, bank records, notes, photographs, medical documents, receipts and vouchers. Ephemera and trivia, bits of information discarded in the wake of the young doctor and his wife. A portrait of a life painted in tiny bits of data, like the points in a Seurat painting.

Judex had been investigating Dr. Wayne and his wife as a matter of course, these past weeks. If the Waynes were good people, Judex would by subtle means attempt to steer them away from investing their money with Favraux. He could not stand idly by and watch another family ruined as his was. If the Waynes themselves were dishonest, unethical people, though, then they deserved whatever fate befell them.

Before that morning, Judex had found no reason to suspect their sincerity, nor to believe they were anyone but who they said they were. He had initially suspected that the couple might not be the Waynes at all, but might instead be Raphael Norton and Ethel Florid, Americans who had embezzled $200,000 from American millionaire George Baldwin and fled to Europe. Through careful investigation, though, he had been able to confirm that was not the case. They were, indeed, Dr. and Mrs. Wayne, and their fortune was their own.

Why, then, did Judex feel so strongly that something was amiss? Mrs. Wayne's recounting of the theft of the Girasol this morning, though emotional, was not convincing. It had too much the air of a rehearsed speech, of a dramatic address delivered on queue. She was lying, but about what?

The answer, Judex found, was right in front of him.

Amongst the piles of research materials on the Waynes was a recent clipping from the front page of *Le Mondial*, just starting to yellow with age. The headline boasted of the poisoning of a dancer named Marfa Koutiloff while onstage performing in a ballet entitled *Les Vampires*. The story had caught Judex's eye, as in a photo of stunned theatergoers accompanying the article Dr. and Mrs. Wayne could be seen, eyes wide with shock and horror.

Judex drew a jeweler's loop from the desk drawer and peered at the photo through its magnifying lens. Around the neck of Mrs. Wayne, he could make out the Gotham Girasol, suspended from a silver chain.

Judex laid beside that photo another, clipped from the society pages of *La Chronique de Paris* just a few days before. It was of Mrs. and Dr. Wayne, taken the evening of Baron de Mortesalgues' ball on Avenue Maillot. In the photo, the young couple were smiling happily, unaware that in a few hours' time they would be rendered helpless and unconscious by assailants unknown. Judex studied the photo through the jeweler's loop, as though seeing it for the first time. Dr. Wayne in evening wear, his wife in an elegant gown with a plunging neckline. Judex looked closer, to be certain.

He sat back, his brow creased. There could be no doubt. In the photo, Mrs. Wayne was clearly not wearing the Gotham Girasol. The gem had not been stolen that night at Avenue Maillot, because she had not been wearing it. That could account for why she didn't report the gem's theft the following morning, when the rest of the victims were reciting their losses and woes to the authorities. Why, then, concoct a flimsy tale about the gem's loss at the ball, nearly a week later?

Why was Mrs. Wayne lying?

Perhaps the Waynes were not all they appeared to be, after all.

Judex was convinced that the Vampires were involved in some fashion. There were simply too many points of congruence to dismiss them as coincidence–the Waynes in attendance at the ballet when Koutiloff is poisoned, and again at Avenue Maillot for the most daring robbery of the decade. What other connections might there be?

Judex was committed. He would investigate the Vampires in parallel with his ongoing researches into the Waynes, and determine whether the couple deserved his assistance, or whether they deserved to be damned along with the banker Favraux.

Judex was not the only one investigating the Vampires. The police were involved, naturally, their every available resource assigned the task of searching for the gang. Impatient at the progress of the investigation to date, though, the authorities had called in the assistance of private detectives like "Celeritas" Ribaudet and the famous Rouletabille, and citizens such as Cigale Mystère–a civilian adventurer who assisted the Parisian authorities from time to time, cruising the streets in his electric car, loaded down with futuristic gadgets and devices–and the Nyctalope–who prowled the nights for sign of the Vampires, his keen eyes seeing what others could. But so far no one had been able to track the Vampires to their lair, nor divine the mystery of who led the mysterious organization. There were whispers of a Great Vampire who directed his subordinates' movements from behind closed doors, and perhaps even higher echelons of power above even that, but they remained only whispers, nothing more.

But the police and the other mystery men could busy themselves tracking down the criminals. Judex was interested in matters only as they pertained to Favraux. What deviltry the Vampires did in the larger world was of no concern to him. Until his father had been avenged, there could be no justice.

It seemed to Judex prudent to begin his investigations into the Vampires at the site of their most recent crime. Their earlier exploits–the decapitation of Inspector Dural, the poisoning of Marfa Koutiloff, the mass robbery and possible kidnapping at the home of the Baron de Mortesalgues–he knew well enough from the detailed coverage provided each in the daily news. If there were hidden connections to the Waynes to be found, there might be secrets about this most recent case yet to be disclosed.

It took only a few hours investigation and a few francs placed in the right palms to turn up a number of interesting facts about the case. The victim, who had fallen to his death from a fifth story window, was one Jean Morlet, an associate a Monsieur Oreno who resided at that same address. However, Judex could find no record of this Oreno before the previous week. In addition, he was able to discover that Oreno had rented out the entire fifth floor of the building the day after the events at Avenue Maillot. Most surprising, Judex learned that the night before had not been the first attempted robbery at that address, but the second in less than a week. The police had apprehended the burglar attempting to break into Oreno's suite of room. The burglar, an American, was currently in jail awaiting trial.

The next day, once "Vallières" had completed his duties for the banker Favraux, Judex made for the jail, sure that he was feeling around the edges of some larger puzzle. It took only a few francs to learn the prisoner's name, and a few francs more to convince the policeman on duty that Judex should be allowed a brief counsel with him in private.

"I've already told the other inspector everything I'm going to say," the prisoner said, after Judex had been ushered into his cell. The policeman locked the door.

"Just call when you are ready to go, Monsieur," the policeman said, retreating down the hall.

Judex waited until the jailer was well out of earshot, and turned his attention to the American. He was young, just entering his twenties, with high, narrow cheekbones, a prominent hawk-nose and piercing eyes.

"I am not with the police, Allard," Judex said, drawing his cape tight around him, gazing at the American from beneath the brim of his hat. "I have questions of my own."

The American seemed to squirm beneath Judex's steady gaze.

"All right, then," he finally said, his eyes shifting to the ground. "What is it you want to know? It's not as if I've got anywhere else to be at the moment."

"You were arrested for attempting to burgle the residence of a Monsieur Oreno, which I will come to in a moment. But first, I'm curious to know why you are in Paris, Mr. Allard. Why come to a land in the grips of war, when you could easily live in safety at home?"

Judex could not help but think of Raphael Norton and his embezzled fortune. But if this were he, what had become of his female accomplice, Miss Florid?

"Look," Allard said, raising his chin defiantly, "I'm not about to sit out the war like those cowards back at home in the States, too fat and lazy to come to the defense of their European cousins. If all men don't act to stamp out evil at its root, it'll spread like a weed all across the globe. And then where will we be?"

Judex's mouth drew into a tight line, and he said, "I'm sure I don't know."

"Well, I couldn't sit idly by while others fought for the cause of justice," Allard went on. "I'm a… how do you say it in French?" He paused, and then said the English term, "barnstormer."

Judex nodded slowly, and translated into the French, "An aviator."

"Yes," Allard answered, "I'm an aviator. Anyway, I have relatives in Russia, and one of them, a Major Kentov, has agreed to arrange for me to be given a position in the Czar's air corps. Kentov was supposed to send word for me here in Paris, and then I'd go on and meet him in Russia. But I've been here a few weeks now, and I'm not sure if word is ever going to come. I'm starting to worry that Kentov might have died out on the Eastern Front, and then I might never get a chance to do my part against the Kaiser."

"If you already suspect that this Kentov will never contact you here, why remain in Paris? Why not just continue on to Moscow, come what may?"

Allard's gaze shifted, and a blush raised on his cheek.

"I have been… distracted," he finally said, a faraway sound to his voice.

Judex pulled his cape tighter, but nodded slightly.

"Very well," he said. "Now we come to the matter of Monsieur Oreno. Who is he to you?"

"He's a cheating bastard, and a liar!" Allard scowled, teeth clenched, his eyes flashing. "Oreno stole something of considerable value from me, and I was just trying to get it back."

"How did you know him?"

"I've been going to a cabaret called the *Veuve Joyeuse* a great deal these past few weeks," Allard said, a wistful tone creeping into his voice, "and I met Oreno there one night. We talked a bit about the art of mesmerism, which he claimed to have some special knowledge of. I don't have any proof of this, but I think that he might have clouded my mind in some way. How else could he have known about the…" He paused, and bit down on the next word he'd been about to say. "About the item, that is," he finished, lamely.

"What was it that he stole from you?"

Allard's expression was guarded, his lips drawn tight.

"Something very dear to me," was all he would say.

A few nights later, after fruitless investigations, Judex returned to his apartments late in the evening. He looked forward to the day when his brother returned to Paris. His mission was a solitary one, but it would be nice to pass the time with someone, on occasion. Someone with whom he could lower his guard, drop the masks and just be himself. Whoever that truly was.

Judex's rooms were darkened, but he knew in an instant that something was amiss. A subtle scent on the air, a tingling sensation on the back of his neck. Once the door was shut and locked behind him, he knew. He was not alone.

"Do not turn on the light," came a soft, sultry voice from the darkness. "Or, if you must, turn on only the table lamp. It is so much nicer that way, don't you think?"

Judex's fingers ached for the brace of pistols he kept in the armoire, a dozen steps across the room. He would never go out unarmed again. In a flash, he calculated the path and distance to the armoire, the seconds needed to reach it and open the door, grab and aim the pistol–if the intruder were armed, he'd never reach it in time.

"If you're thinking of these," the voice from the darkness said, followed by the distinctive sound of a pistol's hammer being pulled back, "I liberated them from the cupboard when I came in. I do hope you don't mind."

Judex stood in place, but reached down to the table at his knees and switched on the lamp.

Seated in his chair, with her feet up on the desk, was a woman wearing a skin-tight black jumpsuit. She was covered head to toe, with only her face left revealed. Her smoldering, fierce gaze caught Judex's, and she smiled.

"A pleasure to make your acquaintance, Judex," the woman said, gesturing him towards the couch with the barrel of the pistol, the other held casually in her lap.

"Who are you?" Judex stood his ground, arms crossed.

"Who I am is not of particular importance at this juncture, but whom I represent most definitely is."

"The Vampires," Judex hissed through his teeth.

"Got it in one." The woman smiled. "I have come to tell you something. This murder that you've begun investigating, the man who fell to his death from that building–the Vampires had nothing to do with it. Our leader has only recently become aware of your existence, and has ordered that you be left alone for the moment because he is not yet sure whether you can be of use to us in future. If you interfere in our affairs, though, and go from being a potential asset to being a nuisance, we will be forced to eliminate you."

"And to forestall this you deny one of your crimes? How do you benefit?"

The woman bristled, a cloud passing momentarily across her smooth features.

"We deny none of our actions!" The woman gestured with the pistol, and Judex tensed involuntarily, anticipating a shot. "Did we cut the head from that oaf Dural? Yes! Did we poison that bitch Koutiloff? Yes! But did we throw this Morlet to his death last night? Most definitely not."

"Why should I believe you?" Judex's eyes narrowed.

"Because if we were truly guilty of the killing, we wouldn't be warning you away. We'd just kill you for interfering in our business. But I prefer to kill those who deserve to die." Her mouth drew into a line, and she added in a hushed whisper, "Like that bastard Moreno."

"And what about the Avenue Maillot heist? Do you deny that one, as well?"

The woman jumped to her feet, tossing one of the pistols to the ground with a thud, and pointing the other square at Judex's chest.

"You mention Avenue Maillot to me?" She snarled, white teeth bared behind curled lips. "Would it surprise you to learn that even the Vampires can be victims, at least in this case? That the plunder from that night was stolen from us before we'd even reached the safety of our home?" The woman began to walk to the open window, her expression grave. "If ever I lay hands on that bastard Moreno…" she began, her voice trailing off into silence.

When she reached the window, her attention briefly turned away from him, Judex prepared to rush forward, intending to tackle her to the ground. As though she could sense his intentions, though, the woman spun around, and pointed the barrel of the pistol directly at Judex's face.

"Please don't try that," the woman said, sounding again all sweetness and light. "I don't want to have to hurt you unnecessarily, and it would be a shame to mar such a striking profile."

With that, the woman tossed the pistol to the ground, and stepped over the sill to the ledge beyond. When Judex rushed to the window to look out, she had already disappeared into the night.

Judex could not sleep that night. The information the woman provided, however unintentionally, was the last puzzle piece that he needed. He had only to confirm his suspicions, and all would be clear.

Returning to the night air, his cape wrapped around him and his hat pulled down low over his brown, Judex made his way to the scene of the crime. With ease, he did what Allard and the black-suited burglar had both failed to do, breaking into the home of Monsieur Oreno without once being seen. Oreno was not in, no doubt meeting with his associates at the *Veuve Joyeuse* cabaret at that hour. Crime does not keep workman's hours, after all.

In a locked bedroom in Oreno's suite, Judex found what he was looking for, and more besides, packed into several valises and a few small chests. It was the work of just a few minutes to transfer the contents of the cases and chests to his automobile, parked on the street outside. One item in particular he slipped into his pocket.

Driving to the Public Assistance Bureau to make a donation, Judex cursed himself for his earlier blindness. Monsieur Oreno. "M. Oreno." He should have seen it long before.

Mrs. Wayne was packing up her belongings in their rooms at the Park Hotel. Her husband had concluded his business with Favraux that afternoon, and they would now be returning home to America.

"Your pardon," said a voice from the shadows, and Mrs. Wayne leapt a few inches into the air, her heart in her throat.

"I mean you no harm," the voice continued, and Judex stepped out from a darkened corner, silent as a ghost.

"W-who are you?" Mrs. Wayne clutched a black leotard to her chest, wringing the fabric in her hands, her packing forgotten.

"You can call me Judex."

"Did you say… justice?"

Something like a smile played across Judex's mouth.

"No. Judex. But it is about justice that I've come. I know what you have done, Mrs. Wayne."

Judex pointed to the black leotard in her hands, with scalloped-edge bat wings attached at the shoulders and wrists.

"I see that you even kept the costume you wore that night."

Tears began to stream down her cheeks.

"I hadn't meant for anyone to get hurt, honestly. But that man chased me out onto the ledge, and then he fell, and then… But I just had to... I had to get it back…"

Judex held out his hand and opened his palm, revealing a fire-opal with a faint purple cast and lights dancing deep within. The Gotham Girasol.

"I broke into Oreno's rooms," Judex explained, "and found what remained of the loot from the Avenue Maillot robbery. Ironically, the Girasol had ended up in amongst the other pilfered goods, despite the falsity of your claims. I find that somewhat… amusing."

Mrs. Wayne looked with wide eyes at the gem in Judex's palm, and then met his eyes.

"You mean…?"

"Yes, Mrs. Wayne, I know that you gave away the Gotham Girasol some time before the night of the ball."

Mrs. Wayne struggled to take a breath.

"What will you…?" She paused, swallowing hard. "That is, what will you do with…?"

"I have given the pilfered goods to the Public Assistance Bureau, where they will no doubt serve society better than they ever could have done in the hands of their rightful owners. I am, however, prepared to return the Girasol to you."

"No," she said, turning her eyes away. "I could not bear to hold it. There is another who should have it, who should always keep..." Her words choked off in a stifled sob.

"Allard," Judex said simply.

Mrs. Wayne was shocked, but she nodded, slowly.

"You met him at a cabaret, unless I miss my guess," Judex went on, "and you found him a welcome change to your somewhat brusque and acerbic husband, the good doctor. You wanted to give him a token of your affection, one which you prized above all others. Otherwise, the gesture would be meaningless, no?"

Mrs. Wayne nodded still, as though hypnotized.

"No," she said, then shook her head, as if to clear away cobwebs. "I mean, yes. I mean..." She drew a deep breath, collecting herself. "I met... him... a few weeks ago. My husband had been so busy with his meetings that it was almost as if we weren't going to have a honeymoon at all. I started going out on my own, to the restaurants and cabarets. It was at the *Veuve Joyeuse* that I met... Mr. Allard. So intense, and an aviator. How dashing he was. I suppose you could say that we fell in love. I gave him the gem in a moment of passion, symbol of my feelings for him. But I'd soon have reason to regret it."

Mrs. Wayne glanced at the gem, still resting in Judex's palm.

"The next day, my husband told me that we might need the gem for collateral. I knew that any day he might come and ask me for it, and I wouldn't have it. As soon as I could, I rushed to see Mr. Allard, to get it back, but he told me that it had been stolen by this Oreno character. He promised he'd get it back from Oreno, but the next thing I knew Mr. Allard had been arrested."

"So you had no choice but to steal it yourself," Judex said.

"Yes. I'd heard all the stories about the infamous gang, the Vampires. I hired a costume from the Costumier Pugenc, the same I'd seen in the ballet weeks ago, with the idea that if anyone saw me breaking into Oreno's apartments, the blame would be cast on the Vampires gang. The man came upon me just as I was entering the room, though, and then he fell to his death. After that, I knew I'd never have another chance at stealing it back, so I told my husband it had been stolen that night at the Avenue Maillot ball."

Mrs. Wayne took a deep breath and sighed. She smoothed the fabric of the black leotard in her hands, and then set it gently back on the bed.

"I suppose you will turn me over to the police now," she said, sounding resigned. "I am wanted by the law, after all."

"I wouldn't give a bent *sou* for the law," Judex said, tightening his hand into a fist around the gem. "The law turns a blind eye while villains prosper, allowing a cancer to eat away at society's heart. No, I care nothing for the law. I care only for justice."

Mrs. Wayne shook her head, looking like she wanted to spit.

"Justice? Do you want to know about justice, Monsieur Judex? Then I will tell you. I have just learned today that I am with child. Pregnant. And I don't know whether my husband or my beloved is the father."

"You talk to me of justice? What are your sordid affairs to me or to Lady Justice?"

Mrs. Wayne lifted her chin, defiant.

"Because even if the law never lays a hand on me, I still pay the price for my deeds. My own life is ended here, for the sake of my unborn child. Were it otherwise, I would leave my husband, and my beloved and I would be together forever. But what kind of life would my child have, with a penniless aviator as a father? Always at the fringes of society, living forever in the shadows. No, better to return home with my husband, letting him think the child is his, so that my baby can grow up in comfort, with all the opportunity in the world. So what if my heart belongs to another, and I die inside a little every moment we are apart? I live now for the sake of my child."

Judex stood silent, appraising her, and found he had nothing to say. Justice, the only god Judex worshipped, indeed moved in mysterious ways.

Tucking the gem back into his pocket, Judex strode to the door, making to leave. He drew his cape around him, already seeming to blend into the shadows.

"Wait!" Mrs. Wayne said, stepping forward, raising a tremulous hand. "Will you see…?" Her breath caught in her chest, and she swallowed hard before continuing. "Will you see Mr. Allard again?"

Judex shrugged beneath his cape.

"I do not know, madam."

"If you should see him, could you give him the Girasol for me? As a keepsake to remember me by?"

Judex's expression remained hard, but he nodded. He turned to the door.

"Only," Mrs. Wayne said, taking another step forward, "please don't tell him about the child. He has his own life to lead, and doesn't need a shadow hanging over him."

Judex did not turn around, but nodded again.

"I will," he said softly, and then disappeared into the night, leaving Mrs. Wayne alone with her memories.

The next day, an anonymous party posted bail for the American aviator, and Allard was released on his own recognizance. When his possessions were returned to him, Allard was surprised to find among them an envelope containing a near-priceless fire-opal and a railway ticket. The train left Paris that afternoon, heading east. Allard would take it as far as the state of combat would allow, and make it the rest of the way to Moscow on foot, if need be.

That same afternoon, Dr. Wayne and his wife were already in Le Havre, boarding a luxury liner that would carry them back to the United States.

In the home offices of the banker Favraux, Judex hid behind the mask of Vallières, waiting for his moment to strike.

And in the streets of Paris, the Vampires still prowled the shadows, and the search for them continued.

Robert Sheckley, the masterful author of The Seventh Victim *and* Dimension of Miracles, *walks to his own drummer. Rather than casting his mind's eye towards the past, it is in the future that he chose to locate his story, a future in which pulp heroes–or their descendants!–are still confronted with variations of the same age-old mysteries ...*

Robert Sheckley: *The Paris-Ganymede Clock*

Paris, The Future

For Arthur Wimsey, the Fantômas matter began one morning in the office of Mr. Fairr, representative of Lloyd's of London. Wimsey had not met Fairr before. Fairr was thin and red-headed, with bright blue eyes that seemed to be gazing at the furthest shores of insurance heaven. Fairr lost no time getting straight to the point:

"We would like you to go to Paris to look into the safety arrangements that are in place for the Paris-Ganymede clock."

Wimsey nodded. "The newspapers say the French are taking unusual precautions."

"No doubt. But we want specifics. Only that will satisfy our underwriters."

"The exhibition opens tomorrow, in Paris."

"And you will be there."

Wimsey flew into Paris early the next morning and taxied directly to the Louvre, where the Paris-Ganymede clock was being exhibited. It had been called that since the Ecole Polytechnique-sponsored expedition to the Moons of Jupiter had returned from Ganymede with what was arguably mankind's most important discovery: an artifact attesting to the existence of an alien civilization.

Wimsey was a man of medium height, stockily built, with a full head off close-cut sandy hair, just beginning to go bald on the crown. He was dressed in a tweed suit and solid leather shoes. He carried a small overnight bag and a furled umbrella, both of which he checked as soon as he entered the Louvre. He showed his special pass at the door. He noted the helicopter circling slowly, high overhead. There were a surprising number of armed guards in dark blue uniforms.

Inside the Louvre, Wimsey joined a group moving slowly toward the Paris-Ganymede exhibit, situated not far from Leonardo da Vinci's *Mona Lisa*, previously the main attraction. The natural movement of the crowd, urged along by the guards and attendants, carried him to the line in front of the exhibit room. He joined it.

Wimsey had read extensively about the clock before making this trip. Nevertheless, he wasn't prepared for the shock he received once he got a good look at it. Although roughly circular, there was something about its curves, something about the carefully sculpted irregularities of its surface. It was a large clock, running on no detectable power source, with three hands moving clockwise at different speeds and two moving counterclockwise. The sum of its qualities said that this machine was no product of Earth, nor of any place that Earth had ever visited. No human had built this thing, which was discovered under a mound of slag on the uninhabited world Ganymede. It was proof positive of the existence of an intelligent race other than humans.

Looking over the crowd, Wimsey paid no special attention to the people. He didn't stare at anyone; his eyes were wide and unfocused. Other detectives might look for someone suspicious; Wimsey was looking for quite the opposite. He wanted to find the least suspicious person in the room, the one you could not possibly suspect.

There were several old people in the room. They walked slowly and with evident pain. You could see that they had barely made their way up the steps, much less be suspected of anything more dire. His gaze rested for a moment on them: an old man who walked with the aid of two canes. An obese woman, supported on the arm of a young man, who appeared to be a paid attendant. Another old man, walking with difficulty, this one accompanied by a young girl of 10 or 12, with long blonde hair, dressed in nice clothing and with black patent leather shoes.

The exhibit was held in an almost square room with a door at either end, one an entrance, the other an exit. In the middle of the room, on a raised dais, there was a metal table. On that table, resting on a bronze tray, was the clock.

There were guards in the corridor outside the room, and three guards within the exhibit room itself. They all carried walkie-talkies. There was a huge crowd trying to get to see the artifact. It was the symbol of the new religion of space. For years, this religion had languished, a religion nearly everyone gave lip service to, but few expected to see in any tangible form. But now it was different. The Paris-Ganymede clock was a genuine alien artifact-proof positive of the existence of alien others.

There were about 50 people in the room. Hundreds more were standing in line in the corridor outside, waiting for guards to let them go in. It was 11 a.m. The people waited patiently: this was their appointment with the unknowable future.

Some people took photographs. Some made little sketches on pads. One man was creating a watercolor. He had a pad of watercolor paper, a tiny easel, little tins of paints and pans of tinted water. The guards were suspicious of him at first, thinking he might be a fanatic, prepared to hurl his paints at the clock. But they had grown used to him now; he seemed to represent no danger.

It was all quiet, serene, almost holy. The electric clock on the wall ticked from 11:05 to 11:06. And, at that moment, the lights went out.

There was a moment of stunned silence. A woman gasped. A man essayed a feeble joke. A guard's loud voice called out, "No panic, if you please! Remain calm! Temporary power failure! The lights will return in a moment." There was a rustle of movement. Someone has fainted. Someone said, "Mother! Are you all right?"

Emergency lights, set high on the walls, went on. They were dim, colored red, and gave the room and its contents a rather infernal appearance. The room took on the baleful look of a scene from Hell. The crowd's unease increased. The red lights flickered. Some claimed afterwards that they rippled or flashed. People started moving toward the exit, which quickly became clogged with struggling bodies.

People tried to fight their way through. A guard's bull-like voice bellowed, "Please! Remain calm!" But his shouts only increased the crowd's panic.

The guards' flashlights went on simultaneously. The strong white beams picked out people struggling in the doorways. There was a scream. One of the beams stopped on a small person, lying on the floor. The guard rushed over to help her, shoving several adults out of the way. It was the young girl with long flaxen hair and black patent-leather shoes.

"It will be over soon," the guard said, helping her to her feet.

"That oaf stepped on me!" she told the guard. She shrugged off his arm. "I'm getting out of here!" the girl declared, and moved into the crowd.

Very faintly, Wimsey could hear the sound of sirens outside. The police! Or was it the army? Somebody bumped him from behind; he staggered, but managed to retain his balance.

The lights came back on. Wimsey looked around, but couldn't see the girl. There were people lying in the exit. Guards were clearing up the tangle.

People were hustled out of the exhibition room. Armed soldiers entered, pushing the crowd against one wall.

"Make way! This is official business!"

The head guard took a deep breath, turned off his flashlight and walked over to the soldiers.

"No reason to be so rough. It's all right now."

"All right?" one of the soldiers said. "In that case, where's the gadget?"

"What are you talking about? What gadget?"

"The clock! The Paris-Ganymede clock! Where is it?"

The guard looked at the exhibit. The table was there, the tray was there, but the clock, the priceless exotic alien clock, was missing.

There was only one item on the tray. It was a black calling card. Wimsey was able to get a look at it. It contained, in a swirling white script, the single word–*Fantômas*!

After leaving the Louvre, Wimsey went to the Conciergerie and asked for the officer in charge of the Paris-Ganymede clock case. He was given a name, Commissioner Robin Muscat, but was told that Muscat had no time to see him at present. Wimsey took out his calling card, scribbled a few words on the back and asked that it be delivered to the Commissioner. He waited, and 15 minutes later, a patrolman ushered him to an elevator and then to a room at the end of the third floor. He entered, and took a seat when the receptionist asked him to wait for a moment. Ten minutes later, he was in Muscat's office.

"I didn't know the British were so interested in this," Muscat said. He was a large man, soft-looking in carelessly brushed dark clothing. The expression his face was hard, alert, wary.

"It's an insurance matter," Wimsey said. "Lloyd's sent me out to look over the protection you are–I should say were– affording the Paris-Ganymede clock. I am able to report that your measures seemed impeccable."

"Good of you," Muscat said dryly. "If I could have a framed copy, it will make a nice souvenir to take into my forced retirement."

"I have said that no possible blame could attach to you."

"Yes, but the Ministry will think otherwise. I am supposed to foresee the unforeseeable. Perhaps they will relegate me to some less demanding post–latrine inspector for the New Maginot Line."

Wimsey didn't reply.

Muscat said, "May I inquire of your interest in this, Mr. Wimsey? Is Lloyd's looking for a fall guy?"

"Not at all. Lloyd's wants to recover the clock."

"That may prove more difficult than finding it in the first place. How do you propose to do that?"

"By examining all suspects, to begin with."

"But there are no suspects!" Muscat said.

"Then we need to create some. May I suggest that you look for a girl of 10 or 12 years, with long blonde hair and black patent leather shoes, perhaps accompanied by an older man?"

"How do you know of this girl?"

"She was in the crowd when I visited the exhibition an hour or so ago."

"And you suspect her?"

"She is the least likely suspect. Therefore, she is a suspect."

"I suppose that's to be expected in a case involving the legendary Fantômas. How do you expect me to find this unknown girl?"

"By studying the surveillance tapes you have running all the time at the Louvre."

Muscat smiled faintly. "*You know my methods, Watson*," he quoted. "We have studied the tapes. They were blanked out or somehow malfunctioned 15 minutes on either side of the theft." He studied Wimsey's card. "It says here in very tiny print that you are a psychic investigator."

Wimsey nodded. "I don't talk about it much, but it's a fact."

"You solved the mystery of The New Hebrides liner some years ago."

"I was involved in that case. I wouldn't say I solved it, I discovered an important discrepancy in the testimony."

"And it is a discrepancy that you will look for here?"

Wimsey smiled faintly. "Something that will excite my psychic fancy."

"Fantômas is not enough?"

"Something in addition to Fantômas could be useful."

"You don't believe the man himself was responsible?"

"Anyone could write 'Fantômas' on a calling card. The name hints at a certain presumption rather than an established fact."

"You don't think Fantômas exists?"

"I'm pretty sure something psychic exists here," Wimsey said.

"But, my dear sir, how can this theft be involved with a psychic matter?"

"How can it not, once the name Fantômas is invoked?"

Muscat looked bewildered. "And why do you wish to speak with this girl?"

"I am merely following the clues least likely to succeed, since they are the most promising ones.'

"Oh, have no fear, I will find her. We have her photograph, as you pointed out; and her name will be in the guest book. I should have her by the end of the day."

Wimsey left and returned to his hotel room. Once there, he took off his shoes and put on comfortable slippers. Then he went to his luggage and removed a small leather case. Carrying this to the window, he removed the back with the screwdriver tip of his pocket knife. Within the box, he found a switch and turned it. Then, he said, in a conversational voice, "Mrs. Rosenberg, are you there?"

"I am here, Mr. Wimsey, just as you requested. May I pour myself a cup of tea before we begin?"

"By all means, Mrs. Rosenberg."

He waited. Presently Mrs. Rosenberg's voice came on again. "There! That's much better. I haven't taken my mind off the subject since you contacted me yesterday."

"Did you view the Exhibition room in the Louvre?"

"Indeed I did. I saw you there, Mr. Wimsey. You looked very nice in your new red tie. Was it a present?"

The old lady in Wiltshire was incurably nosy. Wimsey ignored her question and asked, "Did you see the theft of the Paris-Ganymede clock?"

"Of course, sir. It is what I was asked to observe, was it not? I saw everything clearly, as long as conditions permitted, sir. But conditions were not good."

"Was there a problem?"

"A phase shift, sir. Didn't you notice it? It ruins reception as long as it lasts."

"You're quite certain it was a phase shift?"

"Quite certain, sir. The red glow was unmistakable. I tried to get my familiar to look through it, but he refused."

"Did he say why?"

"He said that something unholy was going on. Something that had to do with black science. He refused to look until it was over. By that time, the clock was gone."

"You noted the time, of course?"

"Of course. The shift began at 3:05 p.m. Paris time, and ended 15 minutes later."

"I was there throughout?" Wimsey asked.

"You were, sir. Though you didn't seem to notice a thing."

"Typical of me. Did you notice a little girl with long blonde hair?"

"I did. There seemed to be an accentuation of some sort around her."

"Anything else?"

Mrs. Rosenberg shook her head. "Except that she was there one moment, gone the next. I can't account for her, sir."

"Excellent, Mrs. Rosenberg. I will get back to you presently. But first I must ask a favor of you."

"Of course."

"I need to speak to the Observer."

"How did you know about the Observer, Mr. Wimsey?"

"Never mind. Can you ask him to speak with me?"

"You must know he doesn't like interviews."

"I know. But I have to ask him something."

"Well," Mrs. Rosenberg said, "I'll see what I can do." She broke the connection.

Wimsey had time for a light dinner in a nearby cafe and a short walk along the Seine. Then, he returned to his hotel room. It took him a moment to realize there was a man sitting in one of the chairs near the window.

"You are the Observer?" Wimsey asked.

"I am indeed," the man said. He was short and strongly made, round-headed and with dark curly hair. He wore a plain dark business suit. His shoes were freshly polished, but there were cracks along the caps.

"You asked to see me, sir?" the Observer said.

"I did," Wimsey said. "And I must beg your forgiveness. I know this is unusual, perhaps unprecedented. But I am working on an important case and I didn't know who to turn to–"

The Observer lifted his hand. "Not to worry, Mr. Wimsey. I was glad to come. Frankly, I welcome the break. When they made me Observer, more years ago than I care to remember, they never bothered their heads about providing a relief for me. I had to train my own. They seemed to think I could just go on doing it. Well, that's simply not the way it is."

"I didn't know that."

"Of course not. Nobody knows about the Observer, except perhaps a psychic such as yourself. Oh, to be sure, some scientists have entertained the notion. I believe a fellow called Heisenberg discussed it with some of his colleagues a long time ago, and then published his thoughts in what they call a learned paper. I didn't read it. I may even have the name wrong. Was it Bohr I'm thinking of?"

"I really don't know," Wimsey said.

"Before your time, was it? Well, it was one of those chaps. One of the brilliant ones. It's all pretty obvious, as far as I'm concerned. The only mystery is who appoints the Observer."

"How did you get to be Observer?" Wimsey asked.

"Don't remember any longer. It was a long time ago. Someone told me I was the new Observer. Never mentioned what happened to the old Observer. And that's all there was to it."

"Yes, it works that way sometimes. That's more or less how I became a psychic detective. In my case, the gift ran in the family."

The Observer nodded, but asked no questions.

"I wanted to ask," Wimsey said. "Have you seen a man named Fantômas?"

"I don't know," the Observer said. "I see everyone. But I don't remember their names. It's not required, you know."

"I thought you might have noticed him. He's not a normal human, you know."

"Sorry, sir, I have nothing more to add."

"Thank you very much," Wimsey said.

The Observer left. Wimsey sat quietly in a chair. He noticed a flash of red out of the corner of his eye. Before he could react, he suddenly found himself in a different place.

He was sitting on a rounded boulder on a wide, bleak granite plain. It was growing dark. At the edge of the plain, a swollen red sun was sinking. Above it was a small black object, another sun, perhaps. It, too, was sinking. It was a melancholy sight. Wimsey had the impression of a dying world.

He turned and saw a bald old man sitting on another boulder to his left and slightly behind him. The old man was dressed in a dark blue robe. His features were human-like, but Wimsey didn't think he was human.

"Hello," he said.

"Hello, Mr. Wimsey. I am Adnan. My people sent me to give you some explanation of recent happenings."

"Thank you."

"We do not do this for you, personally. It is for ourselves. To set the accounts as correctly as we can at this point."

"Where does it begin?" Wimsey asked.

"With the clock."

Wimsey listened while Adnan explained that his people once lived on the moon called Ganymede. But it was not their home. During their space-traveling days, they had made a civilization on this world. It was one of many worlds they had settled, and then decided to abandon. There were difficulties with Ganymede. These could have been solved if the will had been there, but the will to populate other worlds had been lost after the paradigm shift that occurred. Adnan's people had decided to give up expanding into space. It was no longer necessary. They had a stable population of several billion on their home world. The home planet was in no danger of imminent catastrophe. It was time to reduce their numbers.

So Ganymede was stripped. All artifacts of their civilization, any evidence pointing to their existence, was taken away.

"Actually," Adnan said, "one thing remained. The artifact you called the Paris-Ganymede clock. There was a person assigned to carry it away. But this person died unexpectedly before this could be done. Knowledge of this did not reach us before your own spaceship landed on Ganymede."

"I am confused," Wimsey said. "Why was it so important for you to remove all artifacts? Why did you not want us to know of your existence? What has happened to the clock now? Who took it?"

"One thing at a time," Adnan said. "My dear friend, you must take what I give you in the limited time available to me and not try to look beyond it. A hundred lifetimes would not be sufficient for me to explain the reasons behind all our actions to you. To address the main point: we did not want to be discovered by you. We wanted to leave no clues as to our existence. The Paris-Ganymede clock was proof that an intelligent alien race did exist."

"What was so wrong about us knowing that?"

"You would have come looking for us. We knew that this quest, once there was some proof, would turn into a planet-wide obsession. It would become tantamount to looking for God–only with a much better chance of accomplishment."

"And what was so wrong about that?"

"From your point of view, nothing. From ours, a great deal. My race has come to a stage of contemplation of, and assistance to, each of its individual member. No one is left out, no one is ignored, no one is considered inferior. This has come about only in fairly recent times. Many other problems had to be solved first. Major political issues had to be settled, or at least a way had to be found to navigate through them. Racial differences had to be addressed. Religions had to be taken into account. This, and much more, had to be accomplished before we could turn to the individual."

Wimsey said, "I don't see where that situation affects your need to remain hidden."

"To remain hidden," Adnan said, "is to exclude. We excluded all other intelligent creatures alien to us. We had never encountered any before, so the point was academic until we encountered you humans."

"I don't see how that will accomplish anything. We have seen the clock. We know that another intelligent race exists."

"Oh, you know now. That is, some of you do. But in years to come, without a miraculous artifact to turn to, how long will your race believe it? Will you still believe it in a hundred years? In a thousand years? With no physical proof? In time, the Paris-Ganymede clock will be relegated to the annals of imaginary or fake history."

"I won't forget it," Wimsey said.

"That is why my people sent me. To satisfy you, personally. But if you tell this story, it and you will be relegated to the region of cranks with interesting but unprovable theories."

Wimsey nodded. He understood that what was happening to him now, was a story he could not tell. Not if he wanted to continue living a reasonably sane life.

"At least, tell me the truth about Fantômas. Is there such a being? Did he take part in what happened here? Is he one of your people, or something else entirely?"

"I can say no more," Adnan said. "You should know better than anyone, Mr. Wimsey, that there is always a mystery remaining. It is not necessary for you or anyone else to know the truth about Fantômas."

Adnan rose from the boulder and gathered his robe around him.

Wimsey said, "Are you just going to leave it at that? Without hope of Earth ever knowing the truth of this matter? It seems to me you're behaving in an underhanded fashion."

"That question will have to be pondered in our Councils. Are we acting ethically here? I don't pretend to know the answer. There is always the hope of a day to come when our race knows how to deal with yours. I doubt that either you or I will live to see that day."

Adnan made a graceful gesture, and vanished.

Wimsey was alone on the dying planet. There was just one thing left. Adnan seemed to have left behind the Paris-Ganymede clock. It was standing at the base of the boulder Adnan had been sitting on. Wimsey walked over and picked it up. As he bent to pick it up, as he touched it, there was a flash of light and a deep musical sound. Wimsey found himself back in his hotel room, without the clock.

No one could close this book better than Brian Stableford; no story could close this book better than The Titan Unwrecked. *Just as we have entered a new century, fraught with new perils, Stableford turns his eyes towards that same transition, a little over a century ago. His stage: a mythical journey where a great cast of writers mingles with an equally superb cast of legends...*

Brian Stableford: *The Titan Unwrecked; or, Futility Revisited*

North Atlantic, 1900

Having narrowly avoided an iceberg on her third return trip the *Titan* had fulfilled all the expectations entertained of her. She had, as anticipated, established the promptitude and regularity of a railway train in shuttling back and forth between New York and Southampton, making the distance between Sandy Hook and Daunt's Rock well within her six-day schedule almost without fail. When she set out westbound from Southampton Water on the evening of Boxing Day in the year 1900, she carried a full complement of passengers, whose expectations of celebrating the dawn of a new century on the night before their disembarkation in New York generated a mood of unparalleled cheerfulness and hopefulness from the moment she slipped anchor.

The *Titan*'s passenger-list was the customary deep cross-section of Anglo-American society, ranging from a duke and several millionaires in the finest staterooms to 2,000 hopeful emigrants in steerage, but the significance of the voyage–the last Atlantic crossing of the 19th century–had attracted an unusually high proportion of romantics of every stripe, including a large company of Frenchmen who had come from Cherbourg to join the ship, and a considerable number of writers–true literary men as well as newspaper reporters–in search of inspiration.

Certain elements of the *Titan*'s cargo were equally exotic, or so it was rumored. In addition to the usual mundane treasures, her secure hold was said to contain the entire contents of a recently-looted Egyptian tomb, and an exotic biological specimen of mysterious nature and origin had allegedly been brought from the Isle of Wight with only hours to spare before the hour of departure. Few, if any, of the crew had actually see these alleged marvels; although many more had seen a large collection of coffin-like boxes that had been stowed in the main luggage-hold, and a series of crates containing an elaborate array of what appeared to be electrical and acoustic apparatus, which had been carefully packed away in the space reserved for fragile items.

Because the purser had a mischievous sense of humor, almost all of the writers found themselves seated at the same table in the first-class dining-room for the evening meal whose serving began while the ship was rounding Land's End. The main course was the breasts of pheasants and partridges shot in the run up to Christmas Eve and hung over the festive season; the legs were, as usual, directed to the second-class dining room, while the offal was added to the sausage-meat reserved for steerage rations. The writers eyed one another suspiciously, all of them anxious for their relative positions on the highest literary ground and each one wondering who among them would be first to describe the *Titan* as a "ship of fools."

"I, for one," said Mr. Henley, seemingly by way of breaking the tension, "will not be sorry to see the very end of the so-called *fin de siècle*. I have had my fill of decadence, and I feel sure that the new century will be a vigorous and prosperous era, in which there will be a new alliance between the manly and aesthetic virtues–an alliance that will revolutionize moral and intellectual life, and quicken the march of progress."

This bold assertion caused some offense to Monsieur Lorrain, whose consumptive cough suggested that New York might be only a stopping-point for him, *en route* to the warm, dry air of Arizona or Nevada. "The century may change," he said, softly, "but the faltering steps of civilization will not recover their sturdy gait by means of optimism alone. We are products of the 19th century ourselves; there is a sense in which the *Titan* is already a ghost-ship, whose parody of life is but painted artifice."

Monsieur Lorrain's immediate neighbors, Mr. Huneker and Mr. Chambers, nodded in polite but half-hearted assent, but stronger support was provided by Mr. Vane. "We are indeed ghosts without knowing it," he said, dolefully, "sailing to judgment while in denial, afraid to confront our sinful souls."

"Well, I feel perfectly fine," said a reporter from the *Daily Telegraph*. "And I'm with Henley. The Boer War is won, the siege of the Peking legations is lifted, the Empire is in the best of health..."

His colleague from the *Daily Mail* took up the refrain: "Oscar Wilde's rotting in Paris; Lillie Langtry's on her way to New York aboard this very vessel, without her new husband in tow; Sherlock Holmes is busy investigating the robberies at Asprey's of Bond Street and St. James's Palace, and all's right with the world."

"Is Miss Langtry really aboard?" asked Miss Lee, who was the only woman at the 13-seater table. She had to turn around to squint myopically through her eyeglasses at the Captain's table, some 20 yards away.

"If it was my fellow Frenchman who robbed Asprey's," Monsieur Apollinaire observed, "your famous detective will be frustrated for once. Arsène Lupin will show him a clean pair of heels."

"Was it Lupin who looted Asprey's?" said Monsieur Jarry. "If so, then it must have been Fantômas who burgled St. James's Palace. The principle is the same, of course; they will both be safe in Paris by now, drinking absinthe with dear Oscar."

"I fear that you are wrong, Messieurs," said Monsieur Féval *fils*. "The unprecedented nature of the double crime strongly suggests that neither Lupin nor Fantômas–nor even the two of them in combination–could have planned and executed it. The *coup* was undoubtedly the work of the Brothers Ténèbre."

"The Brothers Ténèbre have not been heard of since your father's time!" Apollinaire protested. "And they were English, in any case. They merely masqueraded as Frenchmen."

"Not at all," said Monsieur Féval. "They are such masters of disguise that one must penetrate far more layers than that to reach their true identities. At bottom, they are personifications of sin itself, just as Mr. Holmes is a personification of intellect, while d'Artagnan and Cyrano de Bergerac are personifications of gallantry."

"We shall not see *their* like again," murmured Mr. Huneker, not entirely regretfully.

"Don't you believe it!" said the man from the *Daily Mail*. "There's a personification of gallantry sitting not 20 yards away, right up there at the Captain's table between Mr. Edison and the foreign fellow."

"Count Lugard," supplied his colleague from the *Telegraph*. "A Transylvanian, I believe. Old Hearst seems to have taken a dislike to him–can't think why."

"I recognize Tom Edison, of course," said Mr. Robertson, "but I don't know your paragon of gallantry. Who are the four young ladies lined up with them, though? They seem to be putting old Rockefeller and his chum Carnegie in a very sweet mood, and poor Lillie in the shade."

"Three of them are the count's daughters, I believe," Monsieur Féval said. "The fourth is traveling with Quatermain–his ward, I presume. Her name is Ayesha."

"Ah," said Mr. Chambers. "So the *Mail*'s model of gallantry is Allan Quatermain, the legendary discoverer of King Solomon's Mines. I thought he was dead."

"The rumor was exaggerated, apparently," Mr. Twain put in. "Happens all the time."

"Didn't he claim to be something of a coward in his account of the Kukuanaland expedition?" Huneker asked.

"Typical British modesty, my dear sir," said the *Mail* reporter. "Being American, you wouldn't understand that. The man's a shining example to us all–the perfect embodiment of the Imperialist creed."

"With men like him at its beck and call," the *Telegraph* man added, "who can possibly doubt that the Empire is destined to rule the world in the 20th century as it has in the 19th?"

"Every last one of us," murmured Monsieur Lorrain, too softly to be heard by any but his immediate neighbors–who were, of course, in complete sympathy with his judgment.

Meanwhile, at the Captain's 12-seater table, the alleged hero in question was looking around in all apparent satisfaction, while the Count from Transylvania was whispering confidentially in his ear.

"My friend," the Count was saying, "I cannot thank you enough for directing my attention away from Carfax Abbey towards the farther horizon. You are absolutely right–to take a creaky sailing ship for a port like Whitby would have been utter madness, when there is a vessel like this to carry my precious cargo. It was well worth the wait–and there are 2,000 peasants down below, you say, crammed into their bunks like veal in crates?"

"No trouble at all, my dear chap," Quatermain replied, magnanimously. "Had it not been for your suggestion of the ingenious trick of carrying the soil of our homeland with us, carefully secreted in the hold, Brother Ange and I might have been anchored to the Great Hungarian Plain indefinitely. You and I have given one another the precious gift of liberty, whose torch-bearing statue and glorious motto we shall salute side by side as we sail into New York while the century fades into oblivion."

"What motto is that?" asked the Count, curiously.

"Do as thou wilt," Quatermain replied. "It is the American Dream."

"Your charming ward assures me that you're an excellent storyteller, Mr. Quatermain," Captain John Rowland broke in, as he refilled his whisky-glass. "Not just the tale of how you discovered King Solomon's Mines, she says, but any number of other ripping yarns. I hope you'll entertain us with a few of them during the crossing."

"Ayesha flatters me, as always," Quatermain told him. "I'm afraid that my accounts of elephant-hunting and the many lost races of Africa's dark heart have grown a little stale by now. They are unable to compete in the nascent modern era with Dr. Watson's accounts of the amazing ingenuity of Sherlock Holmes–not to mention those delightful ghost stories Mr. James tells. Ah, if only they were with us, we should certainly be obliged to rescue them from the oblivion of the writers' table! Perhaps we should invite Mr. Twain to join us one evening–he's said to be a dab hand with a tall tale, I believe."

"If we ask Mr. Chambers nicely," Mrs. Hugo de Bathe–the former Lillie Langtry–put in, "he might revert to his old self and favor us with another account of *The King in Yellow*."

"We don't allow fellows like that on *this* table, Miss Langtry," Andrew Carnegie said.

"Not our sort at all," echoed John D. Rockefeller. "Two of them are newspaper reporters, you know."

"If there were one of *my* reporters on board," said William Randolph Hearst, "I'd make damn sure that he traveled second class, but these British journalists are too genteel by half. If you want good stories, it's no good looking at them."

"I fear that I'm only a humble white hunter myself," Quatermain said, with a sigh. "But I've been fortunate enough to lead a adventurous life, and to see some passing strange things. If they make good stories, it's generous fate that must be credited with their authorship. I couldn't make anything up to save my life."

"You're not so humble any more," the Captain observed. "You've as many diamonds as were stolen from Asprey's and St. James's put together, so they say. The produce of King Solomon's Mines has made you rich."

"I'm just one more soldier of fortune living on my capital," Quatermain said, with a sigh of regret. "There was one haul and one only–and I still feel guilty about having the monopoly. Such a pity that Good and Curtis never made it back! I might never have made it myself, if not for the loyal devotion of dear old Gagool! I can't compare with people who make money day by day by means of their industry and ingenuity, like Mr. Rockefeller, Mr. Carnegie, Mr. Hearst and Mr. Edison."

"Money makes itself, dear chap!" Rockefeller assured him, "If you let it have its way. Hard cash does hard work."

"That's the wonder of Capitalism," Carnegie added.

"With a little help from the ads," Hearst supplied. "You have to maintain demand to keep the cash registers ringing–but they'll ring in the new century with a mighty peal."

"I'm just a humble inventor," Edison assured the hunter. "Haven't a penny by comparison with these chaps. The utility of my inventions is its own reward. I'm content simply to have given the world such electrical wonders as the incandescent light bulb, the phonograph, the telephone, the perfect woman and the chair, not to mention the machine for communicating with the dead. I need no more financial reward than is adequate to fund my further experiments."

"A machine for communicating with the dead?" the Count queried. "We have not heard of that device in Eastern Europe."

"It's still in the last phase of its development," Edison confessed. "I have the pieces of the prototype carefully lodged below, with all the fragile goods. I put the final touches to the design in London, but I didn't have time to assemble the demonstration model. I thought of taking it to the exhibition in Paris, but I'd rather give the first glimpse of it to American eyes."

"There's no need to wait until New York, then," said Hearst, who had leaned forward attentively as soon as Edison had mentioned his new machine. "You have a better audience in this dining-room than you could hope to get in any exhibition hall in Manhattan. Even if we have to let the British reporters in, they won't be able to get their copy home before my papers hit the streets. Why not bring the machine ashore to a real blaze of publicity?"

"So that Mr. Hearst can steal yet another march on Joe Pulitzer," Rockefeller murmured to Carnegie.

"Be a damn sight more amusing than tales of shooting lions in Africa, at any rate," was Carnegie's whispered reply.

"Well, I don't know about that," Edison said to Hearst. "I'm not sure that the mid-Atlantic's the best place for that kind of chat. I've an idea that the dead might prefer to hang out in cities, just as we do."

"Do you really think so, Mr. Edison?" Ayesha asked, sweetly. "One hears as many tales of haunted wildernesses as of haunted houses–and there's no shortage of tales of haunted ships."

"If they're just like us," Captain Rowland put in, after taking another draught from his whisky-glass, "they probably love the *Titan*. Give them a change of scene, what?"

"Absolutely," Quatermain put in. "We have four more nights at sea ahead of us, and I doubt that my meager ability to emulate Scheherazade can possibly keep a company like this on tenterhooks for all that time. I'd dearly like to see Mr. Edison's machine in operation."

"I'd prefer to see his perfect woman!" the Duke of Buccleuch muttered.

The remark did not seem to be addressed to anyone in particular, but Edison heard it. "That was a private commission," he said, frowning. "And besides, we have five perfect women of flesh and blood seated at this very table, have we not?"

"You're far too kind," Ayesha said–although Mrs. de Bathe, who was now 47 years old, merely acknowledged the compliment with a slight nod of the head. The Count's companions, who did not seem to have a word of English between them, smiled vaguely as they were carefully surveyed by seven pairs of male eyes.

"Well, I guess it *might* be a good idea to try the machine out before we reach New York," Edison said. "It'll take some work, mind–I'll need to borrow a couple of your crewmen, Captain Rowland."

"Granted," Rowland said, generously. "I'll instruct them to set it up in the first-class saloon–under your supervision, of course. When can you have it ready?"

"Not tomorrow or the next night," Edison said. "It's a very tricky assembly. Might be ready on the 29th, I suppose."

"Excellent," said Captain Rowland, refilling his glass yet again. "What a fine voyage this promises to be!"

John Rowland was sleeping dreamlessly, as only a hardened drinker can, when he was awakened by his first officer, Mr. Hodgson.

"I'm afraid there's trouble in steerage, sir," Hodgson reported.

"There's always trouble in steerage," Rowland growled. "Anybody dead?"

"Five, sir–and talk of worse than murder."

"Five!" Rowland sat bolt upright in bed. Deaths in steerage were not uncommon in the course of a westbound journey, because the wretches that huddled into the accommodation in the lower decks by the thousand were often suffering from malnutrition and disease–conditions frequently exacerbated by the sacrifices they had made to purchase their tickets to a new life. To make thing worse, the Irish, in particular, tended to be exceedingly quarrelsome. To lose five on the first night out was, however, highly unusual. "And what the devil do you mean, *worse than murder*?" Rowland added, belatedly.

"Three of the victims are young men, sir, and two of them young women. All were said to be in relatively good health before boarding, although they looked damnably thin to me–but the point is, sir, that they've been exsanguinated."

"What on Earth does that mean?"

"It means they've been drained of all their blood, sir. Each of them has a ragged wound in the throat, in the vicinity of the jugular vein and carotid artery. There's talk of vampires, sir."

"Bats?" said the befuddled Rowland.

"No sir–human vampires, like Sir Francis Varney, who was said to have been hanged several times over, or that Hungarian countess who cut a swathe through Paris when Napoleon was first consul."

"Five bodies, you say?" Rowland repeated, pensively. "Do they think we have five vampires aboard?"

"Yes sir, that's the theory," Hodgson confirmed. "There are vigilantes roaming the lower decks already, sir, saying that if the vampires can't be caught, staked through the heart and beheaded today there'll be five more bodies tonight, and five more every night till we reach New York."

"Staked through the heart and beheaded? What kind of barbarians are these people?"

"Mostly Irish, sir. In fact, that's the moderate view. Some are saying that the five victims will rise from the dead to become vampires themselves, so that there'll be ten victims tonight, 20 tomorrow, 40 on the 29th, 80 on the 30th and a further 160 on New Year's Eve. If we were to be delayed at sea until the 2nd–which isn't so very improbable, if the weather report is to be trusted...."

"Nonsense," said Rowland. "Storms in the Atlantic are water off a duck's back to the *Titan*. We'll be in New York shortly after dawn on New Year's Day, come hell or high water!"

"Well sir, even if that's so, the total casualty figures calculated by the alarmist faction would take a fair bite out of the number of steerage passengers, even though we're riding full. Even if the numbers turn out to be a wild overestimate, there's another kind of alarmist wondering what might happen if the monsters were to turn their attention to the upper decks–in which case there might be a real tragedy, if, in fact, there really were any vampires aboard."

"Which there aren't, of course," said Rowland, confidently. "What have you done so far to quell the panic?"

"Mr. Black tried to reassure the frightened emigrants by pointing out that we'll be burying the five bodies at sea, and that it'd take a damnably clever vampire to find its way back to the *Titan* from the bottom of the Atlantic," Hodgson reported. "That might have been a mistake, in retrospect because it seemed to concede the possibility that there might actually be vampires involved, which it might have been wiser to deny point blank. Sorry about that, sir."

"That's all right, Hodgson," Rowland said, as he pulled on his uniform. "Black was only doing what he thought best, although they're hardly likely to take such assurances seriously from a second mate. It needs a captain's authority to make such things clear. Hand me that bottle of Scotch, would you? I need a nip to clear my head. Tell Mr. Black and the purser to meet me on the bridge–and find that fellow Quatermain. We may need help on this one, and he's a heroic sort, if what they say is true."

Mr. Hodgson hurried off to execute these orders. Rowland finished off the bottle and then made his way forward, lurching slightly in spite of the state-of-the-art stabilizers with which the luxury liner was fitted. Hodgson was already on the bridge, with the second officer and the purser, young Kitchener–but it was to Allan Quatermain that Rowland turned first.

"There's trouble afoot, Quatermain," he said. "Five people dead–steerage people, but paid for their passage nevertheless–and wild talk about vampires. It needs to be nipped in the bud. I'd like you beside me when I go down there to address the mob, if you're willing. It'll give them extra confidence, you see, you being a big game hunter and all. I'll tell them you'll look into the matter personally, if I may."

"You certainly may," Quatermain said. "I'll do everything I can to help, of course."

At that moment, the door burst open. A young man pushed his way past the sailors stationed beside it, muttering what Rowland assumed at first to be "murder," before he realized that this was one of the French contingent who had come over from Cherbourg on the *Deliverance* to meet the *Titan* at Southampton.

"Monsieur," said the Frenchman, "I am Edward Rocambole, the grandson and heir of *the* Rocambole, and I have come to offer my services as a detective!"

"I never heard of anyone called Rocambole," said Rowland. "Did you, Hodgson?"

"No, sir," said Hodgson.

"Nor have I," Black chipped in.

"Nor I," added Kitchener.

"Damn cheek, in any case!" said the Captain. "This is a British ship and I've already recruited the best possible assistance in Mr. Quatermain here." He leaned over to whisper in Quatermain's ear: "We don't need any help from some jumped-up Frog who thinks he's Paris's answer to Sherlock Holmes, do we Mr. Quatermain?"

"I think we can handle the matter between the two of us," Quatermain murmured. "Bud-nipping's a job best left to expert fingers, in my experience. Too many hunters frighten the game, you know."

"Exactly," said Rowland. Then he raised his voice again to say: "Won't be necessary, thanks all the same, Monsieur Cricketball."

"But I am the grandson of Rocambole!" Edward Rocambole protested.

"And I'm very probably the bastard grandson of King George IV, as is every dissatisfied soul in England," Rowland countered. "Not that it matters, given that we're in mid-Atlantic. On the *Titan*, I'm master regardless of my ancestry, grand or humble."

"If I might be so bold as to ask, Mr. Rocambole," Quatermain chipped in, "Are you by any chance a *second-class passenger*?"

Edward Rocambole's face went scarlet–a sight that would surely have stirred the spirit of any vampire–as he seemed to realize, belatedly, what he was up against. He muttered what might have been an apology, despite featuring the words *sang*, *cochon* and *chien*, and hurried away.

"Right," said Captain Rowland. "I'll just take a little nip of whisky, and then we can go below and pour oil on the troubled waters. Meanwhile, Hodgson, better get those burials organized. Don't want dead bodies cluttering up the *Titan*, do we."

"Can't you store them in the refrigeration hold?" Quatermain asked. "They are, after all, the *prima facie* evidence of five heinous crimes."

Rowland exchanged a furtive glance with Hodgson and Black before saying: "No, we can't. All the available space is taken up by provisions for the voyage. We can't put dead bodies in with the food, can we? The *Titan*'s famous for her standards of hygiene. Anyway, if we keep the bodies on ice, we'll only feed anxieties about them rising from the dead."

With that, the Captain led Allan Quatermain away, thanking him profusely for his kindness in offering support and protection.

Quatermain stood silently by Rowland's side, posing impressively, while the Captain made his speech to "the rabble in steerage." The Captain's judgment was proved correct; thanks to the weight of his authority and Quatermain's reputation, the mob's leaders were cowed into submission, and were, in the end, meekly delighted to be reassured that there were no vampires aboard the *Titan*.

At dinner that evening, there was a certain gloom at the writers' table, in spite of the fact that there was Dover sole fried in butter for the fish course, venison pie with roast potatoes for the main course, and spotted dick for dessert. "Three

Irish and two cockneys," the man from the *Daily Mail* complained. "Where's the news value in that?"

"Couldn't agree more," said his colleague from the *Telegraph*. "What vampire worth his salt would go after scum like that when there's flesh of the highest quality on offer." He was staring across the room at the count's three daughters, who were looking even lovelier tonight than they had the previous evening.

"Do vampires take salt with their blood?" Monsieur Apollinaire inquired.

"Sir Edward always had a taste for serving-wenches," Miss Lee pointed out. "If he'd only stuck to them, he wouldn't have been hanged nearly as many times as he was."

"In any case," said Mr. Vane, "we're all sailing to judgment–what does it matter if some of us get there a day or two ahead of the rest."

"If I were a vampire," Monsieur Lorrain observed, "I wouldn't bother with the likes of the count's daughters."

"Nor would I," said Monsieur Jarry. "I'd take out Rockefeller, Carnegie and Quatermain. Three vast fortunes to be redistributed at one fell swoop! If they've only had the decency to make substantial bequests to the Arts in their wills..."

"Not likely," said Mr. Huneker, mournfully. "Rockefeller and Carnegie have heirs avid to inherit, who won't let a penny get away if they can help it. Hearst would be a better bet. I don't know about Quatermain, though–does anyone know if this Ayesha's in line for Solomon's diamonds if the old braggart croaks?"

"If there are five vampires aboard," Mr. Twain pointed out, "they could dispose of her too, and the Duke of Buccleuch to boot–and that's just for starters. If the other gossip is reliable, though, they'd all be back again the day after tomorrow to lodge their complaints via Tom Edison's machine."

"It'll never work," Mr. Henley opined. "I knew a man once that tried to sell me a time machine, but it turned out just to be a bicycle with knobs on."

"That Ayesha's a queer one, though," Mr. Chambers said. "Came up to me while I was playing deck quoits this afternoon and asked me if I had a copy of the *King in Yellow* I could lend her. Said she'd always wanted to read it."

"Can I have it after her?" Monsieur Apollinaire put in, swiftly.

"There's no such book, damn it!" Chambers said. "I made it up."

"That's what Dad used to say about vampires," said Monsieur Féval *fils*. "But the bodies keep turning up, don't they?"

"It was probably a fight, a suicide pact and an overdose of laudanum, not necessarily in that order," Mr. Henley opined. "It all happened in steerage, after all."

"I'm astonished that the Captain decided not to preserve the bodies until we reach New York, though," said Mr. Robertson. "Dereliction of duty, in my opinion. One way or another, those five people were murdered. There ought to be an investigation."

"There's some chap in second class pretending to be a detective," the man from the *Mail* chipped in. "One of your lot, I believe." He was looking at Monsieur Lorrain.

"What do you mean, *my lot*?" Lorrain demanded.

"French, of course," supplied the man from the *Telegraph*. Name of Rocambole."

"Isn't he dead?" asked Mr. Huneker.

"The report was probably exaggerated," Mr. Twain put in. "Happens all the time."

"He's the first Monsieur Rocambole's grandson, Edward," Féval *fils* supplied. "Not a bad chap, really. He's been asking questions in the refrigeration hold."

"Probably after some food," said the man from the *Mail*. "If we're only getting venison pie on the second evening out, they must be getting sausages–and what that leaves for steerage, I can't imagine."

"Faggots," said the man from the *Telegraph*.

"What the hell do you mean by that?" demanded M. Lorrain.

Miss Lee put a soothing hand on Monsieur Lorrain's arm. "It's a form of English *cuisine*," she explained.

"There's a phrase to make the blood run cold," Monsieur Jarry observed. "*English cuisine*."

"I rather like venison pie," M. Apollinaire confessed.

"It could have been worse," Miss Lee explained to her neighbor. "It might have been black pudding."

"I thought Britain had put an end to the slave trade," Mr. Chambers said, with ill-disguised irony.

"If we hadn't," Mr. Henley said, dryly, "there might have been a different result to your Civil War.

Meanwhile, at the Captain's table, John Rowland was beaming at Ayesha with eyes softened by a delicate whisky glaze. "You really are the most beautiful woman I've ever seen, Miss Ayesha," he murmured. "Do you have another name, by the way?"

"She Who Must Be Obeyed," the coquette said, seeming to misunderstand his question. "But I'm a bit of an old dragon, I fear, beside Mrs. de Bathe and Count Lugard's daughters. Now they really *are* lovely. I could almost fancy them myself."

"Not as lovely as you, my dear," Rowland insisted.

"Damn it, Quatermain," John D. Rockefeller said to the great white hunter, "I'd rather listen to one of your blessed stories than watch Rowland make love. No lions, though. Ever encountered a vampire, by any chance?"

"As it happens," Quatermain said, "I have." He had not spoken loudly, but such was the authoritative tone of his voice that the other murmurous conversations ongoing around the table immediately died. All eyes turned to the alleged paragon of gallantry.

"It wasn't reported in any of my newspapers," Hearst said, skeptically.

"Ran into Varney, did you?" asked the Duke of Buccleuch, effortlessly exceeding the American's skepticism.

"No," said Quatermain. "I encountered the Brothers Ténèbre. The younger one is a vampire, you know."

"I thought the younger of the two so-called Ténèbres was a thief named Bobby Bobson," said Buccleuch. "Teamed up with William something-or-other. Weren't they hunted down in Hungary way back in the 1820s?"

"They have been hunted down many times," Count Lugard put in, "but they always return, with new names befitting every new era. Always different, and yet always the same: one tall and manly, the other short and gentle. They are English, as you say, but also French, German and... let us say *cosmopolitan*."

"Not American, though," Carnegie put in.

"We'd soon put a stop to their antics," Rockefeller agreed, "if they actually existed, and weren't just phantoms of the Old World's imagination."

"Wouldn't last five minutes in the land of the free," Edison agreed.

"Wouldn't last two in your electric chair, Tom," Hearst added.

"Hold on a minute," said Captain Rowland, banging his glass on the table to call his guests to order. "I want to hear Mr. Quatermain's story. If he says that he's met these two characters, I'm inclined to take his word for it. Was it in Africa, Mr. Quatermain?"

"It was on a ship," Quatermain said. "Not such a fine vessel as this one, of course, but a neat enough rig in her way–the *Pride of Kimberley*, a cargo vessel with two dozen passenger cabins. I came up from Cape Town to Lisbon in her a few years back. First night out, a body turned up, in much the same condition as those we buried at sea today. Just one, mind–a young woman. No one suspected a vampire, at first, until a second body turned up in much the same condition, when the crew started muttering. That was three nights later, mind–if it was a vampire, it wasn't so very hungry. Probably on rations, given that we only had eight women aboard, only three of which could be reasonably described as young. I'm getting ahead of myself, though. Like Captain Rowland, the skipper turned to me for help as soon as the first body was found, and I promised to look into the matter."

As he paused to chew a mouthful of spotted dick, Carnegie whispered to Rockefeller: "Fellow can't even get his plot in the right order."

"Unlike Rowland, who can't get his *hors d'oeuvres* in the right plot," murmured Rockefeller. "He'd do better to set his cap for one of the Count's daughters–at least they wouldn't understand what he's saying."

"Not suspecting a vampire at first," Quatermain went on, "I figured that any skullduggery aboard a ship like the *Pride of Kimberley* was bound to concern diamonds. On a ship like the *Titan* there must be rich and various pickings for any thief clever enough and bold enough to try his luck, but the *Kimberley* was outward bound from Cape Town. I wasn't the only passenger carrying a few stones to cover my traveling expenses–in fact, it would have been hard for a flying fish to skim the deck without hitting someone with a few sparklers stashed away in his luggage.

"At first, when I began asking my fellow passengers to check up on their hidden goods, they all reported that everything was in its place–but within 24 hours of my asking, they began coming back to me to say that they'd checked again, with much less happy results. Nearly half of them had lost their secret savings, and most of the losers were in no position to complain to any authorities in the Cape or England, because the stones were being smuggled. They'd never have confessed it to me if I hadn't shown them my own stones, and explained to them that I reckoned that old King Solomon had probably imposed his duty at source, so I didn't see why Queen Victoria should get a second cut.

"Then, the second body turned up, and the third chap who had a daughter in tow started worrying about losing more than his half-dozen second-rate gems. Even the men who only had wives got a little distracted, by hope if not anxiety. The blood-sucking seemed to me to be a strange business, because I couldn't see why a vampire would get on a boat where he'd be out at sea for days on end, and where his predations would stick out like a sore thumb. You could see why one might get on a great ship like this, I suppose, where there are three thousand potential victims at sea for less than a week, but the *Kimberley* was another kettle of fish. I decided soon enough that the guilty party couldn't have come aboard in search of blood, and that taking the blood he needed to sustain him was just a matter of necessity while he carried out his intended plunder–which meant, I figured, that whoever had taken the diamonds must also be taking the blood.

"Now, one of the first passengers to complain that the secret compartment in his trunk had been emptied was a tall German fellow who clamed to be the Baron von Altenheimer, who was traveling with his brother Benedict, a Catholic priest–a Monsignor, no less. I was suspicious of the Baron from the very beginning, because he claimed to have been at Heidelberg, although he didn't have a single duelling scar and never mentioned G. W. F. Hegel in casual conversation. I set myself to keep a very close watch on the pair of them. He fancied himself a storyteller, but I noticed that his brother kept slipping away when he was telling his tales, protesting that he had heard them all before. I followed the Monsignor the very next evening, and caught him rifling the lining of a three-piece suit hanging up in one of the cabins–which turned out to have seven rough-cut stones sewn under the collar.

"I managed to knife him between the shoulder-blades while his back was still turned, but it wasn't a mortal blow. Actually, he made quite a fight of it–he was a wiry little chap, and he certainly didn't have muscles like a priest–but I turned the tables on him after he'd chased me up on deck and eventually managed to throw him overboard. Not a moment too soon, either, seeing that his brother, having delivered his punch line, immediately came at me with a saber. The Baron was a much bigger fellow than the priest, with quite some reach, but I'd had the presence of mind to secrete one of my hunting-rifles in the scuppers, just in case, and I got to it before he sliced me up. I let him have both barrels, and he went over the side too. He was probably dead before he hit the water, but it wouldn't have mattered if he weren't. The sharks were all around us by then, having been attracted by the younger one, who was bleeding like a stuck pig from the wound in his back.

"We went through their luggage of course–that's how we discovered who they really were–but we didn't find a single diamond. Even the stones that brother Benedict had snatched from the loaded suit must have gone over the side with him. The sharks must have scoffed the lot–but at least the third young lady was saved from becoming a vampire's victim, much to her relief. She was very grateful to me, but as she was much the ugliest of the three, I didn't take advantage of the poor child."

"Ayesha wasn't with you on that trip, I presume?" Captain Rowland asked.

"No, she wasn't. This is her first time out of Africa. It's all a great adventure for her."

"Actually, my dear," the young woman drawled, "it's been a bit of a drag so far. No disrespect to your marvelous ship, Captain, but I'll be glad to get back on dry land, where I can be myself again."

"Meaning no disrespect myself, young lady," the Captain said, "but I'll be very glad to have four more days of your company before you do."

"You don't suppose *we*'re in danger, do you, Mr. Edison?" the former Mrs. Langtry said to her neighbor.

"I doubt that I am," Edison replied, a trifle ungraciously. "These ancient monsters never attack men of science."

Andrew Carnegie, meanwhile, leaned over to whisper in John D. Rockefeller's ear: "Didn't believe a damned word of it myself," he said. "Made the whole thing up, I shouldn't wonder."

"I don't know," said Rockefeller. "If he were making it up, he'd surely have painted his fighting skills in a kinder light–and he'd have added a love interest too. You can be sure that's what Mr. Chambers would have done–or even that Twain fellow. Didn't I read that he was dead, by the way?"

"I read that too," Hearst put in, "in one of my own papers–so it must be true. We won't have far to look for our vampire, if any more poor folk turn up dead, will we?"

Captain Rowland was woken again shortly before dawn on the 28th, this time by Mr. Black. Rowland had been dreaming about chasing a sea serpent, desperate to be hailed as a hero by Mr. Hearst's *New York Sun* and to win the love of the fair Ayesha.

"What is it now?" he demanded.

"Five more dead, sir," Black reported. "Three young men, two young women. Only one Irishwoman this time, though, and two Americans on their way home."

"Americans? Not...."

"No sir–steerage, like the others. Mormons, I believe."

"That's all right, then. Can't imagine Hearst getting excited about that. More rumors, I suppose?"

"Yes sir. They're not going to be fobbed off by a speech this time. And there's been a leak."

"A leak! Which compartment? How bad is it?"

"Not in the hull sir–I mean that someone in the crew's been letting out information about the cargo."

"You mean..."

"No sir, not that. The sarcophagi in the secure hold."

"Damn! That *will* make Hearst excited, for all the wrong reasons. He's very secretive, for a newspaperman. Still, I suppose it's not every day one gets a chance to pick up the contents of a freshly-looted tomb on the cheap while passing through Cairo. You can't blame the man, given that he has the money to spare. So the steerage mob has got the idea that we've got a gang of Egyptian vampire mummies aboard, has it?"

"Yes, sir."

"Very well. You know the drill. Meeting on the bridge. Send for Quatermain–and Hearst too, I suppose."

Black hurried off and Rowland got dressed, cursing his luck. By the time he arrived on the bridge, Hearst was already berating Hodgson, Black and Kitchener. "When I say absolute secrecy, I mean absolute secrecy," the newspaper magnate was shouting, at the top of his voice. "If I wanted people to know my business, I'd print it. I want an armed guard placed on the hold with my treasure in it–a dozen men, the very best you have. If anyone comes near it, they shoot to kill."

"We'll do everything necessary to protect your property, sir," Rowland assured him. "And yours too, sir, of course," he added, turning to Allan Quatermain.

"Oh, don't worry about *my* luggage," Quatermain said. "I don't have any precious stones stashed away in my boxes–just some interesting fossils I picked up in Olduvai Gorge."

"Precious stones!" howled Hearst. "Who told you I had gems? Do you think I'm some kind of smuggler? Why, I'll bet that Carnegie's bullion is worth five times as much as my few trinkets–and as for Rockefeller's suitcase full of bonds..."

"Excuse me, Mr. Hearst," Rowland said, soothingly, "but none of us is supposed to know about any of that. I don't think Mr. Carnegie and Mr. Rockefeller..."

"Don't be an idiot, man, I'm not going to print it. I've got *real* news to print, about preachers' love-nests and actresses' bastards."

"Guards with guns aren't going to quiet rumors, sir," Hodgson said. "if anything, they'll just inflame them further. Will you try to talk to the people in steerage again, Captain?"

"If you'll pardon the suggestion," Quatermain put in, "I think it might be a good idea to change our tactics. Instead of going down to the steps of the third-class deck to talk to anyone who cares to listen, perhaps we might invite a few of the ringleaders up to your stateroom–sit them down, offer them a cigar and a few bottles of champagne, talk about the situation like civilized men. I'm sure we can make them see sense and convert them into ambassadors of reason. Especially if Mr. Hearst can promise to give due acknowledgement to their contribution in the *Sun*. Perhaps Mr. Carnegie and Mr. Rockefeller might offer their services in finding the anxious gentlemen employment, when they reach New York."

"That's exactly what I was about to suggest," said Rowland. "A capital plan, worthy of a true naval strategist. Organize it, Hodgson. Put the armed guards on the hold anyway, though. Can you see to that, Black? As soon you've arranged for the disposal of the bodies."

"Yes, sir," said the two mates, in unison.

"Have you really got *fossils* in those boxes of yours, Quatermain?" Hearst asked, in the meantime, having evidently calmed down. "Dinosaurs, do you mean?"

"Not dinosaurs, Mr. Hearst," Quatermain said. "I've seen a few dinosaurs in my time, but I never managed to bag one, worse luck. These are humanoid bones. I intend to make a gift of them to the New York Museum of Natural History."

"Who told you about that, damn it?" said Rowland, whose attention had only just returned to his passengers' conversation.

"I didn't know it was a secret," Quatermain said, equably. "Surely everyone knows that New York has the second best Natural History Museum in the world?"

"Not for long," Hearst assured him. "It'll be the best soon enough."

"It certainly will," Rowland agreed, in spite of being an Englishman.

"It would be if we could catch one of these vampires for its exhibition halls," Quatermain said. "Especially if it turned out to be a mummy. Two attractions for the price of one!"

"If anyone touches one of my sarcophagi," Hearst said, darkly, "they'll end up wrapped in bandages themselves."

By mid-afternoon on the 28th, Allan Quatermain's plan seemed to have worked like a charm. Harmony had been restored to the lower decks, and everything was running smoothly on the *Titan* in spite of the worsening weather. The vessel was sailing into the teeth of a force nine gale from noon till 6 p.m., and the rain was torrential, but the wind slackened in the evening and the deluge relented. As the crew were about to go into dinner, Black reported that a good proportion of the steerage passengers were dreadfully seasick, and that more than one had expressed the thought that exsanguination by a vampire would be a mercy.

There were a few absentees from the first-class dining-room too, but the writers' table was full. Several of the faces on display were a trifle green, but these were men with nibs of steel, and they were not about to let a little nausea prevent them from enjoying a meal whose price had been included in their tickets. The fish was only cod, but the main course was roast lamb with mint sauce, with prune *flan* to follow.

"You don't suppose that Hearst's mummies are really rising from their coffins by night to steep their bandages in blood, do you?" said the man from the *Telegraph* to the man from the *Mail.*

"Who cares?" said the man from the *Mail.* "It'd be a great story if we were ever able to print it, but your editor wouldn't wear it any more than mine would. We could try hawking it to Pulitzer, I suppose."

"He wouldn't touch it either," said the *Telegraph* man. "The good old days are long gone; it's all one big cartel now. These other chaps might make something of it, though–benefits of poetic license and all."

"I'm afraid not," said Mr. Twain. "The trouble with being an honest liar is that you have to maintain plausibility. A Yankee at King Arthur's Court is one thing–vampire mummies on a transatlantic liner is another."

"Perhaps so," said Monsieur Féval *fils*, regretfully. "Although..."

"I do hope there isn't going to be a mutiny," said Mr. Henley.

"Really?" said Monsieur Apollinaire. "Why?"

"A mutiny might be quite amusing," Monsieur Jarry agreed.

"There isn't going to be a mutiny," Mr. Huneker said, "unless the vampires start picking on the crew. The passengers might let off a little steam, but nobody with an ounce of common sense goes in for serious rioting on a ship in mid-Atlantic, especially in the dead of winter."

"We shall meet our fate soon enough," opined Mr. Vane.

"You talk like a one-book writer, Mr. Vane," said Mr. Chambers, a trifle snappishly. "Think of the delights awaiting us in New York. Think of the romance of America, and the newborn century!"

"We've got to get to New York first," Miss Lee pointed out. "Have you been out on the promenade deck today?"

"Certainly not," said Monsieur Lorrain.

"We'll get to New York all right," said Mr. Robertson. "A little late, perhaps, but we'll get there. I trust this ship implicitly."

"Everyone trusts his ship implicitly, until it starts to sink," Monsieur Jarry observed.

"An allegory of life," said Monsieur Apollinaire, with a sigh. "I must mention it to Mallarmé when I get back."

"Didn't I read that he was dead?" Mr. Henley put in.

"Probably an exaggerated report," said Mr. Twain.

"Happens all the time," 12 voices chorused, before Mr. Twain could draw breath.

"The deaths in steerage weren't exaggerated, though," said Mr. Chambers, pensively. "We've another four nights at sea yet–maybe five if the storm sets us back a long way. That's 20 or 25 more bodies, at the present rate."

"Enough to devastate the whole of our table," Mr. Huneker agreed, "if the vampires get tired of slumming. Except, of course, that we all have ink in our veins instead of blood."

"There might be worse things aboard than vampires," said Mr. Twain, who had recovered quickly enough from his momentary embarrassment. "I talked to your friend Rocambole today, Monsieur Féval, and he dropped a few dark hints about secret lockers in the refrigeration hold. Now, it happens that I was also talking to the crewman who's in charge of the refrigeration unit–that Kitchener fellow–and he jumped like a jackrabbit when I asked him what he had in his secret locker. Denied everything, of course–just ice, he said–but one of his kitchen staff muttered something about monsters of the deep that never really died, even if they were cut to pieces."

"Sea serpents, you mean?" said the man from the *Mail.*

"Not likely," said the man from the *Telegraph.* "I heard a rumor about that ship that went down in the Channel last week–the *Dunlin,* I think it was, or maybe the *Sandwich.* There was talk of that being sunk by a monster that should have been dead but wasn't."

"There can't be any sea serpents in the Solent," Mr. Henley put in. "They'd never get away unobserved in Cowes week."

"That's just the point," said the man from the *Telegraph.* "This was something tinged with a far more sinister superstition than any mere sea serpent."

"Like vampire mummies, you mean?" asked Mr. Chambers.

"Something of the same order, I suppose," the man from the *Telegraph* admitted, "but there was talk of Madeira...."

"Rowland's favorite tipple seems to be Scotch," Monsieur Jarry put in.

"Mine's absinthe," Monsieur Apollinaire added.

"*I* heard a rumor that these sarcophagi in the hold don't actually have mummies in them at all," the man from the *Mail* told his colleague, competitively. "They're actually stuffed full of gems, bullion and bonds. All shady, of course–but that's how these millionaires stay ahead of the pack, isn't it?"

"Let's hope it's all still there when we reach New York," said the *Telegraph* man. "I'd hate to think of those French bandits who robbed Asprey's and the palace making off with it, wouldn't you?"

Meanwhile, Allan Quatermain was responding to a query from the Duke of Buccleuch as to whether he had ever encountered a mummy."

"Several," Quatermain answered. "But only one that was given to wandering around."

"And was it a vampire, too?" inquired Hearst, sarcastically.

"Not at all. He was a rather plaintive chap, actually, animated by the desire to be reunited with his long-lost love, Queen Nefertiti. He choked a few people to death, but only because they got in his way. I had to do something about it, though–the business was getting out of hand."

"Blew him away with your elephant-gun, I suppose," Carnegie suggested.

"I did try that," Quatermain admitted, "but the bullets went clean through him, and the dust they blew out simply spiraled around for a few minutes before getting sucked back into his body. I could have been in a sticky situation myself then, but he wasn't much of a runner."

"How fortunate," murmured Mrs. de Bathe.

"I had to set a trap for him instead," Quatermain went on. "Happily, he was none too bright–the ancient Egyptians used to take a mummy's brain out through the nostrils with a kind of hook, you know, and put it in its own canopic jar–so he fell right in. I'd filled the pit with oil, and laid a gunpowder fuse, so it seemed like a mere matter of striking a match and retiring to a safe distance."

"Seemed?" said Rockefeller. "You mean that it didn't work?"

"Oh, he went up like a Roman candle. The resin that Egyptian mummifiers use to stick the bandages together is very flammable, and what was left of his body was as dry as a stick. If anything, the operation was a little too successful. It turned him into a cloud of thick black smoke in a matter of seconds. The trouble was that the trick he had of sucking back his dust after bullets went through him worked just as well on smoke. One minute there was nothing but a cloud settling slowly to ground-level, the next he was reformulating, a little larger than before and in a far darker mood."

"How terrible, my dear fellow!" said the Count. "What on Earth did you do next?"

"Ran like hell, old man. He was a little nippier on his pins now, but I still had the legs of him. I needed to rethink the whole problem, but once I'd figured out what was what, it wasn't too hard to come up with a new plan. Given that fire hadn't worked, the logical thing to try seemed to be water, for which he seemed to have something of an aversion–but transporting water from the Nile is a tricky business, and he wasn't about to be lured into the stream."

"So you buried him, did you?" Hearst suggested. "Got him back into his pyramid and slammed the door behind him."

"That might have worked, I suppose," Quatermain said, judiciously, "but it didn't seem to me to qualify as a final solution. Besides which, I already knew that he was a sucker for pitfall traps–so it was just a matter of figuring out what kind of filling might work better than oil." He paused for dramatic effect.

"What did you use?" Rowland asked, impatiently.

"Molasses," Quatermain said. "Nice, thick, sticky molasses. After a couple of days of impotent struggling, he'd virtually dissolved in the stuff. After two days more, it had set rock hard. We broke up the mass and sold the pieces in the souk as dark candy. I didn't eat any myself, but those who did said it was delicious. I think I've got a few pieces left in my cabin, if anyone wants to try some."

"Doesn't that qualify as cannibalism?" Edison asked.

"No more so than enjoying this delightful repast," Quatermain said, indicating the lamb shoulder on his plate. "Or, for that matter, breathing. Where do you think the carbon in our bodies goes when it's recycled? Julius Caesar's atoms have been redistributed so widely by now that there's one in every mouthful we eat, another in every breath we take. And Attila the Hun's too, of course, not to mention Cain and Solomon, Herod and Apollonius of Tyana. There's a little of everything human in every one of us, gentlemen–and a little of everything unhuman too: cats and bats, mice and elephants, snakes and dragons. Everything circulates–except wealth, of course. Wealth always flows uphill, from the pockets of the poor to the coffers of the rich. Isn't that so, Mr. Rockefeller, Mr. Carnegie?"

Hearst burst out laughing. "I concede, Mr. Quatermain," he said, "that you're a cleverer storyteller than I thought. Except, of course, that you're contradicting yourself. The story you told last night, about the infamous Brothers Ténèbre, suggests that wealth sometimes vanishes into the maws of sharks."

"Was that really the moral of my story?" Quatermain said. "Well, perhaps–I'm just a humble white hunter. If you know anything at all about the Brothers Ténèbre, though, you'll know that they're infinitely more skilled at self-reconstitution than any mere mummy. They always come back, and they always have another robbery to execute–but they're just fleas on an elephant's back when it comes to questions of serious wealth. I'll wager that they could clear out the hold of this ship–and the first-class cabins too–without putting any one of you gentlemen to any serious inconvenience, even though your luggage would seem a fabulous fortune to any of those poor folk down in steerage. They'll have little chance in life but to be vampires' victims, I fear, even if they reach New York with the blood still coursing in their veins."

"Not so," said Edison. "Were your immortal bandits to make off with my machine for communicating with the dead, I'd be the loser and so would the world. It's irreplaceable. Light-bulbs, phonographs and electric chairs can be mass-produced; once you have the trick of their making, it can't ever be unlearned, but the machine for communicating with the dead is a different thing altogether–a radically new departure. Its operation isn't based on the laws of physics, but the principles of pataphysics."

"What on Earth is pataphysics?" demanded the Duke of Buccleuch.

"It's the scientific discipline that deals with exceptions rather than rules."

"It sounds more like scientific indiscipline to me," said Carnegie.

"In a manner of speaking, it is," Edison admitted. "It's a tricky basis on which to build a technology. Every fugitive principle of pataphysics is good for one unique machine, but mass production is awkward. The factory principle doesn't apply, you see–every one would have to be hand-crafted."

"Sounds un-American to me," Rockefeller observed.

"Is it really unique?" Quatermain asked. "I had not imagined that we might have anything so rare and priceless aboard. What about you, my dear? Had you any inkling of this?"

"No," said Ayesha. "I had not. And yet, we are to be privileged to witness the machine's debut tomorrow night, are we not?"

"I'm afraid it won't be tomorrow, ma'am," Edison said, sorrowfully. "The crewmen Captain Rowland lent me are doing their best, and the ship's stabilizers are working wonders, but the storm is making things difficult even so. It'll be the 30th now, I fear."

"What a pity!" said the count.

"I have no doubt that it will be worth the wait," said the former Lillie Langtry. "And the pleasures of anticipation will be all the more piquant."

"I'll drink to that," said Rowland.

"We shall all look forward to it immensely," Ayesha assured the inventor.

Later that night, when the last of the first-class passengers had retired to their cabins, Ayesha came into Allan Quatermain's cabin. Once through the door, she changed her stance slightly, and when she spoke, her voice seemed a good deal deeper than it had in the dining room.

"You can steal Edison's machine if you want to," she said, "but we have to take the rest too. I'm not going without the gems from Hearst's treasure-trove, Carnegie's bullion or Rockefeller's bonds just so you can tinker with some idiot machine. What would we want with a machine for communicating with the dead, anyway? It's not as if we haven't been dead often enough ourselves–if our peers had wanted a chat, they could have dropped in on our graves then."

"It would all depend on which dead people we'd be able to talk to," Quatermain told his companion, stretching himself out on the bed as he spoke. His Africa-tinged British accent had vanished; one might almost have taken him for a Frenchman by the timbre of his voice. "Some dead people–the aristocracy of the astral plane, you might say–must know many interesting and valuable secrets."

"You want us to go hunting buried treasure under the advice of ancient pirates and plunderers?"

"The more recently-dead have their secrets too. I've always thought that blackmail is a more civilized crime than burglary–and so much more modern. We ought to move with the times, Brother Ange, lest we make strangers of ourselves in a world we no longer comprehend."

"I comprehend Carnegie's bullion as well as he does, Brother Jean," the false Ayesha said. "Nor have I the slightest difficult in comprehending Rockefeller's bonds. No matter how the world changes, there'll always be money, and where there's money, there'll always be thieves. We are timeless, brother; that is the very essence of our nature. We are the shadows of the love of money that is the root of all evil, and we shall never lose touch with the world, no matter how many times we are banished from it, only to return."

"The love of money is not the only kind we shadow," the false Quatermain observed. "You might consider leaving your grosser appetite unslaked tonight. Exsanguinated corpses are a trifle conspicuous on a ship, even one of this gargantuan size."

"Have you mentioned that to the Count and his harem?" the cross-dressing brother retorted. "They have been starved too long to be moderate in circumstances like these. And I've been hunting alone for far too long not to enjoy the company. You should come with us tonight, you know–you're supposed to be a great white hunter, aren't you? Stalking Irish colleens is so much more fun than stalking elephants, and one can take so much more pleasure from them, even before one drains them dry."

"*Chacun a son goût*," said the false Quatermain. "I am the Chevalier Ténèbre; I treat courtship in a very different fashion."

"More fool you. Given that the count's ladies are spoken for and Lillie Langtry's past it, there's nothing in first-class worth making your kind of effort for, but the lower decks are full of girls who fondly imagine that there's something better awaiting them in New York but whoredom. Think of the disillusionment I'm saving them! Anyway, it's the swordplay that attracts you to the knightly life, not chaste courtly love. You must be aching for a good fight. You might try picking one with one of those frightful writers–the world could do with a few less of their kind."

"Once we're in Manhattan," the pretended Quatermain said, "you can gorge yourself to your heart's content. It won't do you any harm to go easy for a couple of nights."

"It's a couple now, is it? And I expect you want me to talk to the Count and his brides, vampire to vampire?"

"If you wouldn't mind. If we stir up a hornet's nest here, it'll be that much more difficult to lay our hands on the loot, and I'm sure that the Count would rather not advertise his arrival in New York too loudly. I know that we're not much given to virtues, but a little patience might help our cause here. If you explain it to the count, he'll keep his brides in line. He doesn't tolerate disobedience."

"Neither do I," said Ayesha, reverting momentarily to her role. "I'll do it–but only on the understanding that we take every last penny of whatever Hearst, Carnegie and Rockefeller have stashed away. If Edison's machine is heavy, it goes on to your share of the load, not mine."

"Agreed," said Allan Quatermain.

The fake white hunter turned over on the bunk then, intending to go to sleep–but five minutes after Ayesha had left, there was a knock on his cabin door.

At first, Quatermain did not recognize the man who entered in response to his invitation, but after a few moments, he remembered where he had seen the other before. "Mr. Rocambole," he said. "What can I do for you?"

"I came to see you, Mr. Quatermain, because I don't trust that drunken fool of a Captain," Rocambole said. "It seems to me that you're one of the few men on this damned boat with a head on his shoulders. I've been carrying out some investigations down below, and I'd like to share my findings with you, if you don't mind."

"Not at all," said Quatermain. "I'd be interested to hear what you've found out. You decided to inquire into the murders despite the Captain's rude refusal of your help, I presume?"

"I did. I've conducted more than a hundred interviews with relatives and friends of the murdered individuals, and people who were close to the locations in which they were killed. I've got some pretty good descriptions of characters who had no reason to be around on the nights in question. I'd have taken the information to the Captain in spite of the way he treated me, but... well, they're first-class passengers, you see."

"Ah," said Quatermain. "That would make the matter rather delicate."

"They're not British, though," Rocambole added. "Or French, of course. Would that make a difference, do you suppose?"

"I don't know. Who are we talking about?"

"Count Lugard and his three daughters, and a man I haven't been able to identify–short, slim and fair-haired. I've asked Féval and Apollinaire to see if they can spot him in the first-class dining room, but they both said that the description doesn't ring a bell. The Count doesn't have anyone else traveling with him, I suppose, except for his daughters."

"I don't believe so. Are you actually alleging that the Count and his three daughters are vampires?"

"Of course not–that would be preposterous. My grandfather told me some tall tales, but he always told me to leave the impossible out and stick to real possibilities, however unlikely. I suppose they might be members of some secret society of assassins, but I think it far more likely that they're gathering blood for some kind of medical research. I think they're experimenting with blood transfusions–or, rather, preparing to carry out such experiments when they reach New York. Surgeons are attempting to use the technique to compensate for blood loss during amputations, I believe."

"It seems rather far-fetched," Quatermain observed, "but it does have the virtue of avoiding the supernatural. Where do you suppose the Count and his assistants are storing the blood?"

"In the refrigerated hold. It's the logical place. I bribed one of the cooks to let me check out the food storage units, and I couldn't see anything suspicious there, but I'm certain there's a secret compartment or two behind one of the bulkheads. If I could get hold of a plan of the ship, I might be able to figure out where they are."

"And you think that I might be able to obtain one from the Captain or one of the mates?"

"The purser, Kitchener, might be your best bet–but you'll have to be careful. I don't want to arouse the suspicions of whichever crewman is in on the conspiracy."

"Are you sure that one of them is?" Quatermain asked.

"Yes. Someone's responsible for the Captain's churlish attitude to my offer of help. He's just a drunken dupe, of course, but one of the two mates must be pulling the strings. That Hodgson's a rum chap–has a camera, you know, takes pictures up on deck when there's no one there to take pictures of. Scribbles, too. On the other hand, Black's got political ideas. I never trust a man with political ideas. I like a straightforward man like yourself, sir–a man who faces his problems squarely, with an elephant gun. Grandfather would have approved of you."

"The feeling would have been mutual, I'm sure," Quatermain said. "Very well, Mr. Rocambole–I'll try to get you your plan, and I'll make some inquiries of my own. Can't let a gang of blood-runners operate unchecked on one of Her Majesty's merchant ships, can we? You can depend on me."

"Do you know who the other man might be, Mr. Quatermain? The short one, I mean."

"I'll inquire into that too," Quatermain assured him. "Can't say I've noticed him, but he may be a crewmen or a second-class passenger. Villains of the count's type always have minions, in my experience."

"Thank you, Mr. Quatermain," Edward Rocambole said, stepping forward to shake the hunter's hand before withdrawing.

"If I were you," Quatermain said, "I'd keep a very careful lookout tonight."

"I will," Rocambole promised. "Not a wink of sleep for me. If I catch a glimpse of any one of them, I'll find out what they're up to."

By the time the Captain was woken by his cabin boy on the 29th, the Sun was over the horizon and his hangover had taken so strong a hold that he had to quaff half a bottle of cognac to bring it under control.

"Nobody died, then?" he said, as soon as his tongue was unfurred.

"Nobody drained of blood, sir," the cabin boy reported. "Last night's only casualties were two old men who died of hypothermia for lack of decent overcoats. Nobody's panicking over that, sir."

"Excellent! Tell Black to heave the bodies over the side forthwith, and let's hope for a day's plain steaming. How's the weather?"

"There's a lull at the moment, sir, but the bosun says that there's another storm-front visible in the southwest, heading our way. Going to be a rough afternoon."

"Damn. Passengers are always in a better mood when they've chucked a few deck quoits around. I suppose it'll still be blowing this evening, so the orchestra in the ballroom will be playing so many extra notes that every waltz will turn into the Gay Gordons. Never mind–there's still the casino."

By the time the Captain had refreshed himself and climbed up to the bridge, the storm-front was almost upon the vessel, and the sky in the southwest was very dark indeed.

"Wouldn't have fancied that in the old days, Hodgson," Rowland said to the first mate. "Enough to put a sailing ship's schedule back two days, and fill the bilges with vomit. Nothing to fear here, though: the *Titan*'s unshakable and unstoppable as well as unsinkable. No icebergs in sight, I hope?"

"None, sir," Hodgson confirmed. "May I take my camera out on deck to photograph the storm?"

"If you like. Silly idea, mind. Where's the fun in looking at postcards of clouds and corposants when you can have French whores in any pose you fancy?"

"It's a hobby, sir," the mate said.

The Captain's excessive claim regarding the unshakability of the *Titan* proved woefully unfounded, especially when her second funnel was struck by lightning. The bolt burned out the wires of the ship's internal telegraph, causing all kinds of problems in the transmission of orders. By the time he had to dress for dinner again, John Rowland felt that he had been run ragged, and he was direly in need of a stiff drink. When he descended to the dining room, the meal was in full flow, and he was forced to bolt his mock-turtle soup in order to catch up with the next course. It wasn't until the halibut had been cleared away and his roast beef and Yorkshire pudding arrived that he began to relax, aided by his eighth glass of claret.

By this time, Allan Quatermain was reaching the conclusion of yet another story. Popular demand seemed to have dragged him back to the subject of King Solomon's Mines. "Yes," he was saying, in answer to a question from the count. "Old Gagool was with me for a year or two after we got back from Kukuanaland. She was a fount of esoteric knowledge. It was she who told me where I could find Kôr, in fact, where I met Ayesha. It was a crying shame that she was immolated by that pillar of flame–but she was very old, you know, and she really did believe that it would rejuvenate her; that was the whole reason she guided me there. I admire the way that natives place such tremendous faith in their superstitions, though. Humans ought to live according to our beliefs, don't you think? We need to be true to our nature, or we're guilty of a terrible cowardice."

"Don't like all this talk of true nature," Carnegie said. "People decide for themselves what they want to be. I'm a self-made man, through and through."

"Me too," said Rockefeller. "What about you, Hearst?"

"Can't see the difference," Hearst growled. "If your nature's to be a self-made man, that's what you'll be. If not, you'll be what other people make of you."

"Sophistry," said Carnegie.

"Not at all," said Count Lugard. "Mr. Hearst is right, and so is Mr. Quatermain. We do not come innocent into the world; we are what we are. Some are shaped to take destiny by the horns and transform themselves, thus entering the next phase of human progress. Others are shaped to submit, and thus to slide back towards the animal. Most people, thankfully, are cattle with delusions of grandeur."

"Thankfully, Count?" Edison queried.

"But of course. Life is a struggle; for the few to succeed, it is necessary that the many must fail. Power is, by definition, power over others; the more one man has, the more his underlings must be deprived of it. Those of us who have it can only be glad that the majority of humankind is submissive, eager to be led... and bled."

"The man has a point," Rockefeller admitted.

"A very good point," the Duke of Buccleuch agreed.

"It's a very harsh way of thinking," Mrs. de Bathe objected.

"It's a very obsolete way of thinking," Edison put in. "Power is no longer limited to the authority to command the muscles of animals and men. Power nowadays is oil and coal, electricity and steel. Power nowadays is *machinery*. In the 20th century, all men will be better able to remake themselves, by means of their technology. Nor will it be merely a matter of their material conditions; with the assistance of a vast array of instruments of discovery whose nature you can hardly imagine, men will become a great deal wiser. Knowledge is power too, and the 20th century will be an era of information. We ought to envy the generations that will come after us, gentlemen."

"A little knowledge is a dangerous thing," Buccleuch muttered.

"And too much is a truly terrible thing," murmured Count Lugard. "Mankind cannot bear overmuch enlightenment."

"We invariably do envy the generations that will come after us, as we gradually grow older," Carnegie said, in a louder voice. "And when we die... ah, how envious the dead must be of the living!"

"We'll have a chance to find that out, won't we?" Hearst said. "This time tomorrow, eh, Mr. Edison? No further delays, I hope?"

"Everything will be in order by the time we have dined tomorrow, Mr. Hearst," Edison confirmed. "We shall give the dead yet another opportunity to envy our repast before we consult their wisdom."

"If this storm doesn't let up," Hearst muttered, "we'll probably give them the chance to envy us queuing on deck to throw up over the side. Are you sure this beef hasn't spoiled, Rowland?"

"Perfectly sure, Mr. Hearst," the Captain said. "We have excellent refrigeration facilities in the hold behind the galley. Nothing ever spoils aboard the *Titan*."

"The perfect place to store fresh blood," Quatermain whispered in Ayesha's ear, "if one were a clandestine medical researcher devoid of ethics."

"Or any other kind of uncanny flesh," Ayesha whispered in her turn, "if it so happened that all the blood had been quaffed by more scrupulous predators."

Coincidentally, the conversation at the writers' table had reached exactly the same topic. "Searched the refrigeration hold, did he?" Monsieur Jarry said to Monsieur Apollinaire, while he contemplated a slice of Yorkshire pudding impaled on his fork.

"Yes," said Monsieur Apollinaire, "but he thinks there's a secret compartment there, where the blood's being carefully stocked up."

"For transfusion, you say?" Mr. Robertson asked.

"We don't say anything," Monsieur Féval *fils* corrected him. "We're merely repeating what he told us. According to him, it's definitely a matter of transfusion. He might be right. He's the detective, after all."

"It's disgusting," said Mr. Henley. "I don't know how people come up with these ideas. I used to like horror stories when they had ghosts and *natural* monsters, but I don't approve of this *medical* horror. It's all mad scientists and gruesome violations of the body–practically pornographic."

"And Monsieur Rocambole thinks that Count Lugard and those three lovely girls of his are the blood-burglars?" Mr. Chambers asked, seemingly anxious to get back to the point.

"Yes," M. Apollinaire confirmed. "Transylvanian, you see. No reverence for the Hippocratic oath. Very amusing, isn't it?"

"He isn't spreading this around the lower decks, I hope," Mr. Twain put in. "We don't want mobs of unruly peasants marching into the ballroom with torches and pitchforks, demanding that we hand the Count and his daughters over to them, do we?"

"Don't we?" said Monsieur Jarry. "Why not?"

"Because we're English gentlemen, you oaf," said the man from the *Telegraph*. "We'd be obliged to defend the honor of the three young ladies–and their lives too of course–even if they are dagoes. We'd be obliged to wade in, even at the risk of our lives. By the way, do you mind my asking why you're wearing bicycle shorts?"

"Because I make 30 circuits of the promenade deck on my velocipede every day, Monsieur, even when it is raining," Jarry informed him.

"It's all blown over now, anyhow," the man from the *Mail* put in. "There might be a few more deaths from hypothermia tonight, and if another funnel gets struck by lightning, we could all wake up with a shock, but the vampire business seems to be over and done with, more's the pity. If only the count's daughters had been victims... *that* would have been a story."

"Not unless old Buccleuch turned out to be the vampire," his colleague from the *Telegraph* put in.

"Ayesha would make a far better vampire than the Duke," Miss Lee suggested.

"Except that female vampires don't usually target female victims," Mr. Henley observed.

"They do in le Fanu's story," Mr. Huneker corrected him. "And there was that poem of Coleridge's..."

"*Is* there a secret compartment in the refrigeration hold?" Mr. Vane interrupted. His face was so drawn and haggard that he might have been intending to crawl into it and die.

"Oddly enough," said Apollinaire, "I believe that there's more than one. After I'd talked to Rocambole, I took a look myself. There's definitely one extra locker down there–he didn't notice it because it's behind a stack of herring-boxes. I couldn't tell how big it might be just from looking at the door, but I bumped into Mr. Kitchener, who was taking a plan of the ship to Quatermain's cabin, and he let me take a quick look at it. It's there all right–and another one whose door I hadn't spotted. Of course, they might be ice stores–but if so, why does the one I noticed have such a huge padlock on it?"

"You don't suppose it's the safe where old Rockefeller's bonds are stashed?" Mr. Huneker suggested.

"Not unless the guys with guns are a bluff," Mr. Twain said. "They certainly act as if the bonds and Carnegie's bullion are exactly where you'd expect them to be, in the secure hold along with Hearst's Egyptian loot."

"What did Quatermain want with a plan of the ship?" Mr. Robertson asked.

"I think Rocambole asked him to get it," Monsieur Féval answered. "Quatermain's the man who can get things done, it seems. He has the Captain eating out of his hand."

"Not a pretty image," Mr. Chambers observed. "To have Ayesha eating out of one's hand, though..."

"It works the other way round, according to rumor," Mr. Twain told him. "Her name means She Who Must Be Obeyed, supposedly."

"Whatever," said Mr. Chambers. "So, if there are two hidden chambers in the refrigeration hold, and one's full of pirated blood, what's in the other one?"

"Did you know," Apollinaire said, "that the *Titan* has 19 watertight compartments, with a total of 92 doors, all of which can be closed within half a minute if the hull's breached. It was all on Quatermain's plan."

"I think you mean *could*, not *can*," Mr. Robertson put in.

"What's that supposed to mean?" Miss Lee asked.

"It means that they *could* have been closed within half a minute before the funnel got struck by lightning," Mr. Robertson told her. "Now that the internal telegraph system has been damaged, though, they probably can't. If we were to be holed tonight–by hitting an iceberg, say–the subsequent flooding might not be containable. Or, indeed, if we were holed tomorrow or the day after, unless the crew can make adequate running repairs."

"We're all sailing to judgment," groaned Mr. Vane. "Soon, we shall be face-to-face with God. And how shall we answer, when he asks us whether we have sinned?"

"Well, I for one," said Monsieur Jarry, "shall say *mais oui*."

"May we what?" asked the man from the *Telegraph*.

"We certainly may," said Monsieur Lorrain, as the dessert arrived. Every eye on the table regarded the ice cream with slight suspicion, but the heroes of letters raised their spoons as one, and set to work.

On the morning of the 30th, Captain Rowland was woken by Mr. Hodgson, who informed him that eight bodies had been discovered during the night, of whom only three were victims of hypothermia and poor clothing.

"Not vampires *again*?" the Captain wailed.

"I'm afraid so, sir," Hodgson replied.

The obligatory meeting on the bridge was called.

Allan Quatermain was late arriving at the meeting, having been buttonholed *en route* by Edward Rocambole, who had explained regretfully that he had tried with all his might to stay awake all night for a second night running but had proven sadly unequal to the task.

"But now we know about the hidden compartments," Rocambole had said, as Quatermain hurried off, "we'll be sure of finding the secret blood bank! The scoundrels won't get away with their nefarious scheme!"

"We'd better have the ringleaders up to my stateroom again," Rowland told Mr. Black, when the council was finally complete. "This time, I suppose they ought to have brandy with their cigars."

"That might not be enough, sir," Mr. Black opined.

"On its own, no," Quatermain agreed. "We should invite them to return later, as guests in the first class saloon, when Mr. Edison demonstrates his machine for communicating with the dead. They won't want to miss an unprecedented demonstration of that sort. We can even suggest that the occasion might be an opportunity to solve the mystery–that the dead with whom we communicate might be able to tell us who the guilty parties are."

"Excellent thinking, Quatermain," said Rowland. "I'm extremely glad that you're with us this trip."

"A further suggestion, if I may," the hunter added. "It might be worth including Mr. Rocambole in the party. He's been doing a little investigating on his own behalf, and it would be as well to put a lid on any rumors he might be spreading."

"Damned Frenchman!" said Rowland. "Oh well, if you think it advisable, we'll do it. Take care of it will you, Black. How's the work on the internal telegraph coming along, Hodgson?"

"Not terribly well, sir. If Mr. Edison hadn't tired himself out working all night on his machine, I'd have asked for his assistance, but he's put the DO NOT DISTURB sign on his cabin door. The weather's no better, alas–but they do say that lightning never strikes twice in the same place, so we'll probably be fine."

"Actually," Quatermain said, "I remember once..."

"Not now, Mr. Quatermain," said the Captain. "I'm sure that your story is an excellent one, but please save it for dinner. We need to get to work."

"One more point of information, if I may, sir," said the hunter, meekly. "What *is* in the two storage lockers connected to the refrigeration hold?"

Silence fell upon the entire company, as the Captain and his two mates exchanged uneasy glances.

After a few seconds silence, Captain Rowland said: "Ice, Mr. Quatermain. Just ice."

"That's what I thought," said Quatermain, mildly. "I'll pass the information on to Mr. Rocambole, just to set his mind at rest."

That night, at dinner, Allan Quatermain held the Captain's table enthralled with his account of multiple lightning strikes on an unnamed peak in the Mitumba Mountains, which had fortunately put an end to a number of hideously grotesque multitentacular creatures that had been directing a murderous native cult for centuries.

"I don't understand what a gang of whistling octopi were doing up a mountain in darkest Africa in the first place," Carnegie muttered to Edison, as fluttering hearts slowed in their paces and the members of the audience began to breathe more easily again.

"Actually," said Edison, "the plural of octopus is *octopodes*, and the creatures described by Mr. Quatermain appear to have had more than eight tentacles in any case. There've been rumors of such creatures from a dozen different parts of the world. Traces of them have recently been discovered at several archaeological sites, but they don't appear to have been bony enough to fossilize conveniently, so their taxonomic status remains dubious, and it's difficult to tell how long they've been around–millions of years, probably. Some of their relatives still live in the sea, apparently; while I was at the Royal Society in London,

I heard a rumor that some body-parts had been caught in the net of a vessel fishing off Madeira. The locals were terrified, for some reason–said they weren't really dead, even though they were mere fragments, and that they were inherently evil. They were dispatched to London for examination, but they never reached England, alas–they were aboard the *S.S. Dunwich*, which sank off Selsey Bill the week before Christmas."

Meanwhile, Ayesha was saying: "The lightning was a blessing. We had heard rumors of these creatures and their unspeakable depredations even in Kôr. The natives who worshipped them as gods–or as the petty representatives of gods even more unspeakably dreadful–had become excited of late, anticipating the imminent return of some ultimate horror that would put an end to man's dominion over the Earth."

"Savages believe all kinds of weird things," said Rowland, staring into her wide blue eyes. "Mind you, we old seamen know better than to laugh at all their superstitions. We've encountered monsters in our time, haven't we, Mr. Hodgson?"

"We have indeed, sir," Hodgson said.

"Hodgson could tell you tales of the South Seas that might even startle Mr. Quatermain," the Captain went on. "Mind you, you don't have to go as far as that to find bizarre creatures nowadays. The beaches on the Isle of Wight..." He stopped suddenly as Hodgson put a hand on his arm. "Oh, of course," he said. "Sorry."

"Horror stories are all very well," the Duke of Buccleuch opined, "but I'm not sure they're fit accompaniment for roasted mallard and baked Alaska, especially when there are ladies present. I can see why a fellow's mind might turn to morbid matters when we've got Mr. Edison's phantasmagoria show to look forward to with our brandy and cigars, but I think a little self-control's in order while we're eating. Don't you agree, Mrs. de Bathe?"

"I don't mind at all," the former Lillie Langtry hastened to assure Quatermain and Edison.

"I am not a stage magician," Edison said. "My machine is not a phantasmagoria. What you will see tonight is one of the greatest experiments in history, more important by far than Roentgen's games with X-rays or Marconi's attempts to develop wireless telegraphy. When my machine is connected up to the ship's generators, everyone present will be privileged to witness the dawn of a new era in human history. It will advance the cause of Enlightenment by an order of magnitude."

"Don't know about that," Buccleuch muttered. "Damn spiritualists have been pestering the dead for years, and all we have to show for it is stupid gossip."

"The Duke has a point," said Hearst. "If you're aiming to horn in on the medium business, you'll have to be careful of your overheads. It's a limited market, and the clients aren't big spenders, for the most part."

"The marketing strategy will be a bit awkward," Carnegie agreed. "A machine for talking to the dead isn't like the electric light bulb–something that every home needs and has to buy repeatedly because of built-in obsolescence. Do you envisage it as a domestic appliance, like your phonograph, or will it be an institutional sort of thing, like the electric chair?"

"I've already explained that the machine isn't amenable to mass production," Edison said. "I envisage it as a wonder of the world, which might be placed in its own custom-built building as a modern oracle."

"And what will it actually *do* for us?" Rockefeller wanted to know. "When you get down to the nitty-gritty, what'll the news be *worth*?"

"I think that rather depends on exactly what the dead have to say for themselves when Mr. Edison opens his channel of communication," Quatermain interjected. "Even if spiritualist mediums are honest–not that I doubt them all, mind–their links with the world beyond seem to be tenuous and discontinuous. If Mr. Edison can open a channel capable of carrying much heavier traffic for sustained periods, the dead may become a good deal more voluble."

"That is my hope," Edison confirmed. "At present, our forefathers can only communicate with us, if at all, in fragmentary whispers. My machine will hopefully give them the ability to speak clearly, at far greater length and in far greater detail."

"But it might not work in the way you envisage," Count Lugard suggested. "And even if it does... it has occurred to you, I suppose, that at least some of the dead may bear us some ill will–and that they might be at least as prone to mendacity, malice, inarticulacy, false belief and insanity as they were when they were alive."

"Come now, Lugard," Quatermain said. "Even aristocrats like yourself and the Duke of Buccleuch, who are heirs to centuries of feudal oppression, surely have nothing to fear from the bitter slanders of a few wretched peasants? Why, I dare say that there are hundreds of elephants, dozens of lions and not a few giraffes whose souls might harbor resentments against me, but I'd be willing to face them all as squarely now as I did when I gunned them down."

"And what about the unspeakable *octopodes* from the Mituba Mountains?" Carnegie asked. "Are you willing to hear what *their* immortal souls have to whistle in your ear?"

"Of course," said Quatermain. "That would be a small price to pay for such opportunities as the privilege of meeting up with my old friends Curtis and Good again."

"You don't think they might be a little envious that you walked away with all King Solomon's treasure while they stayed behind to feed the vultures?" Hearst suggested.

"They have the treasures of Heaven now," Quatermain said. "They were virtuous and generous men, and I cannot imagine that they would bear me any grudge."

"They're likely in a very small minority, then," Hearst said. "What about the majority whose members are suffering the torments of Hell and the rigors of Purgatory? Shall we hear their screams of agony when Edison switches on his machine, do you think?"

"My machine will hopefully put an end to all such idiot superstitions," Edison said, stiffly. "I am confident that it will demonstrate the infinite mercy of God–or His utter indifference to the condition of the dead, whose echoes beyond the grave must be natural phenomena, like electricity and X-rays, waiting to be revealed by the march of progress."

"And exploited, of course," Carnegie added. "After discovery comes utility."

"Just so," said Rockefeller. "Still can't see exactly how you'll make your money, though."

Edison raised his eyes to the Heaven in which he did not seem to believe, but he remained silent. Presumably, there seemed to him to be no point in correcting the millionaires' misconceptions yet again.

"I'll drink to that," said Captain Rowland, although it was unclear to his 11 dinner companions exactly what he meant by "that."

At the writers' table, the talk was similarly dominated by Mr. Edison's impending demonstration.

"It will be interesting to converse with Shakespeare," said Mr. Huneker.

"Chaucer and Malory," Mr. Robertson speculated.

"King Arthur himself, and Sir Perceval, too," suggested Mr. Twain.

"Plato, Aristotle and Epicurus," added Mr. Chambers.

"Charles Baudelaire and Villiers de l'Isle-Adam," Monsieur Lorrain put in.

"Sappho and Catherine the Great," mused Ms. Lee.

"Napoleon Bonaparte and Georges Cadoudal," was Monsieur Féval's slightly mischievous suggestion.

"Horatio Nelson and the Duke of Wellington," countered the man from the *Telegraph.*

"Walter Raleigh and Elizabeth I," supplied the man from the *Mail.*

"Simon Magus and Apollonius of Tyana," said Monsieur Apollinaire.

"Attila the Hun and Genghis Khan," Monsieur Jarry contributed.

"All mere flights of destiny's fancy," Mr. Vane opined. "We shall all meet the Lord, whether Mr. Edison's machine works or not, and we shall all be judged."

"Percy Shelley and John Keats," Mr. Huneker went on, blithely.

"Samuel Johnson and Jonathan Swift," Mr. Robertson added.

"George Washington and Julius Caesar," said Mr. Twain.

"Homer and General Custer," added Mr. Chambers.

"Salome and Cleopatra," was Monsieur Lorrain's second contribution.

"Michelangelo and Leonardo da Vinci," Ms. Lee suggested.

"Fra Diavolo and Cartouche," said Monsieur Féval *fils*.

"Jack Sheppard and Dick Turpin," riposted the man from the *Telegraph*.

"Richard III and Henry VIII," said the man from the *Mail*.

"Merlin and *la fée* Morgane," said Monsieur Apollinaire.

"Gilles de Rais and Jeanne d'Arc," said Monsieur Jarry.

"If the lines of communication remain open, of course," Monsieur Féval observed. "We'll have some stiff competition in the new century. If every home in the world acquires one of Mr. Edison's machines, Father will want me to serve as his amanuensis, I'm sure. Now that we have the electric light bulb and the typewriter, the transcription of the dead's pent-up literary works could become a long and arduous task."

"It could be worse," said Mr. Twain. "We might be historians."

When the dining room had emptied again, the gentlemen reassembled in the saloon, where they brought out their pipes and cigars as usual–except for those who preferred a glass of absinthe, with or without a dash of ether.

Mr. Edison's machine had already been set up, and connected to the ship's generator. In appearance it was somewhat reminiscent of a cross between a telephone exchange and a church organ, its manifold pipes being tuned to catch and amplify the voices of the dead, while its multitudinous switches were designed to secure and facilitate connections between the mundane and astral planes.

There was a stool at the front, from which all the indicators were visible and all the controls accessible, but Edison did not take his seat immediately; he busied himself checking the various connections for a full 15 minutes, during which interval his audience–augmented now by Edward Rocambole, a select handful of his fellow second-class passengers and an equal number of representatives of the third-class–shuffled for position. Almost all of the watchers were standing up, the seating in the saloon being arranged about the walls, offering a very poor view. Thanks to the *Titan*'s stabilizers, the waiting men were only swaying gently from side to side even though the storm outside was raging as never before.

Finally, the moment of truth arrived. Mr. Edison turned to his audience, bowed and opened his mouth to make a speech.

"Oh, get on with it, man!" said the Duke of Buccleuch, rudely. "We all know why we're here. Let's hear what the dead have to say, if anything."

Edison was obviously not pleased by this demand but he scanned the faces of the crowd, as if in order to measure their opinion. What he saw there evidently disposed him against further delay, and he sat down. He reached out his right hand to take the lever that would activate the machine's electricity supply, and pulled it down decisively.

The machine crackled and hummed. The pipes emitted eerie sounds, reminiscent of harpstrings stirred by a wayward wind–but then the voices began to come through.

They *were* voices–no one in the saloon could have any doubt about that–but it was quite impossible to distinguish what any one of them might be saying. There were thousands, perhaps millions, all attempting to speak at the same time, in every living language and at least as many that were no longer extant.

None of the voices was shouting, at first; they were all speaking in a conversational tone, as if they did not realize how much competition there was to be heard. As the minutes went by, however, this intelligence seemed to filter back to wherever the dead were lodged. The voices were raised a little–and then more than a little. Fortunately, the volume of their clamor was limited by the power of the amplifiers that Mr. Edison had fitted to his machine, and he immediately reached out to turn the knob that would quiet the chorus–with the result that the voices of the dead became a mere murmurous blur, denied all insistency as well as all coherency.

Edison's own voice was clearly audible over the muted hubbub when he turned to his audience to say: "If you will be patient, gentlemen, I am certain that our friends on the Other Side will begin to sort themselves out, and make arrangements to address us by turns, in order that each of them might make himself heard. It is just a matter..."

He was interrupted then, by an unexpected event.

Allan Quatermain, who happened to be looking out of one of the portholes, observed four bolts of lightning descend simultaneously from widely disparate parts of the sky, converging upon the funnels of the *Titan.* All four struck at the same instant, each one picking out a funnel with unerring accuracy.

The cables connecting the ship's internal telegraph system had been imperfectly repaired, but there was nevertheless a continuous circuit running from the bow to the stern, and from the crow's nest to the keel. It ran through every bulkhead and every compartment, every cabin on every deck, every hold and locker, every davit and stanchion, every rivet and joint. The lightning surged through the hull, possessing every fiber of the vessel's being.

The *Titan*'s wiring burnt out within a fraction of a second and Mr. Edison's machine collapsed in a heap of slag, although it left the man himself miraculously untouched, perched upon his stool. So diffuse was the shock, in fact, that the men standing in the saloon, their womenfolk in their cabins, and even the masses huddled in steerage felt nothing more than a tingling in their nerves, more stimulant than injury.

Nobody aboard the *Titan* died as a direct result of the multiple lightning strike, but the flood of electrical energy was by no means inconsequential. Communication between the *Titan* and the world of the dead was cut off almost instantly–but *almost* instantly was still a measurable time, and the interval was enough to permit a considerable effect.

Exactly what that effect was, no one aboard the *Titan* could accurately discern, and the only man aboard with wit enough even to form a hypothesis was

Jean Ténèbre, who had briefly borrowed the identity of the elephant-hunter Allan Quatermain.

If the real Quatermain had made any posthumous protest, his voice went unheard.

What the Chevalier Ténèbre hypothesized was that by far the greater portion of the power of the multiple lightning-strike, which had so conspicuously failed to blast the *Titan* to smithereens or strike dead its crew and passengers, had actually passed through the ship's telegraph system and Mr. Edison's machine *into* the realm of the dead, where it had wreaked havoc.

What the realm of the dead might be, or where it might be located, the Chevalier had no idea–but he supposed that its fabric must be delicate and that the souls of the dead must be electrical phenomena of a far gentler kind than the lighting of Atlantic storms.

Thomas Edison had presumably been correct to dispute William Randolph Hearst's claim that Edison's machine might only enable the *Titan*'s passengers to hear the screams of the damned in Hell–but if the souls of dead humankind had not been in Hell when Edison closed his master-switch, they obtained a taste of it now.

And they screamed.

They screamed inaudibly, for the most part, because the pipes of Edison's machines had melted and their connections had been dissolved–but there was one exception to this rule.

The Brothers Ténèbre and Count Lugard's party were not the only individuals on board the *Titan* who might have been classified as "undead." The fragment of the creature that had washed up on the beach at Nettlestone Point, having earlier been found by a fishing-vessel off Madeira and lost again from the *Dunwich*, also had an exotic kind of life left in it. Like many supposedly primitive invertebrates, the part was capable of reproducing the whole, under the right existential conditions and with the appropriate energy intake.

When this seemingly dead creature screamed, its scream had only to wait for a few microseconds before it was translated back from the fragile realm of the dead into the robust land of the living.

It was a strange scream, more sibilant than strident, and it was a strangely powerful scream.

As Edison's machine had briefly demonstrated–confounding all the skeptics who had refused for centuries to believe in spiritualists and necromancers, ghostly visitations and revelatory dreams–the boundary between the human and astral planes was not unbreachable. When the unnamable creature, whose close kin had died by lightning in the Mituba Mountains, was resurrected by lightning, its scream tore a breach in that boundary, opening a way between the worlds–and through that breach, the newly-agonized souls of the human dead poured in an unimaginable and irresistible cataract.

The breach, Jean Ténèbre subsequently decided, could only have lasted for a few microseconds more than it took to make the scream audible in the first place–but while it lasted, the souls of the dead had a chance to assert themselves in the world of the living, of a kind they had never had before–not, at any rate, in such quantities.

The souls of the dead vied with one another to dispossess the souls of the living: to claim the bodies of the *Titan*'s 3,000 passengers for their own use and purposes.

The competition was understandably fierce.

There were eight people aboard the *Titan* whose souls could not, as it turned out, be dispossessed. The two Brothers Ténèbre, the Count who had inverted his name and his three lovely brides were six of them. The seventh was Edward Rocambole, whose opinion of his own heroism was so unshakable that he simply could not be persuaded to vacate his mortal habitation. The eighth was an 11-year-old girl in steerage, by the name of Myra, who was just lucky.

As December 31, 1900, whiled away, Jean Ténèbre made some slight attempt to figure out who might now be inhabiting the bodies of his fellow passengers and the *Titan*'s crew. He spoke seven languages himself, so he made a little more progress than another man might have, but it was still an impossible task. The dead turned out to be very discreet, and they clung to their assumed identities as stubbornly as the Chevalier had ever clung to any of his multitudinous pseudonyms.

By the time he had to dress for dinner, Jean Ténèbre had found some reason to suspect that Captain John Rowland might once have been Edward Teach, nicknamed Blackbeard; that Mr. Hodgson might once have been an American gentleman named Edgar Poe; that Mr. Black might once have been Niccolo Machiavelli; that William Randolph Hearst might once have been Judas Iscariot; that John D. Rockefeller might once have been Nebuchadnezzar; that Andrew Carnegie might once have been Cyrus the Great; that the Duke of Buccleuch might once have been Wat Tyler; that Edison might once have been Daedalus; and that the former Lillie Langtry might now be the former Catherine de Medici, but he could not be sure.

The one thing of which he was sure was that, in the struggle for repossession of the Earth, the meek had, in general, not prevailed.

That night, however, dinner was served as usual, although the only meat left aboard was chicken, all the remaining pork and beef having mysteriously vanished into one of the storage-lockers adjoining the refrigeration hold.

At the writers' table, the conversation ran along lines that were a trifle unusual, but nevertheless perfectly civilized.

"Are you going to stay in the writing game?" Mr. Robertson asked Mr. Twain.

"I doubt it," said Mr. Twain. "Not unless Edison hurries the development of moving pictures. That's where writers will make money in future–that and broadcasting, Marconi-style. How about you, Chambers?"

"I'm heading for Texas," Mr. Chambers said. "Going into the oil business, I think. The 20th century is going to need power, and there's an ocean of black gold lying around just waiting to be sucked out. Are you with me, Huneker?"

"All the way," Mr. Huneker agreed. "But I might just get into automobiles. They're not much to write home about just now, but I have a feeling there's scope in them–and a market for your oil, Chambers."

"You're staying with the *Mail*, I suppose?" said the man from the *Telegraph* to his friend.

"Just for a while," his colleague agreed. "Provided I make editor within two years. It shouldn't be difficult. Within five, I'll have Middle England eating out of my hand and every advertiser and propagandist in the country licking my arse. You?"

"I fancy that I might found a tabloid of my own. *The Daily Mirror*, say–or *The Sun*, if I could be sure that swine Hearst wouldn't sue me. I'll not be in competition with you, mind. Wouldn't want to confuse the poor lambs with debates or the truth, would we?"

"We should be thinking in terms of an all-round information cartel," Mr. Henley added. "Sew up the print media, telegraphy and telephones to begin with, then join forces with Twain, and keep a lookout for anything new that comes along."

"Europe," Monsieur Jarry said to Monsieur Apollinaire, "is ripe for looting. England and Germany will be at one another's throats even if we don't stir the pot, with France caught between them. Given that the Sun never sets on their various imperial adventures, that puts the whole world up for grabs or very nearly."

"There's going to be big money in armaments," opined Monsieur Féval. "Bigger and better guns, tougher and thicker armor. Civilians won't be able to stay out of 20th century wars, with fleets of airships raining down bombs on cities."

"And big money in medicine too," Monsieur Lorrain put in. "It always pays to have both sides covered in a major conflict–killing and healing always go hand in hand. There'll be fortunes to be made out of any method of combating infection and syphilis. Armies are wonderful instruments for spreading the plague–all that camaraderie and rape."

"High explosives are passé," Apollinaire mused. "Poison gas is the way forward. Atom bombs, maybe a little further down the line. Germ warfare too, if your medicines can provide the means to protect the folks at home."

"The long-term future's in morphine and human trafficking," Ms. Lee opined. "Even if populations aren't displaced *en masse* by wars, there's bound to be migration on a scale that beggars the imagination, and even the people who aren't physically wounded in your universal wars will be in dire need of pain relief."

"We shall be judged by our actions," Mr. Vane asserted, cheerfully. "Let's make sure that we make more profitable use of our second chances than we were granted time to do with our first."

As soon as dinner was over, the entire company repaired to the grand ballroom. Guards were posted at the doors to make sure that there was no eruption from the third class decks, although a number of second-class passengers were admitted in order to remake old acquaintances. Edward Rocambole was not among them.

Although three-quarters of the former members of the orchestra were no longer able to play their instruments, it did not take long to assemble a new company, which made up in enthusiasm for what it lacked in polish. No waltzes were played that night, but polkas by the score and tangos by the dozen, punctuated by the occasional tarantella. The former Mrs. Langtry was only one of the singers persuaded to perform, although the ballads she performed had never previously been in her repertoire. Individual dance performances included a spirited rendition of the Dance of the Seven Veils by one of the second-class passengers, which proved such a success that Allan Quatermain volunteered to entertain the gathering with a saber dance, which he executed with a speed and skill that belied his years.

Down below, the third-class passengers were dancing too.

In one of the storage-lockers connected to the refrigerated hold, something else was dancing in its own eldritch fashion, perfectly oblivious to the cold.

Although Captain Rowland was famous for maintaining a supply of liquor aboard the *Titan* that was impossible to exhaust, the vessel was drunk dry that night–but not until well after midnight, when every member of the assembly in the ballroom filled a glass to the brim with champagne in order that they might drink to the health, wealth and happiness of the new era. It was not until that temporal landmark was passed that the assembly crossed the fine definitive line between a party and an orgy, but once the boundary had been cleared, there was no looking back. The *Titan* had never been host to such a hectic celebration; nor had any other ship in the entire world.

The storm outside died down by slow degrees, but, long into the early hours, its lashing rain and crashing thunder seemed to be beating time to the tempestuous emotions that ran riot within the ballroom.

Everyone there–and, for that matter, everyone aboard the vessel who was excluded from the ball by the accident of social class and lack of useful connections–was glad to be alive.

"You know," Mr. Vane said to Miss Lee, in one particular moment of intimacy, "there's no reason at all why every sea voyage shouldn't climax in this glorious manner. You'd think, wouldn't you, that everyone would be glad to be alive, for every moment of every day, whether they'd actually sampled death or not."

"That's true," Miss Lee agreed. "But you have to bear in mind that this is the first ship in history–and perhaps the last–that has lost its right to be classified as a ship of fools."

The following morning, shortly after dawn, the *Titan* steamed past Sandy Hook. She soon came within sight of the Statue of Liberty.

"It's going to shake things up when this lot get ashore,", said Ange Ténèbre, still playing the role of Ayesha, as he/she drank in his/her first sight of the home of the brave and the land of the free. "If I weren't so incorrigible, I might have thought twice about stealing the bullion and the bonds, let alone Hearst's antique gemstones. Do you think they might go looking for them–and perhaps find them?"

"I doubt it," his brother said. "They're too busy making future plans to care overmuch about minor inconveniences. And if they do go looking, they'll have to be very careful about opening the wrong freezer compartment. The thing in the other one's getting distinctly restless."

"There might be repercussions, though," the shorter brother observed. "More so than usual, I expect."

"We're well used to repercussions," the taller one replied. "We've been hung, beheaded or broken on the wheel in half the capitals of Europe. If we end up in Edison's electric chair, it'll be one more new experience. And if we don't... we'll have a high old time. We can be movers and shakers too, if we only put our minds to it. This could be our century."

"You've always been the one urging discretion in the past," Ange pointed out.

"Times change," Jean said, firmly. "In any case, we'd have to do something rather spectacular to stand out in a crowd like this one. I doubt that America will notice anything out of the ordinary in anything we might do. It's always been a land of opportunity."

"They certainly won't give us a second thought once they've opened the other storage-locker," Ange agreed. "The people from the New York Museum of Natural History are going to get one hell of a shock when they unlock it."

"I expect it'll slip over the side and head for Innsmouth when it's eaten its fill," Jean said. "One shoggoth more or less won't be more than a tiny ripple on the flood tide of history–as will the addition of an extra ounce of rapacity to the characters of men like Hearst and Rockefeller."

They were joined at that moment by Count Lugard and his three delectable brides.

"Did you dine well last night, Monsieur Ange?" the Count asked, politely.

"Yes, indeed," said Ange. "The poor girl seemed a trifle disconcerted, not having expected her second term on Earth to be terminated quite so rapidly, but her blood hadn't curdled at all. You?"

"Likewise–and my three lovelies had a good time also. Irma was a trifle reckless, descending no further than the second-class cabins, but she says that it was worth it, just to see the expression on Monsieur Rocambole's face when he realized that there is, after all, no such thing as a gang of crazed medical technicians covertly collecting donations for medical research."

"The world is full of such misconceptions," Ange lamented. "The only things in life that are dependable are lust and avarice."

"Do you not mean death and taxes?" the Count asked, laughing to emphasize that he was joking. They were, after all, surrounded by conclusive evidence of the evitability of death, and they both knew perfectly well that only little people paid taxes.

"Aren't you afraid that the sunlight will shrivel you up and cause you to burst into flames?" Ange riposted, laughing just as merrily.

The Count looked up into the brightening sky, then lowered his eyes to drink in the sunlight reflected from the myriad windows of a host of skyscrapers. "I shall love it here," he said. "And my brides will have the time of their unlives. We'll soon make ourselves felt in Manhattan. Things will never be the same again."

"Not according to Jean," Ange told him. "He doesn't think the arrival of the *Titan* will change anything significantly. He's a great believer in the irresistible tide of history."

"That's not quite what I meant, Brother," the Chevalier corrected him. "I meant that no one will think that things have changed any more than they would have in any other case. They'll be expecting change regardless, and our contribution to it–not to mention that of the 3,000 reanimates–will seem to be nothing more than a curlicue in a rich and complex pattern. This is a new century, Brother Ange; even if the *Titan* had hit an iceberg and gone straight to the bottom, you and I would still be living in interesting times."

"Always assuming that we still could come back again, if our graves were lying on the ocean floor," Ange said, uncertainly.

"For the Brothers Ténèbre and everything we stand for," Jean assured him, "fate will always find a way."

Credits

Mask of the Monster

Starring:	**Created by:**
"Gouroull"	Mary Shelley, Jean-Claude Carrière
Judex	Arthur Bernède & Louis Feuillade
Jules Maigret	Georges Simenon
Louise Maigret née Leonard	Georges Simenon
Cornelius Kramm	Gustave Le Rouge
Fritz Kramm	Gustave Le Rouge
Jules de Grandin	Seabury Quinn

Written by:
Matthew BAUGH is a 43-year-old ordained minister who lives and works in Sedona, Arizona, with his wife Mary and two cats. He is a longtime fan of pulp fiction, cliffhanger serials, old time radio, and is the proud owner of the silent *Judex* serial on DVD. He has written a number of articles on lesser known pop-culture characters like Dr. Syn, Jules de Grandin, and Sailor Steve Costigan for the Wold-Newton Universe Internet website. His article on Zorro will appear in *Myths for the Modern Age*. *Mask of the Monster* is his first published story.

Cadavres Exquis

Starring:	**Created by:**
Fascinax	Anonymous
Numa Pergyll	Anonymous
Jules de Grandin	Seabury Quinn
Franz Krypfer	Anonymous

Written by:
Bill CUNNINGHAM is a pulp screenwriter-producer specializing in the Direct-to-DVD market. His credits include *Scarecrow*, *Scarecrow Slayer* and *.Com for Murder*. An authority and lecturer on D2DVD movies and marketing with over a decade of experience, he knew that somehow he would become a writer when he saw his creation, *The Pixie*, accepted into DC Comics' *Dial H for Hero* series

(*Adventure Comics* No. 488) right out of high school. When he is not drinking coffee to excess, Bill is not so secretly hatching plans for a multimedia empire out of his Hollywood, CA kitchen, haunting used book and punk rock stores, and researching the exploitation cinema of Hollywood's poverty row urban legend, Titan Studios.

When Lemmy Met Jules

Starring:	**Created by:**
Lemmy Caution	Peter Cheyney
Jules Maigret	Georges Simenon

Written by:
Terrance DICKS managed to escape the world of advertising to build a distinguished career as a writer, then a producer, for the BBC where he masterminded *Doctor Who* from 1968 to 1974, and later produced a variety of classic series such *as Oliver Twist* (1985), *David Copperfield* (1986), *Brat Farrar* (1986) and *Vanity Fair* (1987), amongst others. His being asked to pen early *Doctor Who* novels–an activity which he continues to this day–led him to become a popular author of numerous Young Adult and Children's Books, including *The Baker Street Irregulars*, *Ask Oliver*, *T.R. Bear*, etc. Terrance has also penned two *Doctor Who* stageplays and scripted episodes of *The Avengers* (1961), *Moonbase 3* (1973) and *Space: 1999* (1975).

The Vanishing Devil

Starring:	**Created by:**
Doctor Francis Ardan	Guy d'Armen, Lester Dent
Louise Ducharme	Guy d'Armen
Sherlock Holmes	Arthur Conan Doyle
Roger Gunn	J.T. Edson
Jules Maigret	Georges Simenon
Doctor Natas	Guy d'Armen, Sax Rohmer
Pao Tcheou	Edward Brooker
Dr. Caresco	André Couvreur

Written by:
Win Scott ECKERT graduated with a B.A. in Anthropology and thereafter received his Juris Doctorate, enabling him to practice law. In 1997, he posted the

first site on the Internet devoted to expanding Philip José Farmer's original premise of a Wold Newton Family to encompass a whole Wold Newton Universe. He is the editor of and a contributor to *Myths for the Modern Age: Philip José Farmer's Wold Newton Universe*, forthcoming from MonkeyBrain Books in 2005. Win lives near Denver with his family and four felines, in a house crammed to the rafters with books, comic books and *Star Trek* action figures.

The Three Jewish Horsemen

Starring:	**Created by:**
Lord Baskerville	Arthur Conan Doyle
Josephine Balsamo	Maurice Leblanc
Erik	Gaston Leroux
Arsène Lupin (Jim Barnett)	Maurice Leblanc
Béchoux	Maurice Leblanc
Victoire	Maurice Leblanc

Written by:
Viviane ETRIVERT learned to read in the novels of Jules Verne and the adventures of Arsène Lupin. She is the author of two novels, *Les Mondes du Trickster* (*The Trickster's Worlds*, 2001) and *La Morrigan* (2004). She has also written numerous fantasy and crime short short stories, the latter featuring a 1930s French Police Commissioner named Commissaire Cles. Viviane is married, has three sons and works as a jurist specialized in European Union Law at the Prefecture of Montpellier, where her story takes place.

The Werewolf of Rutherford Grange

Starring:	**Created by:**
Harry Dickson	Anonymous
Sexton Blake	Harry Blyth
The Westenras	Bram Stoker
The Rutherfords	Philip José Farmer
John Roxton	Arthur Conan Doyle
Gianetti Annunciata	Anonymous
Sâr Dubnotal	Anonymous

Written by:
G.L. GICK lives in Indiana and has been a pulp fan since he first picked up a Doc Savage paperback. His other interests include old-time radio, Golden and Silver Age comics, cryptozoology, classic animation, British SF TV and C.S.

Lewis and G.K. Chesterton. He is, in other words, a nerd and damn proud of it. This is his first professional sale.

The Last Vendetta

Starring:	**Created by:**
Arthur Gordon	Emile Gaboriau
Ignacz Djanko	Sergio Corbucci & Bruno Corbucci
Josephine Balsamo	Maurice Leblanc
Loco (a.k.a. Aguirre)	Sergio Corbucci & Mario Amendola
Leonard	Maurice Leblanc
Hong Chen	Guy d'Armen
Huan Tsung Chao	Sax Rohmer
Oliver Haddo	Somerset Maugham
Count Bielowsky	Pierre Benoit
Mr. Washburn	Lowell Ganz & Babaloo Mandel
Satanas	Louis Feuillade
Clyde (a.k.a. Nine Fingers)	Gianfranco Parolini & Renato Izzo
Yolaf Peterson	Sergio Corbucci & Massimo de Rita

Written by:
Rick LAI is a computer programmer living in Bethpage, New York. During the 1980s and 1990s, he wrote articles utilizing Philip José Farmer's Wold Newton Universe concepts for pulp magazine fanzines such as *Nemesis Inc*, *Echoes*, *Golden Perils*, *Pulp Vault* and *Pulp Collector*. Rick has also created chronologies of such heroes as Doc Savage and the Shadow. Several of these articles and chronologies have recently been revised and made available on Win Eckert's Wold Newton Universe website. Rick is also a collector of the works of French detective writers such as Emile Gaboriau, Gaston Leroux and Maurice Leblanc. He has recently developed an interest in Spaghetti Westerns and Kung Fu movies, as shown in *The Last Vendetta*, his first short story.

The Sainte-Geneviève Caper

Starring:	**Created by:**
Arsène Lupin	Maurice Leblanc
Sherlock Holmes	Arthur Conan Doyle
Ganimard	Maurice Leblanc
Also Starring:	
Lord Dunsany	

Written by:
Alain le BUSSY hails from Belgium and studied political and social sciences, before working in human resources for the European division of Caterpillar. Bitten with the fantasy bug as a child, Alain became involved in fandom at an early age and attended the Heidelberg Worldcon in 1970. A prolific writer, Alain has had over 25 novels and 200 short stories published. In 1993, his novel, *Deltas*, the first volume of *The Aqualia Trilogy*, won the Rosny Award, the French equivalent of the Hugo. Other significant works include the heroic-fantasy saga of *Yorg* (1995) and *Equilibre* (*Balance*, 1997), the story of a waterworld which is the sole meeting point between mankind and an alien reptilian race.

Journey to the Center of Chaos

Starring:	**Created by:**
Alexander Whateley	H.P. Lovecraft
JimGrim (a.k.a. John Green)	Talbot Mundy
Dahoor	Guy d'Armen
Robur	Jules Verne
Sâr Dubnotal	Anonymous
Tom Turner	Jules Verne
The Yian-Hos	Helena Blavatsky
Yog-Sothoth	H.P. Lovecraft

Written by:
Jean-Marc & Randy LOFFICIER, the authors of the *Shadowmen* non-fiction series, have also collaborated on five screenplays, a dozen books and numerous comic books and translations, including *Arsène Lupin*, *Doc Ardan*, *Doctor Omega* and *The Phantom of the Opera*, all published by Black Coat Press. They have written a number of animation teleplays, including episodes of *Duck Tales* and *The Real Ghostbusters* and such popular comic book heroes as *Superman* and *Doctor Strange*. In 1999, in recognition of their distinguished career as comic book writers, editors and translators, they were presented with the Inkpot

award for Outstanding Achievement in Comic Arts. Randy is a member of the Writers Guild of America, West and Mystery Writers of America.

Lacunal Visions

Starring:	**Created by:**
C. Auguste Dupin	Edgar Allan Poe
Sergeant Picard	William Kotzwinkle
Maître Zacharius	Jules Verne
Doctor Omega	Arnould Galopin

Written by:
Samuel T. PAYNE was born on the Channel Island of Jersey, in 1982. Throughout the 1990s, he contributed a number of articles for student magazines and literary periodicals before graduating in English Literature in Leeds, North England, in 2004. Aside from writing, he enjoys playing bass guitar, painting and modelwork. His latest modelwork, in the form of a Dalek, can be seen on the covers of the *Dalek Empire* audio CDs. He is currently writing an original *Doctor Omega* novel based on C.I. Defontenay's classic epic, *Star, or Psi Cassiopeia,* both scheduled to be released by Black Coat Press in late 2005.

The Kind-Hearted Torturer

Starring:	**Created by:**
C. Auguste Dupin	Edgar Allan Poe
Comte de Monte-Cristo	Alexandre Dumas
Comtesse de Clare	Paul Féval
Valentine Morrel	Alexandre Dumas
Haydée	Alexandre Dumas

Written by:
John PEEL was born in Nottingham, England, and moved to the U.S. in 1981 to marry. He, his wife Nan ("Mrs. Peel") and their 13 dogs live on Long Island, New York. He has written just over 100 books to date, mostly for young adults. He is the only author to have written novels based on both *Doctor Who* and *Star Trek.* His most popular work is *Diadem,* a fantasy series of which he's currently writing the ninth volume.

Penumbra

Starring:	**Created by:**
Philippe Guerande	Louis Feuillade
Les Vampires	Louis Feuillade
Favraux	Arthur Bernède & Louis Feuillade
Judex (a.k.a. Vallières)	Arthur Bernède & Louis Feuillade
The Waynes	Bob Kane & Bill Finger
Kent Allard	Walter Gibson

Written by:
Chris ROBERSON is a writer, editor and publisher. His novels include the forthcoming *Here, There & Everywhere*, *The Shark Boy and Lava Girl Adventures* with Robert Rodriguez, *The Voyage of Night Shining White* and *Paragaea: A Planetary Romance*. His story "*O One*," which appeared in *Live Without A Net* (2003), won the 2003 Sidewise Award for Best Short-Form Alternate History, was listed as an Honorable Mention in *The 21st Annual Year's Best Science Fiction* and was short-listed for the 2004 World Fantasy Award for Short Fiction. In 2003, Roberson and his business partner and spouse, Allison Baker, launched the independent press MonkeyBrain Books, an imprint specializing in nonfiction genre studies. He lives in Austin, Texas with his wife, their daughter and his library.

The Paris-Ganymede Clock

Starring:	**Created by:**
Arthur Wimsey	Dorothy Sayers
Melville Fairr	Craig Rice
Fantômas	Marcel Allain & Pierre Souvestre
Robin Muscat	Maurice Limat
Mrs. Rosenberg	Joss Whedon

Written by:
Robert SHECKLEY was born in Brooklyn. A veteran science fiction writer, he began to sell stories to science-fiction magazines such as *Galaxy* soon after his graduation. During this time, he also wrote 15 episodes of *Captain Video*. His first novel, *Immortality, Inc.* (1958) was produced as the movie *Freejack* (1992). He also wrote the story which was the basis for the movie *The Tenth Victim* (1965). Robert has, to date, produced about 65 books, including 40 novels and

nine story collections. His best-known works are *Mindswap* (1966) and *Dimension of Miracles* (1968). He has also written a fantasy trilogy in collaboration with Roger Zelazny and a humorous private detective series starring private eye Hob Draconian. Recently, Robert worked on the computer game *Netrunner*.

The Titan Unwrecked; Or, Futility Revisited

Starring:	**Created by:**
Allan Quatermain (a.k.a. Jean Ténèbre)	H. Rider Haggard, Paul Féval
Ayesha (a.k.a. Ange Ténèbre)	H. Rider Haggard, Paul Féval
Dracula (a.k.a. Lugard)	Bram Stoker
Edward Rocambole	Ponson du Terrail, Frédéric Valade
Captain John Rowland	Morgan Robertson
Captain Black	Max Pemberton

Also Starring:
The Writers:
Guillaume Apollinaire
Robert W. Chambers
Paul Féval, *Fils*
William Ernest Henley
James Huneker
Alfred Jarry
Vernon Lee
Jean Lorrain
Morgan Robertson
Mark Twain
Sutton Vane
and
William Hope Hodgson
The Captains of Industry:
Duke of Buccleuch
Andrew Carnegie
Thomas Alva Edison
William Randolph Hearst
John D. Rockefeller
and
Lillie Langtry

Written by:
Brian M. STABLEFORD has been a professional writer since 1965. He has published more than 50 novels and 200 short stories, as well as several non-fiction books, thousands of articles for periodicals and reference books and a number of anthologies. He is also a part-time Lecturer in Creative Writing at King Alfred's College Winchester. Brian's noverls include *The Empire of Fear* (1988), *Young Blood* (1992) and his future history series comprising *Inherit the Earth* (1998), *Architects of Emortality* (1999), *The Fountains of Youth* (2000), *The Cassandra Complex* (2001), *Dark Ararat* (2002) and *The Omega Expedition* (2002). His non-fiction includes *Scientific Romance in Britain* (1985), *Teach Yourself Writing Fantasy and Science Fiction* (1997), *Yesterday's Bestsellers* (1998) and *Glorious Perversity: The Decline and Fall of Literary Decadence* (1998). Brian's translations for Black Coat Press include Paul Féval's *Knightshade, Vampire City, The Vampire Countess, John Devil, The Wandering Jew's Daughter* and the forthcoming *The Black Coats: 'Salem Street.*

Printed in the United States
32825LVS00005B/178